SAVED?

A shadow moved. Dutch let go of Kit. A gun appeared in his hand. She took a step back and he made no move to grab her. None of the men did. They stared into the darkness, hands creeping beneath their shirts for weapons. Kit took another step away, and another. But she did not run. She could not. She heard music. Someone was singing.

A man stepped from the container. Kit could not see his face, but it did not matter; it was his voice she was listening to, and it was like hearting Mozart in a raw sea full of quiet thunder, with darkness as a song. She wanted to play her fiddle against that mournful cry, then maybe lie down and die, because after this stopped, after it was gone, nothing else would ever do. Nothing else would matter. Kit felt ruined; as though she was listening to her heart break and falling in love, both at the same time; a feeling so impossible, so terrible and wonderful, she wanted to scream and cry.

Other books by Marjorie M. Liu:

EYE OF HEAVEN
THE RED HEART OF JADE
SHADOW TOUCH
A TASTE OF CRIMSON (*Crimson City Series*)
TIGER EYE

MORE PRAISE FOR MARJORIE M. LIU!

SHADOW TOUCH

"Liu's screenplay-worthy dialogue, vivid action and gift for the punchy, unexpected metaphor rockets her tale high above the pack. Readers of early Laurell K. Hamilton, Charlaine Harris and the best thrillers out there should try Liu now and catch a rising star."

—*Publishers Weekly* (Starred Review)

"If you have yet to add Liu to your must-read list, you're doing yourself—and your patrons—a disservice."

—*Booklist* (Starred, Boxed Review)

"Liu is a world-class talent. Her stories are filled with extraordinary characters, and plotlines that are ingenious and riveting."

—*Romantic Times BOOKreviews* (Top Pick)

A TASTE OF CRIMSON

"Liu...draws characters with such precision...they practically step off the page."

—*Publishers Weekly*

"Passionate, intense and gritty, this paranormal thriller is a truly enthralling read."

—*Romantic Times BOOKreviews* (Top Pick)

"Ms. Liu expertly grabs the reader with her dark and intensely detailed plot filled with mystery and passion. A must read for those who love paranormal fiction."

—*Affaire de Coeur* (Five Stars, Reviewers Pick!)

TIGER EYE

"I didn't just like this book, I LOVED this book. [Marjorie M. Liu] has a great new voice, a fresh premise, everything I love to read. Anyone who loves my work should love hers."

—*New York Times* Bestselling Author
Christine Feehan

SOUL SONG

MARJORIE M. LIU

LEISURE BOOKS   NEW YORK CITY

To my mother, for the music.
To my father, for the sea.

A LEISURE BOOK®

July 2007

Published by

Dorchester Publishing Co., Inc.
200 Madison Avenue
New York, NY 10016

ISBN-10: 0-8439-5766-2
ISBN-13: 978-0-8439-5766-2

Visit us on the web at www.dorchesterpub.com.

ACKNOWLEDGMENTS

I would like to thank, as always, my agent, Lucienne Diver, for her endless encouragement and spunky good cheer; Chris Keeslar, for being a wonderful (and patient) editor; and Brianna Yamashita, Brooke Borneman, and Diane Stacy, three of Dorchester's finest ladies, who work hard for their authors, and are generous of heart.

Finally, to my readers, a heartfelt thank you for being friends to my words. May we share many more, together.

Full fathom five thy father lies;
  Of his bones are coral made;
Those are pearls that were his eyes:
  Nothing of him that doth fade,
But doth suffer a sea-change
Into something rich and strange...

—William Shakespeare, from *The Tempest*

CHAPTER ONE

She said her name was Elsie, and that she had a gun in her car.

A foolish confession, spoken without promise or bravado. Just the truth, from a woman too frightened for artifice. M'cal tasted her fear in every word, in the brief negotiation of price and time. He knew, without a doubt, that this was her first encounter with the kind of man she believed him to be—a prostitute, a stranger from the street—and though she wanted his services more than she wanted to be safe, M'cal was big and strong, could hurt her with his hands.

M'cal did not care, either way. Taking the human weapon would be easy, if it came to that. He did not think it would. He sat stiffly in the narrow passenger seat of Elsie's little red Jetta, his legs cramped, one shoulder pressed against the cool, rain-spattered window. He was too big for her car. He had to twist so that he would not brush against her body, even by accident. M'cal did not want to touch her. Not ever. Not until he had to.

He expected Elsie to speak to him. Most women did, in her situation. He had become accustomed to the attention, to his position as an object of desire. Had learned to accept it as one more punishment to endure. But Elsie stayed quiet, and her silence made M'cal more curious than was healthy.

He glanced sideways, taking in her soft face and full mouth unevenly lit by passing streetlights. Pretty, solid, pale. Not a woman who should need to pay for sex. Not the kind of woman who would want to.

And not a woman who should die young.

M'cal's wrist hurt. He rubbed the silver cuff chafing his skin. The metal was warm, and a low, tingling shock radiated up his fingers into his bones, worsening as he stroked the rough engravings.

Elsie made a small noise; more breathless than a hiccup, but just as involuntary. She covered her mouth, glanced at M'cal, and said, "I never asked for your name."

"No," he said quietly. "Most don't."

Her gaze flitted away, back to the road. "What do you call yourself?"

M'cal hesitated. "Michael."

"Michael," she echoed, voice still trembling with fear. "How long have you been doing this?"

Long enough, he thought.

Elsie drove down Georgia Street. Coal Harbor was on the right, the shoreline crowded with apartment high-rises. M'cal peered between the buildings, glimpsing slivers of the opposing shore—the Vancouver city skyline glittering against the choppy water. A wet night, windy. Poor visibility.

"A little over a year," he lied, staring at the sea.

Elsie's knuckles turned white around the steering

wheel. "You're older than the other guys. That's why I chose you."

M'cal still watched the water. "Most of the boys on that block are in their teens. The youngest is thirteen."

Elsie said nothing. The car did not slow. Georgia Street curved right, swinging into Stanley Park. They passed the long dock and Tudor style office of the Vancouver Rowing Club, and between the road and rough stone seawall, M'cal observed late-night joggers and bicyclists braving the rain on the paved pedestrian trail. Beyond them, across the harbor, the full expanse of the downtown core perched like a neon gem on the water's edge, trailing light against the waves.

Elsie drove past the first parking lot but edged into the second. Eight totem poles filled the border of a landscaped garden, which was nothing but shadows in the evening dark. Ten o'clock at night, and the parking lot was mostly empty; M'cal saw a few steamy windows.

Elsie parked the car in the most isolated spot, near the totems. M'cal sat quietly, waiting, staring at the sea. The engine ticked. Rain pattered against the windshield.

"I don't know if I can go through with this," Elsie said.

"All right," M'cal replied, though her feelings changed nothing. Elsie let go of the steering wheel and stared at him. He stared back. She could not hold his gaze and ducked her chin, brushing long hair out of her face.

"I'm sorry," she mumbled, and then, softer, "Why do you . . . do this?"

Why did you? M'cal wondered, but stayed silent.

He did not want to know this woman. He did not want to be her friend. He did not want to understand what kind of pain would drive someone like her to risk life and limb to pick a stranger off the street and pay for sex. A death wish, a kind of suicide watch; only slower, harsher.

"Michael?" Elsie whispered, hesitantly. M'cal closed his eyes. The bracelet burned against his wrist and the sensation clawed up his arm into his throat, stirring the old monster to life. M'cal felt a surge of hate so profound he almost choked on it, struggling against himself, trying to center his heart with memories of his old life, fighting with all his strength to swallow the compulsion rising hard and terrible inside his mouth. He heard a woman laugh, somewhere distant in his mind—a fine, high tinkle of joviality—and he bit back a scream.

Run, he thought at Elsie, pressing his head against the cold window. *Run now. Please.*

But she was no mind reader. He heard her body shift, listened to cloth rub. Held his breath. A moment later, Elsie touched his shoulder: Light, it was the faintest brush of her fingertips, though to M'cal it felt like a gun blast inside his heart, the crash of some clumsy human fist. Pain. A lot of it. Followed by that terrible compulsion which forced open his jaw, breath pushing hard and ragged from his lungs.

Elsie gasped. M'cal grabbed her wrist. His hand burned, but he did not let go—could not, though he tried. He stared into her startled eyes, her dark and frightened eyes, and leaned so close he could taste the faint edge of her soul on the brim of her lips.

And then he took that soul with nothing but a song.

* * *

Afterward, if he had been close to a knife, he would have tried to cut off his hand. Again. A hard slash to the wrist, right above the bracelet. Futile, a poor man's defiance, but all he had.

Instead, M'cal sat and held Elsie in his arms, suffering through the pain of her touch, because he understood now, though he wished otherwise. He saw, inside her head, years of abuse. A life wasted. Unfulfilled. No muse to build a dream upon, and now, after a short existence, a desire to be more, to feel again. To be a woman, wild and winsome and free. Free to hate herself. Free to build upon extremes. All or nothing. Death or life.

So, the street. A slick, rainy corner full of men and boys. One choice, the start of a new self, running from the path of caution into devil-may-care. Wasting freedom on humiliation.

M'cal wished very much that Elsie had chosen differently.

She did not speak. She sat against him in the car, very still, staring out the windshield at the harbor. Her face was slack, her eyes dark, empty. All her vitality gone; drained away into a wisp, a shell not long for the world. Her worst nightmare, come to pass.

"Go home," M'cal murmured, gently pushing her away. "Go home and forget about me. Forget tonight."

Elsie turned the key in the ignition. M'cal got out of her car. The cool air and drizzling rain felt good on his face. He walked away, across the parking lot, toward the sea. He did not look back, though he was briefly bathed in headlights, in the sound of the Jetta's engine as it hummed away down the curving road.

Inside his head, Elsie wept.

M'cal crossed the wet grass, the pedestrian trail,

and stepped onto the seawall ledge. He glanced around, found himself alone. Below, high tide had drawn water over the shore, and the sound of it lapping against the wall was a lullaby of whispers, old riddles, dreams. *His* dreams, distant as they had become. M'cal could taste stones hidden beneath the shallow waves, sharp and dangerous. He kicked off his shoes and stood for a moment, toes digging into the stone and staring at the city painted on the sea.

M'cal jumped. Headfirst, it was a giant arcing leap that left him, for a moment, almost parallel to the choppy water. He shot beneath the waves, slithering into a soft, cool spot just above the jagged rocks. A breathless impact, followed by a quick, hard stab of joy. For one brief moment M'cal could pretend things were as they had been long ago. He could imagine.

But then the bracelet burned, and with it the sea, and he stopped pretending to be something he was not and propelled himself with long, easy strokes into deeper waters. He tore away his silk shirt, pushed off his jeans; he sank unencumbered like an arrow, toes pointed, arms crossed over his chest. Allowed his body to finally, desperately, change.

M'cal lost his legs. His thighs fused, then his knees and calves and ankles, feet spreading into a thin fan of metallic flesh, long and flat and scaled. Fine ribbons of silver rippled from hip to fin; and against his neck, another change: skin splitting into deep slits.

M'cal stopped holding his breath. Bubbles fled his throat. He tasted metal, chemicals, the etchings of humanity imprinted upon the sea. The scents on his tongue made him cringe, but he inhaled anyway, swallowing long and deep, both savoring and regretting the coarse liquid that spread into his body. The sea burned. Brine was in his lungs like fire, in his eyes and nostrils, needling the webs between his fingers, his groin, the scales of his tail. The bracelet burned worst of all. Not that M'cal needed any reminders.

He fought his instinct to surface, and instead pushed deeper into the harbor; enduring, taking small pleasure in one of the few acts of free will left to him: cleansing his soul with ocean fire, skirting the edges of home to rattle the bars of his prison. Being himself, if only for a short time.

Voices eddied, low murmurs of fish and storm. They were distant, a golden hum carried by the current, a thread that M'cal reached for with his mind. That music disappeared, replaced by a slight vibration that scurried over his skin, mixing with the burn of the sea. He sensed movement on his left; a sleek body. M'cal followed, heart pounding, and met a starry gaze, dark and sad. *Brother seal, little spy.* The creature melted swiftly into deepwater shadow. M'cal tried to call it back, but his throat closed.

Look, but do not touch, he remembered. *See, but do not speak.*

The bracelet throbbed. He had ventured too far. He tried to resist, but after a brief struggle his muscles twisted, turning him away from the heart of the harbor toward the city shore. He was a puppet man, pulled by invisible strings.

M'cal swam fast. He had no choice. As he neared shore, he heard the low boom of the city against the water: concrete shuddering through rock and earth, the groan of steel and glass and thousands of bodies tossing and turning and roaming. It was a maze of sound, and above him was another labyrinth as he swam beneath the boats moored to the crisscrossing docks.

His body knew the way, compelled by the bracelet. M'cal did not recognize the path; the boat had moved since morning. That was a frequent occurrence of late: shedding old habits, never staying in the same place twice. M'cal might have called such actions evidence of paranoia, but he was not optimistic enough for that. Still, it was curious.

M'cal found the boat eventually—or rather, it found him—and he poked his head above water, staring at the long, white motor yacht like a sleek floating castle made of pearl. No lights burned. The boat was quiet, with an air of emptiness. M'cal was not fooled.

He drifted close, and only at the last moment did he shift shape, reluctantly giving himself up to humanity. His tail split, his fin receded, toes twitching as his gills faded into flesh—but the sea still burned and Elsie still wept, and he had nothing, nothing to show for himself except that he was still alive, and inside his heart was still fighting.

M'cal heaved himself out of the water, naked and dripping and strong. He climbed the short ladder attached to the stern, but when he reached the deck his legs gave out, knocked from under him by a command. He fell hard on his knees, tried to stand but could not. He was forced to remain on all fours, head bowed, muscles trembling. He heard the click of high heels, smelled perfume: white lily, white rose, white lilac. The scent burned his nostrils.

"Oh," purred a low voice. "Oh, the fallen mighty. Merman, mine."

M'cal stayed silent. Ivory stilettos clicked into view. Slender, creamy ankles, smooth and soft. He closed his eyes and a cool hand slipped through his hair, nails biting deep into his scalp as the seawater dripping from his body continued to burn.

And then there was nothing but air beneath him—nothing to hold on to—and he flipped sideways, slamming hard on his back. The night sky spun, rain drizzling against his body, but above him stood a woman clad in white silk, long hair straight and shimmering like liquid silver, and he could look at nothing else.

The witch planted her feet on either side of his chest. Her skirt was very short, revealing long legs, no underwear. M'cal wanted to vomit.

"You have something for me," she murmured, and sank slowly to her knees. Her thighs squeezed his ribs, the touch of her skin taking away the pain left by the drying seawater. M'cal wished it would not. He preferred discomfort to the alternative. He tried to move, to kick her off. His body refused him. As usual.

The witch smiled, long fingers dancing against his chest and throat. She bent to kiss the corner of his mouth, and he felt the draw of her power tug on Elsie's soul.

"My prince," whispered the witch. "Give me your voice."

M'cal did not speak. The witch reached between their bodies and touched his stomach, lower still, caressing him with deft, long strokes. M'cal willed himself not to respond, but there was magic in her fingers—literally—and his control meant nothing. He grew hard in moments, his human body a betrayal, and the witch slid herself onto his shaft with a sigh.

"Your voice," she said, swaying upon him. "Your voice, and I will stop." A sly smile touched her mouth. "Unless you *want* me to finish you. Unless you want *me*."

M'cal tried to look away, but the witch held his gaze and rocked harder, forcing terrible pleasure through his body. The sensation tore at him. Disgusting, thrilling; his defiance was the same as defeat, which was the custom of their dance. Killing him softly, breaking him one impossible choice at a time when all she had to do was command by force what she wanted.

But the witch surprised him. She stopped her movements, gave up her pleasure, his humiliation, for a long, quiet stare that was far more thoughtful than anything she had thus far allowed him to see. It made him uneasy—a feat, given his already desperate circumstances.

M'cal returned her gaze, studying her flawless face, the crystalline perfection of her eyes, cold as some blue belly of arctic ice. He tried to remember why he had loved her, so long ago, and thought it must have been for beauty alone. He could not remember for certain. He did not want to.

From behind the witch a shadow lumbered close—a slow, gray hulk with a fat, pasty face and red spots the size of nickels on his cheeks; silver eyes like shark teeth and a mouth just as sharp. The hulk watched M'cal just as carefully as the witch. Licked his lips, once.

The witch leaned forward, silver hair spilling over M'cal's face. He tried to move his head. No luck. All he could do was watch. He did not close his eyes.

The witch kissed him. Inside his head, Elsie screamed. M'cal almost cried out with her, but he swallowed his voice and held on to the woman's stolen soul with all his strength, fighting and fighting. His fault, his fault—but this time would be different; he would make it *different*—

The witch inhaled, and it was like being kissed by a hurricane. For one brief moment, everything inside M'cal felt loosened from its anchor: heart, bones, lungs. Essentials, floating in blood. Drifting. Elsie, drifting, torn away from his grasp. Until she was gone, stolen. Again. Just like all the others. So easy. The witch always made it look easy. And him, useless, unable to redeem himself. Nothing but a tool.

The witch leaned back, breathing hard. Shuddering. Her eyes were closed and she touched her mouth, dragging her fingertips over her lips.

"Ivan," she murmured, and the hulking man behind her shuffled close. He held out a soft silver robe, which he helped drape over her narrow shoulders. His hand, a palm the size of a football, came down to rest heavy against the curve of her long, pale neck. M'cal glimpsed a silver band glinting against that thick wrist; smooth and seamless, it was not quite a twin to his own, but close enough.

The witch rose slowly off M'cal's body. Power leaked through her skin; he felt scratchy with it, as though barnacles or steel wool rubbed against him. The sensation did not fade when she stopped touching him. Distance was the only cure, as with most things in his life.

The witch stared down her nose at M'cal. "Up, prince. Up, now."

No compulsion. Not yet. And with Elsie gone— *gone, gone*—there was no more need to stay silent. Not that the witch needed his voice to take what she wanted from him.

"No," M'cal said. His throat hurt.

" 'No,' " mocked the witch. "No, evermore, with you. No and no. I grow tired of that word."

"I do not care," M'cal replied. "You know that."

"And I know that you are mine." The witch snapped her fingers. The bracelet burned. M'cal fought the compulsion, but his muscles twisted; he pushed himself off the deck and stood. Exposed. Helpless. Raging. The hulk, Ivan, studied him with a narrow gaze; the line of his mouth tilted just slightly.

"I have another task for you," said the witch, softly. "A specific target this time. You will take this woman's spirit and bring it to me. You will do this now, tonight. I must have her *tonight*."

M'cal listened to her voice. "Something has frightened you."

The witch tilted her head and Ivan moved—fast for a man of his size, almost too fast to see. His fist rocked M'cal off his feet, sending him sliding across the deck. M'cal tasted blood; a tooth jiggled.

"Get dressed," snapped the witch, turning quickly with a flourish of silk and silver hair. "Ivan? Give him the name." She walked away.

Ivan knelt and smiled. His teeth were sharp as knives. He tried to touch M'cal's bloody lip, but the compulsion was gone and M'cal grabbed the big man's meaty index finger. M'cal yanked backward until bone cracked, then twisted so hard it lay perpendicular to the rest of Ivan's fingers. His strength was terrible; he began to crush the bone.

Ivan never flinched. Shrugging, he tossed a slip of paper on the deck beside M'cal, then stood slowly, jamming his heel against M'cal's shoulder, forcing the merman to release him with nothing more than a push and tug. M'cal gritted his teeth, wary, but Ivan did not retaliate. His expression never changed, not even when he grabbed his broken finger and reset it with a sickening crunch.

Ivan turned and lumbered off, following the witch. M'cal watched him go, licking his lip, again tasting blood. A weak breeze brushed his throbbing face; beside him, the paper rustled. He thought about not picking it up, but refusal would only delay the inevitable. The witch would force him, just as she had for years. M'cal preferred to move on his own, even if it was just an illusion.

There was a hotel address on the paper, as well as the whereabouts of the victim, at least for the next several hours. There was also a name. M'cal spoke it out loud, enjoying the rolling delicacy of its sound. It was a short-lived pleasure; he found himself racked by guilt, hatred, a rage so terrible he shuddered with it, his fingers digging into his thigh against the hard deck. The silver cuff glinted against his wrist, the skin just above the metal covered in thin white scars. Again he thought about a knife, a gun—something, anything—to stop himself. Or to stop the witch.

But there was nothing. Nothing he could do. Nothing he had not already tried.

"Kitala Bell," he murmured, gazing once again at the paper in his hands. "Forgive me."

CHAPTER TWO

The woman sitting in the front row of Kit Bell's concert had a knife sticking out of her eye.

It was a big knife. Blood covered her youthful face, running rivers down her low-cut white dress, staining the ends of her long blond hair. She dripped on the carpeted floor, on the old man beside her. No one noticed. Even the woman herself remained oblivious to the fatal wound in her head. She smiled beneath the blood, nodding and clapping her hands to the fast music. Enjoying herself, because it was a perfect night. Simply wonderful.

Kit, who was not prepared, who had gone almost a year without signs of death, almost threw down her fiddle. She caught herself in time, though—made the pause in her music nothing but an extra beat, some artful hitch—and hid her nausea with a grimace that she hoped would pass for a smile. She had no choice. The fifteen hundred individuals seated in the posh Queen Elizabeth Theater had shelled out fifty dollars a ticket to see the final leg of her North American tour.

Screaming *Jesus Christ!* and hauling ass off the stage to puke simply would not do. Kit was a professional that way.

So she gritted her teeth, buckled down. She looked away from the dying woman—anywhere but at that one seat directly in front of her—and rimmed the air with a fine high beat, dancing down the devil inside her mind as she plucked and skimmed, bending her soul around the music running fast from her fiddle—faster, faster—until her skin felt like the strings and the world a bow of light, until the music was so much a part of her that each breath became a note, each heartbeat a melody.

She was alone on the stage. No accompaniment necessary. Few musicians in the world could claim the same, and it was part of her draw. Because when Kit played, there was not a soul on earth who could keep up with her. She played to the death, death down to ashes, and nothing less satisfied. She might burst her heart one day for real on her fiddle, but that would be the perfect way to go: giving it all, dying like one long note on a string, cutting air and ears and souls. No regrets. Just music. Always, music.

Now was no different. Kit forgot bones and blood and knives; her thoughts faded into a baser instinct. No one could play with heart and think; no one could hold such music without a little insanity.

The set ended. The audience began roaring before the last trembling note, but she paid no mind to the applause. The knife was still there.

Kit bowed and left the stage at a run. She wanted to vomit, to take an aspirin, to get back to her hotel for a hot shower and some kind of goofy cartoon to take the edge off the ghoulishness in her head; but as she stood in the shadows offstage, heart pounding, head bent, she could feel the thunder of the audience rumbling in her veins, and she could not run. Not yet.

Kit took a deep breath and raced back on stage. She started playing as soon as she left the wings—Mozart's Violin Concerto in D, but at a breakneck tempo, her bow rocking over the strings until she hit the center of the stage and stopped on her toes, transforming the rondo into something far more earthy, cutting the notes with Irish roots, burning them into a jig. The audience shouted, men and women stamping their feet, clapping hard with the beat.

All except two. The young woman was gone. The old man beside her was missing as well. Their absence caused no relief. It meant only that the woman had gone to die. Die soon or die later, in a year or a lifetime, with terrible violence as the cause. A knife in her eye.

And there isn't a single thing you can do about it, Kit thought bitterly.

She finished with a flourish. The audience begged for more. Kit did not listen. She smiled and waved, kissed the air with her thanks, and then with a sweeping twirl of her patchwork emerald silk skirt, ran lightly off the stage.

Her fiddle case lay on a chair just beyond the wings. Her coat was there, too, as well as her purse. Ready for a quick getaway. Kit had no dressing room; she had come to the theater straight from the hotel, and while the stage manager had tried to press upon her one of the Queen Elizabeth's numerous suites, she had shrugged him off. All Kit needed was her fiddle; bottled water and flower arrangements were unnecessary for her mental health. She was not picky about how or where. All that mattered was that she got to play.

The Queen Elizabeth's stage manager was an older gentleman named Alec Montreuil, a Quebecois born and raised. He and Kit had known each other for some years, enough that words were almost unnecessary as she hugged him good-bye. His brow crinkled when he looked into her eyes. She shook her head.

"I'll tell you some other time," she said.

"Soon," he replied, his accent heavy. "Your father would be worried, I think, by the expression on your face. False smiles do not work on me, Kitala."

"And here I thought I was a fine actress." Kit shook her head. "I'll look you up before I leave town, Alec."

"Yes," he replied solemnly. "You will. *Bonne nuit, ma belle fille.*"

"Good night," Kit replied, and walked away. She could feel Alec watching her, but did not look back. She tried not to feel like a dog for doing so—it was bad manners at its worst—but she had no choice. She had to run. She had to get out. The knife was still in that woman's eye—in Kit's own eye—dangling like a fishhook. Blood was everywhere.

She barely pushed through the stage door in time and hit the poorly lit back alley, gagging. Had to lean against the slick, wet brick wall as her body heaved. Nothing came up—she ate no dinner before performances, ever—but it still hurt, still made her eyes well with tears. She wiped them away with the back of her hand—did the same to her mouth—and took a deep breath. The air was good and sweet. Tasted like medicine in her lungs. She heard low voices and glanced to her left, meeting the startled gazes of some theater employees who stood on the loading dock, smoking. They waved at her, frowning.

Kit waved back but did not wait for a response. She

turned and walked away, fast, trying to ignore the faint sound of her name as the men bandied it about behind her. God only knew what they were saying, what they thought. Not that it mattered. There was only so much she could do to protect her image.

Kit's nausea faded by the time she hit the sidewalk. She took a right on Cambie, avoiding the main press of theatergoers streaming across the street. No one noticed her—or if they did, were polite enough to leave her alone. Away from the stage and spotlight, Kit knew she was just another woman with brown skin and brown eyes; ordinary, normal. The magic lived only in the fiddle, in the theater.

Hotel Georgia was a couple of blocks up the road, a straight line from the theater, but Kit took an alternate route, away from the crowds. It was early enough in the night that she felt safe walking the streets. Not bravado; she had spent the morning scouting out the area, familiarizing herself with the best routes, the most dangerous spots. She knew her way; a cab would not be much faster, and she needed the air. Her stomach was better, but the memory was still poison; she wanted that woman out of her system.

Impossible, maybe. Learning how to forget was one lesson Kit had never mastered. Too stubborn, too much heart to forget those singular prophecies of violent death that sprang upon her like random illnesses. Knowing how people were going to die was a terrible burden.

Let it go, she told herself, clutching her fiddle case. *Let it go. Everyone dies. Everyone goes on. You can't change a thing. You can't.*

"Right," Kit muttered, still miserable.

It was not quite eleven-thirty. Vancouver at night

felt both lovely and dangerous, with an urban shine that was modern, sleek, all fine hard edges with towers and skyscrapers full of electronic stars, glittering bright. A deceptive beauty; the city's underbelly, as Kit knew all too well, was raw with drugs and cold cash and prostitution. No amount of refinement could hide that, though the natural scenery helped. Everything looked better—cleaner—against a backdrop of mountains and ocean.

Just don't look too close, Kit thought, reaching up to touch her eye. She caught herself, but not in time; her fingertips traced a circle around her lashes. She shuddered. *Don't look too close, don't look too close.* Or else risk seeing things that could never be taken back. Suffering. Death. Lingering like a sore.

Just like the woman in white—the woman dying, the woman already murdered with a knife in her eye. That vision, another cut inside Kit's heart, another wound, one of many. Whispering, like all the others, *maybe* and *could have*, and that deadly *what if*.

Kit turned right on Georgia Street, passing coffee shops and wide, clean storefront windows pimping trendy clothes and purses, bright like the eyes of peacock feathers, for show. Yuppie, not much personality. She heard a shout ahead of her, looked sharply and saw two men jump a vehicle parked at a red light. One held a bucket, the other a rag. Guerrilla car washing, for spare change. The men splashed on some water, slopped the rag around the windshield then screamed at the driver until he inched down the window and tossed them several crumpled bills. The light turned green; the car sped away.

Kit crossed the street before the intersection. The men watched her bypass them and she met their gazes, hard and strong. They did not follow. They had more cars coming; bigger fish.

Close to the hotel, only a block away from tourist-friendly Robson Street, Kit encountered more pedestrians. She tried to keep her eyes on the sidewalk, but could not help herself—she watched the faces, searching. All she saw was normal, easy and happy; no murder, no mayhem, no weapons. Just men and women out for a good night, with the promise of more and better.

Nice. She needed that.

Until, ruin. The end. Just ahead, the door to a Starbucks swung open and a blond woman in a white coat stepped out. The old man was with her, swinging a cane.

Kit stopped walking. Stared. No blood or knife, not anymore, but that did not mean the woman's fate had changed. Message delivered, message received; that was all that mattered.

The young woman and her companion stood on the street corner, waiting for the light to change. Kit started walking toward them. Slow at first, then fast. The woman and the old man began walking, too. They crossed the street. Kit followed. She did not know what to do—she had no plan, no words. What could she say? *Hello, excuse me, you're going to be murdered?*

Right. She had tried that once before and gotten nothing for her trouble but ridicule; worse, even. Which by itself was not such a terrible thing, but now she had a career to consider, a profession that put her in the public eye. Silence, no matter how much it hurt, had been her policy for years.

And all those what-ifs? What are those worth? Are

you going to sell yourself out, let a woman who needs your help pass on by? Even crazy people can play the fiddle. There's no one who can take your music away.

Kit took a deep breath. Fine, then. She would do it, this one time. It would probably just freak the woman out, offer no protection whatsoever, but at least she could sleep easy knowing she had tried to give a warning, to divert fate.

Her grandmother slipped into mind. Brown skin shining beneath the New Orleans sun. Strong fingers crushing mint. A smoky voice, talking up such things as destiny, the movements of chance and fortune. Playing games with Death.

Ain't nothing or no one can close that eye once it got its mark on you, old Jazz Marie had rasped, again and again. *So don't you waste precious energy tryin' your hand, Kitty Bella, or else maybe you get the mark instead. And that's something you not strong enough for, not for some time yet.*

Kit pushed away caution and caught up with the young blond woman and her elderly companion. Their heads were bowed together; no laughter, just quiet conversation. Peaceful, serene.

She almost stopped. Almost gave up and turned away. No spine, no courage—or maybe, as her grandmother would say, too much good common sense running through her veins. Old Jazz Marie would let this sleeping dog lie.

And Kit, despite her convictions, was about to do just that when the young woman suddenly slowed and looked over her shoulder, directly into Kit's eyes.

Kit stumbled. So did the woman. Up close the blonde appeared very young, the definition of charming, with a quick intelligence in her pale eyes that focused immediately on Kit's face.

"I know you," she said softly. "You're Kitala Bell."

"I am," Kit said, trying to sound calmer than she felt. "And you?"

"Alice." She hesitated, then held out her hand. Kit had no choice but to take it, and the first contact of their skin made her nauseated all over again. Blood dripped from the woman's wrist—ghost blood—covering Kit's hand; she could feel its warmth. Kit looked into the woman's face and the knife jutted, quivering.

Alice frowned. "Are you okay?"

"Fine," Kit murmured, gently disengaging her hand. The vision faded, but the sickness did not. She swallowed hard.

"My dear," said the old man beside them. "You do not look fine."

Alice glanced at him. "Uncle John, I think she has something in her eye."

Kit's heart lurched painfully. "What did you say?"

"Your eye," Alice repeated, almost sadly. "Your eye."

"Oh, my," said the old man, staring. "Oh my, indeed."

Kit's hand snaked to her throat; she touched the leather cord of the gris-gris and the gold of her cross—charms of protection, worn at the insistence of her grandmother—and around her body felt a tickle of something she had not experienced in years, not since old Jazz Marie lived. The sensation was shocking. Invasive. She backed away, watching Alice and the old man. Wondering at her bad luck.

Don't be a good Samaritan. Backfires every time.

"Wait," said Alice, holding out her hand. "Don't be afraid."

"I'm not," Kit lied. "You're the one who's in trouble."

Alice and the old man shared a look. "What do you mean?"

"You're going to be murdered," Kit said, and the words slipped out so easily she might as well have been speaking of dessert or the weather. Men and women passing her just at that moment did a double-take.

"Please explain," said the old man, glancing again at Alice. He looked quite pale. Kit's vision wavered. She saw blood on his chest. His eyes rolling up in his head.

She looked away, trying not to be sick. Too much, too fast, too strange. These strangers—Alice and her Uncle John—were in a great deal of trouble. More than Kit could handle. Not without making herself a target as well. But that did not stop her from forcing her gaze back to the old man's face, searching for more, another clue. He stared back, a furrow between his eyes, one more wrinkle of consternation in a forehead already full of worry. Kit thought she might like him, given the chance. Dapper, clean. Old school. He reminded her of Tennessee.

"You need to be careful," she whispered, unable to help herself. "Both of you, so careful."

Alice took a step toward her. Kit did not retreat. She held herself strong, fiddle case slung tight against her back like a shield. A thread of music curled through her head, a slippery sword. She watched Alice open her mouth to speak.

Kit heard a soft thud. It sent a chill through her, though she could not place the sound. A moment later, though, the old man stumbled backward, clutching his

chest. He stared at himself—they all three stared—
and Kit watched in horror and dread as a red stain
bloomed against his crisp white shirt. She almost did
not believe it, almost wasted precious moments telling
herself it was merely a vision, the painted future.

But then people began to push and run, screaming,
and she knew it was real. The future had arrived.

The old man collapsed. Alice fell to her knees,
scrabbling at his chest, cradling the man's face. He did
not respond to her touch. Kit knew he would not. She
had already seen him die once before, and a gunshot
wound to the heart did not allow for good-byes or last
words. Neither did a knife in the eye.

There was a humming in her ears; fiddle strings, rising into a scream. Kit gritted her teeth and grabbed
Alice's upper arm, yanking hard, hauling the woman
to her feet. No time for second thoughts or regrets, no
time for questions. She looked into Alice's stricken
eyes and said, "You have to run now."

"We both do," Alice breathed, and as Kit stared,
stunned, the young woman kicked off her heels and
gave the old man one last look so torn and hurt and
hard, Kit felt her own throat thicken with some foreign grief that felt too much at home in her heart.

The hairs on the back of her neck prickled; she did
not turn to look, but instead pulled on Alice's arm.
The woman did not resist. She took Kit's hand and the
two of them dodged into the milling, frightened
crowd. Kit felt eyes watch them; she imagined herself
at the center of a crosshairs.

Not your time, she told herself. *Not now.*

But the woman beside her was another matter entirely. It might be that her death was not scheduled for

a lifetime yet, but, given what had just happened to the old man, better safe than sorry. Not that Kit could fight fate. Not that anyone could.

The hard shell of the fiddle case banged against her back. Kit had the absurd desire to play—could even hear the notes inside her head, wicked and pure. She ran to the music—a whirlygig—searching for someplace safe, well-lit, crowded. But the stores had closed, and it seemed that just when she needed a coffee shop, all of them had disappeared. Just ahead, though, she glimpsed the stone facade of her hotel. Perfect.

Kit heard sirens. Fast response. Two police cruisers sped through a distant intersection on her left; another appeared just ahead and stopped in the middle of the crosswalk, red and blue flashing. Kit slowed, Alice silently mirroring her. The two women shared a quick look but kept moving.

A police officer stepped out of the cruiser: a woman, small and trim, with hard dark eyes and a short bob of black hair that swished around her chin. She looked directly at Kit and Alice. There were no spare glances for any other pedestrians, no question in her gaze, just a clear, unwavering focus that made Kit feel like she was barreling one hundred miles an hour toward a flat stone wall. Kit nudged Alice with her elbow and the two began to turn down an alley that opened up on their right.

The cop took a quick step and touched her gun. "Stay where you are," she said loudly. "Don't move."

Every pedestrian in the police officer's vicinity froze, including Kit and Alice. Pure law-abiding habit, though every instinct screamed at Kit to run. Alice swayed toward the alley. Her face was flushed, her eyes red-rimmed, bright. But there was a hard set to her mouth and a spring to her posture that made Kit think she was just as ready to scuttle.

"You know what this is about," Kit murmured.

"I'm sorry," Alice said. "You were only trying to help."

The cop moved closer. Her gun was out, trained on Kit. Everyone else around them began to move again, sidling away, whispering and staring. Kit wondered, absently, if anyone recognized her.

Not that there was time. Alice grabbed Kit's hand and, in a surprising show of strength, yanked her down the alley in a flat-out run. Kit tried to pull back, but Alice would not let go; her grip was painful, fingers like little iron rods. Kit heard a shout behind them, the sound of shoes slapping pavement. Her shoulder blades tickled. She was a perfect target.

Her breath whistled. She was in such deep shit. Running from the cops—even if it felt right—was a terrible thing to do.

The alley was a glorified garbage dump and drug depot; empty bleach bottles and used syringes covered the ground, as well as broken glass. Alice hissed but kept going. Kit glanced back and saw the cop standing, legs apart, gun raised.

"Crap," she muttered.

A sharp bang echoed through the alley. Alice cried out and fell to the ground. Kit went down with her, still unable to free her hand. She scraped her knees, felt the burn race through her body. She wanted to scream, wanted to keep running; an allegro howled on the back of her tongue, her fiddle wailing in her mind.

Alice's grip finally loosened, but Kit did not run.

The other woman was bleeding from her leg. She tried to stand, ended up falling again.

"Go," she hissed, tears streaking down her cheeks. "Please, go."

But it was too late. The police officer was there. Kit saw flashing lights at the end of the alley. Headlights blinded her—almost as much as the gleam of white teeth as the female cop smiled.

"End of the road," she said, and raised her gun. Kit stiffened, but no shots were fired. Instead; the weapon came down hard against her head. Pain burst through her skull, stunning her—but not enough to render her unconscious. Unfortunately. Kit tried to move, but her body would not work properly. All she could do was crawl, her cheek pressed against the cold, wet cement as she pushed through filth. She did not care. Her head hurt. She needed to get away.

She heard another voice—a man's, low and gruff. She could not see him; the headlights still blinded her. Alice cried out again, fought; the sound of flesh being hit made Kit flinch. A car door opened, slammed—Kit kept crawling—and then a hand grabbed her hair and yanked her head back so hard she choked.

"This one?" rumbled a harsh male voice.

"Take her. She could cause problems."

"Don't know how," muttered the man, but Kit found herself slung into a pair of meaty arms. She tried to fight, but all she managed to do was throw up. Nothing was produced except bile, but it earned her another tap on the head. She was thrust into the back-seat of the police cruiser—landed hard on Alice, who lay very still against the opposite door. Kit felt Alice's chest rise and fall. Still alive, then. For now.

"Bitch got my shirt wet," growled the man climbing

into the front seat. A police officer, Kit noted. Or at least he wore the uniform. The female cop climbed in on the other side. Her hair was mussed. She was breathing hard.

"Docks first," she ordered.

Kit's fiddle case pressed against her back. She tried to pay attention, to memorize the faces of the cops, but there was an axe blade pounding on her skull and her vision kept fading with the passing streetlights. Her eyelids felt heavy, too.

This is a kidnapping, not an arrest, Kit told herself, trying to stay conscious. *They're going to kill you.*

Marked. Death and fate. No turning back. She reached into her shirt and grabbed the gris-gris, feeling the contents in the little leather pouch roll against her palm. Music filled her mind—*T'Aimse 'Im Chodladh*— and she hummed the Celtic tune beneath her breath, centering herself, slowing the pounding of her heart. The pain lessened. Her vision strengthened.

There was no handle on the door beside Kit, and she was separated from the front by wire. All she could do was sit and wait. The city changed; away from the downtown core the buildings grew older, rougher. Kit saw more homeless people curled on the street, some of whom turned away when they saw the police cruiser. *Good idea*, Kit thought. *Wish I were there with you.*

In the distance, Kit saw a cruise ship. She licked her lips and said, "You're not really cops, are you?"

The woman shot her an amused look. "Of course we are. You think we would run around in these uniforms, in this car, if we weren't? Cops know their own. A fake wouldn't last long in this city."

Fake enough, Kit thought. "So, what's going on, then? Why do you want this woman?"

"It's not us who wants her," rumbled the man, but the woman tapped his shoulder and he clamped his mouth shut.

"No more questions," she said, glancing back at Kit. "You don't need the answers."

"I'll be missed," Kit said. "I'm well known. You could ransom me. I don't suppose you make much money as cops."

The man twitched, but the woman stayed cool, showing no emotion. "We're getting paid."

"I'm worth millions," Kit replied. "Worth more alive, that's for sure."

This time, the man glanced into his rearview mirror. Kit met his gaze, unblinking. Again the woman tapped his shoulder. She also removed her gun from its holster and clicked off the safety.

"The wire is wide enough for the muzzle of this gun," she said coolly. "I will shoot you if you do not shut up."

"No, you won't," Kit said, thinking fast, trying to sound calm. "Too much blood to clean, too much risk the bullet will pass through me and damage the car. You want this job to go easy. Without anyone finding out what you're doing."

The woman smiled. "Trust me. I think we can come up with a good cover story. Benefit of the doubt, and all that."

Kit gritted her teeth. "Fine. You're going to kill me anyway. Might as well keep me alive long enough to get some extra money for it."

"Jess," muttered the man. "We could do it. No one would be the wiser."

"Fuck you," replied the woman, glancing at him. "We're doing this by the numbers."

"Which numbers?" Kit struggled to hide her desperation. "You really care what anyone tells you to do?"

"You care or you die," said the woman, and she put away her gun. "Seems my partner here has forgotten that."

"No," he mumbled. "But the money—"

"Shut up," the woman said, sounding weary. "And slow down. You're going to miss the street."

The man tapped on the brakes and swung a hard right. Alice slid across the seat into Kit's lap. She made no sound, but her hand twitched. Maybe she wasn't unconscious after all. Kit pushed her up, smelling blood. Alice's leg. Those cops were going to have to do some cleaning tonight, after all.

Something small pressed into Kit's hand. It felt like a business card. Holding her breath, watching the cops watch the road, she slid it carefully into her coat pocket. No reaction up front. She glanced down at Alice, and found the blonde's face still slack, eyes shut, a touch of drool at the corner of her mouth. Girl deserved an Oscar.

Between the buildings ahead, Kit glimpsed orange cranes, shipping containers. Far on the right, two cruise ships loomed, and on her left, a long, dark freighter. There was very little security, just a chain link fence that stood wide open, without a guard. Some lights, but only at the entrance.

Her captors did not seem at all concerned about being seen. The police cruiser drove into the shipping yard without slowing, taking another hard turn around a mountain of stacked orange containers, and then another, weaving a path through the maze toward the sea. Near the edge of the immense dock platform, Kit saw men standing around smoking. The cruiser pulled up beside them, and the female officer rolled down her window.

Only one of the men drew near. He was big and wide, with a shaved head and mean eyes. Despite the cool air, his shirt was partially unbuttoned. He wore no coat, which made it easy to see the tattoo covering the base of his throat and upper chest. In the poor light, it resembled a woman with her legs spread.

He peered into the backseat at Kit. "Something we can do for you, Officer Yu?"

"Plan B," the cop said.

"Payment as usual?"

"Each of you will be contacted tomorrow."

The man cracked his knuckles and smiled. "Instructions?"

"No." She glanced back at Kit. "Do what you want with her, Dutch, just as long as she's dead at the end of it."

"No," Kit said.

The woman gave her a long, hard look. "You can try your bribes with Dutch and his friends. But to be honest, I think you might find being dead a whole lot easier than being alive with them."

The back door opened. Dutch reached in. Kit started fighting, screaming, trying to make as much noise as she could. Behind her, Alice finally moved. She wrapped her legs around Kit's waist, pulling back, forcing Dutch to contend with the weight of two women.

"Fuckin' shit," muttered the big man as Kit slammed her heel into his face, rocking him back a step. "A little help here?"

The door behind Alice opened. The woman gasped,

Kit heard a thud, and then Alice went limp all over again. This time it did not seem to be an act.

Dutch grabbed Kit's ankles and yanked hard. She grabbed hold of the wire as she slid across the seat, clinging like a leech—until Officer Yu slammed the butt of her gun against Kit's fingers. She had to do it twice before Kit would let go, and Kit hit the pavement hard on her back, kicking and screaming. Dutch swore, looking at Officer Yu. "You sure you don't want to just shoot her?"

She shrugged. "We're on a tight schedule. But you have a gun. Do it yourself."

Dutch grunted and kicked shut the door. The police cruiser sped away, tires squealing as it disappeared around the containers.

Kit stopped fighting for one brief moment, looking around, taking stock—which was one woman against five men, most of whom were just now ambling over, tossing away their cigarettes with a finality that said those would be their last for a good long time.

Goddamn. She was in deep shit.

"I don't suppose I could pay you not to kill me?" Kit craned her neck to look into Dutch's small, narrow eyes.

"Nah," he rumbled. "I'm not that kind of greedy."

"Of course not," she muttered, and let out a piercing scream. Dutch swore—dodged her knee to his groin—and swept his foot under her legs, knocking her flat on the concrete. She fell on the hard shell of her fiddle case, tried to catch a breath, and found a foot on her throat instead.

"Got us some brown sugar," muttered a man, crouching close as Dutch applied more pressure on her vocal cords. Kit felt someone tug on her hair and she bared her teeth, kicking and writhing, trying to fight off the strong hands that caught her limbs and held her down. Her heart thundered. It was hard to breathe. She was going to die. Slow and awful.

She fought harder. The men laughed. Dutch said, "Take her to the container."

A hand clamped over her mouth. It smelled like cigarettes and piss. Kit was lifted, dragged. She heard a loud clanging sound—a container door swinging open. The men still laughed, chatting each other up like it was a Saturday night and some football game was about to start. Kit wondered if there would be beer and chips.

The container loomed. The man who had opened its door disappeared inside. A flashlight beam cut the darkness within—but only for a moment. Kit heard an odd thud, so loud it cut through the laughter of the men, the roar of blood in her ears. The flashlight beam disappeared. Kit heard another thud, followed by a crunch like bone.

Something large flew out of the container, hitting the ground hard at their feet. It was the man who had gone in. He was dead—no question about it. The long pipe lodged in his chest made that fairly obvious. As did the fact that his head had been twisted so far around his body he had a fairly good view of his ass.

"Fuck," breathed one of the men. The hand covering Kit's mouth fell away, but she did not scream. She stayed very quiet, staring into the black mouth of the shipping container.

A shadow moved. Dutch let go of Kit. A gun appeared in his hand. She took a step back, and he made no move to grab her. None of the men did. They stared into the darkness, hands creeping beneath their shirts for weapons. Kit took another step away, and another. But she did not run. She could not. She heard music. Someone was singing.

A man stepped out of the container. Kit could not see his face, but it did not matter; it was his voice she was listening to, and it was like hearing Mozart in a raw sea full of quiet thunder, with darkness as a song. She wanted to play her fiddle against that mournful cry, then maybe lie down and die, because after it stopped, after it was gone, nothing else would ever do. Nothing else would matter. Kit felt ruined, as though she were listening to her heart break and fall in love, both at the same time—a feeling so impossible, so terrible and wonderful, she wanted to scream and cry.

She did neither, just stood there listening, warmth spreading through her body. Telling herself to run. Not caring if she did.

Dutch groaned. He stumbled backward, just one step, but even as he moved away, the other men lurched forward, legs stiff, like zombies. They stumbled right up to the storage container, and the man stepped aside as they entered the dark metal mouth, disappearing into the darkness. Kit watched, breathless, and inside her heart she felt a change in the song, a twist.

Gunfire rocked the air, echoing from within the shipping container like some terrible rack of cannons. Men screamed. Kit imagined them shooting each other, slaughtering one another at pointblank range, and though it was impossible, she also knew it was the truth.

The gunfire lasted only seconds. Kit never stopped watching the man in shadow, whose voice continued to hum. She felt his song change once again, and in her mind heard another melody, heartstrings plucking a tune. It seemed right, the perfect harmony; she sang it beneath her breath.

The man's voice faltered. Dutch shuddered, shoulders sagging. His arm came up with the gun in hand. He aimed.

Kit slammed into Dutch just as he squeezed the trigger. The shot went wild. He hurled a punch at her, but she was ready and dodged. She had no time to duck the second blow, though; his fist rushed toward her face.

It never landed. A hand shot between Kit and Dutch, catching the big man's fist. Kit stumbled away, staring. All she could see was a long, lean back, clad in black silk. A tall man, taller than Dutch. His hair was the color of jet, loose and thick.

He did not speak, nor did he sing, but his silence was almost as compelling. Kit heard bone crack, and Dutch went down on his knees, shuddering. His gun hand came up, but the dark man grabbed his wrist and bent it so far back his knuckles almost touched his forearm. Dutch screamed. His weapon clattered to the concrete.

"You should not have touched her," said the stranger; quiet, soft, voice aching with power. "You should not have dreamed of it."

Dutch's scream died into a whimper. Kit backed away. She did not look where she was going; only, she suddenly knew what was going to happen, could see it in her head, painted upon Dutch's red face, and she wanted distance, no more violence. Even if it was well deserved.

She kept moving, watched the man in black place his hands on either side of Dutch's head. Closed her eyes at the last moment and suffered only the loud crack of a neck breaking.

Kit opened her eyes. Dutch slumped to the concrete. Dead, he did not look particularly big or strong. She liked him better that way. Not breathing.

His murderer, her rescuer, stood for a long moment staring at Dutch's body. Kit did not think about being in danger. The violence she had just endured and witnessed went so far beyond anything she had experienced that the idea of one more threat seemed somehow trite. Still, she kept her mouth shut, gaze locked on that lean, strong back, tracing the lines of a body holding a voice that could only belong to someone not completely human.

And when the man finally turned to look at her, *not human* seemed entirely appropriate.

He was beautiful. Utterly, fantastically beautiful. Even in the poor light of the shipping yard, his skin seemed to glow; pale, flawless, his face full of elegant classical lines. Breathtakingly masculine.

Her awe did not last. She blinked and discovered blood. Blood against his throat, gushing from a hole the size of a baseball: a death sentence, wailing in her vision. The man in front of her was slated for murder. The future was turning on him. On her, as well.

Raw misery roared through her heart. If there was a final straw, then this was it, because this man who had saved her life—no matter who he was—did not deserve such an end. She did not deserve to see it. Not when the sound of his voice made her feel so much; not when the sight of his face, combined with what he had just done for her, made her feel something else entirely.

You can't save him. You can't even save Alice. Give it up. Let go.

But Kit could not look away, and she stumbled backward, staring into the stranger's eyes. It was impossible to see their color, but his gaze was hot, piercing. The hard line of his mouth softened just a fraction.

"Are you hurt?" he asked, and again his voice put a hook into her heart; sinking, sinking deep. The lethal wound in his throat vanished, but not the memory. She put it away, though. She had spoken the truth earlier in the night, summoned up her courage for Alice—but that was different. This man was different. She could not tell him he was going to die.

"No," Kit breathed, fighting the urge to close the distance between them. "You?"

He shook his head, giving Dutch a second glance. "I feel better."

Kit did not know how to respond. She never had a chance to try. She glimpsed movement on her left, someone standing just within the shadow of another shipping container. Her brain registered the glint of metal held at waist level; a long barrel. She thought, *not again,* and stumbled backward.

The man in front of her moved. He ran toward her. He was very fast, but Kit still heard the gun fire, felt a burning against the side of her neck. She began to fall.

Strong arms caught her body, picked her up. Kit touched her neck. It was wet, hot. She was bleeding.

And then she was falling into the sea.

CHAPTER THREE

To survive amongst humans, solitude had always been a necessary part of M'cal's life. He had spent much of his youth on land, a willing exile because of his ties and his blood—which was a deviation, impure by the standards of other, less tolerant Krackeni—and while that isolation had for a time become a burden, he could look back now with the wisdom of a man considerably hardened, and appreciate it for what it had been.

Peace. Freedom. Safety.

But despite the way he had been raised—with care and warnings, years and years distant—he had given it all away in a heartbeat. One bad choice. For love, or the illusion of it. And of all the mistakes he could have made, that was the worst. A gesture of apocalyptic foolhardiness; an act of extreme madness. He had lost his soul in love. He had lost the souls of others.

And until he saw Kitala Bell, he would have sworn on his life that he would never make the same mistake again.

He drove to the Queen Elizabeth. Gaining access to the theatre was simple—his voice gave him an unfair advantage over weak minds—but he was unprepared for what followed, for what he encountered as he entered that cold dark auditorium.

Power. Power and beauty. M'cal had never heard anything to match, not even amongst the Krackeni, and he recalled, like some idol of an ancient religion, his brief vision of Kitala on stage, her entire spirit coiled like a diamond spring; strong, vital, shining. Blinding his eyes and heart with terrible brilliance.

He had stood there, staring, enveloped in wild sounds that danced like heartbreak; crazed, giant. Listening to her made him feel things he should not. Made him remember things that hurt. Such as the witch and why he had loved her so—for her smile, her body, her face, for shallow pleasures that had overwhelmed and now shamed him.

But this woman, Kitala—her music went beyond beauty into the elemental, and thus, was far more dangerous. Because it was not shallow. And he was not ashamed to love it; to love each note like freedom, like peace, like the cold soft sweep of the sea or the thunder or the light of the moon. Her music made him remember he was not yet dead. It made him feel hope, and that was a cruel drug.

He could still hear Kitala's music inside his head as he carried her over the edge of the shipping yard platform, turning as they fell so that he would bear the impact of the free fall into the water some fifteen feet below. He held her tight in his arms, this woman he was supposed to kill.

She did not scream, but he remembered that sound. Like murder. Like fear and loathing and all those emotions M'cal wished he could express every time the witch touched his body. Every time she forced him to hunt.

He hit the water hard and sank beneath the waves. Kitala struggled, but M'cal refused to release her. For good reason. A small object hissed past his ear—a bullet. Someone was shooting into the water. He took them deeper.

The sea burned his skin. So did Kitala's touch. He ignored the pain, shifting his lungs, feeling gills spread against his neck, just beneath his hairline. Kit's eyes were squeezed shut, mouth clamped tight. Bubbles fled her nose. He felt the strain in her body, her frantic desperation as she thrashed against him. Drowning, slowly.

M'cal breathed, endured the agony of saltwater, and grabbed her nose with his free hand. He pinched it shut. Placed his mouth over hers. Waited for her to run out of air.

It happened fast. Poor lung capacity combined with too much stress. She opened her mouth and he pressed hard against her, breathing into her body. She fought him, but only for a moment, and he patiently held tight, waiting for her to grow accustomed to breathing in such an odd—and intimate—manner.

Kitala tasted like mint. Her mouth was soft and warm. So was her body. It did not matter that touching her felt like being wrapped in jellyfish venom. He could feel her past the pain; could still hear her remarkable music. Singing right down to his soul.

Do not think too hard. Do not feel. Her soul is yours. You must take it. Either way, the witch will compel you.

He could do it now. It would be so easy. Just one

breath. One song, rising from his throat. He could feel the monster waiting.

But the compulsion was not there, not yet. The witch was still giving him the opportunity to choose—that awful choice, which she took such pleasure in. Kitala still had a chance, just as long as she could get away from him. Far and fast, that was the only answer. Assuming she survived long enough to leave the city. That was another mystery—that someone else should want her dead—because what he had just seen and followed and prevented was nothing short of a very focused extermination. And once the last gunman revealed that Kitala still lived, while her would-be murderers did not . . .

M'cal's hand tightened around her waist. Kitala's eyes opened just a sliver. He doubted very much she could see anything, but he pretended that she could, that she knew him, that he was not alone. And when her mouth moved beneath his, he pretended, for a moment, that it was a kiss. Something more than mere survival.

Kitala's fingers dug into his shoulders. She still tasted good. No pain in that, at least. He almost wished there would be. He was feeling things that were entirely unhealthy. And unexpected.

He kicked gently, propelling them through the water. He could hear her heartbeat throbbing with the pulse of the city, with his own blood, and felt her fiddle case bang against his wrist. He carried them out into Coal Harbor, away from the shipping yard and its ghosts and guns, and slowly brought them to the surface.

The moment their heads broke free of the water, Kitala pushed away from his mouth, gasping and blinking water out of her eyes. M'cal did not let her go far; he kept her within the circle of his arms, treading water as she clung to him, orienting herself. Her neck looked raw, but the rest of her was still perfect. A wild mass of curls, weighed down by seawater, framed a delicate face. High cheekbones, dark eyes, skin the color of caramel. Earthy, wild, raw and lovely. Just like her music.

I wish I never saw you, he thought. *I wish I did not know you existed.*

He expected Kitala to speak, but she did not; she merely stared at him, haunted. She shuddered inside the circle of his arms, and he realized his mistake. She was cold. The water was freezing. He had to get her out, fast. For a moment, though, all he could do was look into her eyes, watching that lingering fear fade into something intelligent and far too perceptive.

"You kept me alive down there," she said faintly, teeth beginning to chatter. "You, and nothing else."

Very perceptive. M'cal ignored her unspoken question, tearing his gaze away to study the shore. His car was parked near the shipping yard, but that area was still dangerous. The marina was farther away and little better; the witch would feel him near, posing another, worse risk. M'cal drew Kitala close. Her body hurt him, but he savored the contact; just the same as he embraced the sea, which was a far greater agony.

"Put your arms around my neck," he told her softly, trying to keep his voice steady. "Wrap your legs around my waist."

Kitala stared. "I don't understand."

"Hypothermia," he replied. "The water is too cold for you. I need to swim you back to shore. I was foolish to bring you out here."

"No alternative." She touched her neck with a shaking hand. "There was a gun."

M'cal pulled her hand away and rested his own along her collarbone, his palm burning as he peered at the long red welt, rough enough to have bled. He tried not to think of it deeper, the bullet true, and he looked into her dark eyes. "Why were those men going to kill you?"

Kitala's jaw tightened. "I saw something I shouldn't. Got involved."

"Just that?" he pressed.

"Isn't that enough?" Kitala looked away from him, back to shore. "Are you going to breathe for me again?"

M'cal brushed his thumb against her cheek. She burned him, but he swallowed the pain and said, "Hold tight."

"Do I have a choice?" she asked, but her arms settled around his neck and those long legs curled tight against his hips. He tugged her even closer. Her mouth quirked. "A little too friendly, don't you think?"

Yes, M'cal thought, but all he said was, "You should pinch your nose."

She did, with only a moment's hesitation and a deep breath. M'cal sank them beneath the waves.

He did not wait to kiss her. Nor did she resist. The moment his mouth pressed over hers, she parted her lips, breathing carefully. He lost himself for a moment, had to concentrate to manage swimming and holding her at the same time. He wished he could shift his body, but the clothes confined him, as did Kitala's presence. Breathing for her would create questions enough.

Not that it mattered. For the first time in years he

wanted to hold someone. He wanted to hold *her*. He wanted to keep her safe. He wanted that fear in her eyes—the cold fear those men had made her feel—to disappear. He did not understand those feelings; familiar, but not. So much had been taken from him.

It was difficult to maintain contact. The pain worsened, as did his unease. At any moment the witch might force the compulsion upon him, as she had earlier in the night with Elsie. She played tricks, always changing from one victim to the next. The witch could not read his thoughts or know what he was doing, but that did not mean she would shy away from enforcing her power. She seemed to want Kitala so badly. A mystery; one he was distracted from for a brief moment when he felt something brush close. *Brother seal, still spying.*

M'cal did not take Kitala back to the shipping yard, but instead to a tiny inlet on its outskirts. There was a beach, a park, with easy access by foot to where he had left his car. It was quite possible the last gunman would think to look for them there, but M'cal was ready this time, as he had been for the others.

They surfaced thirty feet off the shore, like seals, poking their heads above water. There were people on the beach, but not many, and those M'cal saw seemed engaged in activities that would preclude caring about a man and woman dragging themselves out of the harbor.

The last stretch was difficult for him. In his other body, the body of his birth, he might have lasted longer, but his skin felt like it was on fire, like he was soaking in acid, and it was too much. He had to let go of Kitala, but she was a stronger swimmer than he imagined and kept pace with him until their knees banged against the rocks and they could stand.

Kitala fell several times before she found her balance. M'cal sensed it had less to do with weariness than a sudden loss of adrenaline and the punch of shattered nerves. Either way, the last time she stumbled it was quite clear she was almost ready to give up and crawl. M'cal did not want to see that. He wrapped his arm around her waist, helping her stand, holding her steady.

"Thank you," she mumbled, her hand buried in the front of his shirt. A tremor raced through her body, a bone-deep chill. Her fiddle case banged against his burning arm.

He grunted. "Can you walk? My car—"

"I can get there," she interrupted, shivering. "Just point me in the right direction."

They sloshed out of the ocean, dripping, and walked from the beach to the grass, cutting across the small park to the road. M'cal let go of Kitala when he thought she could stand on her own. He did not want to, but he needed the distance. He touched his bracelet. The metal was warm.

They arrived at the road and turned left. M'cal focused on staying upright. His clothing was soaked in seawater; until he stripped down and dried off, he was going to be very uncomfortable.

"What's your name?" Kitala asked. Her teeth chattered.

"M'cal," he answered, without thinking.

"Interesting," she said, rubbing her arms. "That doesn't sound like a western name."

"I did not choose it."

"I didn't mean anything." She gave him a curious look, her gaze flickering down to his throat. She seemed to flinch, though it might have been the cold.

Glancing away from him, she said, "My name is Kit. Kit Bell."

Not Kitala? M'cal wanted to ask, but he stayed silent.

The street was dark. M'cal heard men talking, glass shattering, but nothing near. No sign of that last gunman. He moved a little closer to Kitala. She glanced up at him, a question in her eyes. No fear. Nothing like that. He thought of the violence she had experienced—the violence she had seen him commit—and wondered how she could still be so calm. How she could look at him as a man, a person, when no one else seemed to.

"Thank you," she said quietly. "For everything."

He could feel the monster inside his throat, waiting. "Do not thank me."

Again, that sharpness in her eyes. "Why?"

He didn't answer. He saw his car, parked beneath a tree, between a truck and a rusty minivan. He had a Porsche, a gleaming black Cayman. A gift from the witch for services rendered. She bought him everything he needed, but only because she knew he hated it. His clothes, the vehicle—all were reminders that she owned him. That he was her toy.

M'cal unlocked the car and gave Kitala the keys. "Take it. Go."

She stood there, staring. "Aren't you coming with me?"

He opened the driver-side door. "It is safer for you without me."

Kit stared. "You saved my life."

M'cal grabbed her arm. His palm burned, but he held on tight and tried shoving her inside the Porsche, mercilessly using his strength. She slammed one foot against the side of the car and pushed back. M'cal leaned close to her ear. She smelled like the sea.

"I was sent here to kill you," he rasped, jerking her around to face him. "I am still supposed to kill you. And I will, if you do not leave this place. *Right now.*"

She did not blink, though he could hear her heart fluttering, wild. "You rescued me."

"No," he breathed. "Do not trust that."

"I trust what I see." Kit's voice hardened. "I trust what I feel."

"You should not trust. Eyes betray. As do hearts." M'cal suppressed a shiver, desperation rising in his throat. His heart ached. The bracelet grew even warmer. "Go back to your hotel. Pack your bags. Leave this city. Get as far from here as you can."

Horror flickered through her gaze; he steeled himself against it, pushing again on her body. But she still resisted.

"No," she breathed, fear in her voice. "No, I won't be bullied. Tell me what's going on. Were you part of the group who kidnapped Alice?"

"I do not know any Alice," M'cal said wearily. "Just you. You were my target. I would have taken you after your concert, at the hotel. I parked there, waiting for you. I had a good view of the street. I saw everything, and followed."

Kitala shivered. M'cal reached past her into the car. She swayed away from him, but that was all. So stubborn. It was going to get her killed.

He had a coat in the front seat. He did not need one—the cold rarely affected him—but he had been caught naked enough times leaving the sea that having a spare set of clothes seemed practical. He found the plastic bag holding his extra pants and shirt. Keeping those, he draped the coat over Kit's slender shoulders. She let him, without comment. The black wool hung loose and huge. His hands stayed on her shoulders, burning and burning. Right through to his heart.

"Who hired you?" she asked again, keeping completely still.

M'cal did not answer. This was taking too long. He opened his mouth and began to sing.

He did not steal her soul; that monster still slept. What poured through his throat was another kind of beast, elegant and full of the old dark deep. A siren call, an incubus song, a lure to rocks and storm and dream. His heart pounded a triple beat, inhuman; quick and strong.

Kitala swayed, eyelids fluttering. Her lips parted. M'cal remembered the taste of her mouth and found himself bending close, his throat humming his wordless song, wrapping her mind in his need, his desire for her to—*go, go now, forget me, be safe and forget*—enter the car and drive away.

I do not know you, he thought. *But I will miss you.*

He could not help himself. M'cal kissed her again, for real this time. It hurt, but her lips were warmer than the burning, and her breath still tasted of mint. He did not press—the contact was light—but she leaned into him, and through his song he heard another melody, a counter harmony. Kitala was singing softly, barely louder than his own deep-throated whispering hum.

He remembered hearing her sing once before, in the shipping yard; it had distracted him, made him falter. It did the same again. There was something in her voice, something he could not name, a sister to the notes plucked from her fiddle: a strong and soft and powerful music. It lulled him, just the same as he was doing to her; except she was still not moving, not obeying, and he realized, quite suddenly, that he was no longer in pain.

Touching her. Still wet with seawater. Not in pain.

He broke off the kiss and stumbled back. Kitala opened her eyes and stopped singing. The pain returned, but only just; the discomfort was a dull echo of what it had been.

"What did you do to me?" M'cal whispered, staring. The bracelet thrummed against his skin.

Kitala touched her mouth, eyes wide. "Nothing."

M'cal took a step, then stopped, holding back. "You *sang*."

"So did you." Her voice shook. She jerked her head toward the shipping yard. "You've done a lot of that tonight. A lot of strange things."

No *stranger than you*, he thought, fingering the bracelet. It made his skin tingle, the sensation traveling right down to the bone. In his throat, the monster stirred.

The witch. He had taken too long to come home.

"Go," M'cal muttered, shutting his eyes, fighting the compulsion. He succeeded—shockingly—but only for a moment. Whatever immunity Kitala had given him was slipping fast. Too fast.

And she was still too close. She said his name. He could feel her reaching out to touch him.

No. No, no, *no*—

"Go!" he screamed. Kitala flinched, and he rushed her, stopping less than a foot away with his fists raised. This time she did not argue. She slipped backward into the car, slammed the door and locked it. Stared at him through the glass for one long moment, confusion and anger in her eyes. M'cal pointed to the road, hand shaking, and she started the engine. Gave him one last look that made his heart ache.

She pulled out and drove away. Fast. M'cal watched the brake lights disappear. The only shred of hope he had found in years, and he had just let her go.

Better than stealing her soul.

The urge to follow was overwhelming. Even after years of being subjected to it, M'cal still did not understand the witch's curse; only that she had set him like a hound to the scent, and while distance would lessen the compulsion to hunt Kitala, as long as the witch wanted her, the desire would remain. Unfortunately, there was a part of M'cal that *wanted* to find her. Hoped he would as long as he did not hurt her. Poor chance of that.

He started walking down the road. It was late, and the air was quiet. He wanted to stop, but his legs were compelled to keep moving. He still carried his bag of clothes. He yanked his shirt over his head without stopping and tossed it on the ground. Dressed in the new button-up. The material was dry and soft. His skin felt better, though the lower half of his body would have to wait for dry clothes until the compulsion faded. If it ever would. He would not put it past the witch to keep him walking until morning.

M'cal could think of worse ways to spend his time.

Through the trees he could see the shipping containers; the distant bulk of the cruise ships. No streetlights around him. The air was cool and smelled of oil and metal; the pavement was wet from the earlier evening rain.

He pretended not to notice the light tread of footsteps behind him. Nor did he turn when something cold and hard suddenly pressed against the back of his head. A long, strong arm grabbed his shoulder, holding him steady. M'cal managed to stand still, but his legs twitched, feet scuffing the ground.

"Fidgety," said a low voice in his ear. "Guilty conscience?"

"No," M'cal said.

"You killed some friends of mine," said the unseen man. "Don't know how you did it, but it was good work. Good enough that I'm gonna have to fuck you up the ass with some bullets."

"Okay," M'cal said.

"Okay," echoed the man, laughing quietly. "Right. But first, you tell me about that bitch. You tell me where she lives. And maybe I'll put the gun in your mouth instead."

"Who wants her dead?" M'cal asked.

"I do," said the man. "All part of the job."

"Surely you can tell me more."

" 'Surely you can tell me more,' " the man minced. "Jesus. You sound like such a fag. Maybe I'll make you suck my dick for the information, huh? I bet you'd like that."

"We should do something about the gun first," M'cal said.

And he began to sing.

CHAPTER FOUR

Kit remembered the first time she saw a murder.

She was six. Her bedroom was on the second floor of a house her parents rented on the outskirts of Nashville. That was the bad part of town, she later learned, though she did not know the difference or care when she was young. Just that for the first time they had heat in winter and food on the table at every meal, and her mother did not cry when she came home from her job at night. Nashville was a good place. The people liked jazz as much as country, even if the singer was a black woman from Louisiana. Even if her husband was a white fiddler from the Great Smoky Mountains. Even if folks were not supposed to mingle that way.

It was at night. Kit was sitting up in her bed, which was right below the window overlooking Montgomery Street. The moon was out. She saw a woman walking alone down the sidewalk. A man ran toward her. The woman did not turn. He shouted something—her name, maybe—and she stopped, looked.

Then she died. Shot in the face. The man kept on running.

Later, the police questioned Kit. *A crime of passion*, they told her parents, but that did not mean anything. Not when she could still see the moonlit explosion of the woman's head, the splatter of blood, brain.

Everything changed after that. Or, at least, one thing had changed: her vision.

Kit drove the Porsche fast. Her neck throbbed as if little needles made of fire were tattooing the wound. A doctor was out of the question. Someone with a sharp eye might recognize a near miss with a bullet, and she could not risk anyone filing a police report.

You're in deep shit, she told herself. *So deep. And it's only going to get worse.*

Much worse, if her instincts were right. And they usually were.

Kit located the road into downtown, following her memories of maps and landmarks, and found Hotel Georgia after only several missteps and a mile or two spent reacquainting herself with a manual transmission. She parked M'cal's car across the street, which still had some late-night foot traffic. But down the road, where the old man had died, and where Kit and Alice had run, the sidewalk was quiet, empty. Body and trauma were both gone, with only Kit's ghost of a memory to tell her it had happened. She wondered if Officer Yu had been the sniper. Or someone else. The dark alley stared at her, and Kit tore her gaze away, looking at her hands clutching an unfamiliar steering wheel. She tried not to shake.

Her fingers hurt when she finally pried them loose, but even though part of her wanted to run, she took her time and searched the car's interior for anything revealing. She found nothing—except the registration in the glove compartment, which listed a Michael Oberon as the Porsche's owner.

"Michael Oberon," she murmured. Not *M'cal*.

But that's his name. That's the name that suits.

Whatever. It did not matter. After tonight she would never see him again, and that was good. He was a dead man walking. Same with every other person on the planet, but having it shoved in Kit's face— the violence and certainty of it—hurt more than she wanted to admit. A lifetime of trying to desensitize herself, and in one night all those walls were crumbling down.

She tried to harden herself. It should have been easy. The man had said outright that he had been sent to take her life—something that should have made her run the first time he said it, though she had not. Instead she had engaged him, pressing him with questions because his eyes told a different story than his voice, and the way he touched her, protected her, spoke a different language than death.

And if someone had hired him to kill her, why and who was a mystery. Kit had no stalkers, never received obscene letters, rarely had people asking for her autograph; she was boring offstage, plain and simple.

Not so boring. Not if people knew what your eyes tell you.

Which made Kit stop for a moment, trying to recall if there was anyone—*anyone*—who might possibly know her secret. Only her parents and grandmother came to mind; she had always been careful with anyone else. And she trusted her family above all others to keep secret what she could do. Not that it was enough to kill over.

M'cal would not have killed you, whispered a persistent little voice. *He saved you. He was still trying to save you when he scared you away.*

Kit just wished she understood why. She could still feel the warmth and pressure of his mouth, the strength of his arms. All of it, burned into her memory. Just like his face. And his future murder.

Blood filled her mind; she grasped for something else, anything.

Blue eyes, she thought. The man—Michael, *M'cal*—had blue eyes the color of a cold winter sky, clear and sharp. Unforgiving eyes, hard eyes, but with flickers of such raw emotion, Kit could still feel her heart aching for him. She did not understand her feelings. She could blame her lack of fear on the fact that he had saved her life, but as for rest . . .

Feeling anything at all for him was dangerous. M'cal was not safe.

Safe enough to keep you alive. On land and *underwater.* Another riddle Kit did not feel like contemplating.

She left the Porsche's keys inside the glove compartment and locked the car, then went up to her hotel room, looking over her shoulder the entire time. Changed clothes. Packed. Checked out over the phone and asked the front desk to call her a cab. Realized, at the last moment, that she still had M'cal's coat. It was a nice big coat. Her own was still wet. She hesitated, then slipped her arms into the loose, long sleeves. Found herself imagining, for a moment, that it was his body keeping her warm. M'cal had radiated a great deal of heat. She remembered that, too. Along with darker things.

Kit did not go to the airport. It crossed her mind, for all of ten seconds. Instead, she traveled a grand distance of five blocks and paid cash for a room at the Hyatt. The clerk gave her a strange look but said nothing. Kit got her key and fled up the elevator. By the time she reached her room, she had begun to shiver. Inside, with the door locked behind her, the shivering turned into a teeth-jarring shudder that racked her bones with violent chills.

Kit dumped all her belongings on the floor and collapsed on the bed. Her heart hammered against her ribs; her head was dizzy, it was hard to breathe, and each rough inhalation managed to feel like the prelude to vomit. Murder, kidnapping, mayhem—all were finally catching up with her. Kit felt like she was having a heart attack. Drowning. Her body no longer belonged to her. The terrible throbbing in her neck did not help either. She probably had an infection.

It's just panic, she told herself, trying to catch a breath. *Nothing more. Calm. Think calm.*

But thinking good thoughts was not enough, nor was the tune she hummed, and after a brief internal struggle she crawled off the bed for her purse. She found her Xanax in a small bottle at the bottom. She kept the medicine for air travel, but this was as good an exception as any. Kit popped half of a pill in her mouth and let it dissolve, grimacing at the bitter taste.

It helped, though. Her heart began to slow. She stopped shivering. Breathed easier, without that frightening tightness in her chest, or the nausea. The medication made her drowsy, too. She closed her eyes and fell asleep.

She dreamed. Sharp dreams, strong; more vision than fantasy, which made her afraid. She dreamed like she was awake, and she knew the feeling for what it was: a blood legacy, like her glimpses of murder.

She dreamed of M'cal. It was not a good dream. He lay on his back in a circle of sand, naked, but the lower half of his body was inhuman. He had the tail of a fish, iridescent and straining with long, rippling muscles. His body glistened with water, and his hair was wet, plastered against his face, framing eyes so anguished, so heartbroken, Kit could feel his pain like a punch in the gut.

There was blood on him. Bite marks. Nothing held him down, yet he seemed unable to sit up. Kit listened to him scream. Felt herself begin to do the same.

The dream changed. Kit staggered, temporarily blind to everything but M'cal's voice inside her head, begging for help. Not her help. Not the help of any one person. But just someone. *Someone, please.*

Kit choked back tears, terrible inexplicable grief. She felt seared to the soul by his pain, by his impossible appearance, which had no precedent in her life or mind even if it was just a dream. She *knew* it was just a dream. It could not be more. Not after what she had just seen. It was too impossible.

Kit smelled mint. Her dream changed. M'cal's voice died away, replaced by John Fogerty's "Born on the Bayou," turned way up on some radio. Beneath the pump and brawl of the song, she heard her grandmother singing along.

Old Jazz Marie, a woman of round curves, perched on a stool on the veranda, with the hot summer wind blowing through the cypresses from the swamp. Kit held her breath, staring. It had been a long time since she dreamed of her grandmother. A year, to be exact. The last time had been on the night of her death.

"Storm coming," said the old woman, a thick bone needle in her hand. She threaded a narrow leather cord through a piece of hide. In front of her, on the battered table, Kit saw herbs and roots; a chicken foot, some bits of fur; a cup brimming with soft, rich dirt. Little stones. Little dolls. Little bones.

Kit watched her grandmother's face, studying the high, wide cheeks, the polished amber undertones of her dark skin. Her hair had been gray for years—as steely and sharp as a thundercloud—and she wore it wild, held back only by a dark red scarf.

"You always say that," Kit said. "There's always a storm."

"Hush. Don't go twisting words on an old woman." Her grandmother stopped sewing and looked at her, straight and clear. "You caught the mark on this one, Kitty Bella. Got eyes on you, for sure. Knew it would happen eventually. Women like us can't go 'round without drawing attention. Bad and good."

"I'm nothing like you," Kit said gently. "Despite what I see."

"*Because* of what you see." Old Jazz Marie spat into the leather, rubbing it hard with her thumb. "Because of what you do. You got power, little cat. And you're gonna need it."

"Tell me. I don't understand."

"You never did. Enough talent to choke a volcano, but you still don't know your ass from a hole in the ground. Hell, child. Come here."

Kit did as she was told, and watched her grandmother pierce her thumb with the bone needle. Blood welled. Just enough to smear across Kit's neck wound. Old Jazz Marie's breath quickened, and she mumbled a string of words in some indecipherable patois. She ended with a high mighty cry that cut Kit right down to the bone.

The old woman slumped over, closing her eyes. She looked tired, weary, as she had only days before her death. Kit reached out to touch her, but her grandmother knocked away her hand. Her eyes were still closed.

"Get going," she murmured, breath whistling through her teeth. "Get gone. You been dreamin' too long."

"No," Kit said. "I miss you."

"No time." The old woman's shoulders hunched even more. "You gotta be strong, girl. Strong in the heart. Trust yourself. Trust *him*."

"Him?" she echoed, startled; but it was too late. Her grandmother died again, slipped away with a breath, and Kit opened her eyes, awake. Her cheeks were wet. She was still crying.

Morning. Light outside. Kit stared at the ceiling and pulled her heart back together, listening to "Raglan Road" curl through her mind as she sewed and mended the cuts caused by seeing her grandmother again. By seeing M'cal.

She touched her neck, searching. Found no blood. No wound either. Her skin was smooth. The pain was gone.

Kit closed her eyes, suffering a deep chill, heartache. She did not bother rising to look into a mirror. It was not the first healing Old Jazz Marie had performed on her granddaughter. Of course, the last time she had done it, she had been alive.

Granny, Granny, Kit called out silently, touching the gris-gris tangled tight with her cross. *What is going on?*

No one answered. Of course.

Kit wiped her face and rolled over to look at the

clock. It was eight. She had slept the whole night. Wasted all that time. Alice might be dead.

She's already dead—today, tomorrow, or next week. You can't change fate. Just walk away.

Walk away, as she should have done in the first place. As she had with so many others, including M'cal, who had saved her life. She'd taken the path of the cold heart, because there were just too many people needing help, and not one of them would have believed Kit if she had told the truth—which was unpleasant, unhelpful. *Don't get murdered* were not words to inspire hope.

But this time was different. Kit had taken that step and Alice had believed her. For what good it had done.

Kit sat up slowly. Her muscles ached, and her mouth tasted rotten. She perched for a moment on the edge of the bed, staring out the window. The city was gray in the daylight. Gray skies, gray buildings. She could see Coal Harbor between the high-rises, wondered how many people could say they had ever almost drowned in that cold water. Probably more than she wanted to know.

Kit found her fiddle case and popped the latch. The airtight seal caused a sucking sound, but that only made her smile. She bought nothing but the best for her fiddle, which had a smooth sweet tone courtesy of a backwoods genius in Tennessee, retired from the craft except for the occasional custom job. Old Earl, who happened to be a friend of her father's, could make violins that rivaled any Stradivarius. Not that the man was prone to bragging. Kit's fiddle had been a gift on her tenth birthday, and it was made of Smokey Mountain blood and bones, with a sound just as powerful.

The interior velvet of the case, purple as a summer iris, was still dry. Thank goodness she had insisted on a waterproof construction, and a custom tight fit. The fiddle lay in its soft foam bed like an amber jewel, fit for the hand of a queen. And when Kit played her music, she felt like one. She removed the instrument, made herself comfortable, and laid it on her stomach. Plucked a tune while she stared at the ceiling.

So. Men had tried to kill her. Men who worked for corrupt police officers. Corrupt police officers hired to murder and kidnap. She wondered if Officer Yu and her partner knew who she was. If they would come looking for her once they found out she was still alive.

Of course they'll come. You saw everything.

And there was M'cal to think of, as well. What he had told her. Someone else wanted her dead.

Trust yourself. Trust him.

Him. M'cal. Kit recalled her dream, her vision: a hole in his throat gushing blood; his eyes, burning with heartbreak; his body, transformed.

He breathed underwater, said a little voice. *He breathed for you both.*

Kit still wore his coat. She buried her nose in the thick wool collar, caught a scent, strong and masculine; but it was nothing she could identify. Only, it was warm and dark, and made her think of the sea.

Kit set aside her fiddle and curled deeper inside M'cal's coat, surrounding herself with the shadow of his presence, once again pretending it was his arms, his long, lean body. It made her feel safe. And stupid. The man was a killer. No matter his reasons.

Trust him, echoed her grandmother's voice. Easier said than done. *If* he was the man she was referring to.

Kit forced herself to sit up and went searching for her jacket, which was still wet. She rummaged through the pockets and found the soggy remains of the business card Alice had slipped her. The card was simple and white. It belonged to an Alice Hardon, Youth Counselor, at 300 Templar Street.

A youth counselor worth killing over? Worth paying cops to break the law?

Kit blew out her breath. Alice had given her the card for a reason. Perhaps someone at her workplace would know what kind of trouble she was in. Maybe even how to find her. Not that Kit could go to the police with that information. She wasn't sure she could trust any cop now.

Kit drummed her fingers against the bed, weighing her options. There were only two: run or fight. Both were poor. She was no Rambo Tomb Raider Amazon who kicked ass on her days off.

But she was no coward either. Not even close.

Kit grabbed the phone. Hesitated, then dialed a number. Held her breath. Because when times were tough, it was good to have a best friend. Maybe her only friend, given that Kit socialized about as much as a rock. Delilah Reese was another fine artist, but her medium was metal, not music. Not that it mattered. Their grandmothers had been friends, and had introduced the two girls at the tender ages of twelve and thirteen. No looking back after that.

But Dela was more than a good friend; she was a friend with connections. The kind that carried guns.

She answered on the third ring, sounding calm, alert. Probably up to her elbows in hot metal. She had an art exhibit soon.

Kit exhaled. "It's good to hear your voice."

"Hello to you, too," Dela said slowly. "But why do I get the feeling this isn't a pleasure call?"

"Because it's not," Kit replied, and after making sure her friend was sitting down, told her entire story. Mostly. She left out the part about how she knew Alice was going to die. Nor did she mention how M'cal had breathed for her underwater, or forced men to kill themselves with nothing but his voice. That was too . . . strange. And disturbing. Something Dela would never believe. Something Kit did not want to explain. She had secrets, just as Dela, she suspected, had her own.

Her friend remained silent for a very long time. Kit said, "Hey."

"Hey. Would it be impolite of me to say that you're screwed?"

Kit rolled her eyes. "Anything else?"

"You need to get out of town?"

"I wish."

"Well, wish your way onto an airplane. I'll even spring for the ticket."

"It's not that easy, Dela. I can't go until I know this woman is safe."

"Bullshit. You've done your duty with this phone call. The agency will handle the rest. They're the best, Kit."

They, meaning Dirk & Steele, the detective agency Dela's grandparents had founded and run for the better part of sixty years. According to her, it had one of the finest reputations in the world; and Kit believed it. She had even dated one of its agents—Blue Perrineau, a real boy scout. All of the agents were to some degree, best as she had seen. She doubted Dela and her family would settle for less.

"I have to be involved," Kit said.

"You're in danger. On more than one front."

"Doesn't matter. I feel responsible for Alice. You'd feel the same if you had been there. They were brutal, Dela. Ruthless. But she still tried to help me. Those men were forcing me out of the car, and she . . ." Kit stopped, swallowing hard. "I have to do this." Had to help one person, as if it would make up for all the others. Though if Alice, then why not M'cal as well? Why had she resisted telling him?

He said he was going to kill you. What do you owe him for that?

Easy answer. She owed him her life. Kit counted heartbeats. Listened to the wind howl outside the hotel window. A storm was coming.

Dela finally sighed. "We need to find out what Alice Hardon and her uncle were into."

"Hope you're not planning on involving the cops," Kit said.

"No. Not yet. Just the Gunslingers." That was Dela's pet name for the men and women of the detective agency.

M'cal's coat collar still pressed against Kit's cheek. She did not push it away. Inside her head, a passage from Mussorgsky's *Night on Bald Mountain* pounded, keeping time with her heart. The music reminded her of M'cal's eyes. She inhaled, tugging the coat closer.

Crazy. You are so damn crazy to still want his scent.

But it was a shield; better than thinking about those men, what they had done to her. What they would have done. Better to remember M'cal and his scent. His mouth. His arms. His hands.

Hands that had broken Dutch's neck. Hands that belonged to a man who could sing others to death, who had impaled another with a long steel pipe.

Kit closed her eyes. "I appreciate your help, Dela. More than I can say."

"You're my friend," Dela said quietly. "I would come myself if I could, but Mahari is sick, and even if I could find someone to watch him, I shouldn't travel right now. I shouldn't even be at the forge."

"Three months left, right?" Kit smiled, feeling wistful. "I'm surprised you can walk."

"I think I'm having a litter," Dela said, with so little humor Kit bit back a joke that sprang to mind. "Just you wait until it's your turn."

"Never," she replied, making her voice light, breezy. "Never going to happen."

Dela, thankfully, was a good enough friend not to give her the obvious lecture. Like, *It won't happen if you don't make time for it*, or, *It'll happen when you least expect it*. She left it alone. Moved on.

"It just so happens that Hari is in Seattle for the weekend," she said. "He's with some of the other guys. They're, um, having a reunion of sorts."

Hari was Dela's husband, a giant of a man who looked like a warrior out of a fairytale but who held his wife's hand like it was made of snow and glass; precious, delicate. Dela had met him in China under mysterious circumstances—which she had *still* not shared—and dragged him home, willing that he was, like a prize from war. The two had been joined at the hip ever since.

Kit could only imagine the trouble those other guys

were getting him in. "Did the big men bring teddy bears and matching pajamas?"

"You have no idea."

"Darn," Kit said. "My world for a camera."

Dela snorted. "They can get to you in less than three hours, maybe two. Think you can stay put for that long?"

"Sure."

"*Kit.*"

"Relax," Kit replied, fingering Alice's business card. "Where could I possibly go?"

She took a shower after she got off the phone with Dela. Washed away the night. Touched her neck, prodding the skin. There was no sign of any wound, not even on her scalp where she had been hit. A chill settled through her. She pretended it was her grandmother, and the cold turned warm.

Her hair remained a soft mess—more frizz than curls—but Kit tied it back with a red scarf that draped over the collar of her denim jacket. Shades of Jazz Marie. Thinking for a moment, Kit slipped on her reading glasses with their thick tortoiseshell frames, trying to pull a fast Clark Kent. Secret Identity 101. She looked into the mirror and studied her face. She imagined her grandmother staring back; she had the old woman's eyes.

Uncanny, her father had once said. *Uncanny and beautiful.*

Kit almost called her parents. She wanted to hear their voices; something warm, familiar. Someone to reassure her. Someone to say good-bye to, just in case.

She checked her cell phone. It was wet, much like

everything else in her green leather purse. She tried to turn it on, and nothing happened. Busted. She tossed it back into her bag, glanced at the hotel phone, and looked away. Grabbed her fiddle case and left the room.

There was an ATM in the marble lobby. Kit withdrew as much as she could and paid for another night. Pocketing the rest, she grabbed one of the idling cabs waiting in the cramped drive just outside the glass doors.

The cabbie was a swarthy man; dark beard, sharp eyes, white turban. He had an Indian accent. He looked at the address on Alice's business card and said, "That's right off East Hastings. Not a good neighborhood. You sure you want to go there?"

"Have to," Kit said. "You won't take me?"

"No, no," he said, handing back the card. "Just a warning. You stay in this place, you have money. People with money don't go to that street. Not on purpose. Too much shit."

Kit did not say anything. She knew poor. Poor did not frighten her. Finding Alice dead with a knife in her eye, on the other hand, did. Ending up like Alice, or worse, scared her even more.

The cabbie drove fast. Downtown spirited by in a rush, sleek and tall and modern. It was a Saturday, and the sidewalks were full of youthful athleticism, cool charm. Vancouver felt like a young city. Kit wanted to stand on some street corner and play her fiddle, to busk as she had on the sidewalks of New York and Nashville with her father.

Good training, he liked to say. *Nothing keeps an artist sharper than trying to reel in folks who don't want to be reeled.*

Kit wondered what else she needed to sharpen up on. Maybe kickboxing. Swimming. Running like hell. Or better yet, shutting off her mind so she never saw another murdered man or woman in her life.

They drove through Gastown; all brick and cobblestone, buildings that reeked of the historic, spilling over with shops and restaurants; quaint, elegant, hip. Just like any other tourist-trap shopping district in any other city in the world. Kit thought it needed music to make it click.

Then the neighborhood changed. Several turns down some narrow streets and the city crumbled, right before her eyes, transforming like Cinderella's pumpkin carriage at midnight into a street of torn facades and broken windows, boarded-up restaurants plastered in paper advertisements of indie concerts and movies. There were some signs of life: several 99-cent stores, some diners, a liquor depot. Billboards painted on tall buildings declared them to be hotels—rooms rented by the week or the hour. Nothing Kit hadn't seen before. Or hadn't lived in.

Templar Street appeared to be in the heart of the Hastings district, a block down from a long line of homeless people waiting to enter a soup kitchen. It was chilly out, overcast, but women trawled the street corner in short skirts and high heels, jacket collars piled high with fake fur rubbing their cheeks. Some of them were marked as dead—strangled, beaten, shot. Hard to look at; visions of murder swam hot in Kit's head.

Kit glimpsed their pimp sitting on a folding chair just inside the old arching doorway of an apartment building. He had long blond hair, a pale skinny face, hard, narrow eyes that reminded her of Dutch. No future murder for him, but that didn't mean much. There was a girl in his lap. He watched the cab as it drove by—Kit felt like he watched her, too.

The cabbie stopped less than a hundred feet away, beside a pale white building with a low roof and tall windows. It looked old, probably historic; a folding placard sat outside the tinted glass double doors. YOUTH CENTER, it said, but the cheerfully painted balloons, hearts, and flowers would have given that away even without the big letters.

"You want me to wait?" asked the cab driver. "Might be hard to get another ride."

"I'll be fine," she said. "But thanks."

The air outside the cab smelled like piss and vomit. A lot of piss and vomit. Kit glanced down the street. The pimp was watching her. She hardened her expression and walked into the Youth Center.

It was clean inside, and large, like a warehouse. Smelled like vanilla and candy and tennis shoes. The walls had all been turned into long, sprawling murals, one of which was currently in the process of being painted by some teenagers whose dreadlocks probably weighed more than their bodies. In one corner, a miniature library had been set up; in another, pinball machines. There were several long tables filled with board games, and off to the left a row of doors that Kit thought just might lead to offices.

But at the front of the Youth Center, directly to Kit's left, there was a desk with a pale, slender brunette seated behind it, whose smile was so big she was either a magnificently unhappy person or just slightly deranged. She wore a nametag that looked like a clown. It said MOLLY! in big letters.

"Hello," Molly said. "Are you here for the pregnancy screening?"

Kit stared. "Um, no. I need to speak to someone about Alice Hardon."

"Alice isn't in today." Molly's smile slipped just a fraction. "She'll be back on Monday."

If only. "I don't need to speak *to* Alice. Just—"

"About her. Yes, I heard you the first time." Molly leaned forward, hands clasped. "But see, we don't just let *anyone* in here to *talk*. Especially *about* our colleagues. It's against policy. So if you have a problem with Alice—"

"That's not it at all—"

"—you are more than welcome to send a letter to our head counselor, Edith, who will determine whether or not to speak further with you. About Alice."

Kit fought her temper. "You're not listening to me. I really need to speak to someone."

"You're speaking to me," Molly said, smile gone. "And you're the one who's not listening."

"This is an emergency."

"It always is with you people," replied the woman coldly, and reached for her book.

Well, fuck that. Kit pulled out Alice's business card and leaned over Molly's desk, shoving it under her nose. "Now you listen," she said in a hard voice. "Alice gave me this card last night. She *asked* me to come here. So you tell me who the heck I should talk to, *right now,* or else the next time I see Alice, I am going to tell her exactly how her *secretary* shot her shit up. You got that, bitch?"

"It would be hard not to," said a low familiar voice, rumbling like the distant edge of some terrible thunder.

Kit felt all the blood drain from her face. She turned around.

M'cal stood behind her, one hand holding open the front door. The corner of his mouth tilted up, but it was a small, sad smile.

"You should have taken my advice," he said.

CHAPTER FIVE

The witch made him walk. Fortunately, the compulsion seemed specific only to finding Kitala, and because M'cal had every intention of doing just that—in the slowest, most roundabout way possible—he'd been able to choose the direction his roving feet took him. He'd done so, determinedly following the limited information given to him by a dead man who now lay shut inside a shipping container with seven other bloody bodies.

One thing was clear: Kitala Bell, musician extraordinaire, had landed herself in a great deal of trouble. M'cal wanted to know why. His reasons were not rational. It was merely a need to know. A suspicion that one answer might lead to another. *Why those men? Why the witch? Why her? Why now?* Because the other women M'cal had brought home, like Elsie, were just food. Random catches. Kitala was different. The *urgency* was different. And if the witch *needed* her—

He'd stopped himself, startled once again at the strength of his thoughts. He had forgotten what that felt like. He could not imagine forgetting, but there—*there*—he could feel the difference, burning in his spirit. Hunger. Raw and burning.

You used to fight harder, he told himself, still hearing Elsie's screams inside his head. *You used to do everything you could to save lives, to defy the witch. And now you make excuses when she gives you a command. Now you say it does not matter, because it will happen anyway, because she will force you. You are giving up responsibility for yourself. That is no way to live.*

But it was the only way he had—the only way he might ever have, for the rest of his life. The brief taste of freedom Kitala had given him was more torture than pleasure.

Ivan found him only an hour before dawn, three blocks away from Hotel Georgia. A bad time of day for the big man. It was a sign of desperation on the witch's part that she would send him to fetch M'cal at such a late hour.

Ivan drove a black Jaguar. The car had a loud engine, because the witch's man tended to drive his vehicles without any kind of maintenance until they broke down around him. Buying cars was a sport, something Ivan enjoyed almost as much as murder.

He'd heard Ivan coming a block before he actually appeared, and waited on a street corner until the big man pulled up beside him. Ivan left the engine running. He rolled down the driver's-side window and stared, shark eyes sharp and glinting.

"I think she already knows there was a mishap," M'cal said. "Telling her myself would be redundant."

Ivan continued to watch him, unblinking. M'cal tapped the bracelet. "Tell her to make me."

Ivan picked up his cell phone, his bracelet peeking from underneath his dark sleeve. He began to type out a text message. It was painful to watch, like asking a sea manatee to perform sign language with one flipper. And it made M'cal question, once again, the peculiar limits of the witch's powers. Surely if she could enslave a merman, a Krackeni—bind him, curse him, torture him—drink human souls like the wine she so greatly enjoyed with every meal, she could read Ivan's little mind from a grand distance of several miles.

Or not. Ivan continued the laborious process of typing. M'cal, itching to move again, tried not to think of Kitala, wherever she might be.

He glanced around, looking for anyone who might be watching. Downtown was quiet this time of day; he had seen only one police cruiser. He wondered if it was the same car that had dumped Kitala off at the docks.

M'cal thought he heard a crunching sound; distant, hard to place, followed by an odd snap, almost like billowing sail. He glanced around, searching, and his gaze traveled up to the skyscrapers. He saw something move. Very high, above his head. A shadow, gliding. Not a bird. Not a plane. It disappeared around a building, and though M'cal waited and watched, it did not reappear.

M'cal looked at Ivan, and found the big man staring at the same piece of sky. His eyes narrowed to slits, his jowls shook and the nickel spots of red burned so bright they looked painted on.

Ivan gave no warning. He gunned the Jaguar's rattling engine and sped away from the curb, leaving M'cal in a cloud of exhaust.

Interesting. Very curious.

M'cal searched the skies again, his tingling fingers tapping his thick bracelet. He tried to remember his history, all those legends and truths his father had been so keen on him learning. Several options sprang to mind, all of them remote. Nor did anything offer a ready connection to his current predicament.

Something had happened to frighten the witch. Something that made her believe she needed Kitala Bell and the power of Kitala's soul. Whatever power that might be.

Power enough to save your life. Strong enough to free you from the witch.

If only. M'cal swallowed down a bitter taste, fighting regret. He had done the right thing tonight. The first right thing in a long time. No matter what happened, at least he could rest easy with that. And he had believed that if Kitala had any sense, she was already gone from this city. Safe and whole and able to keep making that lovely incandescent music.

But just in case—because M'cal took nothing for granted, not anymore—he had planned to solve one last problem for her. The only gift he could give Kitala, even though she would never know of it: He was going to make her safe again. He was going to kill the people who had ordered her death. He was going to eliminate their bosses, burn them to the ground, scatter the ashes and make it known: *Do not touch, do not kill, do not go close.* Anything to keep them from hunting Kitala, wherever she might go.

A place, apparently, not so far away after all.

Kitala was beautiful. M'cal had not forgotten, but now, in the clear, sharp light of day, her vitality, her glow, was almost blinding. He stopped breathing when she turned to look at him; felt his world lurch, collapse. But he remembered the danger in the same moment their eyes met, and it stole his joy. His shocking, surprising joy.

"How did you find me?" Kitala asked, staring. M'cal found himself wondering the exact same thing. He glanced behind her at the woman sitting behind the desk. She was staring at him, expression startled, verging on dreamy, her mouth just slightly agape. A flush touched her pale cheeks. Kitala glanced over her shoulder, rolled her eyes—and met his gaze again, this time with a small, wry smile that curled hard into his gut. It felt good. Unfamiliar, but good.

But it could not last. One of them needed to leave this place. Immediately. The bracelet was cool, the compulsion had quieted . . . yet it was still there, simmering in his throat. The witch had not removed it. He was only surprised she had not encouraged it, set the monster raging. But then, he had never hunted for her in the daylight, and like Ivan, the witch preferred the dark.

As with Elsie, though, if Kitala touched him, even by accident—

"Excuse us for a moment," M'cal said to the woman behind the desk, who smiled so widely he thought her jaw might crack. He held open the front door for Kitala, and without a word she walked out of the Youth Center and stood on the sidewalk. The strap of her fiddle case fit neatly between her breasts. She was dressed simply. Around her neck hung a golden cross and a small beaded leather pouch. He liked her glasses.

They stood looking at each other. Kit took a step toward him, and M'cal moved quickly away.

"Do not touch me," he said firmly. "Not if you value your life."

Hard emotions flickered through her eyes; more confusion, perhaps even hurt. M'cal wished he could take her in his arms again. He wanted to feel her warmth. He wanted to know if it felt as good as he remembered, despite the pain.

"Contagious, huh?" Kitala said, swallowing hard.

"It is not safe," he replied, fighting himself. "And you should *not* be here. There are people who will hurt you if they can."

"Like you?" She lifted her chin, staring at him over her glasses, which were sliding down her nose.

"Like me," he agreed heavily.

Her expression faltered. "Are you here to finish the job?"

M'cal hesitated, unsure what to say, except the truth. "I never expected to see you again."

Never, not in his wildest dreams. Last night should have been enough warning for anyone, man or woman. Which meant that Kitala Bell was very dense, very brave, or very crazy. A breeding ground for a bad outcome. M'cal did not want to be responsible for her death.

He almost turned and walked away. Some feat, if he could. However unintentionally, he had found Kitala. The first part of the witch's compulsion, fulfilled. His feet refused to move.

But his heart was little better. He remembered the men who had tried to kill Kitala. They might be dead, but there were others, and it was dangerous for her to be here alone. Dangerous for him to be with her.

But if you are careful, very careful, you might just be the lesser of two evils.

If he could not convince her to leave, that was. She was still watching him. He could feel the tension radiating off her body. Ready to run, maybe. He hoped so.

"You followed me," she said.

"I encountered the last gunman after you left," he corrected her. "I . . . persuaded him to tell me what he knew."

"And?"

"And he was muscle, some hired thug there for dirty work. He did not know much, except for bits and pieces about the woman you mentioned. Her home address. Her place of work. This"—he waved at the Youth Center—"was closer. I decided to come and ask questions."

Kit narrowed her eyes, betraying no trust, only conflict. Frustration eddied through him. The woman had no reason to trust his intentions—it was better that way, better to keep her on the edge, frightened—but there was a part of him still standing in that darkened auditorium, falling in love with her music, and those notes were still buried deep, opening a place of softness where he had forgotten a soft touch could exist. He could not be cruel to her.

So M'cal struggled for words instead. It was difficult. It had been too long since he had held an actual conversation. Women in cars did not count. Neither did the witch.

He settled for taking another step away from Kitala, checking their surroundings for anything more dangerous than himself. All he found was a squirrel nosing a discarded syringe, one of many that seemed to litter the sidewalk. "You should go, Kitala," he said in a low voice. "Find someplace safe and stay there."

Kitala also noticed the squirrel and waved her foot

at the animal, scaring it from the needle. "Who hired you to kill me?"

M'cal hesitated. "It is complicated."

"Of course it is." She began to walk around him, back to the Youth Center. M'cal blocked her, fear and anger making his throat thick, stirring the monster. He pressed his fist against his thigh, fighting himself, and looked Kitala straight in the eye. "Please. I did not help you last night just to have you toss away your safety like it means nothing. Like killing those men meant *nothing*."

It worked. Her breath caught, her body stilled. Guilt rumbled through her eyes, which he instantly regretted. He did not apologize, though. Just held her gaze.

Kitala stepped close. M'cal could not move fast enough to escape her; she stopped with just a hairsbreadth between them, peering up into his eyes with a caged hunger that he felt in his bones, in the answering ache of his heart.

"Why do you care?" she breathed. "Why *did* you save my life?"

M'cal said nothing. He had no words, no reason. Just need and desire, an imperative that had shot down to his soul. *Keep her safe* had been the words running through his head; that, and rage. Rage that anyone could hurt her. Kitala, who could make music to rival the Sirens.

But he could not say that to her. He wished instead that he could use his voice to drive her away—but that had failed on the previous night, and he was afraid of what might happen if he tried again.

Kitala, still gazing into his eyes, shivered. "Fine. Don't tell me. But I'm not going anywhere, M'cal. Not until I find Alice. Please. I *have* to find her, alive or dead. I need to know."

"I thought you were strangers."

Her face softened. "You yourself are putting in an awful lot of effort just for a stranger. You're going to get in trouble for it, too, aren't you?"

"Yes," he said quietly. "But I will not die for my trouble. You might."

It was her turn for silence, but it was a stubborn quiet; no anger, just resolve. *Little warrior heart, so strong.* She reminded him of the old tales, the myths his father told of the human world. The ancient world, when the Krackeni had shown their faces and bodies to humans, and the two had mingled, if uneasily. A time of gods and monsters walking the earth as one.

Then and now. Times had changed. Mostly.

He gestured toward the Youth Center door. "Come, we are wasting time."

Kitala's eyelid twitched. "You're staying with me?"

"As long as I am able," M'cal promised. "If you want."

"We'll have to work together." Her voice was soft with challenge. "Unless that's a problem."

"If I kill you, it is."

"You say that like you don't have any control over your actions."

"Because I do not," he told her quietly. "Not nearly enough."

That made her stop. He could see it in the way her posture changed, the frozen cut of her expression. Kitala studied his face; he thought she finally understood, and it both pained and relieved him. But all she did was slowly nod, her dark eyes thoughtful, and in a quiet voice she said, "I think I'll take my chances."

M'cal stepped away from her. He wanted to run.

There was a knot in his throat, hot and bitter, and he could not swallow past it.

"Whatever happens," he said hoarsely, "do not touch me."

"Okay," she replied, and he thought that this time she took him seriously.

They entered the Youth Center for a second time. The woman at the desk watched them, a bit more warily than before. M'cal waited for Kitala to say something, but she raised an eyebrow, a faint smile playing on her lips, and murmured, "You ask. I think she likes you better."

He also knew how to get quick results. "Alice Hardon's boss, please," he said in his smoothest voice, teasing each syllable with enough hints of song that he was able to infuse his request with real power.

The woman blinked once. "Just follow me."

Kitala gave him a sharp look, the humor that had been playing across her face fading into an expression of intense curiosity. He wondered if she had heard the music in his voice. He wondered what she had made of the previous night, the things he had done to save her. He had committed violence, but more than that, he had used his voice to kill. And right now, he thought she was remembering that.

All he could do, though, was gesture for her to precede him. The woman led them past a row of doors, down a long narrow hall that was dark, like a tunnel to a cage. M'cal forced himself not to think about the walls, but focused instead on Kitala's slender, shapely back. She had a very lovely bottom.

At the end of the hall there was a closed door upon which the woman leading them knocked. M'cal heard a muffled voice answer, and the door opened to reveal the chaos of a small office overrun by too much work. Dangerously tilting bookshelves lined the walls, while file folders reared up in stumpy stacks as tall as the desk, which was hardly big enough for a laptop and a cup of coffee.

A woman sat behind the desk. She was gray and round and wore old tinted glasses the size of teacups. Gold-plated earrings shaped like cats in cowboy hats dangled from her ears to her shoulders—jewelry matched only by the fierce red bandana tied around her forehead. A giant eye had been painted in the center of the cloth. It stared at M'cal.

No smiles from the old woman. She looked ready to shoot someone.

"Edith," said the secretary. "These are friends of Alice. They want to talk to you about her."

The old woman sat back in her chair, staring. "Get out and shut the door, Molly."

Edith's voice was sharp, and Molly blinked hard—shaking free of M'cal's mesmerizing power. She flushed so red her skin almost matched the bandana around Edith's head, then departed fast, head down, leaving M'cal and Kitala standing in front of the desk. Edith did not invite them to sit, nor did M'cal feel so inclined. Given the look on her face, neither did Kitala.

"Well, well, well," Edith said, glancing at the necklaces hanging from Kitala's neck. "This should be good."

"That would depend on what you are expecting," M'cal replied.

"Not a pretty boy like you, that's for sure." Edith took a swig from her mug and smacked her lips. "You, young man, are definitely a piece of work."

Kitala frowned. "We didn't come here to talk about us."

"Just Alice, huh?" Edith smiled grimly. "And who are you, to be asking?"

"Kit," she said, holding out her hand. "And this is—"

"Michael," he interrupted. "Michael Oberon." He did not offer to shake Edith's hand. The old woman noticed, and snorted, gripping her mug. Her knuckles were white.

Stress. Anger. Fear? M'cal wondered. He glanced at Kitala, and saw her gaze flicker to the woman's straining hand. If Edith held that mug any tighter, it might crack.

"Molly called you friends of Alice," said the old woman, her eyes sharp behind her tinted glasses. "Friends, my ass. You two wouldn't know Alice from a dog turd."

"She gave me her card," Kitala said, revealing the scrap of paper. Edith gave it a perfunctory glance and waved it away.

"Doesn't mean squat. Alice was always giving out her cards. You could have gotten it off anyone."

"Not just anyone," Kitala replied.

Edith frowned, tapping the side of her face with a short, fat finger. "You look familiar to me."

Kitala grimaced, bent down, and grabbed a CD case lying on top of a stack of files. She held it beside her face, and sure enough, M'cal saw a very fine photograph of Kitala playing her fiddle, her expression caught in a breathtaking moment of wild joy.

"Oh," Edith said.

"Alice has been kidnapped," Kitala went on in a flat voice. "We were taken together. I got loose. She didn't. She slipped me her card before I escaped. I thought it might mean something." She hesitated, catching her breath. "Tell me it means something, Edith."

Edith looked down. "John?"

"Dead," Kitala said. "Shot in the chest. I'm sorry."

The old woman nodded, her expression still empty. Her hand tightened even more around the mug. "I take it you didn't call the police."

"Two cops were in on it." Kit waited a moment, studying the old woman's face. "You're not surprised by any of this, are you? Alice wasn't, either."

Edith merely shrugged, still looking down. "They'll find out you escaped. They'll come after you."

"Yes," Kitala said, glancing at M'cal. "Can you tell us what this is about?"

"No," Edith said.

M'cal was not entirely surprised by the woman's answer, but her reticence was just another waste of time that he could not afford. If the witch compelled him to return to her—and he was surprised that she had not already—he would have little choice but to go. Leaving Kitala behind. Without protection.

"Tell us what you know," M'cal said, pouring power into each word, letting the syllables lilt closely into song. Simply speaking would not be enough; it was the limitation of his kind, an occasionally deadly weakness that mattered only on land, and never in the sea. He felt Kitala glance at him, wondered again if she heard the difference in his voice.

Edith finally looked up. She took off her glasses. Her eyes were ice; sharp, gray, unblinking. She stared at M'cal—a piercing gaze, bitter—and a thread of unease passed through him.

But then her expression relaxed into grief; quiet, reserved. As though Edith was a woman who had suffered a great deal in her life, so much that the heart was simply not strong enough for yet another wild rage of sorrow.

"Alice is as good as dead," said the woman, her voice cracking. She pried her hand off the mug; it resembled a claw. "I doubt anyone can help her."

Kitala and M'cal shared a brief glance. A tremor raced through her body, and he imagined reaching out to her, just one hand, one brush of comfort. He saw her own hand twitch and shifted his feet, ready to move in case she forgot. In case she wanted to touch him.

But she did not try. Kitala looked at Edith. "You sound like you've already given up."

A flush touched the old woman's cheeks. Again she looked down at her hands, splaying her fingers against the table. Her lower jaw trembled.

"This is a dangerous neighborhood. A lot of bad things pass through here. We do our best to stay safe, to keep our noses out of business that doesn't concern us, but . . ." She stopped, and gestured at the office. "We have one of the highest success rates in the city for youth turnaround. Kids come here, they leave changed. Doesn't matter how screwed up they are. All these files? Lives."

Edith gripped the edge of the table; her nails dug into the wood. "Alice began poking around in something she shouldn't. She never told me what, or with whom, only that there were people in trouble. Big trouble. Enough that she got her uncle involved. The man used to be an investigator. She said if they ever got hurt . . ."

The old woman did not finish. Kitala said, "I'm sorry. I am so sorry to be the one to bring you this news. But I'm trying to find Alice. I *will* find her. Do you think you could help? Maybe ask around, find out what and who she was investigating?"

"Yes," Edith whispered. "I think I could do that."

"About the police," Kitala began hesitantly, but the old woman flashed her a hard look.

"I'm not stupid, Ms. Bell." Edith reached around to the purse hanging from the back of her chair. She removed a business card and gave it to Kitala. "My cell phone number is there. Call me anytime. Where can I contact you if I find anything?"

Kitala hesitated, tucking the card into her purse. "My cell phone isn't working, and I might be changing hotels soon. I'll let you know when I have a stable number where I can be reached."

"If you had any sense, you'd leave town," Edith said. "You don't owe Alice anything."

You are a poor friend, thought M'cal. He wondered if Kitala felt the same; she gave the woman a long, thoughtful look, and then quietly, carefully said thank you and good-bye. M'cal followed her example, with far less grace, and they left.

Molly was back at her desk. She ignored them, and they did the same to her. Outside, it had begun to rain.

Kitala raised a hand to her hair, grimaced, and sighed. "Why do I feel like we just wasted our time?"

M'cal turned his face to the sky, savoring the raindrops as they hit his skin. "It was not a complete waste."

"Do you think Edith was hiding anything?"

He glanced at her, frowning. "Do you?"

"I don't know." Kitala kicked at the wet sidewalk, shaking her head. "Alice went to all the trouble of giving me her card, and all we got was more mystery.

There has to be something else we're missing. Unless the whole point of sending me here was not to help her, but just . . . to let someone know she was gone."

"That possibility bothers you."

"Of course." Kitala gazed up at him, and again it took all his willpower not to touch her. His desire frightened him. Kitala seemed nothing like the witch, but he had been deceived before. The risk was terrible. *He* was terrible—to fantasize, knowing the danger to her. The monster slept, but the witch's curse had too many layers; once she set the compulsion, he could not touch or be touched; not without causing death; not without creating a shell out of human flesh. Soul stealer, soul singer. Hardly better than a demon.

Kitala's skin looked soft, her cheeks high, her eyes dark and large behind her glasses. The shirt she wore beneath her denim jacket was low-cut; the swell of her breasts made M'cal's mouth dry. He tried to look away from her, but all he managed was to stare at her odd jewelry, her throat, her neck.

Her neck.

M'cal leaned closer than was safe, his gaze tracking over her smooth, rich skin. Kitala held very still, staring at him.

"What," she said slowly, "are you doing?"

She smelled good. Clean, fresh. "Your neck. You were injured last night. There should be a mark."

"Ah." Kitala looked uncomfortable. "I heal fast."

M'cal raised his eyebrow. "Not that fast."

Kitala turned up her collar, her long, elegant fingers staying near her throat. "Curiosity runs both ways. In there, you did something to those women. You . . . manipulated them. With your voice."

So she *had* noticed. M'cal started walking. Kitala

kept pace, her gaze locked on his face. "You tried something similar with me last night. But when I sang with you—"

"You were immune to me even before you sang," he told her gruffly. "But your voice . . . your voice did something different."

Kitala stopped walking. "What are you, M'cal?"

He turned around to face her. "Does it matter?"

"Yes," she said quietly. "I . . . had a dream last night. In it, you weren't human."

He fought to keep his expression neutral. "Do you always believe your dreams?"

"Sometimes," she admitted. "I might have a good reason to believe the one I had last night."

M'cal looked at her neck. "What was I, in your dream?"

It was hard to tell if she blushed, but her cheeks seemed to suddenly warm with soft pink undertones. Her gaze faltered. "You were a . . . merman."

Merman. A flush trembled down his body. He could not think. He could not speak. All he could do was stare, that one word echoing through his head. It was impossible she should know. Impossible.

He was silent too long. Kitala's expression changed, growing shocked then alarmed. And then something else crept into her eyes, something almost like compassion, which was as unexpected as anything else she could have said to him. As astonishing as *merman.*

"M'cal," she breathed, gaze flickering down to his throat, and there was so much pain in her voice, so little fear, he forgot himself. He forgot everything but Kitala, and his heart hurt—his heart hurt so bad—because for the first time in a long while he could imagine that someone cared. Someone *cared.*

The moment died fast. He was not careful, not paying attention. Kitala touched him, her fingers lacing around his hand. Pain rained down on his muscles.

The monster woke up.

CHAPTER SIX

Kit remembered, but too late. It was instinct, desire, too much that she could not name that made her take M'cal's hand—including the look on his face, the shock, the fear. The dreamt memory of his screams, which she was certain now were real. Real as his body, which was forever burned into her mind.

M'cal flinched, staggering away from her, curling in on himself with his arms tight against his belly. Holding himself, holding back. His face turned ashen; anguish tore through his eyes.

"Run," he hissed, but in that one word she heard enough to make her skin crawl, the hairs on her nape rise, and all she could do was stand as he screamed at her, his howl rising into a high, wailing note that was part song, part cry, and all power.

It was like being hit with the sharp edge of a merry-go-round railing—hard, fast, spinning—and when she closed her eyes, holding her head, there were so many lights inside her mind she might have been looking at the night sky on a roller coaster, taking a nosedive out of her world.

Her world. Her life. Her memories. Watching her life pass before her eyes, all of it flickering and fading and burning like falling stars, a shower of them streaking through her and leaving nothing behind. She could not catch them, she could not fight. All she could do was listen to M'cal's voice, the terrible beauty of it sliding like a dark rainbow into her soul. And though Kit knew she should be afraid, each unearthly note seared her with such lovely sympathy, such twisted delight, she could feel her own music rising and rising, the strings of her fiddle arcing light inside her mind. Until, quite suddenly, the stars disappeared and she could no longer hear M'cal's voice. She could not hear anything at all, except for her blood roaring in her ears and the pounding of her heart against her ribs. Her body was moving; bouncing. Her neck hurt.

Kit opened her eyes. It was difficult to see. The world tilted at a dizzying angle. Distant, in her mind, she heard the strings of a fiddle singing. A mournful cry.

She tilted her head again and found M'cal. He was not looking at her, but she could see his face and it was twisted, covered in rain, his black hair plastered against his pale skin. His eyes were haunted, framed in shadows. He was carrying her.

What happened? wondered Kit, but when she tried to ask, her voice slurred into nonsense and her tongue felt thick as a brick. M'cal glanced at her, his mouth set in a hard line. He said nothing. He looked beautiful and terrible.

She heard catcalls, shouts; caught the flash of thighs and high, shining boots; fishnet, cleavage, red lipstick.

A blond man with a familiar narrow face and sharp eyes. M'cal said something to him—let go of her long enough to pull a wad of cash from his pocket—and then suddenly they were moving again, into a building that smelled like cigarettes and dirty sheets. It was blindingly dark—no lights, all shadow—and she closed her eyes, dizzy. She felt M'cal run upstairs, fast and graceful, and she clung to him, inhaled him, fingers clutching the soft fabric of his black shirt. He smelled like his coat—warm—and his body was hard and strong.

Safe, she thought dimly, and then, *Trust him.*

M'cal stopped. Kit opened her eyes. They were in front of a door, which he nudged open with his foot. No lights were inside, but there were windows. The walls were painted pink. There was a couch and a bed, both narrow, both old. M'cal lay Kit down on a quilted comforter that was supposed to be white but had been stained after long use into a camouflage of grays and browns.

Kit tried to sit up, but she was too weak. M'cal began to help, but stopped. He suddenly seemed afraid to touch her; his fingers darted nervously above her shoulders, not quite making contact, and after a moment he retreated, backing away until he hit the wall opposite the bed. He slid down into a loose crouch. His eyes were haunted. He was breathing hard.

Kit tried to speak, but her voice refused to rise above a whisper. Her throat hurt. "What happened?"

"I almost took your soul," he rasped, and the raw emotion on his face was awful to see.

But his words echoed through her, again and again, and she knew they were true. Impossible, but true. Kit wondered if her dismay showed; M'cal rocked hard to his feet, turning away from her, pressing his head and hands against the pink wall. His entire body trembled; his fingers curled into fists.

"M'cal," she murmured brokenly. "M'cal, please."

"I hurt you," he whispered.

"I'm still here," she said. "Please."

M'cal turned back around, standing in the half-light and shadows, his body long and lean, coiled. His wet hair curled around his hard face; his eyes glinted like a gasp of sky on the other side of a thundercloud.

He walked to her, and for the first time she was able to appreciate how he moved—like a dancer, utterly in control of his body; elegant and agile. Dangerous.

She tried to sit up again. He was there in an instant, his hand hovering over her shoulder. He did not touch her, but he was close—so close.

Kit did not let him pull away. She grabbed his hand. He flinched, but that was it. Nothing happened. Slowly, slowly, his fingers curled around her palm. She let out a shaky breath. M'cal swallowed hard and sat down beside her, perching so far off the edge of the bed she thought he might fall.

"Talk to me," she said.

"And tell you what?" he replied softly, staring at their clasped hands. "That I am a murderer? That I almost took your life?"

"You said soul."

"It is the same. You cannot live without a soul. The body . . . gives up." He looked into her eyes with a gaze that was cold and hard and wild. "I had no choice, Kitala. If you had not stopped me . . ."

He could not finish. He tried to let go of her hand, but Kit hung on. She knew it was dangerous—could feel it in her weakened body, in his strength—but there was a part of her that recognized this moment as something vital, infinitely important. Something to fight for.

Even if it's for nothing. Even if it breaks your heart. Kit glanced down at the strong lean lines of M'cal's throat and found his skin pale, free of blood and holes. Memory lingered, though. Death. She had caught more glimpses of it outside the Youth Center, inside Edith's office. Almost tasted the scent of his murder.

But he's not dead yet. Forget the how or why or when. You'll never know the answer until it is too late. Focus on now.

Now. What a concept. Forgetting the future had never been an easy thing to do.

Kit's back hurt; the fiddle case still hung against her. She tried to pull the strap over her head. Her arms were stronger, but it was still an effort. M'cal leaned in close to help her. Close enough to feel his warmth flow over her body; close enough to inhale his scent; close enough to kiss.

"How did I save myself?" Her voice sounded low, husky.

M'cal took his time pulling the strap over her head. She leaned in even more. His eyes flickered to her face. "Your music, Kitala. There is power in your music. You defended yourself with it."

"I didn't feel like I was defending myself." On the contrary; Kit had felt like she was making the best music of her life.

The strap got caught in her wild mass of hair. She placed her hand on M'cal's hard chest, tilting her head so that he could free the case. The arch of her neck lay exposed. M'cal faltered; one hand curled behind her back, supporting her. The other still held the fiddle case.

Kit met his gaze, and for a moment time stretched like a moonbeam reaching through a cloud, and she heard inside her head soft notes that could have been a voice, his voice, lilting like a ghost unseen. Music to love, even if everything else was strange. Music as blood and bone, another heart. Music that called to her soul.

M'cal's gaze drifted down to her neck. She did not look at his, just kept her eyes locked on his face, suffering confusion, desire, fear and something more, deeper; the sense that once again this moment meant more than any other. That her life as she knew it was gone, dead, changed.

He kissed her neck. Kit closed her eyes, savoring the heat of his mouth, feeling it move through her, pool in her heart like a slow rhapsody. He kissed her again, and then once more, his lips trailing up her throat, and just when she thought her mouth would be next, he pulled her against him, tucking her close, in what had to be the most gentle embrace of her life.

"This cannot last," he murmured. "Whatever you did will not last."

Kit's hand crept to his shoulder. "I don't understand."

M'cal began to pull away from her. Kit grabbed the front of his shirt. He covered her hands—one hand was large enough to warm both of hers—and crooked his mouth into a brief, faint smile.

"Playing rough," he said. "That might be dangerous."

"Only if you don't explain some things to me," she replied. She found it difficult to think, to speak, when

he was so very near. "Make it simple, M'cal. I'm confused enough as it is."

M'cal brushed his lips against her forehead. "Nothing is simple, Kitala."

"Please tell me."

" 'Please,' " he rasped. "You have said that word to
me more than any other person has in years. *Please*.
No one says that to me, Kitala. No one."

"They should," she murmured. And then: "I saw it
in your eyes, but I want to hear it from your lips.
You're not human."

"Not human," he echoed, his voice catching. "Not
fully."

"Show me."

He exhaled sharply. "I think you have seen
enough."

Kit looked into his eyes. "Please, M'cal."

His jaw tightened. He held up his hand. At first
nothing happened, but then as she watched, unblinking, odd faint lines formed against his pale skin; ridges
that took on a glimmering iridescence, a sheen that
looked like crushed pearls. Scales like tiny jewels.
They spread higher, growing and growing until loose
webbing draped between his fingertips. His nails
lengthened into small, sharp hooks, darkening in
color to silver blue.

Kit touched his hand, breathless. Here was proof, if
she could believe her eyes and touch. Astonishing,
shocking, ridiculous. His hand closed around hers,
and the heat of it was immense. All she could do was
stare, her mind blank for one brief moment, until
something woke inside her and she analyzed his touch,
the smoothness of his skin, like a snake. She was not

afraid of snakes. It took a moment, though, to reconcile that she was touching the flesh of a man, a person *not human* but still with humanity.

"You are only the second person I have shown myself to," M'cal said, which made her look at him. His entire body was tense, his eyes cold, hard. For a moment she felt threatened, but as she met his gaze, she glimpsed a glimmer of doubt roll through his face— one heartbeat, then gone—and she knew, without any uncertainty, that he was just as unnerved.

She squeezed his hand. He flinched when she did, almost like it hurt, and he stared at her. His cold mask fractured.

"Who was the first?" she asked, his skin still gleaming; inhuman, iridescent.

His fingers twitched. "Another woman. It ended badly between us."

"How badly?"

M'cal looked away and pulled his hand free. "Badly enough that I often think it would have been better to die than to have ever met her."

Screams—Kit could still hear his screams. She thought she might hear them forever. "What has this woman done to you, M'cal?"

"She owns me." M'cal's smile was raw, bitter. "I belong to her. She controls my actions. Makes me hunt." He held up his arm and rolled back his sleeve, revealing a silver bracelet almost half the length of his forearm. The metal was engraved with odd figures and symbols, none of which Kit recognized. There was a multitude of white scars on his skin above the bracelet. "This forms the link. It binds me to her. Nor can I remove it. I have even tried cutting off my arm, but the blade does not sink far before I am compelled to stop."

Kit stared. On any other day, with any other man, she might have called him a liar. But she had seen too much that she could not explain—felt too much of the same. She touched the bracelet and found the metal warm. "What else?"

He said nothing for a moment, simply studied her face. She let him, meeting his gaze, allowing him to see without fear everything she was feeling. She reached up slowly and brushed her thumb against his cheek. He caught her hand, kissed her palm, closed his eyes.

"The woman who did this to me is a witch," he rumbled. "Or whatever you call a woman who wields magic as she does."

Witch. Magic. Hard words to swallow. Nothing should have shocked her—not given her background, her grandmother, the things she could do—but somehow this did.

If Granny were here, she'd already be rolling up her sleeves, taking charge. None of this would make her bat an eye.

Hell, Old Jazz Marie had probably known that all of this fantastic stuff existed and just kept it to herself. The woman was probably looking over Kit's shoulder even now, shaking her head.

Which made Kit take a deep breath, swallow hard, and summon up her courage. *Just take it one step at a time. Go with the flow. Play it by ear.*

In a slow, careful voice, Kit said, "This . . . witch. She's the one who wants me dead, isn't she?"

M'cal's gaze darkened. "She asked for you specifically. I do not know how she learned about your abilities, Kitala, but after seeing some of what you can do, I understand her interest."

"My abilities," she echoed, thinking of murder and death. Of M'cal with a hole in his throat. "Just what do you think I can do?"

He hesitated. "Magic."

"Magic." This time it was Kit who tried to pull away, but M'cal held her, and she did not fight him. Just sighed, closing her eyes. She felt weak, lightheaded. "I know about magic, M'cal. But what I do isn't that. I don't know what you call it, but I'm no . . . witch." Not like her grandmother.

"You have power, Kitala. A great deal of it. And even if you are using nothing more than instinct to direct it, your potential is immense. You would not have been able to save yourself otherwise. No one turns aside such a call. Not even the witch can do that. It is why she protects herself with this." He tapped the bracelet.

"That's not what I do," Kit protested. Yet, even as she spoke, the fiddle strings sang in her mind, and she felt something new within the music: a lightness, like a shot of sunlight in her soul, as though in her heart she stood on the edge of a cliff, ready to fly.

M'cal's eyes narrowed; his hand flexed against her waist. "Then what do you think you do, Kitala? What are you sure of?"

"Death," she said, the word slipping from her lips. She could not believe how easily it happened; for a moment she thought she imagined it. But, no. *Death*. She had said it, and M'cal was still looking at her, frowning.

He had no chance to ask. Kit heard a soft knocking

sound. They both flinched, but there was not enough time to move before the door opened. A boy poked his head into the room. He could not have been older than sixteen, but there was something in his eyes that looked more ancient than dirt. He was painfully skinny, dressed in a loose T-shirt and black jeans, with a metal-studded belt slung loose around his hips. He wore a Mohawk, spiked blue, and a tattoo of a dragon curled around his forearm. A cigarette slanted from his mouth.

"Fuck," said the kid, staring at M'cal. "It really is you."

"Billy," M'cal said quietly, shocking Kit. He said nothing else, but very gently untangled himself from her, continuing to pull the fiddle-case strap over her head. When that was done he stood and faced the boy. Each movement was careful, methodical, controlled. He did not look Kit in the eye. His expression was totally flat, all his raw emotion gone. It made her afraid—and curious.

Billy entered the room and shut the door behind him. He gave Kit a cautious glance, and to M'cal said, "I'm not interrupting anything, right?"

M'cal said nothing, and Billy shrugged. "Well, okay, yeah, I get it. I'm interrupting. But I thought I saw you come in, and it looked . . . bad. Not normal. And it's been a while. You left."

There was an accusation in those last two words; hurt, as well. A thread of emotion entered M'cal's eyes: pain, regret. "I had to go away, Billy. I had no choice."

"You picked up somewhere else."

"Like I said."

"Yeah. S'okay." Billy scuffed his tennis shoes on the

floor and gave Kit a sharp look. "You Mikey's friend?"

M'cal hesitated. Kit said, "Yes. I'm his friend."

"You sick?"

"I was." Kit glanced at M'cal. He still refused to look at her.

The boy seemed satisfied with her answer, and took another step toward M'cal—hesitant, like some beaten dog ready to run. Kit checked for track marks on his arms. She did not see any, but there was a nervous quality to the boy that was either natural or the edge of some high. He scratched his arms, the side of his head; fidgeted.

"Cooley's dead," Billy blurted out.

"Is that so?" replied M'cal.

"Reena said you were talking to him the night he died."

"I do not remember."

"Right." The corner of the boy's mouth curled; it was a surprising expression, both sweet and sinister. "Just wanted to say thank you."

M'cal did not bat an eye. "Who is the new management?"

"No one. We're, uh, taking care of ourselves. Each other."

"What about the man downstairs?"

"He won't try anything. He only handles women. Fags make him sick."

"You live in this neighborhood?" Kit asked. The boy looked surprised that she spoke, but he nodded, still scuffing the floor, swinging back and forth on one foot. "You ever go down to that Youth Center on Templar? Talk to an Alice Hardon?"

Billy looked affronted. "Fuck, no. Those bitches don't know shit."

"But have you heard of Alice?" M'cal asked.

The boy's eyes narrowed. "What's going on?"

"She was kidnapped," Kit said. "According to her friend, she was looking into something she shouldn't."

"People need to mind their own fucking business," muttered Billy. "All kinds of shit someone could get into."

"Something the cops have a hand in?"

Billy snorted. "Take your pick."

Kit hoped he was exaggerating.

M'cal stirred, taking a step toward the boy. "If you hear anything, will you let me know?"

Billy did not immediately answer. He looked at M'cal with a hard, clear gaze, and then glanced at Kit, studying her with the same intensity.

"You're done, aren't you?" he said to M'cal. "You're leaving."

"If I can," M'cal replied, without hesitation. "You should, too."

For a brief, startling moment the curtain dropped and all Kit could see on Billy's face was raw, naked sorrow—but it disappeared in the blink of an eye, and he became once again nothing but a shuffling punk.

"I'll ask around," he mumbled, eyes downcast. "I owe you."

"You do not—" began, but the boy walked to the door. He stopped just before leaving.

"Where do I find you?" he asked Kit.

"My hotel," she said. "The Hyatt. I might not be staying there long, but I'll leave a message. Ask for Kit Bell, room 2610." Her room number, so casually given, when with Edith she could not say the same. Something had made her hold back.

Billy nodded, gave M'cal one long last look—a hungry, hard gaze—and left.

Kit watched him go. She did not say a word, just sat staring at the door as it closed. Sat some more, thinking about everything she had just seen and heard. She looked at M'cal, and found him staring back. She could not read his expression. He looked bored, but she knew it was an illusion. M'cal was not, she thought, the kind of man who ever felt bored about anything. He was too smart for that, his life too difficult.

"Billy seems like a good kid," she said carefully.

"He is," M'cal replied.

"He's also a prostitute."

Long silence. "Yes."

"So are you."

M'cal's gaze finally faltered. "I have done such work. In this neighborhood and others. It was how I knew we could come here to rest and hide. I have . . . used this room before."

Kit tried to get off the bed and stand. Her legs gave out, but M'cal was suddenly at her side, his arms around her waist, holding her up, engulfing her.

"The witch made you do it," she murmured, and a tremor passed through him; all that fine control finally melting away. His arms tightened, and he carried them both back to the bed, where they lay on their sides, curled around each other; a cocoon, made of them. The mask was gone. His eyes were haunted but not broken. She saw resolve, acceptance. Anger.

"It was part of the hunt," he told her. "But it was also one of her ways of degrading me. Breaking me."

"By having sex with strangers?"

"There was no sex," M'cal said, though there was a bleakness to his voice that made Kit sick. "Sex was not her objective. Not in those situations. What she wanted—what she has always wanted—was my soul. And because she could not take it, she found other ways to shame and corrupt me."

"By making you feel like a thing, an object for sale. Nothing but flesh. No soul, no heart that mattered."

"You understand."

She understood that she wanted to find this woman and beat the living shit out of her. Acts of cruelty were nothing new to Kit—she had seen enough of it in her life—but this, no matter how strange or impossible, went beyond what her sense of justice could accept. It was too terrible.

Maybe her anger showed; maybe her disgust. A faint sad smile passed over M'cal's face.

"Little warrior heart," he murmured. "I wish I had met you first."

Kit closed her eyes. No words, no thoughts—all she could do was feel, and what flowed through her, slow and warm, was a familiar mix of loneliness and sorrow, her secret companion, a cold, hard knot only music could soften. Always on the go, always on her own, with only her fiddle as a friend.

But this time, what she felt was not for herself alone, but for M'cal too; his isolation, his grief, his forced betrayal of dignity and heart. She felt raw for him, cut; so full of emotion she could not speak with it.

So she touched him. She opened her eyes and brushed her thumb over his lips. He seemed to savor it, more than she expected, as though he was unused to such a thing. Perhaps he was. His eyes darkened, and his hand crept up her waist; slow, tentative.

Do not touch me, Kit remembered him saying outside the Youth Center, and she imagined what that would be like, to live knowing that one touch could compel murder.

You already know, she told herself. *Just one look and you know. Every time you look at someone, you run the risk of seeing death. Alice, M'cal, so many others.*

But at least she did not run the risk of killing. Not by her own hand. Though she wondered if doing nothing was not the same. A more distant murder. Her fault for staying silent.

She almost told him right then. Almost said, You are going to die. But the words would not come, and her own throat felt raw, broken.

You are accepting his murder with your silence. Even though he did not accept yours. Even though for Alice, a woman you barely know, you are risking your life. You made the leap for her. Why not him?

Because Alice was a stranger, Kit realized. An unknown, distant. Even now, Alice was fixed in her head as a woman little better than a caricature, someone in trouble who needed help. Help that Kit could not deny, despite herself. But M'cal, on the other hand . . .

It's become personal with you. You care.

Shocking, how much she cared. It was an involuntary emotion, a compulsion not unlike falling in love with Mozart or the fast pluck of a rangy banjo, the crest of the sun on some rosy spring morning in the Smoky Mountains with the dew glittering like diamonds on the green crisp leaves of trees. Natural, brilliant, easy. And though she had struggled not to think of it, to refuse those emotions, they bubbled up inside her heart like laughter or acid or a sob. The truth hurt. The truth overwhelmed.

She did not want to tell M'cal, because saying the words would make it real. She did not want to tell M'cal, because for the first time in her life, after all her careful isolation, her efforts to keep her heart free of entanglements that she knew would end in violence, she had finally found someone she was afraid of losing and whom she knew, without a doubt, would be lost. Sooner, rather than later. Against his will.

I need to tell you something, she said in her mind, but the words remained frozen on her tongue. No strength.

Later, she thought. *You still have time. He's not going anywhere. Not yet.*

But soon. She had to tell him soon. She only hoped he believed her, that he did not call her a freak, a liar, crazy—like others had, so long ago.

As if, whispered a small voice. *M'cal will believe you.*

Kit watched his eyes: so blue, so haunting. Inhuman. "The woman who . . . holds you. She makes you kill. Why?"

"Power. My kind have a gift for song. Music is at the core of our culture. But some of us can do more with that gift than others."

"Like steal souls."

"Yes," he said gravely. "And more. It is a warrior trait, passed down from a time when there were great battles within the world. So much strife that it touched even my kind, within the sea. My ancestors could turn back armies with nothing but their voices. Kill with nothing but a song."

M'cal traced his fingers over her cheek; light as a

feather, easy and gentle. "What I take is the essence of a human, everything that makes that individual want to live. It is a terrible thing to do, Kitala. Better to die outright, I think. But that desire, that vitality, is immensely powerful. It is the essence of life. The quickening of it. And the witch has learned to harness it. She takes what I steal, and it makes her strong and young. Gives her, temporarily, the skills and knowledge of those who have been stolen."

Bitterness touched his gaze as he added, "There is a great irony in this, Kitala. What I do to others is exactly what the witch has done to me. Forcing those women at the Youth Center to speak to us. Forcing the men who hurt you to kill themselves."

She caught his hand, held it. "You fought for me. You implied that was impossible."

"It depends on the compulsion, on the witch's mood. Though I would be lying if I did not admit that she has . . . relaxed . . . when it comes to controlling me."

"What does that mean?"

"It means that in the beginning, when she first captured me, I always fought. *Always.* I suppose I had convinced myself that I was still fighting." M'cal shook his head, a look of disbelief flickering over his face. His voice softened with incredulity. "I now see that was not the case. The witch wore me down, and I never realized it, until you."

"M'cal—" Kit began, but he rolled away, looking at the window.

"I can still hear them," he told her, his voice deadly quiet. "Strangers, random individuals whom I killed for the witch. Making me pretend I was a prostitute was part of that. The men and women who paid for my time were always my victims—and one more way for the witch to demonstrate her absolute control. Showing me how futile it was to fight her. So I told myself I had no choice, or better, that I was choosing my battles. Like I did with you when she gave me your name."

Choosing battles. Remembering faces, voices. Something Kit understood too well. She forced him to look at her—poured into her gaze all her anger, her determination—and in a low, hard voice said, "We will stop this." *I will stop this. I will save your life.*

He said nothing, and Kit sank into herself, listening to her heart, the echo of strings singing; around her, more distant: cars honking, a baby crying; somewhere above, the springs of a mattress heaving; laughter, screams. Life, teeming. All of it, like music.

"We should go," M'cal said quietly.

"Yeah," she said, wetting her lips, noting how he watched her mouth. "Whatever I did to you . . . how long do you think it will last?"

"I do not know." He pushed a little closer, still staring. Kit remembered his mouth on hers, in the water— the heat of it, the power of his body as he kept her alive. She closed the distance between them, but did not kiss him. Hesitating, breathless, she waited for M'cal.

He kissed her. Gently at first, taking his time with electrifying tenderness; a brush of his lips, barely a taste. Savoring. Kit's breath caught—and then caught some more as he deepened the kiss, crushing her mouth. His intensity was desperate, starved. Kit felt her eyes burn with unshed tears as she grappled with him, fighting to match his passion as her heart bubbled into her throat, singing.

They broke apart, panting, trembling, lips still brushing. M'cal's hand had found its way beneath her T-shirt, his fingers hot against her back. Her hand was buried in his hair. She did not loosen her grip. Part of her was afraid he might slip away, fade like a dream. There was no room in the world for a man like him, no such thing as magic.

M'cal brushed his lips against the corner of her mouth, trailing kisses across her cheek, her neck, ending at her ear.

"I had to taste you again," he whispered. "Just in case."

"You touched me last night. No urge to hurt me then."

"But you remember it did not last." M'cal ran his finger down her throat. "It is complicated, Kitala. More than you realize."

She caught his hand and kissed it. She did not mean to, but it felt natural, right. Like holding her fiddle and sliding the bow across the strings. Music was in her heart, in her ears. She watched M'cal's eyes, and he leaned in close and kissed her again. He tasted clean, almost salty.

They untangled themselves and moved off the bed. M'cal helped Kit stand. She was stronger—her knees wobbled only a little—and he presented her fiddle case.

"I want you to play for me," he said.

"Tonight," she replied, and the promise sent a small thrill through her.

They left. It was indeed a squalid room—and an awful shade of pink—but Kit felt a pang when they closed the door behind them. She could have stayed longer; there were things she would have liked to do— one look at M'cal told her he felt the same.

As they descended the creaking wooden stairs, Kit told him about her friend Dela's offer of help. She told him what she knew of Dirk & Steele.

"You trust them?" he asked. They walked slowly, open air on one side, and on the other, a wall pitted with bullet holes, wide, hairy cracks, exposed rusty wiring stripped down to nubs. Cockroaches darted along the steps between cigarette butts, whiskey bottles, and used condoms. A scrawny tomcat took a break from chasing insects to spray the wall directly in front of them. The odor was foul.

"Yes," Kit replied. "And I don't say that often."

M'cal hesitated. "And me?"

She stopped, turning so she could look him in the eyes. She had to climb two steps to do it; he was quite tall. "Tell me why you care how I answer."

"I think you know," he said. "It should be obvious."

It was not obvious—not entirely—but Kit could not bring herself to push the issue. "Would you believe my answer?"

"I would hear it in your voice."

"I trust you," Kit said quietly.

M'cal briefly closed his eyes. "But you are afraid."

"Aren't you?"

"Terrified," he whispered.

At the bottom of the stairs, two flights down, Kit heard a door slam, followed by rough protests, shouts. One of the voices sounded like Billy. She and M'cal glanced at each other and peered over the railing.

Kit saw the edge of a white T-shirt—a black bob, a lithe figure, racing up the stairs. She was out of uniform but very familiar—and holding a gun.

"Run," M'cal said.

CHAPTER SEVEN

Over the years, Kit had lost track of the exact number of murders she had witnessed. As a child she had kept a special diary, one with dates and descriptions, but her mother had found it when she was ten and the little book disappeared. After that, Kit stopped writing things down.

Kit had never witnessed her own death, her own future possible murder, and while that was a good thing, she had to wonder as she raced up the stairs, M'cal at her side, if that was merely an oversight of her gift, as sometimes happened, and whether it was her true fate to meet a grisly end, her life taken by another.

"Can't you just sing at her or something?" she gasped.

"Too many people inside the building would hear me," M'cal replied in a hard voice. "I don't play games with souls."

And what about us? Kit wanted to ask, but she understood and did not blame him. She pushed harder, trying to force her weakened body to save itself from the woman chasing them.

"Here." M'cal opened a door and shoved Kit into an empty room. Locking them in, he ran to the window. He moved like an animal, loose-limbed and graceful. The window had been painted shut, but M'cal grunted and yanked it open with hardly any hesitation. Cold, wet air blew in, and right beneath them, not more than three feet down, was a long, flat roof.

He helped Kit out, following quickly. Behind them, Kit heard the door smash open and a familiar voice yell, "Stop!"

M'cal stopped, but only to sing. As the first notes began curling from his mouth, Kit saw movement from the corner of her eye. She looked to find a fire escape, ascending from below the rooftop, and saw a man appear—Officer Yu's partner, also out of uniform. He had a gun. He looked surprised to see them, but that was all the hesitation they were given. He shot M'cal through the throat. The exit wound exploded. Blood sprayed Kit's face.

Time stopped—visions of the future becoming reality—and she screamed as M'cal collapsed, falling to her knees beside him. She could not believe—*could not believe*—but he was still and pale, staring sightless at the sky, and all that vitality—all that power and grace—was leaking into a red puddle around his body, against her knees. She touched him. His chest was still warm.

Too late. You waited too late.

Guilt raged through her, swallowed quickly by fury and a loss so profound she felt like part of her soul was draining away in M'cal's flowing blood. A hand snaked into her hair; Kit was yanked backward, hard on her ass, dragged for several feet until a gun muzzle drilled into her cheek. Officer Yu stared at her, eyes cold. Kit felt colder. That woman was dead. Dead, if it was the last thing she ever did.

"Up," said Yu.

"Fuck you," whispered Kit.

"Dick," said the woman, and her partner appeared, holstering his gun. His composure was not as finely tuned as Yu's, but he managed to look sufficiently bored as he stuck his hands under Kit's armpits and hauled her up. She fought him, but not enough; all she could do was stare at M'cal, at the blood. She could taste the blood. She could taste her shame. Kit bent over, gagging, but Yu still gripped her hair, and yanked her into a stumbling walk away from M'cal's still body.

The buildings on Hastings Street were old and connected, with the joined rooftops all at the same height, covered with gravel and exposed tarpaper. Steam rose from vents. Kit splashed through puddles. No one talked. Yu and Dick were all business. There was an access door, locked with a padlock. Dick shot it open, and he and Yu marched Kit down the narrow stairs, pushing so fast Kit thought she might lurch and tumble down with every step. Fiddle strings flinched inside her head; music bit and gasped: the edge of *Danse Macabre*, a hint of the *Valkyries* . . . something totally new.

The building they were in was one of the abandoned monoliths lining the street. Kit caught saw some signs of life—empty cans, syringes, bleach bottles, clothing, battery-operated lamps; heard the structure creak and groan, the echo of distant human voices—but none of it meant anything. She was still alone with two corrupt police officers. Heart breaking.

"How did you find us?" Kit finally asked. She did not recognize her own voice.

"In this neighborhood?" Yu pushed her gun harder against Kit's back. "How many people do you think we own?"

Too many, she realized. "When did you find out I was still alive?"

"This morning," Dick said gruffly, glancing over his shoulder. "Sorry about your friend."

Kit swallowed hard. "You didn't have to."

"Yes," Yu said. "We did."

Tears rolled down Kit's cheeks. She could not hide them, could not fight them. She hurt like hell, right in her heart, like there was a fork covered with the venom of a black mamba, stirring and poking and cutting. She had not hurt this badly since her grandmother's death. She could not believe how much she hurt.

You killed him. You did not warn him. You were selfish and now he's dead.

M'cal, whispered her heart. *M'cal, please.*

She thought of her grandmother—how Old Jazz Marie had reached from beyond the grave to heal her neck. If Jazz Marie could do it—as she had so many times while alive—then Kit suddenly wondered if she herself could do the same. Heal. Bring back to life. Perform a concert of miracles.

But only if she could get back to him in time. Right now.

Kit whirled, body-slamming Yu. Surprise was on her side—the woman gasped and fell hard on the stairs. Kit leapt past her, but the officer grabbed her ankle and held on. Kit tripped, landed on her hands, kicking and screaming. She caught Yu in the face—the woman loosened her grip—but then Dick was there and for the second time in two days, Kit was hit in the head. Pain exploded—*his neck, the blood, hurry*—but Kit kept trying to move, to fight. Dick grabbed her around the waist and hauled her back. Yu punched Kit's stomach. Kit's reading glasses, hanging from one ear, fell off completely.

"Fucking cunt," Yu muttered, brushing back her hair with a trembling hand. She hit Kit again, but Dick turned at the last moment so that her blow slammed Kit's hip instead of her gut.

"Easy," he said to Yu. "Cool head, remember? You're always telling me that."

Yu drew in a shuddering breath, giving him the coldest stare Kit had ever seen on a woman's face. But after a moment, Yu nodded sharply and turned to walk down the stairs. She did not look back.

Dick exhaled, and dragged Kit after his partner. She could not fight him; her body hurt too badly. She would have fallen down except for the man beside her. Having him touch her was almost as bad as being beaten.

"Just shoot me now," Kit mumbled, hardly able to speak past the pain in her head. "Get it over with."

"Sorry," Dick said. "You made waves. You're wanted alive this time."

Kit stumbled. "Who?"

"Big boss," Dick replied.

"Stop talking to her," Yu called. Dick clamped his mouth shut.

They reached the bottom of the stairs and wound around a narrow hallway. Kit heard footsteps skittering away from them, saw signs of more life—squatters, drug addicts—and then Yu pushed open a door and Kit closed her eyes against the gray wet light.

They stepped into an alley. The air smelled like rotting garbage and feces. Yu said, "I'll get the car," and then she jogged away, disappearing around the corner.

Kit thought of M'cal holding her, kissing her. His face, his faint smiles. Her heart broke again, and she swallowed a sob.

"My offer still stands," she choked out. "Money if you let me go."

Dick shifted his feet. He was a big man, with hands as leathery as footballs. His blond buzz was too short for the size of his head, which was craggy and full of dull round edges.

"How much money?" he asked.

"Enough for you to retire and live comfortably for the rest of your life. In some places, more than comfortably."

"Mexico?"

"You would be a king."

He hesitated. "She'll kill me."

"Yu?" Kit pushed past her pain to look him in the eye. She imagined shooting him with his own gun—bang, bang, right through the neck. "You're a big guy. You could take care of her first."

"We're partners," he said.

"You're a survivor," Kit replied. "And you have your priorities, same as her. Money. Power. You wouldn't be doing this otherwise. But you're just getting scraps, aren't you? Not worth the effort you're putting in."

Dick stared, something wild curling through his eyes. "Give me a number."

"Two million." Kit was not lying. She had that much in the bank, straight-up cash from all her record deals, royalties, and advertising fees. Easy to accumulate; she was not a big spender. And she was willing to throw it all away if it meant saving her life.

Dick liked that amount. Kit could see it plain as day on his face. But he waited too long to say anything. A dark red sedan pulled down the alley. It looked like a personal vehicle. She memorized the license plate.

Dick pushed Kit into the backseat and climbed in beside her. Yu was in front. She did not immediately drive away; she was on a cell phone, listening to someone talk. She said very little, simply nodding. Her face was drawn, pale.

"Yes," she said. "Yes, we're coming now." And then, with a note of surprise in her voice: "No, we didn't . . . cut off his head."

Kit's breath caught. Beside her, Dick went very still. Yu said, "Yes, of course," and ended the call. She glanced back, over her shoulder.

Dick said, "No fucking way."

"One of us has to go back."

"You do it," Dick said, his hand flexing around Kit's arm. "I killed him. It's your turn to do the shit work."

Yu said nothing. She gave him a hard look and popped open the trunk. Got out of the car. Came back around with an axe and a plastic grocery back. Kit snarled, fighting Dick, beating her fists against the glass. Yu ignored her and disappeared into the building.

Dick grabbed Kit's hair and pulled her head so far back her neck cracked. She did not care.

"Who the fuck do you work for?" she ground out, fighting for control, for breath.

"Jess handles that part," Dick said. "All I know is they're scary motherfuckers. Got their hands in all kinds of shit. They think being nice to a person is cutting off their privates instead of putting a bullet in their brain."

"You still want that two million?" Kit asked.

"Fuck, yeah," he muttered, and let go of her hair. The keys were in the ignition. Dick gave her a cautious look and turned his back to sidle out of the back seat. The moment he was out, Kit slid the strap of her fiddle case over her head. Quick, easy. Dick got into the front seat, gun in one hand, his other on the keys. He started the engine and glanced back at her.

"Just you remember," he said. "Try anything and I hurt you."

"I understand," Kit said. Tears were still running down her face. It added to the effect.

Dick nodded and put the car in gear. Hit the accelerator. Kit waited for that first lurch of speed and then threw the strap of her fiddle case over Dick's head, around his neck. She hauled back with all her strength. Dick took his hands off the wheel. The car swerved. Kit put her foot on the back of the front seat, bracing herself as they slammed into a Dumpster.

Everything flew forward. The strap loosened just enough for Dick to catch a breath and aim his gun into the back of the car. Kit threw herself down, still holding on to the fiddle case. Dick fired. The bullet missed, slamming into the seat beside her. Kit sat back up and pulled harder. Dick made a gurgling sound. He fired again, but the shot went into the rear window. Glass shattered. Kit did not loosen her grip. She thought of M'cal and gritted her teeth. Jerked and yanked and wrenched, sliding her arm between the case and the back of his seat, feeling his body shake and writhe in front of her.

Until he stopped.

Kit let go of the fiddle case. She was shaking. Shaking so badly her teeth rattled in her head. Her heart slammed her ribs; she could not hear past the roaring in her ears. Swallowing hard, she reached around to touch Dick's neck. He was still alive. Just passed out. Kit freed her fiddle case and looped the strap back over her head. Saw Dick's gun lying on his lap and strained to reach it.

The back door opened. Kit's hand wrapped around the gun and she slammed backward, weapon aimed, finger on the trigger—

—only to find herself staring at M'cal. Alive, covered in blood, with a wound in his throat that looked raw and deep and red. No longer a gaping hole. He was alive. Breathing. Staring at her.

Kit almost shot him. Her finger had already begun to close—reflex—but he caught the gun and took it from her. *Oh, my God*—she reached out to touch him. M'cal grabbed her hand, kissed it fiercely, and dragged her from the car. He tried to speak, but his voice would not work.

Kit did not ask him how. No time. M'cal hesitated, glanced up and down the alley, and shoved Kit back into the car. He closed the door, opened up the front, and pulled out Dick. Dumping the man on the ground, he jumped in, reversed, accelerated, and then they were on their way, squealing out of the alley. Kit looked back. No sign of Yu.

She climbed awkwardly over the back of the front seat, banging her shoulder on the dashboard as she tried to right herself. M'cal glanced down at her. There was blood on his mouth, all over his face. He was doused, bathed in it. All Kit could do was stare.

She touched his arm, his shoulder—reached up to press her fingertips against his face.

"How?" she murmured, still unbelieving, heart in her throat.

M'cal tried to speak. This time he made a gurgling sound, a ghost of a word, but that was it. Frustration filled his face; he tapped the bracelet cuffed to his wrist.

"Part of your . . . imprisonment?" Kit asked incredulously. "You can't be killed?"

He shrugged, as if to say that was not entirely correct; but either way, it was good enough for her. She could suspend belief if it meant M'cal was alive.

Kit pressed her forehead on his arm, savoring his warmth, his strength. She tried not to cry—but could not help herself. She managed to be quiet about it, but M'cal touched her hair and that only made her shake harder. Too much. All of this was too much.

"I wish I had known," she mumbled brokenly. "I thought you were dead. You don't know what that felt like." *How it felt to know I could have warned you.*

He tapped her shoulder, making her look at him. His eyes were solemn, so very grave, and he touched his heart. Pointed at her. Made a gun with his fingers and shot at her. Touched his head, pointed at her again. Laid his hand over his heart a second time.

Kit did not know what the hell he was trying to say, but she took a wild guess. "You thought maybe I was dead, too? That they shot me?"

M'cal nodded, his jaw tightening. Raw emotion flickered through his eyes, which were suddenly red-rimmed, bright. Kit wiped away a fresh stream of tears and placed her hand over his heart. M'cal covered it with his own, squeezing so tight she could imagine his soul riding against her skin.

"Don't do that to me again," she whispered. "Please."

"Same to you," he whispered hoarsely.

They did not drive far. M'cal was behind the wheel of a stolen car, presumably owned by a police officer, and that was a very bad combination.

And they were also covered in blood, with no change of clothes in sight. Walking into a department store to do some quick shopping was out of the question, and entering her hotel looking like a victim in a slasher film would be far too shocking a sight. Someone might call the police.

Kit's cell phone was still waterlogged from the night before, and M'cal did not carry one. They drove for five minutes into Chinatown, where they found a pay phone. Kit, being a bit more presentable, jumped out and made a collect call to Dela. She watched the street as she dialed, but except for some curious looks from several beggars—who began to walk toward her, saw the blood, and turned away—no one seemed at all threatening or inclined to point their fingers. Not yet anyway.

"Hari's at the hotel," said Dela. "And you're not there."

"Um, yeah," Kit said. "I happen to be in Chinatown at the moment, covered in blood, and in possession of a stolen car that belongs to the corrupt police officer who tried to murder me. I could use some help. Like *now*."

"Oh, Kit," Dela muttered. "What part of 'stay put' didn't you understand?"

"Lecture me later." There was a parking garage nearby—Kit could see it from where she stood—and she told Dela to ask Hari and the others to meet them there, on the top level. She also asked for a fresh change of clothes—for both her and M'cal.

"You're not alone?" Dela asked, sounding surprised.

"Long story," Kit replied. "Thanks, Dela. Later."

Kit hung up the phone and dove back into the car. M'cal made a straight line to the parking garage, where they drove to the very top of the structure. Kit peered out the window, looking for a security camera. She did not find one, but that was poor comfort. M'cal backed the car into a corner slot—better to hide the broken rear window—and then turned off the engine. Time to wait.

Kit hid Dick's gun in her purse. M'cal watched her.

"You did well," he rasped, and cringed, swallowing hard. Kit winced in sympathy and touched his face, fingers gently tugging aside his collar so she could better see his throat. It was almost healed, but there was an imprint the size of a quarter—the last remains of the hole that had blasted through his neck.

"You were dead," she said.

"But the witch is not," he replied. "I told you it was complicated."

"Any other surprises?" she asked sharply.

He hesitated. "I cannot touch the sea without being consumed by pain. I cannot touch any human other than the witch without the same."

Kit's hand flew off his throat. He caught it and brought her palm to his lips.

"I do not feel pain now," he said quietly. "That was your gift to me, what you did when you stopped me from taking your soul."

"But you don't think it will last."

"The bracelet remains."

"We need to get it off you."

"Perhaps you can use your magic."

Kit shook her head. "I don't know what I do, but it's not magic."

"Kitala—"

"I knew you were going to die," she interrupted. "I knew, and I didn't tell you."

M'cal's eyes darkened, and her stomach lurched like she was falling, but when he spoke there was no condemnation, no anger. He brushed his thumb against her cheek and said, "Earlier you mentioned death."

Years of death. Too much. She almost said that out loud, but stopped herself, fighting for different words. She did not know why it mattered—surely there was nothing she could say that would surprise M'cal—but she cared how it sounded. Too much pride, too much fear. Too much guilt.

"Sometimes," Kit said slowly, "I see when people are going to die. When they're going to be . . . murdered."

M'cal's face showed nothing. "Only murder?"

She nodded. "But it's useless. I don't know when or who will murder. Only *how*. Only that it will be violent and awful, and that no matter how good a life someone leads, no matter how kind they are, that's what they'll have to look forward to in their last moments. Not love. Not family. Just pain. Fear. A broken heart." She swallowed hard, trying not to think of the countless people she had encountered who had stood talking to her with bullets in their brains, ropes around their necks, skulls smashed in, stomachs gutted.

M'cal touched her shoulder, the back of her neck, and she flinched. "Every time I meet someone, every time I give a concert or walk down the street . . . I have to be prepared to see violent death. The possible murder of my friends, the ones I love. It's why it's easier to be alone. I give my concerts, I travel. But always by myself. No one else. Because I don't always know right away. Sometimes it takes weeks, years—and then . . ." Kit stopped, sickened. "So many people get hurt in this world, M'cal. So many people hurt each other."

"Yes," he agreed softly. "Sometimes it seems like pain is the price for the time we have. We live, we burn bright, but in the end . . ."

"All we do is burn," she finished.

M'cal sighed. "You knew Alice was fated for murder."

"She was at my concert. Front row. With a knife sticking out of her eye."

"And you warned her." He hesitated. "But not me."

Kit looked away. "I don't expect you to understand."

"You might be surprised." He touched her cheek, his palm large and warm, soft like his voice. "Tell me, Kitala."

Tell him. Say the words.

Tension ran hard through her shoulders, making her cheeks hot. "I was afraid. Afraid to tell you, afraid to admit it."

"Did you think I would hurt you? That I wouldn't believe you?"

"No, not that." Kit finally looked into his eyes. "You told me that you started to give up on helping others. Because you knew it was futile, that no matter what you did, the outcome would be the same. It's no different for me. But I've never . . . I've never been with anyone I was so frightened of losing." Her voice dropped to a whisper. "I've never been with anyone, *knowing* they would be lost."

M'cal said nothing and she closed her eyes, frustrated, ashamed. "I'm sorry. It's hard to explain."

His thumb stroked her cheek; a moment later she was shocked to feel his lips press against her forehead. But still, silence. Nothing but his slow steady breathing as he pulled her near, tucking her gently against his chest. His heart beat beneath her ear like the slow drum of some mountain storm, thunder thudding against cloud and tree and stone.

"You and I are too much the same," M'cal murmured. "Ruled by powers we have no control over, forced to endure the pain of others. I murder because I am compelled to. You *see* murder, without any ability to stop it. And both of us bear the guilt and shame." He pulled back just far enough to look into her eyes. "Why was Alice different?"

"I don't know," Kit told him, still unsure what was happening between them. "It was . . . impulse, spur of the moment. I didn't have time to think about it. Unlike you. But I *was* going to tell you. I just thought we had more time."

"I used to take time for granted." M'cal smoothed back her hair, his gaze thoughtful, troubled. "Why do you do it? Why put yourself in the public eye, if seeing the public puts you at risk of pain?"

"I have to. My music."

"You love your music more than you hate your fear." M'cal's jaw tightened. "Last night I was there for the latter half of your concert. You were . . . unearthly. You do more with your violin than make notes and melodies. You . . . make reality. You change reality. Inside here." He touched his chest. "That, I think, is a more precious gift that knowing when someone will die. That is worth fighting for, Kitala."

If words could be hands, then Kit felt like M'cal had just placed his around her heart. Warmth spread. She tried to say something, but could not. She hardly thought she deserved it.

"I kept the truth from you," she finally said.

"You did," he agreed. "Am I supposed to punish you for that?"

"You should be angry."

M'cal smiled faintly. "There is a story I read once, about an iron house, airtight, no windows, no escape. People, trapped inside. All of them asleep but one—and the one person had the knowledge they were going to suffocate. But he let them sleep, Kitala. He did not wake them, because there was nothing for him to do. Mercy won out, and they died in peace."

Kit frowned. "Are you saying I did the right thing?"

"I am saying that there is no easy answer in these situations, and that I understand your reluctance to tell me." He leaned close, tilting up her face. "Do not be sorry, Kitala. I am not."

It was difficult to look at him. She felt wrecked with too much emotion she could not hide, and M'cal's own eyes were a study in contrasts; the raw physicality of his body translating into the piercing intensity of his gaze, which was tempered with an inexplicable tenderness that made her heart soften, her shoulders relax.

"I'm glad," she breathed. "I'm so glad you're still breathing."

M'cal smiled and touched her face. His hand shook, just slightly, and Kit wrapped her fingers around his wrist to steady him. He gave her the very faintest of nods, and then, with infinite care, kissed her softly on the lips.

This time it was Kit who shook, and his arms curled around her body, holding her close as he deepened his kiss. She loved the strength of his arms, the power of his body—how he held her so carefully in his lean hungry embrace.

His mouth trailed from her mouth to her cheek. "All this time . . . you have not been alone, have you? There must have been someone you trusted with your secret."

"My parents." Kit closed her eyes, savoring his warmth, his closeness. "My grandmother. She had a gift, too. Real power. She tried to help teach me, but I was a poor student. I wanted the visions gone, and I was more interested in music than her voodoo. She died a year ago."

His long fingers flicked the beaded pouch hanging around her neck. "Is this from her?"

"Yes." Kit touched the leather, feeling the movement of the tiny objects hidden within. "She said it would protect me."

He kissed her forehead. "Then never take it off. Let her love take care of you."

Like last night, thought Kit, remembering her grandmother's touch, her words, her urgency—set against the backdrop of her swamp home, safe and distant from the world. Kit missed that creaky house, which Old Jazz Marie had left to her. If she got out of this alive, she was going back there to sit a spell. Play her fiddle to the spirits and the alligators. Maybe try to learn about some things she had refused to accept while her grandmother still lived.

And how will M'cal play into that life? Would he be satisfied with it, if he could choose?

A merman living in the bayou, sitting pretty on the veranda of a rambling yellow house, centuries old and the home of former slaves and witches, music and voodoo; blessed with the love of a priestess queen. Or better yet, she could take him to the Smoky Mountains, to the old haunts where fiddling men still beat the ground with their feet in the shadows of dusk, plucking strings while the wind cried. She would lead him to the forest graves of her father's parents, lay a red rose down, or maybe a lilac, and tell him stories. So many stories, and more that she wanted to hear from him. If they ever got the chance. If she could find the courage to take such a chance. If he would accept such an offer, given with all the fear and hope one heart could muster.

He is not human and you do not care. He is a stranger and it does not matter.

Like thunder. Like the crack of dawn. A new day blooming. She felt that in his kiss, his voice, the way he looked at her. Infatuation, maybe; a crush, possible; but Kit had never felt so strongly about anyone. Not that the path promised to be easy.

Kit peered into his eyes. "There's something else you should know. Those cops don't want me dead anymore. I'm supposed to be brought in alive. And as for you . . . the person who seemed to be giving the orders wanted your head. Literally."

"My head?" M'cal frowned. "I suppose decapitation might kill me. Perhaps the witch, as well, given our link."

"Or the axe could bounce. But I'm not inclined to test that theory."

"Nor am I. But that implies someone knows about my ability. And if that is the case . . ."

"Bad news." Kit drummed her fingers against her thigh. "Could be coincidence. Maybe they found out you stopped those men last night, so they want your head as a trophy?"

"I did not leave anyone alive to talk. And there were no cameras, no witnesses." M'cal shook his head. "There are only two people who know about me. But they would not work this way. It would not be like them."

Rain pattered on the windshield. In the distance, Kit heard police sirens. She stiffened for a moment, but the sound faded. M'cal let out his breath, and once again he wrapped his arm around her shoulders, pulling her in close. Kit closed her eyes. Her head still hurt, as did her stomach where Yu had punched her.

"How did you avoid that female cop?" Kit peered up into his face. "She was on her way with an axe."

"I heard her coming. I hid in one of the side rooms. I almost confronted her, but because she was alone, I thought it possible you might be nearby. *If you were still alive. I had to know.*" He swallowed hard, the intensity of his gaze faltering for one brief moment, becoming so weary and full of quiet horror, Kit placed her hand over his mouth when he tried to continue. They stared at each other, and after a moment he kissed her fingertips, closing his eyes with a shudder. Kit closed her eyes as well, her entire focus, every part of her, concentrating on those few small spots in contact with his lips. Her breathing quickened.

M'cal's hand brushed the swell of her breast. She strained against him, silently begging for more, running her own hands under his shirt, seeking skin. His body was smooth, hard, hot. He made a sound, low in his throat—almost like pain—and kissed her so deeply it was all she could do to keep breathing.

Kit's hand trailed lower, her fingers moving lightly over the hard bulge in his slacks. He broke off their kiss and threw back his head as she touched him more firmly. Kit bit down a fierce smile, and glanced around. No one was watching. They were alone.

Isolated, but no chaste nun, Kit had managed a few relationships, all with varying success given that she had never expected any of them to last. She had no faith in her ability to endure, not with her fear of seeing some murder of the man in her bed, or having her secrets revealed. Still, she had picked up some things. Learned about her own appetites, as well. But even now, she was surprised.

She quickly unbuttoned M'cal's pants and slid her hand inside. His hips thrust against her and she kissed him hard, welcoming his tongue as it slid inside her mouth. Lust; Kit had never been so overcome, so instantly wet with desire. Covered in blood, on the run, terrified as hell—and none of that mattered; all was insignificant to the overwhelming sense of *rightness* in her heart when she kissed M'cal. Being with him was like being filled with music—true, pure. She had never felt that with another person. Had never imagined it was possible.

She wanted M'cal inside her. Barring that, she wanted to taste him. She had to. She had to feel more of him. She thought he might want the same thing. His large hands would not stop moving; he tugged her blouse down so far her breast lay exposed. He ducked his head, taking her nipple into his mouth, sucking lightly. Kit gasped, grabbing his shoulder with one hand, squeezing him gently with the other. He made a rough sound, and she freed him from his pants, her breasts aching, her thighs shifting restlessly.

M'cal was built the same as a human man—only bigger—and she bent down, taking him in her mouth. He cried out, burying his hands in Kit's hair as her tongue swirled around the tip of him.

"Do you like this?" she asked, blowing lightly on his damp skin. He shivered, looking down at her with such lust and longing that for a moment Kit forgot herself, could see only the old hurt lurking at the back of his gaze, and she knew with utter clarity that this was the first time he had ever been touched intimately by someone who did not want to use or hurt him.

Kit rose up and kissed his mouth. He attacked her with equal ferocity. She tasted tears—hers, his, she did know—but her heart swelled so big she thought she might burst with it.

M'cal broke away, breathing hard, shuddering. "I hear a car coming."

Kit nodded, chest heaving, but she kissed him again, drawing out his lower lip between her teeth. M'cal exhaled, sharp—and then smiled like a shark as he ran his hand over her aching breast, tucking it back inside her blouse. She returned the favor, watching him watch her as she slipped his hard erection inside his slacks. There was still a bulge, but she hoped no one would care or notice. *She* certainly did not mind.

A long black Suburban, windows tinted, peeled around the entrance to the rooftop parking lot. Even from a distance, Kit recognized Hari in the passenger seat. She did not know the person driving—a young man, was all she could tell from far away. M'cal and Kit climbed out of the car just as the Suburban pulled up. The back door opened. A darkly handsome man with scraggly black hair and golden eyes poked his head out. He smiled briefly at Kit, but his expression froze when he saw M'cal. M'cal, too, stiffened.

"Get your asses in here," said the man after a brief hesitation. He voice was low, gruff. A tattoo peeked out from beneath the collar of his scrappy leather jacket.

Kit climbed in first, M'cal close behind her. The moment the doors closed, the Suburban sped off. The interior was dark, soft; it felt like a tomb. All the faces that looked back at her, except Hari's, were unfamiliar. Much to her relief, not one of them appeared to have been fated to a violent death. Not yet.

On her left was the man who had let them in the car, who looked vaguely familiar; behind him was another individual with skin as dark as coal and short black hair streaked gold—a color that matched his eyes, which studied her and M'cal with eerie solemnity.

Kit reached forward to shake Hari's hand in greeting, then met the brief gaze of the Surburban's driver: a young man with golden skin and dark hair laced with unusually natural-looking streaks of blue and green. He had golden eyes, too. All the men did—something she had thought was unique to Hari. The oddity tickled her mind—with uneasiness, perhaps.

Take nothing for granted, whispered a tiny voice. *Not a thing.*

"It is good to see you again," Hari rumbled. His hair—wild in color, like the others; *just* like the others—was pulled back from his face, revealing a physical perfection she might have once said had no equal—until M'cal.

"Same to you," she said, trying to ignore how Hari studied, so gravely, the blood on her face and body. She touched M'cal's hand, and was shocked at the tension running through him; he was almost quivering with it. She looked at him, and his jaw was tight, his eyes sharp.

Hari met M'cal's gaze, nodding once with a somber, knowing expression that said more than Kit was comfortable with. "You are safe here, friend."

"Not a friend yet," M'cal replied in a cool voice.

"M'cal," Kit said, but the man beside her laughed, low and hard. She looked at him. "What's so funny?"

"It must be in the fucking air," he said roughly. He raised an eyebrow, and his golden eyes seemed to glow for one brief moment. "I go my entire life, quiet and normal, but in the past three years I've seen more shit coming out of hiding than I know what to do with. Hell, we might as well put up a sign." He looked across Kit at M'cal, and shook his head. "My *God*."

"Koni," growled Hari, and the other man shut his mouth and looked out the window.

"I don't understand," Kit said, but even as she spoke those words, she felt some piece of her, deep down in that primitive part of her heart, lift up like some red bleeding flag, and all that sudden uneasiness—the hair, those golden eyes—screamed at her in ways she would never have noticed or acknowledged before M'cal. Before the events of the past night and day. Her eyes had been opened, and could never be closed. Her grandmother, she thought, would be very pleased.

"Tell me," Kit said, steeling herself.

No one said a word. No one looked at her. Except M'cal. He took her hand and squeezed it gently.

"What it means," he said slowly, "is that none of the men in this car are human."

"Oh," she said. "Oh, *damn.*"

CHAPTER EIGHT

Not human. A case of biology and magic, one stronger than the other, combined in flesh and blood, creating life. M'cal was not human, not entirely, but he had always had the comfort of knowing he was not alone—that there were others even beyond his kind. Because the world was larger than the ocean's heart, and in the old days, the first days, true humans had been outnumbered by the swift and furious, beings of magic. Wars of magic.

And he knew, too, that such creatures were hard to kill. The evidence for that had never been clearer. He was now sitting in a car with four shape-shifters, in a day and age when finding even one in a lifetime would have seemed like a miracle.

He did not trust it. He was not sure what Kitala felt. She was very quiet. Too quiet.

"Rik," Hari said to the young man driving. "Find a place to stop."

Two bottles of water appeared between M'cal and Kit. "You must drink," said the man behind them. His voice was soft, clear, touched by an African accent. "You have been through an ordeal. There is food here, too, if you like."

"Thank you," Kitala said hesitantly, taking the water. M'cal, after a moment, grudgingly did the same.

The man smiled at him, his teeth blindingly white. "I am Amiri. The gentleman beside Kit is called Koni. And there, Hari. The young man driving is Rik. As I am sure you surmised."

What M'cal had surmised was that the young man behind the wheel was definitely one of the water folk—confirmed when the man glanced backward for a better look at M'cal and almost swerved off the road.

"Sorry," muttered Rik as they all grappled with their seat belts and armrests, listening to cars honk and brakes squeal. He veered into a small, grisly parking lot, where M'cal watched two gaunt men lean on the hood of a Cadillac and shoot heroin straight into their legs.

"Christ," Koni muttered. "I should have flown."

Kitala leaned away from him. "I need some answers. I want to know exactly what is meant by *not human.*"

"They are shape-shifters," M'cal said. "You did not know this?"

"Of course not," she snapped, "I don't even understand what that means."

The men all looked at each other. Koni shrugged and pulled back his sleeve. Tattoos covered his sinewy arm, which he held up in front of Kitala. As M'cal watched, golden light curled against his skin—a swimming light, like the sun through water—and within that glow his arm began to change.

Black feathers sprouted—dark buds unfurling sleek

and dry, rippling through his skin—his entire arm shifting, cutting in length, his hand shriveling beneath long, silky quills. It was a disturbing sight; beautiful, maybe, but M'cal was only used to seeing his own kind shift, and this was different. More elemental. He tried not to feel anything else as he watched the shape-shifter work his magic, but this was difficult; it reminded him too much of what he could do, what he wanted to do even now: enter the sea, while he still could, without the pain, and be himself. To be free.

Free without Kitala, he wondered. *Is such a thing possible? Could you leave her even if you were allowed?*

Beside him, Kitala swallowed hard, leaning against his shoulder. She was utterly silent, eyes wide. Staring. The shape-shifter raised an eyebrow and smiled. He smelled like cigarettes. "Unless you'd like to see me naked, sweetheart, this as far as I'm going to go."

M'cal frowned, putting his arm around Kitala's shoulders. Koni watched him, the edge of his smile fading just slightly. But not the appreciation in his eyes when he looked at the woman beside him.

Kitala did not appear to notice. She reached out, slow and careful, to touch one of Koni's feathers. Her hand had to pass through the golden light—which made her flinch—but she did not stop until she laid her fingers upon Koni's transformed arm. She sucked in her breath.

Koni glanced at M'cal. "You want to feel me up, too?"

"Not particularly," he replied. Kitala withdrew her hand and reached up to grip the leather pouch and cross hanging from her neck. Her expression was raw—raw with wonder, raw with unease, raw with confusion.

"This is crazy," she said quietly. "How much more am I supposed to take?"

"I am sorry," Hari said, and gave Koni a dark look. "You should never have found out. Not like this."

Koni's feathers receded. He rolled down his sleeve. "So much for always being the careful one. But she would have learned the truth." He glanced at M'cal. "She already knows about *him*. I could tell."

"But imagine if you had been wrong," M'cal said. "You took a grave risk."

Kitala gave him a sharp look. "Do you know these men?"

"No. But there is magic in us. We can see it, recognize it. Smell it," M'cal said.

She closed her eyes. "So, there are a lot of you."

"Not at all," put in Amiri, his voice floating softly from the backseat. "If only."

M'cal glanced at him. "But there are four of you here. So many. Your numbers must be increasing. This is not normal."

"Tell me about it," Koni muttered.

Hari inclined his head. "It is true that in recent years we have been . . . discovering more of our kind. The oddity—and risk—of that has not escaped our attention."

Kitala held up her hands. "Dela knows about this, doesn't she? All of you work for Dirk & Steele. Are there . . . more . . . like you? At the agency?"

The men stayed silent, which was all the answer M'cal needed—though listening to their voices had given him plenty. Kitala closed her eyes, shaking her head. "I cannot believe this."

"Please," Hari said. "Do not be angry with Delilah. She meant no harm. There are simply too many individuals who must be protected. Those are not her secrets to tell."

Kitala said nothing. Koni rolled down his window and removed a cigarette from his leather jacket. He lit up, taking a long drag that he blew out into the cold, wet air. M'cal's bracelet tingled. He touched the metal and found it still cold, but it was only a matter of time. His throat hurt. The witch most certainly would have felt that wound.

"You are here to help us?" M'cal asked Hari.

"Yes," said the man solemnly. "Perhaps you can tell us what has transpired since Kit last spoke with my wife."

"Or who was shot," Amiri said.

"I was," M'cal replied. "Here, in the throat."

The men stared. Kitala sighed.

"Right," Koni muttered, tossing away his cigarette. "Like I said. Fucking air."

They drove away from the grit and grease of Chinatown, through the glistening skyrocket buildings of the city center, and entered a quiet neighborhood filled with pale pink stucco and yards too small for the grandiose homes bulging inside their finely manicured plots. It was an environment for the rich, but nevertheless depressing in its bland uniformity. If East Hastings Street looked like the physical embodiment of a sexual disease, M'cal thought that North John Avenue might be in the running for Best Perpetual Case of Constipation.

Rik pulled down a narrow alley that ran behind the houses on the street. Two homes down, he stopped and slid the Suburban into a garage, the door of which was already open. He clicked a remote on the dashboard, and the door slowly shut behind them.

"Who owns this place?" Kitala asked.

"The agency," Rik said. His gaze darted to M'cal and then flicked away. Kitala glanced at M'cal, but all he could do was shrug. He had an idea of what was making Rik uncomfortable, but now was not the time to discuss it. He was not entirely certain there would ever be a good time.

The garage was empty. The interior of the house was nearly so. Just the basics: a round dining table, a long couch, and a television. The men carried in several suitcases, one of which was handed over to Kitala, along with M'cal's coat. He was surprised she still had it.

"How did you guys get into my room?" Kitala asked.

"I told them I was your husband," Koni replied blandly. "I said we'd had a fight and I wanted to surprise you. Thank God you didn't unpack," he said, grinning at M'cal. "I'm not sure what would have happened if I'd had to touch your frilly underthings."

"I probably wouldn't be able to wear them anymore," she said dryly.

"And you would no longer have a pair of hands," M'cal added.

"That so?" Koni smiled, folding his arms over his chest. "You know, other than the fact that I can tell you're not human, I still don't know quite *what* you are. Nothing I've encountered before, that's for sure. Care to share?"

Rik began to leave the room. Koni held out his hand and stopped him. "Don't think I haven't noticed your googly eyes, kid. What do you know that I don't?"

"Manners?" Amiri murmured. Hari emerged from the kitchen, a phone in his hand. The man was even bigger than M'cal had realized—a good six inches taller, around seven feet—and broad through the chest. There was a sharpness to his gaze as well. Watching everything, analyzing.

Warrior, he thought. Born and bred to it—and to a degree that no one, not even M'cal with his legacy, could match. Hari was a relic.

Rik glanced at M'cal with a great deal of fear and respect. "He's one of the Krackeni."

Kitala looked at him. "*Krackeni?* Is that what you're called?"

"It is one name," M'cal said slowly.

"For the Kracken," Rik added. "For what they control in the sea."

"That is where you are from?" Amiri asked, coming around to stand beside Rik. M'cal could hear the genuine curiosity in his voice, a root of kindness, and it set him more at ease. He did not like talking about himself to these strangers—shape-shifters or not—but he did not see any way around it. He needed their help, and Kitala seemed to trust them. As long as this latest revelation concerning their backgrounds had not tarnished her opinion.

"I am a . . . merman." M'cal found it difficult to speak the word. To hear Kitala say it was one thing, but from his lips, it simply sounded . . . odd. As though he should be lounging on some rocky beach with a conch shell in one hand and a trident in the other.

"Merman," Hari echoed. "I am not familiar with that term."

M'cal and Kitala shared a quick look of surprise, but the others did not seem at all taken aback. Amiri said, "It describes an individual who lives beneath the sea, who can take breath from water, and who has the tail of a fish rather than the legs of a man." The shape-shifter met M'cal's eyes. "That is correct, is it not?"

"It is." M'cal turned his attention back on Rik. "Krakeni is an obscure term. How did you know it?"

"I swim as a dolphin," said the young man. "I'm also from the sea."

"That is no answer."

Rik hesitated. Amiri moved close and put his hand on the young man's shoulder, which seemed to relax him for a moment. Then he tensed up again, looked M'cal in the eyes, and said, "I've known your kind. A long time ago."

The uneasy tone of his voice was not a ringing endorsement of M'cal's people. He wondered which of the colonies Rik had encountered. Some, he knew, were more territorial than others. And some, as he was painfully aware, were just plain dangerous. Even to their own kind.

Kitala brushed against his hip. The brief contact made him warm, his heart jump. Even around so many others, he was affected—could not help himself. He wanted to touch her so very badly—to touch without pain, to touch a woman of his own choosing, to touch and be touched, and not be afraid. It gave him a sense of peace and wonder that he had forgotten— incredible, that he should forget—but being with the witch had made him lose more of himself than he had ever realized.

Kitala had saved his life. She made him remember what it was to be himself. Fully himself. And that was a gift that could never be repaid. Never. Because even if the witch recaptured him—and she would, without a doubt—this time M'cal would refuse to let himself forget. Never again.

Hari held up the phone. "There is news regarding Kit."

Kitala frowned, pulling the strap of her fiddle case over her head. "What kind of news?"

He hesitated. "According to the agency's contacts, you are wanted for questioning in the disappearance of Alice Hardon."

She froze. "Are you serious?"

Hari nodded. "Police in the Vancouver and Seattle area have been alerted. They have your name and picture."

Kitala closed her eyes. "I'm gonna kill someone."

"They probably already think you did," Koni muttered.

She gave him a dirty look and laid her fiddle case on the dining table. Flipped the catches. Pushed back the lid. Her instrument rested on its bed of purple velvet. The color of the wood was a deep, gleaming amber. Kitala plucked a string, and the note shivered through M'cal like a cold wind.

"Are you well?" Amiri asked him.

"Fine," M'cal replied, unable to look away from the fiddle.

Kitala glanced at him, and there was a darkness in her eyes, an understanding; a promise. And then she tore her gaze away to look at Hari. "Was there anything else? Mention of a stolen car? Attacking two police officers?"

"You attacked cops?" Rik asked.

"Who do you think shot M'cal?" Kit said to him.

Hari stared at the healing wound on M'cal's throat.

His eyes darkened into something threatening, wild. "There was no mention of an attack. Alice's family reported her missing, a claim taken far more seriously given that her uncle John Hardon was gunned down in public last night."

"I was there." Kitala gazed down at her fiddle. "We need to find her."

You need to stay alive, M'cal thought. One glance at the other men told him they felt the same, but no one said a word.

Kitala closed the fiddle case, laid her hand upon the hard plastic shell with a thoughtfulness that bothered him. Like she was saying good-bye. But she put the case under her arm, picked up her suitcase with the other, and walked to M'cal. Kissed his shoulder and said, "I'll be upstairs."

He watched her go. He wanted to follow, but stayed still. Looked at the other men. Waited until he heard the floor above them creak, then said, "Do you know how to find Alice Hardon?"

"No," Hari said quietly. "And that does not mean we will not try, but our first priority is keeping Kit safe."

"Keeping her safe means we *must* find Alice. We have no choice. And not simply because Kitala wishes it. If you do not find the woman, and the police continue this line of inquiry, it will ruin her life. Her entire career."

"She cannot go to the police to clear her name," Amiri stroked his jaw with long, elegant fingers. "Only Alice Hardon can do that."

"*If* she's alive," Koni muttered, giving M'cal a hard look. "We know why *we're* here. Why are you?

What's a *merman* doing on land anyway?" He shook his head. "I can't believe I said that word."

"This, coming from a shape-shifter."

"Takes all kinds, man. I thought I'd seen everything." Koni flung himself down on the couch and removed the pack of cigarettes from his jacket.

Hari moved closer, his golden eyes sharp, intense. "Your throat. I can see the remains of your wound. That is where you were shot, yes?"

"It is almost healed," Amiri noted quietly. "Is that a trait of your kind?"

M'cal did not answer.

Hari closed his eyes, as if it pained him to look at the injury. "Did someone give you the ability? Was it against your will?"

A striking question, full of implication. M'cal hesitated. "You know this. You have seen it before."

Hari unbuttoned his shirt and pulled the material apart. On his chest was a grotesque mass of burn tissue—scars—in the shape of words. The other men looked away. M'cal stared.

"This was done to me," Hari rumbled. "By someone who also gave me the power of regeneration. Of immortality. But it made me a slave as well, and I was compelled to do anything asked of me. I was a prisoner for more years than I care to think of."

M'cal's breath snagged in his throat. He held up his arm and tapped his bracelet. "You and me both."

"Christ," Koni muttered. Rik slumped down over the dining table. Amiri approached M'cal and peered at the engravings, his long fingers touching the air above the metal. The air smelled like power, old magic; mystery. Even M'cal could not escape the sense that this was a moment that might not come again; that perhaps it was the first of its kind in this modern age. Men who had become nothing better than myth, together, breathing the same air. And if this should become normal—if the world had changed so much, if the circle had come around again . . . then M'cal could not predict the changes he might live to see; he did not dare.

Hari buttoned up his shirt, very slowly, his eyes hooded, dangerous. "Who did this to you?"

"A woman," M'cal replied, choosing his words carefully. "A witch. She also wants Kitala dead."

"There are two groups that want her life? Why her?"

M'cal hesitated, weighing his trust, what he had heard in the voices of the men around him. Truth, honesty. Nothing hidden, except their own uncertainty.

You must trust. For Kitala, you must.

He stepped closer to Hari, better to see his eyes. "I cannot speak for those who came after us today, but as for the witch . . . I believe she is interested in Kitala because Kitala is gifted in magic. She was able to temporarily free me from my bonds. Though not, thankfully, of the regenerative power the bracelet provides."

Koni sat up sharply. "What kind of magic?"

"Enough," Hari interjected. "We should not discuss Kit outside her presence." He gave M'cal a long, steady look and clapped a hand on his shoulder, shaking him slightly. "Go, rest. We will begin looking for Alice. And we will find a way to free you. I promise."

M'cal nodded and began to back away. He stopped, though, staring thoughtfully at his hands. "My knowledge of this matter is limited, but it seems that it should be highly unusual—even impossible—for two spells, from two different individuals, to be so similar in power and direction. Not unless there is a substantial connection between them. Would you agree?"

"Yes," Hari rumbled, his expression deadly. "I most definitely would."

It was a big house, with at least four bedrooms on the top floor. Sterile, empty, just a shell. Dust bunnies swirled around M'cal's feet as he walked down the long hall, searching for Kitala. He found her in the last room, the master suite, sitting on the edge of the bed with her fiddle case in her lap. She was still covered in his dried blood.

M'cal closed the door and went to her, dropping to his knees. He took her hands, found them cold to the bone. Her face was gaunt, her eyes tired, skirting the edge of hollow. It made M'cal afraid. He blew on her hands, rubbed them. When she did not immediately respond, he set aside her fiddle case and pulled her up into his arms. He forced her to look at him, and finally she gave him a crooked smile.

"Don't look at me like I'm done for," she murmured, running her fingers down his face. "I'm tired, not beat or broken."

M'cal began to breathe again. "You worried me."

"It's you we should be worried about."

"Not yet," he said, though he felt the pressure, the fear, building inside his heart like a bomb. It made him clumsy as he crushed her against him. Every moment was precious; every act, every word, something that might have to anchor and strengthen him for a very long time to come. Nothing could be taken for granted.

Kitala clung to him, her arm snaking around his ribs. He could feel the power in her body—physical and spiritual—could still remember the taste of her soul as he had begun to draw it into his body. That was a terrifying memory, but M'cal had a love for human myth, and in that moment between life and death, he had imagined her as the fire from the phoenix, raging and dying and ready to be born again. A fire deep as her soul—a fire that *was* her soul.

Kitala pulled away just far enough to look into his face. The weary tenderness in her eyes made his heart ache. He could not recall anyone ever looking at him like that; he was not certain anyone ever would again. She touched his face, very lightly, and brushed back his hair. No words—no words that would be enough—but her eyes spoke, as did her hands as she slowly began to unbutton his shirt.

He stood very still as she undressed him. It was a somewhat grisly task; his shirt stuck to his body because of the blood. But they shared grim smiles, and it was all right, fine, because with Kitala he needed no explanations, no hesitation. She simply understood.

His shirt dropped to the floor. She touched his chest. Her hands were no longer cold. She stood on her toes and kissed his throat, and the heat of her mouth raked a fierce path to his sex, which had remained semihard ever since their encounter in the stolen car.

The memory of her lips and tongue made his blood surge even more, and he was suddenly quite hard, quite constricted, and quite ready—a sensation that intensified as Kitala zeroed in on his chest, slowly licking in a circle around his nipple, circling closer and closer. She flicked it with her tongue, then gently bit down.

M'cal's control shattered. He dragged them both to

the floor, attacking her mouth in a raw, wet kiss that sent her writhing against him, wrapping her legs around his hips and thrusting up. The sensation of her moving against him made him wild, and he pushed her blouse over her breasts—round, lovely, so firm she did not need to wear a bra. Her skin was a lovely rich shade of caramel, toned and silken—so good to touch—and her taste turned his body into one long endless ache.

Kitala's hands gripped his hair. She flung back her head, gasping, and he leaned over to recapture her mouth as his fingers slid beneath the waistband of her jeans into her underwear. She was wet, hot, but he struck a rhythm that made her cry out, her breathing so ragged it sounded like she was dying.

She fumbled with his pants buttons. He tried to help her, but she batted his hand away with a fierce grin—so lovely to see her smile—and then she was pushing his slacks down to his knees, wrapping her warm hand around him. He shuddered, and she laughed—then stopped laughing as he kissed her again and undid her jeans. He wanted to see her naked. He wanted to feel her naked beneath him, around him, holding him.

In moments he had his wish. Kitala lay before him, propped on her elbows, her chin up and her perfect breasts jutting. Her legs were impossibly long, smooth and soft. Spread wide. Blood covered her face, but she was still the most beautiful creature he had ever seen. His heart pounded so hard he thought he might die, but looking at her made him feel something else—like he had come home to fate, destiny. Like he should get down on his knees and pray to some God he did not believe in, because surely, surely, what he was feeling must be proof of something greater.

M'cal crawled over her body, fighting for control—
an almost impossible feat when she reached down,
smiling unrepentantly as her fingers stroked him in
places that made his back arch, his breath rattle in his
throat. He wanted to give up, to collapse, but he kept
himself together, even when she guided him right
against her slick, wet heat, rubbing and rubbing,
rolling her hips. M'cal thought he heard music in his
head; strings, voices.

"Kitala," he rasped, pouring all his heart into her
name. Her eyes darkened with understanding. No
fear. No manipulation. Just honest, breathless desire.

He pushed into her body, and the sheer pleasure
that rocked through him almost made M'cal lose himself. Her legs wrapped around his hips, her feet digging into his buttocks, goading him harder, faster, the
both of them violently taking each other's pleasure,
swallowing breath and sound and thunderous heartbeat. A stream of images passed through his mind—
the witch, riding him; men and women, touching his
body, right before their deaths—but then he looked
into Kitala's eyes—her sparkling, pleasure-heavy
eyes—and all of that old pain burned away.

He felt the swell of her body as he brought her
close, could hear it in her gasps and cries, and he knew
the moment she broke. He gathered her close in her
arms, savoring her pulsing shudders as he finally let
himself go, his senses rocking with pleasure as he
buried himself thick and furious with one long last
thrust. She cried out, writhing against him so fiercely
he almost became hard all over again. She kept moving, and he rolled on his back, taking her with him as
she reached between them, touching herself, swiftly

climaxing for a second time. At which point he was truly—and impossibly—hard and ready again.

Kitala threw back her head and began riding him, slowly swiveling her hips. He reached for her breasts, straining, thrusting up to meet her as she played with his senses. Until finally, *finally*, she took mercy and stretched out against him, bringing her legs together until their two bodies pressed so close there was not a hairbreadth between them. Rocking, rocking, rocking into another break of pleasure so powerful, M'cal almost went blind with it.

Everything stilled. He could not move. He lay on the floor with Kitala on top of him, listening to her make small sounds of pleasure with every ragged breath. Sleek and brown and beautiful, totally limp within his arms.

After a while, they managed to make it to the bed, but they did not talk. M'cal curled around Kitala, tucking her into the curve of his body, sharing warmth, comfort. She held his hand in an iron grip, which did not relax—not until her breathing eventually evened out, deepening, drifting her into sleep. M'cal tried to do the same, but he could not settle down. Too much fear. Time was running out. The compulsion could return at any moment, and he had taken enough risks, touched Kitala too many times than was safe for either of them.

Only, her presence was a drug, a lifeline, and he could not stop. So he stayed awake, watching her, holding her, listening to the sleeping monster inside his throat, and tried to think of all the ways he might stop himself from killing the one person who suddenly meant most to him.

He came up with nothing. No answer, no solution that he could manage on his own. Unless the witch changed her mind—or unless he and Kitala could find a way to permanently break the spell—he was going to be a constant threat to her. One merely postponed.

And in that case, the witch might just kill Kitala herself. If no one else did it first.

CHAPTER NINE

"I Put a Spell on You" was playing softly on the radio when Kit, dreaming, opened her eyes and found herself back on her grandmother's screened veranda, some wild bird crying all lonesome and heartbroken from the swamp. It was twilight. Candles burned. Old Jazz Marie sat on her stool. The pouch was done, but the hard part had come: mixing magic, sparking life. Not real voodoo, according to her grandmother, but something she had taught herself, learned through hard years of scrabbling for some understanding of the power flowing through her mind. Old Jazz Marie's own grandmother had had the gift, but she died too young. Kit was luckier. Except she had not been so interested in learning. Irony could run both ways.

"Mmm, mmm," murmured the old woman. "I told you *trust*, and you just ran all the way, didn't you, girl?"

Kit tried not to blush. "Not that I don't love seeing you, but why am I here? I know this isn't a normal dream."

"Nothing in life is normal," replied Old Jazz Marie. "But folks sure try to convince themselves. Never could figure out why."

Because the alternative is too frightening, Kit thought. Her grandmother gave her a sharp look.

"Wouldn't be so frightening if you had listened to me while I was still alive and kicking. When it came to learning about your heritage, though, you were always about as happy as a dead pig in sunshine. No worries, no cares—not about the possible dangers. Playing opossum with your life, Kitty Bella. That's what you did."

"I didn't want any part of it," Kit said. "All those dead people—"

"But you're still seeing them, and it won't ever go away. Least you can do is learn to control it. That's all I ever wanted."

"Didn't seem like that at the time." Kit scuffed the floor with her bare feet. "Just felt like more nightmares."

Old Jazz Marie sighed. "Stubborn as a mule. And in such danger, too. Things are not what they seem, child. Illusions are being cast. And the one responsible is worse than you can imagine."

Her grandmother picked up a conch shell from her small worktable, a pale fine thing the color of bone. She held it out to Kit. "Put that to your ear, little cat. Tell me what you hear."

Kit did as she was told, pressing the shell close. She listened, and at first heard nothing but the thrum of blood in her ears, the thud of her heart, like a drum. But that did not last, and in its place came something that at first seemed like a soft breeze full of dawn, all blushing rose and promise. A hushed sound, perfect and still. But that, too, did not last, and what followed was the lonely wail of something more than strings— as if strings could be made of earth and thunder, rolling and rolling like the first note of some distant creation.

Primitive. Primal. Perfect.

"What is this?" Kit breathed, cut with a sense of bitter disappointment as the music faded.

Old Jazz Marie regarded her solemnly. "That is the song of your soul, Kitty Bella. A song of power. You hear that song in your head, you can do anything. You can move the stars, breathe life into a butterfly, walk that swamp outside and take a nap in the mouth of a 'gator. You can even reach out to the dead. Talk a spell or two. All depends on how well you hear, and what you do."

"And what do I do?" Kit whispered.

Old Jazz Marie smiled, gentle, and pressed her thumb against her granddaughter's forehead. "Be good, little cat. Just be good."

Kit opened her eyes. This time, she was in a bedroom, on a bed, surrounded by strong arms and a strong body. Naked.

She remembered. M'cal. Warmth flooded her, a true and delicious contentment. *A well-loved woman*— that was what she felt like. Up until now, Kit might have said she had felt that way a time or two; but no more. This was the real thing. This warmth—this bone-deep, down-to-the-soul satisfaction, tempered with heart—was what it meant for a woman to be well loved. Taken and reformed, made new from the old—because part of her now was composed of M'cal, and she had never felt that way about any other man. Never imagined that she could, if only because she had so much to hide. No trust, not really.

But events had put her on the edge of a volcano, teetering above the lava, and there was nothing like almost losing one's life to bring out the best or worst. Kit didn't think it was possible to learn a person's true mettle unless you put them in the fire. M'cal had not disappointed. She hoped he felt the same about her—but even if he did not, Kit thought she had held up fairly well. Kidnapped, shot at, still covered in blood; her career likely ruined; lives hanging in the balance, including her own—and oh, the fact that no one around her appeared to be fully human.

No screams yet. No pleas of insanity. And only half a Xanax in a twenty-four-hour period. Fantastic.

There were two windows, both curtains drawn, but with enough gaps for her to see that it was dusk. Kit had to go to the bathroom. Her skin felt disgusting. She tried to wriggle out of M'cal's loose grip, but his arms immediately tightened. She smiled to herself and lifted his large hand to her mouth, kissing his palm. His skin was callused, the sinews and tendons of his wrist and fingers chiseled, smooth, and strong.

"Hello," he murmured, his breath stirring her cheek.

"Hello," she whispered, rolling over to look at him. He was a mess. Soaking in a bath of blood would have been kinder. His hair was crusty with it, his entire upper body dark and red and rough. But it was *his* blood, not a stranger's—*he is strange, unknown*—and for some reason, that made all the difference. Gross, but not intolerable. In an odd way, even sexy. M'cal looked as if he had gone to battle in hell and had come out the other side, raw and ready for more. Ready for *her*.

She remembered, too, how it had felt to have him moving inside her body, making love to her with such ferocity and tenderness—how all that mattered was his eyes, the way he looked at her. Like he would die if he did not touch her. Like he would die if he did.

But he can't die. He's safe, no matter what you see. Safe for now, anyway. Which would just have to be enough. No turning back. She stroked his cheek with her fingers, marveling at his warmth. "I was going to take a shower. You want to join me?"

M'cal smiled, but it was ragged, weary. His eyes were bloodshot. Kit frowned, touching his face. "Did you sleep?"

He shook his head. "I was afraid the compulsion would return."

"You need to rest. Don't be afraid."

"You are asking the impossible. If I hurt you—"

Kit covered his mouth with her hand and then carefully, slowly, scooted backward until she left his embrace. She felt cold without his arms around her. "How about this? Better?"

"No," he said ruefully.

"Tough," she said, rolling onto her back and stretching, wriggling her hips, arching her spine. M'cal watched her body. He reached out to touch her breast. Kit swatted his hand.

"No touching," she said. "You need to rest."

"You make it impossible." He lifted up the covers, revealing just how impossible. Kit laughed quietly and rolled back on her side, cushioning her head on her arms.

"Merman," she said. "Man of the sea."

M'cal scooted closer, his hand resting just a breath from her own. "Do you have trouble believing?"

Kit hesitated. "Not exactly. I trust my eyes. I trust what you tell me. But it is . . . alien. I have trouble reconciling it, even understanding how something like you—you, who look so human in every way—could exist."

"And the men downstairs?"

Kit closed her eyes. "They make it worse. I still don't know what the hell is going on with that. I should call my friend. Ask her. But I don't want to. I can't."

"You feel betrayed?"

"No," she said, and it was true, so true. "Something that big? I wouldn't tell. I certainly never mentioned what I can do. But it's just . . . too much. I don't want to deal with it. All I can handle right now is you and me. And Alice."

"Alice," M'cal murmured. "If we find her alive, I hope she appreciates all the things you have done to help her."

"It wouldn't matter if she did." Kit sighed. "I don't know what I'm doing, trying to circumvent fate. For all I know, I'm putting into motion the events that will kill her."

"All you can do is follow your heart." M'cal traced the air above her face. "Be good, Kitala. No matter what else happens, if you are good, you can have no regrets."

"Be good," she echoed, feeling a tingle run up her spine. "You know, the path to hell is paved with good intentions."

M'cal smiled crookedly. "So?"

Kit laughed quietly. "So, tell me about your . . . people? Is that the right term?"

"It is as good as any. And there is not much to tell. We are like humans in many ways, though the Krackeni are fierce isolationists. Xenophobic, even. There is no real sense of property, but there are territories, fiercely guarded, with a great deal of ceremony required before entering such waterlands."

"Pity the unwary sailor?"

M'cal frowned. "Human myth has its Amazons. The Krackeni have their version as well. Once, in the distant past, a particular colony of Krackeni females wanted to take revenge on human sailors for an unfortunate encounter they'd had with them."

"Huh." Kit chewed on her bottom lip. "What happened?"

"Others of our kind stopped them. By that point, we had already begun retreating from human activity. It had become unsafe to mingle—though it had not always been so. In the ancient ports of the old world, we lived side by side with humans—trading the fruits of the sea, selling our services as guides and musicians. Some of us even ventured farther inland—into two lost colonies that disappeared into what is now Europe and Asia. We were searching for new water alternatives, new trade routes. I suppose remnants of those bloodlines might still exist."

Kit shook her head. "I never imagined that the world could be so big."

"Even with what you can do?"

"It's not the same."

M'cal shrugged, his eyes drooping slightly; sleep, finally. But his voice still sounded strong when he said, "It has become more difficult for us. Every year my kind must go farther, deeper than we ever have before. And it is still difficult to avoid discovery."

"It's only a matter of time."

"Which is why some of us have been sent away to live on land, why our colonies have been split and divided, and flung across the ocean. It is dangerous for all of us to be in one place. And for those like me, on the surface, we are here to watch and learn, and if necessary, fight."

"Fight," Kit echoed, surprised. "Why not try to get along? If you are discovered—"

"We will be treated like animals. Experimented upon. And even if we are not, there will be those who fear us, who will try to control us. Humans scarcely tolerate each other. How will they accept us?"

"I accept you. Would your people accept me?"

M'cal said nothing, which was all the answer she needed. She began to pull away, but he grabbed her hand.

"My mother was human," he said quietly.

Kit stared. "Is that common?"

"No. But my father was one of those sent to live on land, and he met a woman he could not live without. It caused . . . a stir, you might say. Mostly because there were those who felt that mixing with a human would contaminate the bloodline."

"The *bloodline?*" Kit tried not to smile. "Are we talking Krackeni Supremacists here? Do they wear little hoods made of white seaweed and have clandestine meetings around lava vents?"

M'cal choked back a laugh. "Some of them probably would if they had any concept of such a thing. But no . . . the bloodline does indeed refer to something . . . rather unique."

"Unique, huh? You're not a prince, are you? Because that would totally cap off the fairy-tale moment I'm having."

His mouth twitched. "Sorry to disappoint. Although, if there were such a thing as royalty amongst the Krackeni, I suppose you could say I am it."

"Rock on." Kit slapped his hand. "So, what's so special that mixing with a human gets all those tails in a twist?"

"You have already had a taste of it."

"I've had a taste of quite a few things, M'cal. And I've been impressed by every one of them."

He smiled. "My voice. What I can do."

"Ah." Kit thought for a moment. "I remember you said it was a warrior trait."

"There used to be more of us, but now there are only a dozen families left that still carry the gift. They are encouraged to . . . intermingle."

"You mean have babies. Lots and lots of babies." She wondered what Krackeni babies looked like. She wondered, quite suddenly, if her birth-control method was enough. She wondered, too, why she was not so afraid of the possibilities.

M'cal's eyes turned distant. "I think the trait is just as likely to be passed on no matter who one's mate is, but I am somewhat biased."

"And what a rebel your father was. Where is he now?"

"Home, somewhere in the South Pacific. He . . . retired. My mother died several years ago from cancer, and after that, he had no desire to remain. I took his place."

"I'm sorry," Kit said. M'cal slid his hand over hers, entwining their fingers.

"She had no regrets," he told her softly, his eyes distant. "Except, perhaps, that she could not join my father in the sea. That bothered her. She wanted to be able to share his life in every way, but that essential part of his nature was denied to her. My father did not care, and she knew it . . . but it still hurt."

"Do you have siblings?"

"None by blood. You?"

"Only child. I think one was all my parents could afford, or handle." Kit looked at their joined hands, dark and pale, and thought of her mother and father. She wondered if the police had contacted them. They would be worried sick.

She did not reach for the bedside phone, though. She kept looking at M'cal, thinking about what he had told her. "You mentioned that you were prepared to fight if things go wrong. You believe that any threat to your people will originate from land."

"There is no doubt of it."

"So, how many generations have you been doing this? Coming to land, acting as . . . some kind of secret defense?"

"My father was one of the first. There have always been Krackeni who left the sea to wander the world. We are as much explorers as humans. But this was different. After your Second World War, we decided it would be in our interest to become more organized. Just in case."

In case mermen ever hit CNN and end up in some lab. "Will you go back to wherever home is?"

"If I can. But it will never be for long. This . . . commitment I made is lifelong."

"Must be lonely."

"I should have appreciated the solitude more than I

did," M'cal replied darkly. "My loneliness made me vulnerable."

"The witch."

He smiled bitterly. "Just before I was captured, I began attending a human university. I had spent the previous years wandering, learning on the sly, but I wanted something . . . more concrete. Stability, I suppose. The witch was one of my professors. Theology, to be specific."

"I would crack a joke about the sins of sleeping with one's teacher, but given the circumstances—"

"Not very funny," M'cal agreed. "She was beautiful, very charming. But she had cold eyes. I noticed that from the beginning, but I was so taken . . ." He stopped, heartbreak flickering across his face. Kit pushed close to wrap herself around him. He held her tight, burying his face in the crook of her neck. She felt the metal of the bracelet press against her skin.

"I thought you said no touching," he whispered.

"I won't tell if you don't," she murmured.

They took a shower together. It went unspoken, but Kit thought they were both afraid that a moment apart would mean forever—that, despite the danger posed by the compulsion, it was still better to take what time they had, as long as they still had it.

Kit helped M'cal scrub his face and wash his hair. It took hard work and a considerable amount of soap and hot water to sluice off the dried blood. Under the bright bathroom lights, Kit noticed a sheen to M'cal's pale skin that she had not seen previously. Like mother-of-pearl; very faint, almost translucent.

"It is the water," M'cal said when she pointed it out. "My body reacts. Instinct." He touched her breasts, which had been aching for his hands for quite some time. Kit sighed, arching her back.

"I like your instincts," she murmured, and then sighed some more as he moved around behind her. He slid her arms over her head, placing her hands upon the wall of the shower stall, kissed the back of her neck, his fingers trailing a slow path to her shoulders, where he lingered, slowly massaging her, pressing the tension out of her muscles. Kit soaked it up, moaning as his hands moved down and around to her breasts, kneading them gently. She began to take her hands from the wall, but M'cal stopped her, made her remain still.

His hands drifted lower. Her thighs shifted restlessly, a fierce, low ache spreading through her as he pressed his leg between hers, spreading her wide as his fingers sank into her body. Kit closed her eyes, savoring the sensation, each pulse of pleasure, combined with the hard, solid muscle of his thigh between her legs; the heat of his body, the hot water beating down upon her; even the steam. She rocked against him, harder and faster, until quite suddenly his hand disappeared. He grabbed her hips, and it was instinct for her as well; she bent forward, stood with her legs apart, and let him take her hard.

As with their first encounter, she found herself astonished at how big he felt inside her, how deep he could move within her body. He filled every part of her, and the pleasure of that as he hauled her close, thrusting faster and faster, made her head swim and her heart rocket into her throat. It did not take him long to push her over the edge, and she staggered, so weak in the knees he had to catch her around the waist and hold her up as he came hard, shuddering against her back. He coiled around her, his arms strong as steel—like being cocooned in the most perfect shield against the world.

Even if that touch triggers him to sing away your soul?

Uneasiness curled, stealing some of her pleasure. She tried not to dwell; she wanted to be with M'cal, no matter the risk. It seemed impossible to feel this strongly about someone, but she could not help it. Her grandmother was right: she had run all the way.

But you saved yourself once, and you can do it again. You can save M'cal, too. Some way, somehow.

Music filled her head: a dawn-light song, a roll of thunder—her soul song, her power.

You can move the stars, echoed her grandmother's voice. Move the stars or save her own life. Save the life of a merman. Save the life of a strange woman.

Right. Easy as pie.

They got out of the shower, stumbling against each other. Too much exertion in too much heat. It affected Kit more than M'cal, but she made herself keep moving, and got dressed, using the clothes the men had brought in her suitcase. There was nothing for M'cal, though. He put his slacks back on, left his shirt off, and joined her as they went downstairs. Kit brought her fiddle case. Silly, but she felt naked without it.

The only men there were Koni and Rik, sitting at the dining table, four boxes of pizza in front of them. The television was on. They were watching *The A-Team.* Mr. T had some skinny white boy in a headlock.

Kit's stomach growled. Koni said, "Hello to you, too, sunshine."

"Hey," she said, flipping open a pizza-box lid. These guys were definitely meat-lovers. She grabbed a slice laden with pepperoni, sausage, ham, and pineapple, folded it up, and stuffed it in her mouth. It was so good she wanted to cry.

"If I time you," Koni drawled, "do you think you could eat that whole pizza in under a minute?"

Kit gave him the finger, listened to him laugh quietly, and took another slice. M'cal joined her, reaching into the box.

"Krackeni eat junk food?" she asked him as he took a bite.

M'cal swallowed, and smiled. "If my people knew what they were missing, you land types would be in a great deal of trouble."

"Good times, I'm sure." Koni glanced at Rik. "Here's a question, though. Care to explain why you never mentioned the existence of mermen? We've certainly gotten you drunk enough."

Rik looked uncomfortable. "It never came up."

"Well, hey, here's a question for *you*," Kit said to Koni. "How come all of you look so human?"

"Why wouldn't we?"

"Because you aren't."

"Don't focus on the small things, sister. It's not important."

Kit narrowed her eyes. "It is to me, *brother*. How many of you are out there?"

"Not enough," Koni replied. "Not nearly enough. Which is why to have four of us together at one time . . ."

"It should be impossible," M'cal said. "And yet, you say you all work for the same organization. Forgive me if I find it difficult to trust that."

"The agency or us?" Koni sat back in his chair and shrugged. "I can understand that. I didn't want any part of it at first, either. But Hari was the first shifter outside of my family who I had seen in years, and there were . . . extenuating circumstances. I hopped on board for a trial period, and never left. It's good work."

"I still don't understand," Kit said. "I thought Dirk & Steele was a detective agency."

"It is," Rik said, his hands fidgeting over a rather gnawed piece of crust. "But we get to use our . . . abilities. And it gives us a chance to look for others of our kind."

"Just shape-shifters?" M'cal asked. Kit thought of Dela.

Koni hesitated. "Not just shape-shifters. Humans, too. Though . . . I wouldn't exactly describe them as normal, either."

"Oh, boy," Kit muttered. "What, they can read minds? Light fires with their ass—" She stopped, a sudden terrible thought coming to her. "What about Blue?"

"Blue?" M'cal echoed.

"Um, someone I dated briefly." Kit frowned. "Well?"

Koni held up his hands. "You should probably let him tell you himself. But, hey, don't get too pissed off. It's not like you mentioned your own mumbo jumbo."

"My *what?*"

M'cal stirred. "I told them that you had some . . . magical abilities."

"Fantastic," she muttered, and opened another box of pizza. This one was chicken and onion. "How is he?"

"Married to a circus performer, with a baby on the way."

Kit choked, coughing. "I just spoke to him six months ago."

Koni shrugged. "Man moves fast."

Apparently so. Of course, Kit was moving pretty damn fast herself. She looked at M'cal and found him watching her with a tiny furrow between his eyes. He looked both concerned and irritated.

Jealous, she thought, with a brief sense of wonderment. *Maybe he even thinks you still feel something for Blue.*

What she felt was stupid. Stupid, to have been around all these people and never noticed that something was odd, or different. She might as well have been blind, walking through life, paying attention to nothing but what was right in front of her. Never mind her visions, although those were partly to blame. Kit never liked looking too close. She simply had not realized how much she was missing.

Kit reached out and took M'cal's hand. There was nothing she could say to reassure him—not in front of witnesses, anyway—but she hoped he would understand. That he would trust her—a trust that was already fragile. She had held back from him once already; perhaps he would think her capable of it again.

Her fingers squeezed lightly. He squeezed back. His eyes did not soften, though. Still thinking, wheels turning. Some possessive streak she had not imagined. With anyone else, it would be a deal breaker. But with M'cal . . . she liked it.

Koni coughed, pushing back his chair. "Hari and Amiri headed out to sniff around for your Alice Hardon. I was supposed to wait here until you . . . woke up; so now that you have . . ." He saluted them both and began walking to the door. Stopping, halfway there, he turned around. "By the way, just how is it that you both met, if your . . . witch—whatever you call her—wants Kit dead?"

Not dead, exactly, Kit thought, recalling the sensation of her soul being sung away. She glanced at M'cal, who suddenly, once again, looked very uncomfortable.

"I was sent to kill her," M'cal said.

Rik sat up. Koni stared. "You're shitting me."

"I wish."

Koni briefly shut his eyes. "Did you know this, Kit?"

"Of course," she replied.

"*Of course?* He told you that he was sent to *kill your ass,* and you're still with him?"

"For the record," M'cal said, "I *did* try to convince her to leave me."

"You must not have tried very hard."

"Hey." Kit held up her hand. "I have my reasons for trusting M'cal. Not the least of which is that he *saved* my life."

Koni grumbled something mostly inaudible and gave M'cal a scathing look. "You don't trust us, fine. I don't trust you. But we're here to take care of Kit, and if you get in the way—"

"Stop me," M'cal said simply. "Do anything you have to. Do not let me hurt her."

Koni narrowed his eyes. "If you cared that much, you would leave with me right now. No questions, no second thoughts."

"Absolutely not," Kit said, but M'cal's face settled into a hard mask and he nodded slowly. She stepped in front of him, palms out. "No, please. Think about this. If the compulsion returns, you'll be forced to go back to the witch. Or hunt me. But if I'm with you, if you give me warning, maybe we can duplicate what happened earlier. Better to try, anyway."

"Better not put you at risk," he said sadly. "Which I have done far too much of today."

"Come on," Koni said gruffly. "Hari left you some clothes. You can change and we'll go."

Kit turned. "Who the hell do you think you are?"

"The help you asked for," he said in a far more gentle voice than she expected. Or, perhaps, deserved.

M'cal placed his hand on her shoulder and steered her away from the other two men, just around the bend in the living room, out of sight. He held her at arm's length, staring into her eyes. For a moment, there was such a terrible strain on his face, she was convinced that he was angry with her. And then something shifted in his eyes—raw, cut—and she realized that he was, in a horrifically restrained way, afraid.

"Stay safe," he whispered. "Whatever you do, Kitala, stay safe. Do not try to follow me."

"You're coming back to me."

"Yes. But whether it will be as I am now, or under the witch's compulsion, is another matter entirely."

"It will still be you." Kit pushed his hands aside and leaned into him, resting her palm over his heart. "She can't take that away, M'cal. Remember that. Remember yourself."

"Remember myself, remember you." He smiled faintly. "The two are the same at this point."

Her throat felt thick. She nodded hard, trying to ignore the burning in her eyes, and leaned close. It was worse, kissing him. His mouth was firm, hot, with that clean taste she was beginning to love—like a wind swept from the sea, bracing and strong and effortlessly powerful. He pulled her close, curling around her body.

And then, without much fanfare, he went to dress in

the clothes Koni showed him. He kissed her good-bye one last time, gave her a long, searching look that she felt right down to her toes, and then left. Gone. Door closed.

There was, apparently, a spare car parked on the street in front of the house. Kit did not stand at the window to watch him drive away. Seeing him get in was enough. Anything more would be pathetic—the act of a moon cow—although she was already close enough to being one that it hardly mattered.

She sat down at the table, fiddle case in front of her. Rik stayed on her right. He looked very uncomfortable.

"Is making you babysit me some kind of punishment?" Kit asked him.

"I'm still in training," he replied, which was not exactly an answer.

She studied his hands. "And you're a shape-shifter? A . . . dolphin? Can you change into anything else?"

"No."

"Why?"

Rik looked bewildered. "I don't know. Why are you asking?"

Kit raised her eyebrow. "Think about it for a minute. I bet you'll come up with an answer."

His expression soured, but not in any way that seemed angry. "Sorry. I'm just not used to talking about it."

"I'm sorry, too," Kit said. "This is all very new to me. And my temper is not at its best."

"S'okay." Rik gave her a faint smile. "I've been through something similar. I was an asshole about it, too."

"Thanks," she muttered, and flipped open her fiddle case. The instrument lay gleaming, polished and untouched by the violence that had plagued her. Good old reliable. Kit went to the kitchen to wash any remnants of pizza grease from her hands. Returned, stared for a moment at the gleaming wood, and then picked up her fiddle and bow. She wished M'cal were there.

"You're going to play?" Rik asked.

"I need to," she said, and it was true. She needed to play her fiddle like she needed to breathe, and if she waited a moment longer, something inside her just might break.

Kit had no song in mind. Nothing written. She merely set the bow to the strings and let her heart guide the music, flinging herself wildly into a twisting riddle of notes, ripping into melodies, distorting them just at the points where they would become beautiful. It was angry music—music of war—and it told Kit something about her state of mind as everything that poured out of her remained violent, thick with battle.

She thought of Alice. Alice so calm, Alice with a knife in her eye, Alice apologizing, trying to protect her. Alice, slipping her that damn card which had led to nothing. Alice, who even now might be dead.

Where the hell are you? Kit wondered, her music growing in fury. She was dimly aware of Rik watching, slack-jawed, but she paid him no mind. Inside her head, something was brewing, building; she felt it like a scream.

Until, quite suddenly, the room around her disappeared and she was lost in darkness—absolute, bone-chilling, and damp, like the heart of an oubliette cast down into the bowels of the world.

She could hear breathing not her own. Rustling, coming from all around. More than one body. A lot more.

And then, as though someone had lit a match, she could see. Not much, but just outlines, shapes. People sitting. Crouched, curled. Kit moved forward. She saw long hair, long legs; nearby, a heavily muscled arm. Men and women both. No one moved, not really. Restless shifting, that was all.

Something made her turn around. She looked hard into the shadows, and the light in her eyes pushed and pushed until she glimpsed, with breathtaking clarity, a shock of blond hair and pale skin, a body clad in a dirty white dress.

Kit stumbled forward, falling to her knees. It was Alice. Alice, with wrists cuffed in chains attached to the wall she leaned upon. Her skin was raw, and there was a bruise forming on her face. But she was alive. Very much so. She lifted her gaze and looked Kit in the eyes with a strength that felt like a punch.

"Be careful," Alice rasped, blue eyes blazing. "You're next."

"Where are you?" Kit cried out, but it was too late. The woman faded—the darkness, the other people, the sounds and smell—swirling away from her like the end of a bad dream. Kit blinked once, and found herself back in the house with Rik, her fiddle still in hand, wailing and wailing like her voice.

She stopped playing—would have fallen if Rik had not caught her. He pulled out a chair and set her down in it, crouching beside her with a steadying hand on her arm. His golden eyes were disturbed, even frightened.

"You were playing," he said. "Something changed. What happened?"

"I saw Alice," Kit croaked, and then, "I need some water, please."

He ran to get it. She heard the refrigerator door open. Beyond the living room, she heard another door creak. Someone had come back.

But the man who appeared in front of her was an utter stranger, a giant dressed in a gray suit, his body round and shaped like a penguin. His head reminded her of a bird as well. Small and puffy, his cheeks so red she thought he must use rouge. His eyes were black, hardly slits. His hands curled like meat hooks.

Danger, fucking danger! screamed a tiny voice inside Kit's mind. She struggled to stand, gaze locked with the man in gray, whose eyes were as cold and hard as gravel chips caught in ice. She heard movement on her left: Rik, emerging from the kitchen. She had no time to warn him. He saw the man—froze—and then threw himself at the stranger with a speed and strength that was astonishing.

"Run!" Rik screamed, and she did—into the kitchen, looking for a weapon. She found a butcher knife and staggered back just in time to see Rik slam into the hardwood floor. She heard a crack, and the shape-shifter went still.

Which left just her and the man in gray. Kit's mind went totally blank. She did not know where to run, how to fight, what to do. She could only stare, breathless, into those sharp, sharp eyes, hearing inside her heart the first violent strokes of a terrible song, a song more like a scream, raging and raging. Her heart thundered like a hurricane.

The man smiled. It was a terrible smile, lips pressed together, the corners of his mouth turning up; worse, because his eyes never changed. If anything, they became colder. Hungry.

Kit moved, but it was not enough. The man rushed

her and he was incredibly fast—one step, and he crossed the room to stand above her, towering like a monolith. He was even more terrifying up close.

She tried to run, but he caught her with his hand, fingers crushing her arm. He yanked her right up against his body—hard as concrete—and lifted her feet off the floor. He smelled like raw meat, with a hint of perfume.

Kit did not think. Her arm swept forward. The butcher knife punctured the suit and sank into the man's side. She screamed as that shuddering impact ran up her arm—in rage, disgust, fear—then pushed as hard as she could, using all her strength, grunting with the effort.

The man in gray did not let go. Kit twisted the blade and he did not let go. She felt hot blood on her hand and still he did not let go. His smile only widened, revealing teeth, and she could not help but gasp as she looked into that mouth. His teeth were sharp—little daggers—filed down to points. Each and every last one of them. It was like gazing into the black, jagged maw of a shark.

But Kit got a good look at something else as he smiled, as he opened his mouth wide. The man in gray had no tongue.

Kit let go of her knife. She went for his eyes instead, but he turned her around, almost juggling her from hand to hand, and slammed his forearm across her throat, cutting off her air. She kept fighting, but the man was too strong. Dizziness hit; vision dimmed. Music, screaming. Alice, whispering.

You are next.

Kit blacked out.

CHAPTER TEN

According to Koni, Dirk & Steele had some very strong connections to Vancouver's law enforcement, enough so that if corruption did exist—and there was no doubt at this point that it did—it would only be a matter of time before the men, armed with Officer Yu's name, found the two bad cops and squeezed some additional information out of them. As well as ruining their careers and putting them behind bars.

All of this M'cal learned on the drive back to Hastings. Hari and Amiri—after rendezvousing with their police friends—were going to meet them near the Youth Center. Home base, as Koni said, for Alice Hardon.

It was seven in the evening. The sun had set. The darkness made M'cal uneasy. The witch would be up and about; Ivan would be mobile. And the compulsion still had not returned. That was not right.

And what is your basis for comparison? Nothing like this ever happened to you before.

No, but he still had his instincts. Whatever this was,

it could not be called good luck. Something was wrong.

He wished he had not left Kitala.

Koni smoked as he drove. "How long have you been in trouble?"

For a moment, the question reminded M'cal of Elsie. Elsie, whom he had almost forgotten. The woman was probably still alive, but not for much longer. Her body would give out in a day or two. If she was lucky, she'd die in her sleep. An autopsy would reveal no obvious cause of death, but doctors were always ready to apply some diagnosis, even if incorrect. No doubt the same would be done to her. And to Kitala.

"Long enough," M'cal said. It was as good an answer as any.

Koni frowned. "She's made you kill?"

"Among other things."

"How do you feel about that?"

M'cal looked at him. Koni shrugged. "Some people take death more seriously than others. You don't seem to be rolling in guilt."

"Are you a mind reader?"

"God, no."

"Then do not presume to know what I feel."

"Fair enough." Koni tossed his cigarette out the window.

M'cal stared through the windshield at the car ahead of them. He listened to the wipers, the rumble of the engine. So normal. So regular. All an illusion, one more thing to take for granted. Kitala had used the word *alien,* and she was right. Even he could feel it, more strongly than ever: the oddity, the strangeness of the situation. Everyone around him—on this road—going about their lives, never guessing that the car behind, beside, in front carried magic, myth; a shape-shifter and a merman.

Ridiculous. Fantastic. Funny even, though M'cal had no urge to laugh. He had never felt so alien as in this moment, so much outside every boundary of human normality.

You are a killer, a slave, he told himself. *Think of human history. That is perfectly normal.*

But not very comforting.

Koni parked the car in front of the Youth Center. The lights were off. All kinds of activity on the street—business as usual, with the women strutting tall and the brake lights shining. M'cal did not particularly want to interact with anyone. Too many people knew him, and it had been difficult enough explaining his past circumstances to Kitala. She had not judged him—not that he could tell—but revealing to her that he had been forced to work as a whore—even if just for show, as a lure to prey—would be a considerably different experience than explaining it to a group of strange men.

But he and Koni did not walk to the street corner. They strolled in the opposite direction, where the shadows gathered more thickly and the tattered doorways of abandoned businesses were filled with skinny kids on cardboard mats, syringes in hand. It was so easy to get needles in this city; just as easy as heroin.

"Any reason why we're going in this direction?" M'cal asked.

"We're grasping at straws right now, but if Alice had trouble in this neighborhood, then that's where we start. I need a place to change, though." Koni smiled grimly. "It's amazing what people will say in front of a bird."

M'cal would have responded, but he saw something across the street that made him stop. It was a dented brown Cadillac, parked by the curb, and inside the passenger seat was a boy with a Mohawk. Billy.

"What's wrong?" Koni asked. M'cal said nothing, still staring, watching the man behind the wheel. His face was twisted and angry. Billy said something, shaking his head, holding up his hands.

Fear. M'cal knew what Billy's fear looked like. He knew what all those children on that old street corner looked like when someone was hurting them. M'cal had put a stop to it as best he could. Protected them. Killed a man to make his point. The one killing he did not regret.

He started running across the street, heard Koni say something but ignored it. He reached the Cadillac in seconds, ran around to the passenger seat, and tried to open the door. It was locked. He rapped on the glass, and Billy looked at him with a mixture of shock and intense relief. Billy tried to unlock the door, but the man behind the wheel held him back. M'cal put his elbow through the window. It hurt, but the glass broke. He stuck his hand in and unlocked the door.

Billy clambered out so fast he almost fell. The driver followed, rushing out of the car. He was a short man, thick with muscle turning to fat. Bald, snub nose, eyes like a shrew, and enough rolls in his chin to almost qualify for a baker's dozen. His belt was undone. M'cal felt sick.

He touched Billy's arm. "Did he hurt you?"

The boy shook his head, but he was scared, pale and shaking. By daylight he could act so tough, like nothing bothered him, but he was probably softer than some of the fourteen-year-old girls M'cal had seen hustling a mile west some nights.

The driver stalked around the hood of the car. "You fucking bastard. You broke my fucking window!"

"You were scaring the boy," M'cal said.

The man's chest heaved. He started fastening his belt. "Little fuck was cheating me. And what are you, his pimp? Fuck you. You're gonna pay for that window, you fag."

"Now, that is some fucking foul language," Koni said, jogging up. "You might want to watch your mouth, mister."

The man sneered at him and looked at Billy. "Think you and I are done? I'll be seeing you again, kid."

M'cal's hand shot out and caught the man around the neck. He slammed him on the hood of his car and held him there.

"You touch that boy again and I will rip off your testicles," M'cal said. "I will not be squeamish. I will not hesitate. You are just a body to me. Do you understand?" He reached into the man's back pocket and pulled out his wallet, flipping it open to see the driver's license. He memorized the name and address. "Mr. Daniel Bodine. I know where you live now. Remember that, should you decide to be stupid again."

M'cal let go of the man, who scrambled sideways, almost falling over his feet in his haste to escape. He crawled back into his car, started the engine, and peeled away.

"I guess you made your point," Koni said dryly. Billy snickered, but it was a weak sound, and M'cal turned to him. The boy's demeanor completely changed; he shrank a little, his face crumpling with embarrassment, shame.

"Don't say it," Billy told him, fidgeting. "I owe you again."

M'cal suddenly felt very tired; his heart ached for Kitala. "You do not owe me. You never did. Are you sure you're not hurt?"

The boy shrugged, but it was tense, brittle. "I thought the police got you."

M'cal remembered hearing the boy yell. "Do you know how they found us?"

He shook his head. "That bitch cop rolled around, started talking directly to Nico. You know, that new blond guy. Says some suspect was seen in the neighborhood. Describes your friend. Bastard gave her everything, even your room number. *Fucker.* I heard shots after that, but no one ever came down." He straightened up and said, "I called your friend's hotel and left a message. Did she get it?"

"No," M'cal said. "What did you find?"

Billy glanced up the street; he still seemed nervous. "Nothing much. Just that I talked to some people who actually dealt with that lady you're looking for. No one knew she was gone. No one knew why. If she was into anything, she kept it real quiet. I even talked to some friends of friends of local gangs, and they don't know shit either. The only shit going down is with some drugs, but from what I heard, that lady never bitched about no drugs. She focused on kids like me."

"So either someone is wrong, lying, or Alice was much more secretive than anyone realized." Koni sighed, shoving his hands into his pockets. "Great."

"There's something else," Billy said, and his voice dropped to a whisper, his eyes darting nervously. "Might not be anything official going on, but some people have been going missing. Regulars, folks who used to come around here a lot. You'd recognize some of them, Mikey."

Probably because he was the reason they had gone missing. On the nights the witch made him hunt—and there had been more and more of them over the past several months—every encounter had resulted in the taking of a soul. Not one had slipped past him. Not until Kitala.

But all he did was nod and say, "Thank you, Billy. I appreciate this."

"You saved my life," said the boy solemnly.

Koni stepped closer, and much to M'cal's surprise said, "You going to hit the street again after we leave you?"

"Have to," Billy told him warily. "Gotta have a place to sleep."

"Not just jump a high?"

Billy pushed up his sleeves and showed off his unmarked arms. "I don't do that shit."

"Other ways to do shit," Koni said easily. "You were doing one of them not two minutes ago."

He bristled. "If you're gonna lecture me—"

"No," both men said at the same time. They glanced at each other, and then Koni slowly reached inside his jacket and pulled out a surprisingly large wad of cash. "You're not a dumb fuck, are you, kid?"

"No," whispered Billy, staring at the money.

"M'cal?"

"Sometimes," he said grimly. "He will not leave this lifestyle."

"Then you'll die," Koni said to Billy with unflinching certainty. He peeled off five one-hundred-dollar bills and gave them to the boy. "Take a couple nights off . . . if your work ethic will let you."

Billy gave him a dirty look, but he pocketed the cash.

M'cal said, "You never accepted my money."

"You're a friend," replied the boy, which made little sense to M'cal but seemed to satisfy some kind of morality within Billy's mind. He looked like he wanted to say something else, but he glanced at Koni, shuffled his feet, and walked away without another word.

M'cal felt Koni looking at him. "Thank you for giving him the cash."

"I would have given him more if I thought he would use it to start something new."

"He is damaged," M'cal said simply, watching Billy turn the corner. "If I had more time . . ." He stopped, shaking his head. "Go ahead and ask."

"None of my business," Koni replied quietly. "Besides, I see Hari and Amiri."

M'cal looked across the street. Sure enough, the two men were there, watching. Hard to miss them; Hari almost seven feet tall and built like a fighter. Amiri was also tall, but not nearly so broad. Slender almost.

"Trouble?" Hari asked when Koni and M'cal crossed the street to join them.

"Only that no one knows what happened to Alice," Koni said. "What did you guys find?"

Amiri smiled. "According to our contact, Officer Yu and her partner have been the subject of an investigation for quite some time. They are suspected of physical abuse, colluding with known criminals, and making false arrests. No evidence, though."

"Nor did they report for work today," rumbled Hari. "They are not responding to any calls."

"I smell the end of two careers," Koni said.

"If they are not killed first for their failure," M'cal added. "Not only did they lose Kitala, but they failed to bring back my head."

"We found something else," Hari said. "Far more disturbing."

"A rash of disappearances," Amiri added. "Men and women vanishing. Not all the victims are from this city—in fact, most of them were visitors—but there have been twelve taken, including Alice, and all the people missing are relatively well off, with no previous inclination to simply disappear."

"None of them the kind to hire prostitutes?" Koni glanced sideways at M'cal.

Hari frowned. "Unlikely. Why?"

"Other folks going missing, that's all." The shapeshifter smiled grimly. "What's the connection between the cops and the out-of-towners?"

Amiri sighed. "There doesn't seem to be one. The possibility that it is all related is only conjecture. But our contact said that some in the department have begun linking them up, speculating that it might be the work of a serial killer."

"Serial killers are more consistent," Koni replied. "You said there's no link between these people."

"None on the surface."

"Alice is a youth counselor," M'cal said.

Amiri shrugged. "According to our contact, she is also extremely wealthy. Her family is American, based in New York City. She used to be an art dealer."

"Huh," Koni replied. "What is a New York art dealer doing in a neighborhood like this, working in a youth center?"

M'cal wondered the same thing. "Did the officer know how long she has been here?"

"Her family reported that she left home nearly six months ago, but that it was only in the past three that she seemed to settle in Vancouver. It was a hasty departure, without warning. She recently requested that her uncle John come visit. It, too, was spur of the moment."

"Woman goes looking for herself," Koni suggested.

"Or woman goes looking for something else," M'cal replied. "Kitala said that Alice was not surprised that someone was planning on killing her."

"She might have been trying to escape someone," Hari said.

"Someone who can pay off cops? Hire men to kill? Who knows enough about me to shoot first for my throat, and then remove my head?" M'cal thought of Kitala. "I do not like this."

Amiri's hip buzzed; his cellphone, ringing. He answered quickly, listening for only a moment before his jaw tightened and his eyes flashed so bright and hot, M'cal flinched, blinking hard.

"Kit has been taken," said Amiri. "Rik is injured."

M'cal went very cold, very still. "Who?"

The shape-shifter hesitated. "It was a man. Large, strong, dressed in gray. Rik says his mouth was odd."

M'cal said nothing. His face gave away nothing. Koni said, "I'm flying," and he pulled off his jacket and handed it to Amiri. He tossed M'cal the keys to the car. "You know your way back?"

"Yes," M'cal lied.

Koni ran into a nearby alley, stripping off his clothes and tossing them to the ground. Golden light seared from his eyes; a thread of black feathers sprouted from his hairline down his throat. And then he disappeared into the shadows, and M'cal took off running, the other men just ahead of him.

He quickly lost track of Hari and Amiri—their car was down another street—but he felt little concern about that. He was not going back to the house. He knew exactly where Kitala had been taken.

You could have told them. Asked for their help. You need their help.

But he knew how delighted the witch would be to find actual shape-shifters, and while they might prove more difficult to enslave than M'cal—who had loved, been blind, given himself freely—he was certain she would not give up such diverse specimens without a fight.

And he did not wish that on anyone. Not ever.

The monster still slept; his bracelet tingled, but remained cold. M'cal gunned the engine of the car, driving straight to the first sea access he could find—a tiny pier off Gastown, near the heliport. He abandoned the car at the side of the road, ignoring the sidewalk as he cut straight over the grass, racing down a steep hill that bled right into the sea. The dock was on his left, but he ignored it. He could hear music. He could feel the water reaching for him; and when he jumped from the shore he sensed, for just one moment, arms spread, ready to hold him.

And they did. He melted into the sea, diving as deep as he could, shooting away from the shore. He tore off his clothes, transforming as he did, and there was no pain—nothing at all but the cool sweetness of the ocean as it caressed and held him. He inhaled so deeply his chest ached, but each breath coursed into his lungs like the cold, clear, crystalline air—*shining, shining*—of some snowy mountain peak, the kind his father and mother had taken him to while he was very young.

He felt young, being in the water. He felt like he was home. Finally, home. It was, he thought, almost as if the curse had been lifted.

Almost.

He swam hard, his body obeying him with perfect ease. His bracelet tingled, but instead of ignoring it, he embraced the sensation, sinking deep within the bond. He let it lead, felt the pull—not as a compulsion, but as merely a line between his body and the witch. For once, useful. For once, something he was glad of.

He heard music, voices—very distant. He sang back, for the first time in years—and the sound cut through the water like the lilting, curling bellow of a crooning whale. Movement on his left. Brother seal. M'cal reached out, and the animal skimmed against his hand.

The seal stayed with M'cal as he soared through the cold, dark waters, gliding and twisting. Within minutes he was joined by others, cutting the shadows, batting fish into his face. He swatted them away. It was just play, but he could not afford to be slowed down, and after a moment he barked an order into the water, and the seals fell into more orderly ranks.

Again, music. M'cal let out another cry, listening to it echo rich and golden through the water. If there were any marine biologists listening, no doubt they would be baffled, but let them chalk it up to a new species, or to a fluke in the machinery.

The pull in the bracelet strengthened, tingling up his arm into his neck. Still no compulsion. The witch was alive, though; he knew that for certain. He let himself sink into instinct, following a trail through the currents. Close to the piers, the water began to run oily. Too many boats, too much city; but no complaints.

He found the boat. It was moored almost twenty feet from the closest dock. Its anchor was down, but as he swam around the boat he felt the vibration of the engine humming through the waters. Ready to run, if need be. He thought of Kitala—imagined Ivan's hands on her— and his rage and fear narrowed to a place in his soul so concentrated, so vile, he thought himself capable of killing with a thought, a breath, one beat of his heart.

If Kitala was hurt, if she was dead . . .

He stopped his thought, and swam around to the ladder. He transformed, regaining his legs, gills receding into his body, and felt Brother Seal brush against his legs like a warm spirit. M'cal poked his head above water. He heard nothing, but that was typical. And likely the witch already knew he was there. No need for subterfuge.

She will take your body all over again. She will compel you to hurt Kitala. You should have asked those shape-shifters to come and help you. You should have never left her alone.

Too late for any of that. M'cal had to handle this on his own.

He climbed out of the sea, dripping and naked, and walked onto the boat. He found the witch immediately. She sat in a chair, a candle burning on the small glass table beside her. Despite the cool air, she wore a silver bikini and nothing else. In one hand she held a glass of wine, and in the other a gun.

"I should have learned a lesson from my sister," she murmured, and shot him through the heart.

CHAPTER ELEVEN

Kit's grandmother woke her up. Another waking dream.

No veranda, no sweet swamp; just darkness, the oubliette. Kit sat naked on some hard surface that looked like nothing more than another part of the endless void. In front of her, laid flat and gleaming golden like a holy relic, was her fiddle and bow. And across from *that* was Old Jazz Marie. Also naked.

"I don't care if I *am* dead," Kit said. "We should both be wearing clothes."

Her grandmother snorted. "You're not dead. *Yet.* And don't go wounding me so quick, child. This is what you'll look like in fifty years. Best to burn it into your memory now, so you don't wake up surprised one day."

"I would have preferred the surprise," Kit said.

Old Jazz Marie smiled. "That's my girl. Now you pick up that fiddle, Kitty Bella, and you get ready to play. Not yet, mind you—you'll know the moment—but when you do, you dance that devil down." Her smile became chilling, more like a snarl. "You dance that bastard right back to hell, you hear? Cut him, little cat. Cut him good."

And Kit woke up for real, her grandmother's voice ringing in her ears.

It took her a moment to orient herself. She lay on a narrow bed in a small room paneled in dark wood. No window, one door, nothing at first glance that could be turned into a weapon. She still wore her clothes.

And there was a woman standing across from her.

The witch, thought Kit, taking in the long, pale hair, the luminous skin, the barely-there clothes: a bikini, of all things, showing off legs so long and smooth, Kit might have called them airbrushed.

The two women stared at each other. The silence was eerie, unnerving, as was the unblinking scrutiny, which after a time seemed like the stare of someone dead—flat and cold.

"Kitala Bell," murmured the witch finally, in a voice surprisingly soft and rich. "Kitala, Kitala."

"Yes," said Kit. "Obviously. What's your name?"

The witch smiled, shaking her head. "So naive. So dangerously naive. Women like us do not share our names, and the names we do give are never real. Names are power. You keep them safe. Your grandmother should have taught you that."

Kit blinked, and like that, her fear began to fade. "You knew my grandmother?"

"Old Jazz Marie," said the witch, and the name curled off her tongue with another slow smile. "She made the name herself, you know. Jazz, for what her daughter sang. Marie, for the charlatan priestess Laveau."

Astonishing. Kit could not speak. The witch pushed off the wall where she had been leaning and sat on the edge of the bed. The mattress did not shift; it was as if she were made of air.

"If you were any other person," said the woman, "I would not be here right now. Ivan would be in my place, making you soft for me. But I knew your grandmother, long ago. We crossed paths. I was doing something. She was doing something. Both of our actions utterly incompatible. We had dinner, debated, ultimately quarreled. And I am not so prideful as to deny that she got the better of me. A very strong woman." The witch looked down at her hands. "Is she well?"

"She died," Kit said. Her throat hurt.

"Ah." It was hard to tell how the witch felt about that, though for one brief moment Kit almost imagined her sorry. The witch's gaze was distant, thoughtful. "That, I believe, is where she and I differed. Your grandmother had no fear of death. She did not fear her age. I, on the other hand, have always preferred the alternative. The price, however, is rather steep."

"You eat souls to keep yourself young."

"Is that what M'cal told you?"

"Yes," Kit admitted. "Why else have him steal for you?"

The witch inclined her head. "I see your reasoning, though it is not entirely accurate. Staying young is only part of why I have him hunt for me. Power is another. That, and knowledge. Imagine for a moment that you could know everything there is about . . . me. All you would have to do is take *me*. Consume *me*. Easy, yes?"

"M'cal has been hunting men and women who

hire prostitutes. How do they know anything worth having?"

"That, my dear, is where the power comes in. Strength, energy. The occasional bank account. It works. Trust me."

"There must be a better way."

"But this is *my* way," said the woman, and she looked at Kit as though marveling at some inexplicable sight; some exotic being, fresh on earth. She murmured, still staring, "You are so innocent. So new and clean and bright. You have only just begun to test yourself, to taste the size of the world and all it can offer. Such as M'cal. You know what he is. How does it feel to you, to be aware of such a flesh-and-blood impossibility?"

"It still feels impossible," Kit said. "But I believe."

"There are other creatures like him. They are the roots of human myth, the first dwellers of the wild lands. Animals who can turn into men, men who can twist reality, reality that can be destroyed in the blink of an eye by a chosen few." The witch smiled coldly. "I had a sister. We were very close. Our . . . aspirations were quite similar. Power, immortality. And yes, I can see from your face that those two things mean little to you, but if you had been forced to endure what we lived through . . ."

She stopped, took a deep breath. "My sister found ways to extend her life, but they were imperfect. Eventually she came upon the idea of harnessing the power of another, and in the course of her experiment, she stumbled upon a family of . . . magically inclined individuals. Not human, if you are at all curious."

Kit found that she was. "What were they?"

The witch smiled. "They call themselves gargoyles.

They can barely go out in public, though they do, with some success. Humans are so easily fooled in this day and age. If someone has the right size and shape, a malformed face and body can be explained away by accident or defect. No one ever imagines the alternative. No one dreams of magic." She tapped Kit's nose. "Even those who have it."

Kit frowned. "So, what happened?"

The witch's smile faded. "She trapped the gargoyles, but one of them managed to find a way around her spell. He and another, a human, killed my sister and freed the remaining gargoyles. All of whom have not forgotten. All of whom are now hunting the rest of our family. One of them is here even now, in this city."

Kit sat back, realization filling her. "And that's why you want my soul—to . . . to give you more power to fight him?"

The witch exhaled sharply, almost with laughter. "No, my dear. No. I am more than capable of fighting one gargoyle on my own. He is not what frightens me."

A cold, hard knot settled in Kit's gut. "So, what does scare you?"

The witch hesitated, and for the first time that cool facade fractured. "What frightens me . . ." she said softly, almost to herself. "What frightens me cannot be put into words. Your grandmother would have known, but I suspect she did not teach you. I doubt that was her choice."

"I was stubborn," Kit said. "Too stubborn."

"The young always are." The witch sighed, and stood. "For what it is worth, young Kitala Bell, I take no pleasure in stealing your soul, or your life. I truly regret it. There are few enough of us as it is, and we are a sisterhood, or should be. Power calls to power. It is why I always respected your grandmother, no matter how far apart we were in thought or method. It is why you and I have just shared words, instead of pain. But this is about survival. Not just mine, but of others." She leaned forward, her voice dropping to a whisper. "You cannot imagine, my dear, the Beast that is coming. You cannot imagine the destruction, or the hate. I know I am not . . . *good*. But I am not evil either. Not in the way I know it to be."

"You're wrong. You enslaved M'cal. You *tortured* him."

"Yes. That *is* what one does. It is part of the game, you see. The mask I must wear."

"No," Kit breathed. "It's not. Why would you enslave him?"

"Because I fear him," said the witch, with astonishing honesty. "Because, like you, I can see the end of days, and I have witnessed mine. M'cal is the man who will kill me."

And with that, she turned and left.

The first paying audience Kit ever played for almost put a bullet through her brain, but that was incidental compared to the comments about her ass. Hooting Harry's was a rough establishment on the edge of Nashville, but she was seventeen, and too desperate and hungry to care that not many of the truckers and bikers fresh from the highway were eager to hear some slip of a black girl play her fiddle on a stage more used to poles, G-strings, and bouncing breasts.

Still, she won them over. She always did.

Unfortunately, her confidence onstage was sorely lacking in all matters of mortal danger, and after the witch left the room, Kit found it extremely difficult to simply sit, think, and wait to die. In fact, it wasn't long before she wanted to puke up her guts like some frat boy on a bender.

She maintained her calm, though. No time to indulge in a panic attack, even if all she could do was replay, again and again and again, with agonizing clarity, every single word of that nuanced, fascinating, and very creepy conversation. The witch was an unexpected woman.

And you believe her. Kit blew out her breath. All of this, pure craziness. She did not want to believe, but everything the witch had said about her grandmother rang true as a bell. But if that was the case, then how peculiar that the old woman had failed to mention anything of the witch in their recent beyond-the-grave tête-à-têtes. Surely, in between all those other warnings, she could have said *something*.

Kit stood and tried the door. It was locked. The room's only piece of furniture was the bed, and its frame was bolted down—though, after pulling up the sheets, she discovered the mattress was held in place by straps. Straps attached to bedsprings. Springs, which could be removed.

To do what? Pick a lock? Poke someone in the eye?

Kit heard footsteps outside the room. A heavy tread. She stood back as the door opened, swinging wide to reveal the man in gray. There was a massive bloodstain on the side of his suit, but he did not seem bothered by pain. He was far too large for the hall in which he stood. His shoulders brushed the walls. His head almost touched the ceiling.

He smiled at her. Kit said, "Your mouth is totally fucked up."

He kept smiling, and Kit thought, *So is your brain.*

The man turned sideways and gestured for her to leave the room. Kit hesitated, but there was no way she could win in a physical struggle with him, so she followed the silent command and squeezed past his round stomach, which was as disturbingly hard as she remembered. Kit hated touching him. Her skin crawled. She felt like his face was a chalkboard and his teeth were the nails.

Walking in front of him, feeling his cold breath against her neck, was almost worse, but she managed to stay calm, observing her surroundings, still looking for a weapon. All she saw, though, as she walked the corridor, was more dark wood, edged in gold-plated metal trim—mirrors in the ceiling—thick shag carpet—a narrow portrait of a naked woman, very tasteful in a seventies-sex-lounge sort of way. All she needed now to make her officially insane was a swinging disco ball, a furred bed in the shape of a heart, and *Shaft* playing loudly over her screams.

Of course, seeing the man in gray naked would probably do the same damage in a shorter amount of time, but she really hoped it did not come to that.

The floor shifted slightly; Kit felt dizzy, nauseated. She choked down bile and climbed a short flight of stairs, tasting cool air, salt—but it was not until her head poked out into a world of night and clouds and damp that she realized she was on a boat. A very big boat—a yacht—anchored on the edge of downtown, with the city lights towering above her head. The deck was long and pale, and near the railing Kit saw a body.

She ran, falling to her knees beside M'cal. There was a hole in his chest. He was not breathing. She tried to tell herself he would recover, but seeing him so still and cold—

"Disconcerting, is it not?" said the witch, coming to stand beside her. "Though I think I prefer him this way."

Kit snarled, throwing her arms around the woman's legs, trying to take her to the ground. Instead she found herself hauled into the air by her hair. The man in gray was impossibly strong; his fist felt like the size of her head. Kit cried out, trying to kick him—punch, scratch—but she felt like a cat held by the scruff of her neck, and no matter how hard she writhed, nothing was effective in making him put her down.

The witch stood back, arms crossed, her eyes narrow and hard. She gave the man a sharp nod, and suddenly Kit could stand again on her own two feet. Her head hurt so bad she felt scalped—and indeed, there was a clump of soft hair in Ivan's hand, which he slowly brought to his nose to smell.

"That was foolish," the witch said to Kit.

Heart pounding—woozy, nauseated—Kit crouched by M'cal and picked up his hand. "You've hurt him enough. I don't care about your reasons."

"I have no regrets," said the witch smoothly. "It is what it is."

A giant hand came down upon Kit's shoulder. She froze, breathless, as the witch said, "You have met Ivan. I suppose you are aware of his peculiarities. He has others, though."

"Really," Kit said, squeezing M'cal's fingers, willing him to wake. The wound above his heart was beginning to close.

"Quite. If you would, please guess Ivan's age."

Guess his age? Kit finally looked at the witch, trying to see if she was joking. The woman appeared serious, though there was something faintly sardonic about the line of her mouth. Kit narrowed her eyes, thought about it for a moment. "I would say he's thirty-five, forty."

The question itself had been a tipoff, but Kit knew for certain that something was wrong with her answer when the witch smiled, eyes glittering—so bright, it seemed chips of diamond were embedded in her gaze. An unnatural light.

Kit forced herself to look at Ivan, studying his face. His skin was smooth and unwrinkled; taut, relatively young.

"Two hundred and a day," said the witch quietly. "Remarkably well preserved for his age, is he not?"

Kit said nothing, staring. Ivan's eyes were as cold and sharp as the edge of a cleaver; his teeth, poking over his bottom lip, were just as bad. A shudder ripped through her; she barely heard the witch add, "You see, my dear, souls are *not* what keep me young."

Ivan's hand shifted, sliding up Kit's neck. She tried to move, but he applied more pressure—more and more—until she felt that struggling too hard just might snap something vital. He arched her neck, exposed it; and as the witch watched, smiling, Kit felt a cold cloud of breath touch her skin. Horror clawed up her throat—a scream—but before she could make a sound, he bit her, his teeth sinking into her neck like a flash of daggers, stabbing and sinking. It hurt like hell, but the only sound Kit could make was a breathless rattle as his cold lips pressed down, drinking her blood.

Her body stopped obeying her; she was paralyzed

from the top of her head to the tips of her toes. Only her vision worked, and Kit watched the witch crouch on the other side of M'cal, leaning close to stare . . . studying Kit like she was a book, a steak, a piece of embroidery ready to be picked apart. Ivan kept drinking. Kit remembered the bite marks on M'cal's body. Dark spots swam in her eyes. Strings murmured; the theme from *Jaws*.

"Ivan is my perfect companion," said the witch softly. "We met some years ago, both with certain needs. He is also a rare breed—not quite like M'cal, but similarly inhuman. Sickened by sunlight, hungry only for blood, remarkably strong and fast. Immortal." She smiled, holding up her hand. There were two rings on her fingers, both silver, both engraved. "My secret—although Ivan has always stayed willing, has always enjoyed his services to me. I saved him, and he remembers."

Ivan stopped drinking. He released Kit, and she hunched over, shivering, touching her neck. Blood dripped down her fingers, but there was no pain. Puncture marks on her neck, though. A row of them, like she was a piece of meat gnawed on by some dog.

Ivan rose and stepped over M'cal. The witch stood to meet him. His lips gleamed red with blood. He bent down, and the woman licked him clean—and then kissed him, slow and careful, her tongue moving inside his mouth. Ivan's hands slid beneath her bikini to cup her buttocks, his fingers moving, pressing, until the witch let out a gasp.

Kit wanted to vomit, but she could not look away; it was too horrible, too strange—the wettest, most disgusting train wreck of her life. And then, as if there had not been enough blood shed, Ivan raised one of his hands to his mouth, bit into his wide wrist, and held it out to the witch.

The woman drank. She did it perfectly, without one wasted drop, closing her eyes and abandoning herself to the act with such need and passion that Kit finally managed to look away unobserved. She saw a gun resting on a chair. Ten feet away. If she could reach it, move fast enough while they were distracted . . .

Kit still held M'cal's hand. His fingers twitched, and, like that, she lost her chance to reach the gun. She squeezed his hand instead, watching his face, but his features remained slack and his fingers did not move again. Just a reflex, perhaps; he was slowly returning to consciousness. *Quick*, she begged silently. *Make it quick.*

The witch made a choking sound; she broke away from Ivan and staggered, touching her mouth. Her eyes were wide. She tried to take another step, but Ivan caught her around the waist and lowered her to the ground. Her weakness was shocking.

"You," she breathed to Kit, dismay rocking through her flawless face. "You . . . *met* her."

Kit shook her head, squeezing M'cal's hand. "I don't understand."

The witch snarled. "Alice. You met *Alice*."

Kit stared, and the witch's entire face contorted; she grabbed Ivan's hand, standing up like her body hurt—all that careful grace and control was spinning away. She kicked M'cal in the ribs. Kit cried out, protesting, but Ivan took one step across M'cal's body and grabbed her shoulders, holding her still. He watched the witch with sharp eyes.

She did not strike a second time, but instead sank into another crouch, grabbing M'cal's bracelet and

holding the metal tight in her hands. She closed her
eyes, murmuring to herself, and Kit remembered the
music she had heard when M'cal tried to take her
soul. It was a hard memory—burning—but as she
held M'cal's hand tight within her own, she poured
that wild melody—that starlight song—into his body,
and imagined it as a shield, a wall around his heart
and soul. Protecting him.

The witch opened her eyes. "Stop. Give him to me."

"Make me," Kit rasped. The woman slapped her
face. M'cal twitched, but his eyes remained closed,
and Kit refused to let go of his hand as the witch
struck her again, her glamour and youth twisting into
something that was, for a moment, ancient, ugly. A
mask—everything was a mask with the witch, except
for this; her rage.

Then, just as the witch was about to slap her again,
M'cal moved, sitting up so fast he was a blur. He
slammed his palm into the witch's chest, and the
woman flew backward, skidding across the deck.

Ivan tossed Kit aside. She banged her chin and
rolled, looking up in time to see M'cal ram the big
man in the gut. They went down together, tangled,
grunting.

Kit scrambled for the gun. She kept expecting someone to stop her, but she made it to the gun and took it in
her hand. She did not know what to do with it except
point—which she did, aiming at the witch. The woman
looked at her; hard, hollow. Kit steeled herself. Fiddle
strings screamed. Her finger tightened on the trigger.

M'cal slammed into the deck, so hard she heard
something crack. Ivan raised a foot above his face. Kit
changed her aim and shot the big man. Pulled the trigger twice. She was too close to miss; blood sprayed

from Ivan's shoulder and gut. He kept standing, but Kit expected that. All she needed was a distraction. M'cal took advantage of it.

He rolled, reaching her in a flash, pulling her to the edge of the boat. He took the gun from her as they moved, looked back over his shoulder, and fired at the witch. The bullet slammed into her leg. She fell, screaming. Ivan kept moving.

A small, dark shape dove from the sky. Black wings fluttered. Ivan slowed, but only for a moment. His fists slashed through the air, and Kit heard a thud. The bird slammed to the deck. A crow.

M'cal hesitated. So did Kit. A mistake. The witch's scream changed, shifting into a double-edged howl . . . splitting into syllables, words. Her eyes glittered diamond-bright, her cutting gaze furious.

Kit tried to move. She could not. Neither could M'cal.

Inside her head she suddenly heard her grandmother's voice—a low shout—and music roared through her like a crash of thunder. The compulsion holding her melted away—

But Ivan's fist slammed into her skull. Kit went down, limp, barely conscious. She heard M'cal screaming, shouting, and then someone kicked her again, in the ribs. Fingers dug into her hair. Rancid breath touched her cheek. She cracked open an eye and found the witch, whose face was pale and blurry.

The woman said something, but all Kit could hear was M'cal. A thread of music hummed through her heart. She surrounded herself in it, threw a line to M'-cal, feeling it hook—a strange sensation, like listening to an echo in her soul—and then the witch said another word and Kit closed her eyes and stopped hearing anything at all.

CHAPTER TWELVE

At sixteen years of age, M'cal had run away from home. A sheltered child—homeschooled—he'd been kept away from others because of his voice. Too unpredictable. There were also blood tests to consider—the threat of accidents, injuries, doctors, secrets revealed through science. His parents were careful that way. Nothing was safe. Especially M'cal.

He understood, for a while. And then he stopped understanding, and left. No word, no letter, no warning. Little bastard. Little adventurer. Sixteen and not human: a combination that should have proven intriguing to a young man's imagination, if for nothing else but the unlimited possibilities, but which instead had become a prison. An impossibly lonely cage for someone built and made for freedom.

It now seemed to M'cal that nothing substantial had changed—only the bars and the keys and the captors. One prison had been made of love, the other of hate. Never able to be his own man except for a brief decade of itinerant travel and work, from one end of the world to another, until he had come home to his family and found his mother dying, too stubborn to tell him until the last moment, too full of love for her son to ruin the freedom he had so ruthlessly stolen without a word of good-bye and only brief letters and phone calls to fill the interim.

Her death had been a hard lesson. A punishment that fit the crime. M'cal had not spoken to his father since the funeral. He suspected he might never again. And, in all honesty, he understood. M'cal did not blame his father. He blamed himself.

Just like he blamed himself for losing Kitala to the witch.

They were taken to different rooms. The yacht was not big enough for a huge separation—they were across the hall from one another—but that was sufficient to make M'cal panic. Anything could happen to her. And here he was, naked and chained to a bed, his arms stretched over his head, his legs shackled. Rope would be too weak to hold him—the witch had learned that the hard way.

Duct tape covered his mouth. It was unnecessary, simply for show. He could not use his voice against the witch. Their link made her—and, by extension, Ivan—immune. Like trying to spell a *geas* upon himself. At least the compulsion was still gone, though the witch had other means of slowing him down.

Stop. Think harder. Find a way.

The boat had finally stopped moving after several hours of travel. The witch never cruised for pleasure. They might be in the Georgia Strait by now, within easy sight of Vancouver Island and only a day's run to Alaska or a midnight stroll to Seattle.

Outside the room, M'cal heard a man scream. Pain

rolled through that cry—surprise, outrage—but no heartbreak. Lucky that way.

Koni. The shape-shifter must have followed him, his lack of trust biting back, though M'cal supposed Koni had lost track of him for a time while he'd traveled underwater.

M'cal closed his eyes as the man screamed again. The sound brought back memories: drinking tea at twilight on a garden bench with the scent of lilacs in the air, a cool, pale hand resting against his face; a question, quietly spoken, the exact words of which he could not remember but were simple, direct: *Do you give yourself to me? Do you give me your soul, your heart, your life?*

And M'cal had said yes. Because he'd loved that woman. He'd trusted her.

The witch did not require trust to make a man her slave. All she needed was submission. And if she worked on Koni long enough, she might just get it. Enough, anyway, to allow her into his mind and soul; to place a hook, a chain, a silver collar.

The witch might try to do the same to Kitala, if she could not swallow her soul directly. Assuming, of course, that the woman still wanted her for the same reasons. Or for any reason at all besides greed.

M'cal tested the handcuffs. He closed his eyes, listening to the boat, the sound of water encasing the hull. He drifted with the slow rock and tumble of the sea, his thoughts spreading deeper into the dark, listening to fish, the dull ticking life of sea anemones and flashing eels; deeper yet, the scuttling of crabs. Lullabies; these were the kinds of things his father had helped him fall asleep to on their camping trips below the ocean waves. Snacking on seaweed, cradled in nets so that the currents would not carry them away as they slept, side by side; staring up into the living darkness, pretending they could see the stars.

M'cal had taken it all for granted. If he ever had children . . .

He stopped himself from finishing that thought, though it bled directly into Kitala, into choking desperation. He calmed himself again, taking deep breaths, still pushing with his mind into the sea, searching.

He found what he was looking for: a pod of orcas, cutting through cold waters. He caught the edge of their thoughts—a complex stream of consciousness; flashes of images, streaks of memory; play and hunger. Orcas never felt fear. Not unless humans were involved. Too many orcas had been stolen from the sea by the violence of heavy nets and cages and rough machinery. Dragged to aquariums and resorts. Caged.

The pod leader was female. She was receptive to his thoughts, though M'cal had trouble telling her what he needed; his voice was better for that. Still, he thought she understood.

There came footsteps outside his room. M'cal broke off contact and opened his eyes. The door pushed open, revealing Ivan. His hands were bloody, as was the corner of his mouth. He smiled, then stepped aside. There was another door behind him, which he opened.

M'cal saw Kitala. She lay on a bed. All he could see was her slack face, the line of her throat . . . the edge of her wrists, tied to the bed frame with rope.

Ivan licked his mouth, still smiling. He cracked his knuckles and pointed at Kitala.

The witch appeared beside him, a sheer silver robe draped over her body. She did not limp, but there was a spot of blood at the corner of her mouth. She stared at M'cal for one long minute, the silence between them hard and thick. Her eyes glittered.

Kitala stirred. M'cal forced himself not to look at her, kept his gaze firmly on the witch.

Come, he thought. *Come here and hurt me. Just leave her alone.*

The witch ran her bloodstained fingertip over her tongue. She made a humming sound, briefly closing her eyes as a terrible strain flashed across her face. It was only a moment before the mask slid back into place.

She entered the room, Ivan at her side, and ripped off the duct tape covering M'cal's mouth.

"You have been busy. So very busy in my absence. Rescuing women, making new friends. And with such abandon, too. Almost as if you forgot your profession." She tapped her ring—a smaller copy of his bracelet. "How will I ever punish you?"

M'cal said nothing. Down the hall, he heard a shout, something wordless, angry. The witch sighed. "A shape-shifter. Magic raining down from the sky. What luck to have a menagerie such as mine."

"He is not yours yet," M'cal replied, counting the rings on her finger.

"The bird is strong," she agreed, holding Ivan's bloody hand to her mouth and licking it. "His friends are remarkable as well. Such secrets they keep. I had no idea."

M'cal gritted his teeth. In the other room, Kitala stirred again, her eyelids fluttering. The witch glanced over her shoulder and smiled. It was a poor smile, one of the least convincing he had ever seen. It surprised him. The witch usually had more poise, but again he sensed a terrible strain. Fear, even.

"How things change. Even in a day." The witch turned back to M'cal, her mask fracturing even more. "I should kill you now. I should have killed you the first time I had you in my bed. It would have been easy. You loved me so."

"I did," M'cal said.

"But you love *her* now." The witch gestured to Kitala. "What makes you think she will not steal your freedom? She is as much witch as I am."

"I trust her," he said.

"You are a fool."

"You are jealous. You did not break me."

"Perhaps not." The witch looked once more at Kitala, whose eyes were finally open, staring. "But *she* could."

"Leave him alone," Kitala muttered hoarsely.

The witch smiled and leaned over M'cal, her robe falling open to reveal her breasts. She traced a finger along his forehead, and then tapped it once. He tried to move, and found himself frozen. Not with the compulsion, though. Something different.

The witch turned again to Kitala. "No matter what you have done, he is still mine. He will always be mine, even if you free him. Memories bind. Memories are forever."

Kitala did not reply; she narrowed her eyes, looking from the witch to M'cal with such intensity he could feel her gaze almost as a touch, right down to his aching heart.

The witch bent, kissing him. He imagined himself biting her mouth, her tongue, but he could not close his jaw. So he lay there, enduring, trying to think of anything but the wet heat caressing his lips.

He felt a tickle in his mind—in his heart—like rage.

Not his own. It seemed foreign, separate. Familiar. He could not reconcile the sensation, but he nursed it.

The witch stopped kissing him. She moved, just enough, and M'cal was able to see Kitala again. She lay unmoving, but her gaze was pure fire, her mouth twisted in disgust. For one brief moment M'cal felt ashamed—a terrible shame that Kitala had seen him so used—but then he buckled down his emotions and it passed.

Again, another tickle—this time accompanied by the faint brush of strings; a hollow music, very soft, more breath than sound. Kitala still stared into his eyes. M'cal felt, again, a thread of some hard emotion that was not his—music, growing louder—and he followed it, down to his heart, suddenly certain of the source.

Kitala, he thought. *What are you doing?*

She did not answer him—perhaps did not hear him—but as the witch leaned in for another kiss, giving Kitala a spiteful look, the music thrumming through his head made a cracking sound.

The witch's hold broke. M'cal flinched. He could move again.

He lunged, snapping his teeth around her nose. Impulse, instinct overriding good sense. She reared back, screaming, blood rushing hot into his mouth. He refused to let go, even when Ivan clubbed the side of his head, again and again—M'cal *wanted* to be hit, needed the force of it—until finally Ivan punched him so hard he knocked M'cal free . . . taking the witch's nose along with him.

She howled, staggering backward, slamming against the wall. Blood gushed between her fingers, spilling down her clothes, her silver hair. Ivan stared, lurching toward her—then stopped, teetering on his toes, glancing back at M'cal with death in his eyes. He bared his sharp teeth, hissing.

M'cal spat out the knob of bloody flesh. It bounced against the shag carpet, landed at Ivan's feet like an odd red button. Somewhere distant, he heard Kitala swearing.

The witch's screams cut off into a strangled sob, and then nothing. Silence. Her hands fell to her sides. Her face was a ruin of flesh and blood, with only a hole where her nose should be, cartilage cut jagged, bubbles forming as she breathed. Not a fatal injury— not for her—but as with Ivan, there were some wounds even the witch could not heal. Not entirely.

"Ivan," said the witch, her voice hoarse, muffled, shaking. "Go to Kitala and hurt her. Any way you see fit. Make her scream."

The blood in M'cal's mouth suddenly tasted like poison. "Stay away from her."

"It was going to happen anyway," whispered the witch, balling up the edge of her robe, her hands covered in blood. "Without the compulsion you have left me no choice." She took a step toward him. "You can make it easy on Ms. Bell. You can make her . . . not care. All you have to do is take her soul, M'cal. Do it now, or she will suffer. For a very long time." She turned to Kitala, still confined to the other bed. "Or you can release him. Give me back his reins."

"Go to hell," Kitala snapped.

"Perhaps Ivan will take your nose," said the witch, each word growing wetter, more muffled with her blood. "Perhaps he will take other things as well."

M'cal snarled, straining against the chains. "My soul could give you the same power. Take me."

The witch's eyes narrowed. "A very tempting offer,

M'cal. After all this time, *very* tempting. But frankly, right at this moment I would rather see you suffer." She turned to Ivan, her profile inhuman, ragged and bloody. "Go. Do as I asked."

Ivan nodded, and shrugged off his suit jacket, laying it carefully over the witch's shoulders. He pressed his lips against her forehead, gave M'cal a hard glance, and then shuffled across the hall toward Kitala, who was struggling to sit up. Her restraints were too tight. Ivan stood above her, staring.

M'cal jerked hard, the handcuffs cutting into his skin. He heard music rising inside his heart, strings shrieking, and he held on to those sounds, willing them to mean something—power, magic, anything that would save her.

"Ivan!" he shouted. "Ivan, punish *me! Ivan!*"

"Give me her soul," said the witch. "Take it, M'cal. You have no choice."

"He has a choice!" screamed Kitala, scooting as far from Ivan as she could. "You leave him alone!"

Ivan grabbed her hair, yanking back her head, and moved so that M'cal's view was blocked. M'cal heard cloth tear. Kitala cried out.

Something in him snapped—a piece of his heart, tearing right out of his chest—and his voice welled so high and fierce in his throat that all he could do was open his mouth and let it out. And what came loose was less a song than a scream, raging wild as a hurricane, howling.

The witch whirled on him, blood spraying from her face. Her eyes were wide, so bright as to be shot through with lightning, and the remains of her nose bubbled violently as if she were underwater, starving for air. She stared at M'cal, but he did not care. All he could do was look at Ivan and sing.

The giant turned. M'cal glimpsed Kitala. Her blouse was torn, but there was steel in her eyes—hard, hot, bright—and she looked at him like she was ready to kill. M'cal was happy to oblige. He had never felt such rage, never felt such power in his voice, and it charged in on him a second time, his jaws snapping like a shark. It felt as if a steep wind were gathering inside that small room; his rage moved cold against his skin, whipping away the witch's voice as she screamed words he could not understand. Her power rolled right off him.

Blood leaked from Ivan's eyes. He raised a hand, touched his face. Looked at the red that painted his fingertips. First, confusion . . . then his mouth screwed up and his eyes bunched into slits and the blood started leaking faster and faster—from his ears as well—and M'cal's voice rose higher, stronger, twisting into something so ugly he could barely stand to hear himself. He had never done such a thing, but it seemed as natural as breathing to curl within Ivan and tell him how to die.

Something struck M'cal—the witch was beating his face with her fists—but her blows meant nothing worse than the tickle of a fin. All he could see was Ivan. The man's skin split, cracks forming against his red cheeks like a patch of dried earth. Blood seeped. Ivan tried to take a step, but his legs gave out and he crashed down hard. Kitala still stared, mouth moving, fierce. M'cal thought he heard her music in his head.

The witch blocked his view, her arm moving. Metal flashed.

He saw it coming, felt the impact, but it took him a moment to overcome his surprise. He looked down and found a long knife sticking out of his chest, still quivering with tension. M'cal did not know where the witch had found it, but the blade was sharp and long and shining, and his voice faltered for one brief moment.

Long enough. The witch grabbed his bracelet, the ring that bound them grating against the engraved metal. She said a word, and this time her power did not slide off him. It hit hard, as if that dagger were a bomb exploding in his heart.

He heard Kitala cry out, but Ivan was still down. M'cal tried to keep his gaze on her face, but the witch blocked him, the pain tearing through his chest, and it was all he could do to keep himself from biting off his own tongue as his jaws snapped together to hold back a scream.

The world rocked. It spun around him like a whirlpool, nothing staying still long enough for his vision to hold on to. For a moment, M'cal thought it was just him—losing himself in the pain—but then the witch slid sideways, hitting the wall, and everything came back into a hard, swift focus.

The boat shuddered, heaving sideways. M'cal would have been flung off the bed if not for his restraints. Instead, he hung in the air for a moment, cuffs digging into his ankles and wrists. From the other room, Kitala yelped; Ivan tried to stand.

And then it happened again, this time with an impact so violent it sounded as if a sharp reef were tearing through the hull of the boat. Once again, the witch was flung down; once again, M'cal hung askew, the dagger still lodged in his chest. He smelled the ocean. He heard water rushing. The boat tipped at a steeper angle.

"We are sinking," hissed the witch. "What have you done?"

"Only what I had to," said M'cal. "I am forcing you to choose."

For the first time in his memory, he saw horror spill through her gaze. She clawed at her face, her fingers inadvertently sinking into the pit of her nose. She flinched, and then flung herself toward him, forced to crawl across the floor toward the bed. The boat shifted again, groaning; M'cal heard whales crying.

"I must have the woman," whispered the witch. "I must be strong enough. There is no alternative."

"Alice!" Kitala cried out, hanging from the bed frame. "What does this have to do with her?"

The witch said nothing. She looked at M'cal—then back at Kitala—and flung herself toward the door, scrambling over Ivan's struggling body to reach the other room.

She never made it. The boat was struck again. Like a roller coaster in slow spin, twisting a loop through the heart of an earthquake. The motion made it difficult to focus, but M'cal saw the witch tumble out of sight down the hall. Ivan followed her, sliding on his stomach as the boat turned completely perpendicular. A man shouted for help. Koni.

"M'cal!" Kitala lat flat on her bed, which might as well have been a standing wall. She hung from the frame, her arms stretched at an agonizing angle.

M'cal heard splashing, and the witch hissing, but no one appeared at the mouth of the door. Just him and Kitala, swinging. And somewhere else, Koni. Trapped. All of them.

The lights went out, plunging all into darkness. M'cal's vision shifted, everything coming back into a sharp focus that swam in shades of gray.

He gritted his teeth and yanked hard on his chains, grunting with pain. The knife was still lodged in him, piercing his sternum. No chance of healing with the blade still there. Koni shouted again; there was something frantic in his voice.

M'cal closed his eyes and reached out to the orcas. They were milling around the sinking boat, whistling and squeaking, coordinating a merry-go-round pattern of circles and lunges, as though the failing vessel were herring and they were ready to feed.

M'cal found the pod leader—an old female. She was ready for him, concerned in the only way an orca could be, which was different from Krackeni or human. The drive to survive was still there, the need to protect. She could feel his pain, and it spread; the rest of the pod began whistling, pinging the boat so strongly he could feel the vibrations through the hull.

We are trapped, he told the female orca. *It is a net.*

Flashed memories of humans appeared in his head; real nets wrapped around flesh with machines grinding and babies squealing, separated from their mothers. The press of wires, the heaviness of air, rough hands and hot sun and noises dull without song.

The boat sank deeper. Koni shouted again. M'cal looked for Kitala and found her, blind in the darkness, her gaze still swimming in his direction. There was trust in her eyes, but fear, too. Her lips were pressed into a hard line. He listened to music sing.

He cut off contact with the orcas. There was nothing the whales could do about handcuffs, and another run at the boat would just make it sink faster. He watched Kitala struggle, fighting to loosen the ropes.

M'cal shifted shape. He had rejected that outright as

an option, but now he had no choice but to try. His legs fused from his groin down, but the transformation stopped at his ankles. The shackles were in the way.

And then they were not. His body transformed around them, leaving a tiny hole in the center of his lower tail for the metal to pass through and around. Unfortunately, his tail was thicker than his ankles, and the exposed shackle cut into his flesh like a dull saw. It hurt worse than the knife, and the chain remained linked to the wall.

The sounds of pouring water grew louder; a resounding crack ricocheted through the boat. M'cal felt the pressure of the sea building around the hull. Sinking deeper, almost gone. He wondered where Ivan and the witch were, if they had already made it off the boat. Maybe the orcas were eating them.

His skin rippled with scales as his neck transformed, gills splitting open. The air instantly dried them out, but M'cal ignored the discomfort—too much to bear already—and yanked hard on the chain screwed into the wall. It did not budge. He thought of Kitala drowning and tried again.

This time it moved. M'cal bared his teeth, trying not to swing, and wrenched down with all his strength. The wall creaked. He jerked again, snarling, and then again and again, until, without warning, the bolt shot out of the wall and sent him falling.

The chain attached to his tail caught him, but the wall buckled from his weight. He yanked the knife out of his chest, stuck it between his teeth, and pulled himself up. Koni's screams were quieter now, muffled. Kitala shouted M'cal's name.

M'cal took the knife out of his mouth and lunged upward, aiming the blade for the wall. It was hard to maneuver with his hands restrained, but he had a long reach and dug the tip into the paneling, prying at the steel bolt with one hand, holding on to the chain with the other. The wide fan of his tail flopped like a flag.

The bolt loosened. M'cal tugged on the chain, swinging in a slow arc, momentum cracking the wood. He did it again, harder, the boat shuddering around him. He heard Kitala breathing in the next room, waters rising, Koni silent—

The wood cracked. The bolt fell free. So did M'cal. He slammed into the wall—now the floor—and felt the breath knocked out of him. It took a moment to gather himself; he had to crawl, to haul himself up by his hands. He could not shift to use his feet—not without finding himself still restrained. Legs useless, either way. He clamped the knife between his teeth and started pulling, hands still bound, trailing chains. Slow going. Too slow.

He wrenched himself over the door, looking down at the hall, which was a steep drop beneath him. Dark water swirled, closer than he liked. He had never been in a sinking ship before; the fact that he could survive it, no matter what, was no comfort at all.

"M'cal!" Kitala shouted.

He threw himself across the hall, landing hard on the edge of her doorway. She hung above him, against the bed. M'cal grabbed the frame, hauling himself up with brute force. Her legs were free, feet digging into the mattress, trying to take the strain off her arms. He touched her, and she cried out, surprised. M'cal grunted. He had forgotten it was pitch dark for her.

He pulled himself all the way up, his tail slithering against Kitala's body. When he could lie flat on top of the bed frame, he took the knife from his mouth and began sawing carefully at the rope binding her wrists—hard work, since his own were still bound together.

"You need to hold the frame," he told her. "Otherwise, when this rope splits, you will fall."

"Okay," she said breathlessly, but she almost slipped anyway when he made the final cut. Her arms were weak from hanging so long. He caught her wrists—felt torn skin, blood—and lowered her carefully so that she stood on the bottom of the bed, her feet on the planks of the frame.

M'cal let him himself down, shifting shape enough so that he could stand on his feet instead of his tail. The relief on his ankles was tremendous. Kitala said, "I can't see a thing."

"I am right here," he murmured. "But we must cross from the bed to the doorway, and the floor is not where it should be."

"I can't see," she said again.

"Wait," M'cal replied, and crouched, flinging out his bound hands so that they hit the edge of the doorway. He still held the knife; the blade bit into his palm, but he ignored the pain, pulling himself over the empty space, bracing his body. "Kitala. Feel where I am. Use me as a guide, a bridge. Walk on my back."

"M'cal—"

"Hurry."

Kitala slid her foot onto his spine, and he gritted his teeth, waiting to bear her weight. Fortunately, she was not heavy, and she danced over him, blind, in one step. He held his breath as she teetered on the edge of the sideways doorframe, bent over to accommodate her height—but then she found her balance, and he hauled himself after her. The water was higher. M'cal thought of Koni.

"Jump," he said. "I will be with you."

"Right," she murmured, and slid into the water, gasping. He followed, shifting his legs, biting back his own gasp as the shackle cut into his tail.

"Take a deep breath," he told her, trying to keep his voice steady. "Put your arms around my neck. We have to find Koni."

They went under, M'cal pulling Kitala with him. His hands were useless for almost anything but holding the knife, but he moved fast, trying to pay attention to her need for air—and also his need to find the shape-shifter.

The yacht was not that big; there were only two other rooms toward the bow. He got lucky on his first try, opening the door into a watery world. There were several electronic devices at the bottom, along with a mesh cage, the door swinging open. Just above it was the lower half of a naked man: arms, torso, two legs, and a waist, blood streaming from cuts. M'cal saw everything but a head.

He swam fast, rising, and much to his surprise, poked his head above water. It was a space only six inches deep—part of an alcove for a television set—but there was air trapped, and Koni was still alive, gripping the edge of a cabinet.

"Son of a bitch," he spluttered, his eyesight apparently just as good in the dark. "What the hell took you so long?"

M'cal pulled Kitala up into the opening, and she gasped, taking a deep breath.

"Busy," he said. "I assume you were in that cage below us."

"For a while," Koni said. "But then that lady did something to keep me from shifting, and her crazy fucking Igor—"

"—Ivan—"

"—whatever, took me out to town. I need a ciga-rette."

"Are you wearing restraints?"

"I've never seen so many fucking handcuffs in my life," replied Koni. "Woman pulled out a chest of them. *Jesus.*"

"Take that as a yes," Kitala said to M'cal, and he ducked back down, seeing what he had missed before: a long chain much like the one trailing behind him, leading to a set of shackles. The witch was not a woman to underestimate inhuman strength. And she was always prepared for guests. The yacht was spe-cially outfitted for such visits.

M'cal still had the knife. He rammed it into the wall, digging against the wood paneling, stabbing and hacking until the ring holding the chain pulled free. He bound it into a coil and swam back to Kitala and Koni.

"Here," he said, handing the links to Koni. "Try shifting again. Outside of the witch's presence, you might—"

Koni did not wait for him to finish. His eyes flashed, golden light spreading down his face into the water. For a moment, M'cal thought it would work—feathers peered out from the man's hairline—but then Koni grunted and the light died.

"Better this time," he said, "but still not there."

"Fine." M'cal tossed aside the knife and reached out with his bound hands. He grabbed Kitala's arm. "I will take her out first, and then return for you. Unless you think you can make it with us?"

"Can you pull me?" Koni asked. "I won't be much of a swimmer with my feet bound like this."

"There is a chain attached to my tail. If you can hold it, and your breath—"

"Consider it done. I want out of here now."

So did M'cal. He let Koni sink and grab the chain, and then pulled him and Kitala out of the room. He had difficulty swimming—all his limbs were encumbered—but he made it down the hall and through the stairwell now pointing downward toward the bottom of the sea, and in less than a minute they were free of the boat and heading toward the surface.

They broke free of the water, Kitala and Koni gasping for air while M'cal drifted around them, listening to the orcas. He could feel their cries in his body, and the old female moved close, her fin splitting the waves. Kitala made a small sound as the pod gathered, rising out of the water to investigate.

"The boat," she said, her teeth beginning to chatter. "They're the ones who capsized it. But where are the witch and Ivan?"

The vessel was almost entirely underwater. M'cal asked the orcas if they had witnessed the escape of a woman and man, but they had seen nothing. He did not dare, however, to imagine that the witch and Ivan were dead.

Kitala shuddered. The waters were clearly too cold for her; any longer and she would have hypothermia to contend with. Koni, however, did not seem especially affected by the ocean's temperature. M'cal saw him looking at Kitala. The two men exchanged glances.

"Are we close to land?" the shape-shifter asked. M'cal glanced around. He saw no lights. But if they were in the Georgia Strait, still near Vancouver, he had a place to go. Maybe. If it was still there.

M'cal sank beneath the waves, reaching out with his

mind and voice to the old female orca. For a moment he expected the witch's compulsion to kick in and stop him. But it did not, and a flush spread through his body. Freedom still felt new. He wondered if he would ever learn to take it for granted again.

The pod leader responded immediately. Scars covered her body, battle wounds. She called out to her pod, and the orcas gathered close, bumping against M'cal's body, pinging him with calls. One of the orcas touched its nose to his bound hands. M'cal hesitated, but the temptation was too great. He asked, and the orca immediately opened her mouth. He placed the link between the cuffs over a tooth the size of his thumb, gingerly shifting his hands as the orca slowly bit down.

A grinding noise echoed through the water. The link snapped. M'cal's cuffs still encircled his wrists, but without them joined he had better mobility. He shifted his tail, re-forming his feet so that the link between those shackles reappeared. It was more difficult to separate them than the handcuffs, but after some brief maneuvering, that link too fell apart in the orca's massive mouth.

He surfaced for a moment and said to Koni, "Hold your legs still."

"What?" said the shape-shifter, but M'cal swam back down and grabbed Koni's ankles, holding him above water as the orca drifted near, her thoughts quite pleased. Snapping links, in her mind, was the same as breaking nets; a satisfying task. Koni flinched when his feet touched the orca's mouth, but the link broke with a crunch, and he kicked out hard, still trailing a chain behind him.

"You're talking to them," Kitala said when M'cal

resurfaced. She was having trouble treading water; her teeth chattered. He gathered her close, hooking her legs around his waist to share his warmth. His tail undulated through the water, keeping them afloat while he used his hands to rub her back. She was shaking. He hoped it was nothing worse than cold.

Koni gave him another concerned look, and M'cal whistled to the orcas, who still jostled for space all around. Curiosity filled them; protectiveness as well. It had been a long time since any of them had met a Krackeni.

M'cal caught Koni's attention and pointed to a dark crest sliding through the water, close on his left. "Grab the dorsal fin of that female and climb onto her back. In front or behind, it does not matter. As long as you are steady."

The shape-shifter hesitated, eyeing the orca with a great deal of wariness. "We hardly know each other. She might get the wrong idea."

"Just do it."

"If I find out later that this is the orca equivalent of grabbing a woman's ass—"

"I will make certain she regurgitates your body parts."

"Fantastic," Koni muttered, and grabbed the dorsal fin, pulling himself up so he straddled her wide body. The orca did not object, though a series of puzzled images flashed through M'cal's brain, accompanied by careful clicks and whistles.

"I felt that," Koni said.

"She has never carried anyone," M'cal explained. "She wants to make certain she does not hurt you. You are quite small to her. Much like a calf."

With one hand, M'cal reached out to grab the dorsal fin of the pod leader, shifting his tail into legs as he hauled himself up to straddle her. He leaned back so that her fin pressed against his spine, and placed Kitala in front of him. She slid her hands along the orca's thick, slick skin and made a small sound.

"Tell me," M'cal whispered in her ear.

"Can't," she replied, shivering so badly that the word was almost inaudible. He wrapped his arm around her waist, used the other to steady himself against the orca's back, and told the old female where to take them.

She pushed through the water, moving slowly, staying as high above the surface as she could. Koni's orca did the same, with the shape-shifter sitting in similar fashion in front of the dorsal fin. The orca's body was wider there; easier to brace oneself as the creatures picked up speed, sliding through the water with breathtaking grace. Heartache bubbled up M'cal's throat, mixed with terrible joy. He had forgotten so much. The cage he had been living in was smaller than his soul.

Music strummed, and he sang—just because he could, for the first time in years, without pretense to harm. It was a different kind of melody than any he remembered; deeper, wilder, with an edge of the power that had filled him on the boat. Each note made him feel like he was prying back the dark cover of something long hidden; primal, untouchable, a ghost from some other, more ancient, past. He could feel it stirring in his chest—another kind of monster.

And he liked it.

CHAPTER THIRTEEN

Take a moment, her mother once said. *Take a moment to breathe in your life, to remember who you are. Then take another, and another, until each breath is that moment and you . . . simply . . . are.*

Kit took a moment—and more—as she rode on the back of the orca, rising and falling through the night sea with the stars peering through the clouds and the scents of cedar and salt mixing cool in her lungs. She took her moments, tasting them with wonder, but it was difficult to remember who she was. Kit felt as though she was no longer in her body, was merely drifting alongside a soaked wild woman whose eyes were full of stars, her body cradled by a man who was not human, who would never be mistaken for human, not with that voice rumbling like sun-soaked honey and thunder. It was like listening to an excerpt of the first dawn, a song of earth and power; part of her, down to the marrow. Genetic memory, a recollection of the soul; dangerous, primeval.

M'cal's arm was strong around her waist, though

his warmth did little to curb the profound chill seeping into her bones. Her hands and feet were numb, past pain; the rest of her body felt like a plastic mannequin fresh from some freezer. If she fell off the orca, she would drown; she had no strength in her body to swim. Not to walk or fight. All she could do was feel, and her emotions carried her into a slipstream of music; strings and voices, and darker, a thrill of something terrible that she could not name.

Here there be monsters, she thought, unable to help herself. *And flights of angels sing thee to thy rest.*

It was difficult to see—there were few lights on this part of the coast—but she glanced sideways and saw a glitter of gold like fireflies in Koni's eyes, and the stars shed enough light to cast a shadow on the dark bodies surrounding them. Kit thought of the witch and Ivan. Her breast hurt.

Not over. Not yet.

M'cal stopped singing. For a moment, she thought her heart stopped beating as well. The loss of his voice, the silence, made the world feel as empty as death. Like a drug; everything lost color in the shadow of that music.

The orcas slowed before the narrow mouth of a small cove. Breath exploded from the blowhole in front of Kit, spraying her with a fine mist of seawater.

"We are here," M'cal said softly, and the orca took them in, followed by the other female carrying Koni. The rest of the pod lingered outside the cove, slapping the water with their fins and tails. The sound followed Kit, echoing against the tree line, the tumble of rocks framing the water like a half-moon.

Thirty feet from shore, M'cal slid off the orca's back, pulling Kit with him. The water no longer felt as cold, and her thoughts were just as numb as her body. Somewhere near, she heard another splash. Koni's voice, murmuring something. She glimpsed a dark eye the size of her fist, peering into her face, and then M'cal started swimming, pulling her away from the orcas toward the shore. She watched the creatures slide away, dorsal fins sharp and proud, and wished she had her fiddle to hold. She needed to make her own music. The moment needed more than breath.

They reached shore quickly. Kit tried to say something as M'cal swung her up in his arms, but her face was numb, and her jaw felt locked in place. They moved through shadows, chains clanking, branches sweeping past her face. She smelled cedar, sap, loam; M'cal's skin, which was clean, fresh, full of the sea. Her heart thudded loud and slow in her chest. Koni kept muttering to himself.

And then Kit heard their footsteps echo hollow, and suddenly the forest was replaced by walls and a ceiling. M'cal laid her down on a hard surface that smelled like dust.

"This place is crap," she heard Koni say. "It's like a tent you can't carry with you."

"You are a poet," M'cal replied. "Really."

"Seriously. No furniture, no *electricity*. You're not going to get her warm in this shack."

"I have blankets," M'cal replied; but moments later loud squeaks filled the air, little bodies scrabbling across the floor. Kit tried to sit up.

"Hantavirus," Koni said. "Bubonic plague."

M'cal sighed. "I have other blankets—*clean* blankets—and a fireplace. As well as some canned food."

"Hallelujah. We're saved."

Another sigh. "There is wood stacked outside. Go get it."

No quips. Footsteps passed close by, and then M'cal was there, pulling off her clothes.

"I am sorry," he murmured, pressing a quick kiss on her forehead. "You will be exposed, but we must get you warm."

If it meant being warm again, Kit would have exposed herself to an entire football team and done a jig. She tried to help him, but he gently pushed her hands aside. Her blouse was already torn; he paused over the rip, his fingers hovering over her exposed breast, which was probably bruising by now.

M'cal stared, his expression unreadable. But then he kissed her again, the heat of his mouth like a balm, and his hands kept moving against her body, tugging and pulling. Kit heard Koni enter the cabin, listened to the hard tumble of wood hitting the floor. Ashes hissed, accompanied by more plunking sounds, the loud tang of metal striking metal. Paper crumpled. Koni said, "Where are the matches?"

"Above the fireplace." M'cal finished pulling off Kit's jeans and underwear. Something dry and warm instantly covered her; slightly scratchy, very thick. A match struck and light flashed, burning brighter as the flame caught hold in the fireplace. Kit could finally see again. She found Koni crouching naked in front of the blaze. Tattoos adorned his body, all the way down his hard thighs. He shoved more wood over the fire.

M'cal scooped Kit into his arms and pulled her close. She started shivering again, violently. Koni said, "Fire isn't going to be enough. She needs body heat." He hesitated, for once looking serious. "She may need the both of us."

Kit coughed. It was laughter, but the men looked at her like she had just landed at death's door with a bout of pneumonia. She could not stop shivering. M'cal stared from her to Koni and picked up her hand. Her fingertips looked odd. Almost blue. He breathed on them, and then tucked her hand back under the covers. He wrapped another blanket around her head and slid in beside her. The heat of his body was delicious, but it did not put a dent in the chill sinking through her bones. Kit felt M'cal hesitate, and watched as he looked up at Koni and said, "All right."

Koni did not say a word. He crawled under the covers carefully, slowly, pushing close until his hips and legs rubbed Kit's. His skin was hot—as much a furnace as M'cal's—and though it was definitely the oddest arrangement Kit had ever found herself in, she could not bring herself to care . . . or to feel uncomfortable. She needed to get warm. Now.

Besides, M'cal was guard dog enough. He placed his arm over Kit's breasts, tugged her shivering body close, and said to Koni, "Keep your hands above the covers."

"Give me a break," Koni replied, staring at the ceiling. "I am not a total pervert. Although, to be honest, consider the night we've been having. First handcuffs, and now this? Way more kinky than I expected."

"Please," M'cal said. "Do not talk."

"You like the strong and silent type, huh?"

"If you do not shut up, I will kill you with my voice."

"I love it when you talk dirty."

"Fine. Which would you prefer to lose first? Your soul or your testicles?"

"You know, you're just a bit obsessed with chopping off balls. Do you have issues with your masculinity?"

Kit coughed again, but this time it sounded more like laughter. Both men looked at her. Koni's mouth quirked. "Do you have something to add to this conversation?"

"No," she whispered, teeth chattering.

M'cal cradled her against his body. "Koni, take her hands. Warm them."

The shape-shifter smiled and cupped Kit's hands inside his. "I am such a trouper."

The three of them talked for a time. It made the situation easier. Nonsense, nothing serious. Trivia about each other, such as favorite colors—ranging from blue to black (sparking a debate about the spiritual themes associated with both); favorite movies—of which M'cal was woefully ignorant, given the somewhat surprising revelation that his parents had disdained television in lieu of books ("barbarians," Koni called them); favorite foods, which led to the discovery that mermen were quite content eating anything and everything except creatures who talked back. And, as with any survivalist slumber party, the requisite worst-date competition cropped up, which M'cal won hands down, given that the first woman he seriously pursued ultimately turned him into her personal slave and assassin.

"Certainly beats being laughed at after sex," Koni said.

"Are you sure she wasn't laughing *with* you?" Kit asked.

"No one has ever laughed at *me*," M'cal added thoughtfully.

"Thanks," Koni said. "Ever so much."

Their voices warmed Kit as much as their bodies, though there was nothing better or sweeter than M'cal

curled tight against her back, each sound he made ruf-
fling her hair, heating her neck. The boat, the witch—
Ivan—faded away. Not entirely, but enough. And
after a while, Kit closed her eyes and fell asleep.

When she woke, the room was dark. The fire had
burned down to embers. Koni was gone. A pair of
shackles lay where he had been, and nearby, another
two sets of cuffs.

M'cal's arms tightened. "Kitala."

She smiled. "How do you do that? Don't you ever
sleep?"

He kissed the back of her neck. "I am afraid you
will disappear if I do."

Kit turned in his arms and pressed close, brushing
his jaw with her lips. "Koni?"

"His ability to transform returned. He left to contact the others."

"Picked some locks, apparently."

"Mine anyway. He merely . . . slipped out of the
others."

"Ah. Right." Kit tried to imagine it and could not.
So much she was taking on faith. "Where are we?"

"A cabin that belonged to my father. When I was
young, this is where we would come when he wanted
to teach me about living in the water. My mother
stayed here while he and I . . . went out."

"I hope it was more comfortable for her back then."

M'cal's smiled; faint, slightly pained. "After she
died, my father cleared out the cabin. He burned the
furniture."

Kit hesitated, peering into his eyes. "And how did
you grieve?"

He swallowed hard and pressed his mouth against
her cheek, so gently it took her breath away. "I grieved

badly. When I was young, I ran away from home. No good-byes, no letters, not for a long time. It broke my mother. It hurt my father. When she died, he never forgave me."

"You said she died of cancer."

"She did. But if I had been there, if I had not *run* . . . perhaps she would have been stronger. Perhaps she would never have become ill." M'cal rolled onto his back, taking Kit with him. "I miss my mother, Kitala. It is hard being here. I should have appreciated the swiftness of time."

"How long were you gone from your family?"

"Almost ten years. I intended to come back sooner. But I kept dreading the idea of facing them. I was sixteen when I left."

"And the witch? How long?"

"Five, perhaps six years. Long enough." M'cal soothed back Kit's curls, gazing into her eyes. "Being with you makes me feel like the man I used to be. Before the witch. I forgot, Kitala. I forgot everything."

"No," she whispered. "You didn't forget. If you had, you would never have saved me. You would never have stuck by me the way you have."

"Never again," he murmured. "I told myself never again."

Kit managed to free one of her hands and touched her neck. Felt puncture marks. She touched her breast, too, and winced.

M'cal's eyes darkened. He covered her hand, and she tried not to remember the sensation of Ivan's mouth, those fat, hard fingers. She buried her face in the crook of M'cal's neck, drawing in his scent, the heat of his skin. Shivered. He drew the covers up around her back. "You are cold."

Kit shook her head. "Just remembering."

His hands stilled. "I remember, too."

She fought for words. "I'm glad you were there. Even if you hadn't stopped him, I would have been glad."

"Glad that I could not keep you safe?"

"Glad that I was not alone," she whispered. "I've seen a lot of things, M'cal. Murders, rapes, hangings . . . even a decapitation or two. I can't forget a single one. But I've never been the victim. I've never been the target, until now. And violence is lonely, M'cal. No matter what side you're on."

He breathed out, slow, his hands sliding up her shoulders. "Before you, Kitala, the only woman who could touch me without causing pain was the witch. Do you understand what that means? For all those years when she . . . took . . . me . . . it was the only pleasure I had. And that was a terrible thing to feel."

Kit swallowed hard, remembering the witch kissing him, how he had lain there unmoving, his face an empty mask. As though he was dead on the inside, and all the witch was doing was touching a shell.

"I was so close to being lost," M'cal whispered. "I had no idea how close. If I had not met you, I would have forgotten myself. I would never have known what it could be to hold someone and not hate myself. Not hate the person in my arms. I would have forgotten how to love."

"Not possible."

"She raped me," he said, and even though Kit had already suspected as much, to hear it said out loud was terrible, shocking. "Every day, in body and mind. It is a wonder I still want anyone at all." He cupped her face between his hands and stared into her eyes with such intensity she forgot to breathe. "But I do. I want *you*. I wanted you the first time I saw you playing your violin on that stage."

"Last night," Kit murmured.

"Last night," he echoed. "Terrifying."

Kit pushed herself up his chest until she could lean over his face and stare directly into his eyes. The heat from the embers of the fire bathed her exposed shoulders and arms. The rest of her was warm. She did not want to talk. There was too much music in her head, too many notes to keep inside, but her fiddle was not there and she could not sing.

But there was a golden thread between her heart and M'cal's; a hook and line she had thrown to him while on the boat. A tenuous connection, one she had no name for, and something she had never considered possible. But it was there, and she used it, adding other strings, playing a symphony on them inside her head.

"I can hear you," M'cal said with a touch of wonder in his voice. "I can hear that music."

"Good," she whispered. "I don't know what that means, but good."

He smiled sadly and kissed her, slow and deep, his hands roving down her body; light, like wings or a melody. He was gentle with her, and she responded in kind, and though they did not go as far as they could have, it was good to be held so tightly; good to look into a face that stared back with as much raw reverence as that with which her own heart ached.

M'cal kissed her throat. He kissed her breast. He kissed her cheek and pressed his mouth close to her ear. "Never again, until I met you. Never again, after."

Kit smiled. "That is an ominous compliment, M'cal."

"But the truth."

"You have a bigger heart than that." She traced a circle over his sinewy shoulder. "Besides, it's a huge world. Lots of ocean. Plenty of hot chicks with tails out there who would probably tie themselves in knots for you. You might find someone you like better than little ol' me."

He pushed her away to look into her eyes. "And you? Do you think there is someone better for you?"

"No," Kit said. "I really don't."

M'cal picked up her hand, and enough light emanated from the hot coals for her to see his skin shift, scales rising from his flesh, which became harder, silkier. Webbing appeared between his long, strong fingers.

"When I left home," he said, "I became a gypsy. I labored at odd jobs across Europe, though I stayed for several years in Greece, helping marine archaeologists search for artifacts in the sea. The work was . . . rewarding. But I moved on eventually. I am a nomad. It is in my blood. My father was the same, but for my mother he found roots. It was difficult for him, though. Krackeni drift, always." M'cal squeezed her hand. "But they do not drift in their hearts. If anything remains constant, it is that."

Kit studied his face, trying to memorize every line; the curve of his brow, the soft sweep of his mouth. "I don't own a home, M'cal. I have enough money to buy ten, but the only home I've ever counted on is my family, and that has always been enough. Because all I need is here." She placed her hand over her heart. "I've been on the road almost as long as you have, since I was seventeen, and I don't plan on slowing down. I don't think I could, not for long. And no one . . . no one has ever been able to keep up with that. Or understand."

"And if I understood? If I could . . . keep up?"

"Then I guess my home would get a little larger," she whispered.

Something fierce entered M'cal's eyes, and he carefully untangled himself and stood. Kit tried to follow, but he laid a hand on her shoulder. She stayed still as he wrapped her tight in a cocoon of blankets; remained silent when he picked her up in his arms and carried her from the cabin.

The forest was dark, but she could see better this time. The sea was close, only a stone's throw away. M'cal carried her to the shore and set her down on the rocks. The air was cool against her face.

"Are you strong enough to enter the water again? It would only be for a moment." His voice was quiet, but held an urgency that made her nod, without question. She unwrapped herself from the blankets, and M'cal helped her lay them aside. He picked her up again, and carried her into the water. She gasped as the waves hit her. It was as cold as she remembered.

M'cal took her all the way in, transforming as he did. She could feel his legs mold together, skin rubbing into scales against her naked legs. His tail undulated gently, keeping them afloat.

"You know," she said to him, fighting a shiver, "I just got over freezing my ass off."

"Forgive me," he replied. "But I am afraid to wait."

It was difficult to see his face, but she could feel the tension in his body. "Wait for what?"

"It is only a ritual," he said, so quiet his voice was almost masked by the lapping of the waves against the shore. "There is nothing binding to it, Kitala. But it means something to my people, and to me."

"What?" she asked again, shivering.

"I give you my protection," he told her, dragging his wet thumb across her forehead. "I give you my song, so that it will keep you safe."

He bent close and placed his mouth over hers. But it was no kiss. Kit felt a rush of air enter her throat, like being plowed with a stiff breeze, and it was followed by sound: his voice, rumbling through her like a mountain shaking free of its roots, or the edge of a tsunami touching the sky. There was no melody, no music; just power, like that same power she had felt while listening to the song of her soul, hidden inside that pale conch shell.

M'cal's soul, whispered a tiny voice. *He is giving you part of it.*

She drank it down, feeling it push back the cold to seep into her bones, her heart. Like being filled with the sky or some endless expanse of blue ocean. M'cal began to pull away, but Kit grabbed the back of his head, holding him to her. She could hear her own song, her own melody of storm and dawn, and though she did not know what she was doing, instinct was enough. She felt that music pouring up her throat, and she willed a piece of it into M'cal. A thread, like the one she had already hooked into him. Her own protection. Her own song.

M'cal shuddered against her, but when he broke free he did not speak. Only stared, eyes haunted. Kit waited, watching him. But still, not a word.

His kiss was more than enough when he leaned in and covered her mouth with his, dragging from her a gasp of pleasure. Kit wrapped her legs around his hips, kissing him back, tasting salt water and heat and everything M'cal. His hands threaded through her hair; she felt something thick press against her lower body. Kit reached down to touch his erection. The skin was different; soft yet bumpy, partially hidden by a pouch in his body. She looked into M'cal's face, hunting to meet his eyes.

She did so, and she found them torn with desire and hunger, a dark intensity Kit found tremendously erotic, because it was for her, because he was suddenly inside her, thick and hot, pushing so deep she cried out, gasping with pleasure. He stayed there for a moment, breathing hard, and then, so slowly she hardly knew what he was doing, he began undulating the lower half of his body—shallow movements at first, and then faster and faster—with a steep arch in his tail that she could feel against her legs as he slammed against her, driving himself again and again into her body. He held on to her hips, leaning her backward as their joined bodies pushed through the water, splashing and writhing around each other, and the pleasure built so fine and hot and hard that when she did finally come it was violent, blinding, shattering.

M'cal gasped her name, shuddering in her arms, and they sank underwater, spinning and twisting. It felt like forever—Kit holding her breath—but then they surfaced and she could breathe again, and M'cal was looking at her, trembling, his gaze so raw she touched his face and asked, "What's wrong?"

"Nothing," he said, but she knew it was a lie. Kit felt M'cal's tension as he swam them back to shore, carrying her free of the water, wrapping her securely in the wool blankets. She hardly felt the cold; it seemed there was a furnace glowing inside her body, as if that piece of M'cal's soul was a tiny sun, spinning heat.

Only when they were inside the cabin, seated in

front of the fireplace, with M'cal stoking the coals and adding more wood, did she say, "Tell me."

He hesitated. "Tell you what?"

She touched his arm. "What happened out there?"

"A ritual—"

"No," she interrupted. "Later. You were upset."

He looked away from her, at the fire. "I have never . . . felt this way about anyone. Never so strongly. And I have never been given so much. I am afraid of losing you, Kitala. I felt it out there, the loss. Almost like it had already happened. And it frightened me."

Kit leaned forward, the blankets slipping off her body. She wrapped her arms around him and squeezed, trying to melt into his damp skin. "Don't be scared. Please, M'cal." *Please. Please don't leave me, either.*

"Ah," he whispered. "Easier said than done."

CHAPTER FOURTEEN

M'cal's father had never been sentimental about anything unless it pertained to his wife, which was why gutting out the cabin had come as such a shock to M'cal the first time he saw it after her death. Not a curtain or rug remained, not her favorite rocks, not even a book. Everything, gone. What was here now had been brought after that time, after his father was long gone. There was nothing left of his mother but memories. Memories he had not confronted in a good long time.

Kitala's presence helped. She lay beside him, curled on her side. Asleep in a nest of blankets. Warm again.

Foolish, dragging her into the ocean without asking, without considering the consequences. Even after all these years, he still acted before thinking. But fear could do that to a man: undermine his common sense. Drive him to any act if it meant protecting what he held most dear.

He had lied to Kitala, if an omission could be counted as a lie. What he had done was more than a ritual, and certainly binding—though only on his end, not hers. She was free, and always would be. But whether she knew it or not, he was part of her now—and there would be no other, not for him, not for the rest of his life. And should she ever meet other Krackenis, they would feel it, too.

His mate. His wife. Carrying a part of his soul in her heart.

Just as you are carrying hers, he told himself, feeling that bright shard lodged like a prism; on one side sunlight, and on the other, a storm. Burning and raging and singing. Kitala Bell. Keeping his soul warm.

He closed his eyes, still marveling, and wondered if she realized, or if it had been only an accident, instinct: claiming him, just as he had claimed her.

M'cal touched her hair, his palm bouncing gently off her thick curls. She stirred, but did not wake. Her skin glowed in the firelight. Looking at her made his throat thick, his chest ache. He remembered love. He remembered what it had felt like to love the witch. If she had not been so hasty in capturing him, he might have performed the ritual with her instead—a monumental mistake, terrifying to imagine. Although, what he felt for Kitala was so much stronger, so much *purer,* he wondered if, down deep, he had even then known the witch could not possibly be the one.

Because it had never been like this. As though just touching Kitala's hand was the same as making love. As though he lived and breathed by the beat of her heart.

But you still belong to the witch. Kitala might have blocked the compulsion, but that woman is still waiting on the other side. She is not dead. And you are endangering Kitala with your presence.

She made a small sound, jerking slightly. A tremor entered M'cal's heart—an uneasiness not his own—and he lay down beside her, curling his arm around her waist. She flinched when he touched her, and then settled back in his embrace. Still asleep.

M'cal closed his eyes, resting. It was a Krackeni trick, much like one used by dolphins and whales—dozing while conscious, semiaware of his surroundings while half of his brain settled into a sleep cycle. Not as good as full sleep, but it would do for now.

"Nifty trick," someone said. M'cal's eyes snapped open, staring.

An old woman crouched in front of the fire beside him. She wore a red skirt and a loose white blouse. Her skin was dark, her hair short and gray. She had features of beauty, but age and weight had taken their toll.

"Inside is what counts." She looked at him sideways with a curt smile. "Not that many could compete with *your* pretty face, though I suspect it's been more burden than aid. Otter like you would have more peace if his pelt weren't so fine."

M'cal sat up slowly, glancing at Kitala. She still slept. The old woman chuckled. "That one always was a log."

"Who are you?" M'cal drew the blanket over his lap. "How did you get in here?"

She smiled. "You dreamed me in, son. And as to who I am, take a gander into these eyes of mine. Maybe dream you an answer, too."

There was nothing overtly dangerous in her voice, so he peered into her eyes, studying them. The answer had already been on the tip of his tongue—instinct—but the dark warmth in her gaze confirmed it. The old woman smiled. "Good. That was a test, you know. See how well you know my little Kitty Bella."

"You are supposed to be dead," M'cal said.

Her smile widened. "Heart stopped beatin', that's all. More to living than flesh and blood. You should know that better than anyone."

He hesitated. "I know Kitala would like to see you."

"Oh, she sees me plenty. It's you I came for this time. Satan loads his cannons with big watermelons, Krackeni. And right now you've got a field of 'em aimed right up your backside."

M'cal's eyes narrowed. "Explain."

The old woman put her hands directly into the fire and held them there with a sigh. "The world is a circle, spins in a circle, and makes our lives the same. Can't be expecting nothing else, except what's come before. Which means, in my wiggly talk, that the bad times are circling 'round again. Days like they were before the big flood, before history started a second time and forgot the darkness." She gave him a hard look. "I think you know what I mean."

"The old wars," he said slowly. "I have heard the stories. Battles of magic."

"Nasty creatures. Demons." The old woman took her hands out of the fire. Smoke rose from her fingertips. "Some of them survived."

Kitala still slept. M'cal said, "What does that have to do with us?"

The old woman did not answer. She held her hand above her granddaughter's head and murmured a soft word. A chill passed over M'cal's skin, and he watched that strong, round body stand straight and tall.

He stood with her, holding the blanket against him. "Please. Tell me."

The old woman shook her head, still gazing at Kitala. "Word of advice, son. Watch out when you're getting all you want. Fattened hogs ain't in luck."

And with that, she disappeared. M'cal stared, ears ringing. A disquieting experience, unnerving. He lay down on his back, staring at the ceiling, fingering the bracelet, which was cold.

The sun was just beginning to rise when Kitala opened her eyes. She yawned, and the cover slipped off. M'cal stared.

"Like the view?" she asked.

"Yes." He brushed his finger against her firm round breast, and she looked down. Her skin was perfect. Not a bruise or scratch. Kitala made a quiet sound, and M'cal reached out to turn her head. The puncture wounds were gone as well.

Kitala touched her neck, eyes darkening. M'cal crouched close and covered her hand with his. Pulled it away. Ran his fingers over her healed skin. She shivered, watching him. "I suppose you want an explanation."

"No," he said. "That is unnecessary."

She gave him an uncertain look, but M'cal said nothing. There was a reason the old woman had not shown herself to her granddaughter. He could not guess what it was, but he was willing to take it on faith. As with many things in his life.

"I am glad you are healed," he said carefully.

Kitala glanced at her breast. M'cal tilted up her chin, forcing her to look at him. He said nothing, simply drinking in her face, the quick emotion passing through her eyes; the lines and curves of her cheeks and brow and chin. Her skin, smooth and soft as dark cream, framed by a crown of brown curls streaked with gold.

"What?" she asked, but the corner of her mouth curved and her eyes were warm. He kissed her, and Kitala leaned into him, smiling against his mouth.

She stood, clutching the blanket around her body. Tall and lovely as a queen. She turned in a slow circle, gazing at the cabin, which was—as Koni had said—little better than a stationary tent. No furniture, except for a tall metal cabinet in the corner that contained small sundries, more blankets, canned food. M'cal had planned on stocking more things, but time had run away, as had his freedom.

Kitala's stomach growled. M'cal smiled, and stood. Walked to the cabinet. Felt her gaze roving over his naked body. It aroused him, but his back was to her as he opened the metal doors—caught the flash of a mouse's tail—and said, "We have peaches, spinach. Bottled water."

"Did you bring this food for yourself? I would think you could just . . . fish . . . for your supper."

"I suppose," he said. "Call it nostalgia."

"Ah," she replied gently. "Do you have a can opener?"

M'cal found one, and turned. Kitala was naked, the blanket pooled around her feet. She glanced down and smiled almost shyly.

"You know," she said, "I'm having trouble deciding what to eat first."

His erection got harder, more painful. Kitala sidled close and took away the can opener. She reached around him to place it back in the cabinet, her entire body rubbing warm and soft against him. Her long, clever fingers slid down his stomach, stroking, and her smile became dark, hungry.

Kitala dropped to her knees. M'cal could not have

stopped her even if he wanted to—and he did not. Her hands were magic, sliding like tight rings up and down his shaft, stroking in opposite directions. Her mouth touched him, sucking lightly—engulfing him entirely—and the twisting sensation, the wet heat, was too much for restraint. He dragged them both down to the floor, Kitala letting go of him for only a moment before he pushed her flat. Instead of entering her, though, he twisted, crawling down her body on his hands and knees. She spread her legs, and as he bent to lap at her, her mouth touched his shaft once again, her swirling tongue running a racetrack around his throbbing erection.

He did the same with his own tongue, and Kitala gasped, her back arching. He did it again and again, becoming more excited with her every cry and touch, and it became a game, them mirroring each other, taking each other higher and higher with their fingers and mouths until they were coiled so tight with pleasure that when Kitala broke, he was there with her, shuddering and thrusting against her tight, wicked hands.

They collapsed into a tangled heap of arms and legs. Kitala started laughing weakly. M'cal dragged her close for a long, wet kiss that made her writhe beneath him, laughter still bubbling against his mouth. She sounded like music. Tasted the same.

But her stomach growled again. There was a box of plastic forks in the cabinet; they ate from the cans. M'cal was not hungry, but he forced himself to take each bite, soaking up the moment, every sound and breath and taste. The mundane felt fresh and new, like seeing a rainbow in color for the first time.

"Please tell me you have an outhouse and toilet paper," Kitala suddenly said, putting down her can of peaches. He hesitated, staring, and she closed her eyes like it suddenly hurt to look at him.

"Right," she muttered. "This is going to be ugly."

She wrapped the blanket around her body and with a brief, strained smile, marched out the front door. He hoped she knew better than to get close to nettles. Or poison ivy.

The thought made him stand up and go after her. Better safe than sorry. He was halfway to the door when he heard her scream.

M'cal ran. The air was cool outside, the sky blue. Evergreens glittered with dew. He could see the ocean and the edges of the cove, curling like rocky hands. But no Kitala. No sounds either. He did not call out to her. He listened inside his heart and looked for her the Krackeni way, as though separated with miles of ocean between them: soul to soul, because they were linked now, forever.

He found her, and the sensation felt like strings cutting into his skin. He ran, his voice rising out of his throat like a tidal wave, roaring. Through the trees he saw movement, dark clothing, and then Kitala cried out again, an angry shout. M'cal sang to her, savoring the surge of power twisting in his mouth. It was a different kind of melody; darker, savage. He had changed after Ivan. Something had changed.

He burst into a clearing filled with men, at least six, dressed in hunting fatigues, holding rifles. Not one of them moved, but their eyes rolled in his direction, and their breath rattled high and sharp in their throats. It was easy to control them. He could taste their souls fluttering, but he crushed those tiny wings, asserting his control. Like the witch, he was the puppeteer and his song was their strings. M'cal's voice snarled a harsher note and they fell to their knees.

Kitala stood on the far side of the clearing, clutching the blanket to her breasts. A woman held her around the throat, a pistol to her head. Black hair, dark eyes, lithe figure. Very familiar. Another man stood at her side. M'cal also knew his face. His throat was covered in a raw red line.

Both of the pair wore massive plastic guards over their ears, thin black wires trailing to pouches on their belts. Neither seemed affected by his voice. Nor did they appear surprised that he still lived.

"Close your mouth or I will shoot her," shouted the woman. *Yu*, he remembered. She spoke with an odd inflection, as though she could not hear herself. Her voice wavered, too; perhaps with stress.

M'cal looked at Kitala. Her eyes were wide, but her mouth was set, jaw tight. *Keep singing*, he imagined her saying, but then he heard those words again, louder inside his mind, and they felt like something more than just imagination. Intrusive, even.

Please, she whispered. *Run.*

The man beside Yu aimed his rifle at M'cal. There was a hand-axe strapped to his side. One shot, one hack. Game over. He did not think he could grow a new head.

But putting Kitala in the line of fire was no answer. There was no way to know how bad—or good—a shot these men on their knees really were. And he did not know how far her body could heal. No grandmother in sight, either.

Run, Kit pleaded, her gaze sliding sideways to the rifle pointed at his head. *They don't want me dead. You can find me. Please, M'cal.*

"Dick," said the woman, and the man's hand tightened on the trigger. Kitala cried out. M'cal changed his song—yanked a string.

One of the kneeling men threw himself at Dick, pushing aside the rifle just as it went off. The shot blasted a tree trunk near M'cal's head, but he was already moving, the men around him providing cover. His puppets jerked to their feet like unwilling zombies, eyes wild as they lay down their guns and shambled toward Dick. The man's rifle was torn out of his hands; he started screaming, swinging his fists. Yu staggered back, pale, dragging Kitala with her.

"I'll shoot her!" Yu screamed. "I'll fucking shoot her if you don't stop now!"

But Yu's finger did not tighten on the trigger, nor did she try to fend off Dick's attackers. She was too smart for that. She kept the gun right at Kitala's head, the best threat, the only way to keep herself safe.

One of the men ripped off Dick's earphones. A thick orange plug was also stuffed into his ear, but M'cal's voice penetrated and the man stopped fighting. Yu shouted his name, but it was too late. Dick pulled out the earplug. M'cal's voice was distorted, the monster in him rising with a howl.

Blood streamed from Dick's ears. The man went down hard, slamming his chin to the ground with a crack. His body jerked and shuddered; his heels drummed the ground. Blood leaked from his eyes and mouth. M'cal told him to die.

Yu finally fired her gun at M'cal, but her aim was bad and the bullet only grazed his arm. He ran. Heard thumps behind him as all the men he had been controlling fell unconscious. Once he felt them go down, he stopped singing and threw himself flat on the ground behind a broken tree trunk. Nettles burned his shoulder and thigh.

"Motherfucker!" Yu screamed brokenly. "I'm going to kill you!"

M'cal closed his eyes, reaching out to Kitala, following his instincts to track her along the bond he had made. He heard music in his head, a rumble of drums, and very tentatively called out her name. No response.

Yu still muttered to herself, followed by some sharp words to Kitala—but then branches started breaking and M'cal peered over the tree trunk and watched the two women march away through the forest, down to the shore. He followed them, quiet, and through the trees glimpsed something that had not been visible from the cabin: a small black speedboat, with oars attached. Silent entry, a loud fast escape. There was no other way to reach this place, unless a person wanted to hike ten miles from the highway. He could not imagine how they had been found. The witch he might understand tracking him, but Yu and those men . . .

M'cal crept down the hill. Yu still wore her earphones. Kitala did not struggle, nor did she look around for him. He tried reaching out to her again, pushing with all his strength along their bond, but nothing happened.

Yu stopped beside the boat and turned to gaze at the shore, the woods. M'cal kept his head down, peering through ferns. Kitala looked directly at his hiding place. She still had the blanket pressed to her breasts, her shoulders thrown back, her chin up. She stared right at him.

Yu stayed quiet, still watching the forest. The pistol dug harder into Kitala's temple. No one said a word.

The only sound was the water, lapping against the shore. Even the birds were quiet.

The woman pushed Kitala toward the boat. They waded out into the water, climbed up the short ladder, and stood for a moment, staring at each other. They said a few words that M'cal could not hear, but that resulted in Yu kicking Kitala in the stomach, sending her sprawling on the deck. M'cal flinched, digging his fingers into the ground so hard his nails tore.

Yu knelt. Her hands disappeared for a moment, but came back with handcuffs. She snapped one end around Kitala's right wrist, then hauled back Kit's left foot and clicked the other cuff around the ankle. Yu kicked away the blanket.

Kitala rolled herself around until she faced the forest. She looked again at M'cal's hiding place. Behind her, Yu dumped the oars and raised the anchor. She started the engine. The speedboat roared, spun like a top in the water, and then sliced a path toward the mouth of the cove. M'cal started running, hurtling toward the shore so quickly that when his foot touched sea, one leap was all it took to take him into deep water. He transformed, and swam after the speedboat.

He followed the boat north, up the coast, arms pressed tight against his sides as he made himself as long and straight as possible. He had raced dolphins as a teen, marked himself a winner on some occasions, a loser on others. Either way, he was fast. The problem was endurance. It had been a long time since he had pushed himself so hard. The witch's curse, the pain of the water, had made that impossible.

His body grew tired, the muscles in his tail aching, but he did not slow. He sang as he swam: great bellows of sound he pumped into the sea. He pushed harder, his voice building, power crackling through the water as he reached and reached, trying to do something—anything—to make himself faster, that boat slower. The orca pod was some distance away, but he heard their response.

He had no chance to reply. Something hard rammed his stomach, flipping him out of the water. He caught sight of Yu's boat, farther away than he had imagined, and then the sea closed over his head and he took another blow to the back, a slam to his head. Pain rushed in. He tried to use his voice, but hands clamped over his mouth, swiftly replaced by a sea sponge shoved hard against his tongue. He thrashed wildly, fighting the strong fingers squeezing his arms; glimpsed faces and flowing hair, the flash of scales. And then a net pressed upon his body, fibers cutting, and he was dragged down and down, screaming inside his mind, screaming for Kitala.

CHAPTER FIFTEEN

As the child of two musicians who could not in their wildest dreams afford day care—and who, as artists, might never consider day care as an option even if they *could* pay for it—Kit had spent much of her youth either alone at home, doors barred, or in the back rooms of bars, with a bag of books to keep her busy while one parent or another performed. Her mother and father were almost never on the same stage—different times, miles apart—but every bar was the same, as was the isolation, which was something that Kit had begun to view as the only way to be safe. Out of necessity, sheer desperation, her parents had taught her to be careful of strangers. To be wary, paranoid. To follow her gut. It was the best protection they could offer when the alternative was to starve. Or send her away.

Kit had learned the lesson well. So well it had become a way of life. Few friends, few enemies. Until now.

She did not bother trying to talk to Yu. The woman still wore earphones. Up close, Kit had heard music blaring out of them. Heavy metal, turned up to the max. Anything to drown out M'cal.

Someone knows who he is. Someone knows what he can do.

Dangerous. Unnerving. As was the fact they had been found at all, which implied an inside job—though Kit could think of no enemy except the witch—and it just did not seem her style. There was also Alice to consider, and the witch's interest in her.

It's all connected. What a mess you stumbled into. Marked for sure. Twisted up in fate.

No such thing as coincidence, her grandmother would say. Just threads, twining and weaving into something resembling free will, choice. But to Kit, that free will suddenly felt like sitting in the eye of a needle with a big fat piece of thread poking and poking, trying to spear her through. And out there, holding that thread, was some unseen force whose only goal was to knock her out and dead.

She managed to sit up, craning her neck to peer over the edge of the boat. The ride was rough, the winds strong. She searched the sea behind them and saw nothing except one brief flash above the water—a long, pale shape catching the sun and disappearing. Kit kept watch, but saw nothing else.

M'cal, she thought, reaching out. For a moment, she imagined a real connection, but the emotions that crowded her were so tumultuous, so full of fear and anger and desperation, she jerked away from them, gasping. Yu glanced back at her, mouth twisting open—the edge of a shout, a scream—but all those contortions ended in nothing but silence and a knowing, chilling smile.

Kit took a deep breath, tearing away her gaze,

steadying herself, pretending she had a fiddle in her hands, her precious fiddle, bow streaking sound like lightning crashing in the clouds. Hot, bright, quick. A symphony running ragged in her ears and heart, building secret strains, mystery. She remembered her grandmother; remembered holding out her eight-year-old hand, being touched on the palm and feeling a spark run through her, flinching as actual light flashed beneath their two bits of flesh.

Magic, Old Jazz Marie had whispered. *Magic in your soul. In all you do, little cat. All you need, right there. So open your heart. Believe.*

Believe. That was the problem. Kit believed, and did not want to. Had always restricted herself to the straight and narrow—or as straight and narrow as an artist could be. Professionally, she was a hurricane. Personally, just a trickle in a narrow stream.

And this . . . magic that she could supposedly do was too new. It frightened her. Even trying to connect with M'cal, though she seemed to have done it several times already, felt too new and uncertain to be trusted as fact and not some odd rambling of her imagination. That old resistance coming through.

She saw islands in the distance, small hills of rock and evergreen pushing up from the sea like living gems. It was only the second time Kitala had ever been up close to similar natural features; she had used part of her first big paycheck from the record company to pay for a family vacation to Nova Scotia so that her father could meet members of his family whom he had not seen in almost twenty years. Musicians, too; sometimes it seemed like her entire family had songs in their blood, tapping out melodies in the womb. The land was similar there as well. As had been Kit's sense of mystery, staring at the ocean. Not so far wrong, to imagine so many riddles beneath the waves.

There were other boats in the vicinity, but none near enough to see her awkward situation. Yu kept a wide distance, though she suddenly glanced sharply left. Kit followed her gaze and saw tall black fins sweep up from the water. Air blasted high and loud from blowholes. A great surge of hope leapt into her throat as the orcas drew near. Yu frowned, steering away from them. The speedboat increased its velocity, bouncing harder against the waves. The orcas fell slightly behind, but did not disappear. The pod spread out, flanking them like a pack of wolves, hunting. Kit thought she recognized the old female she had ridden, but maybe it was instinct, a gut reaction to the orca leading the fringe.

Yu glanced over her shoulder, staring. "What is this?"

The cop could read lips—Kit had discovered that during their brief exchange after climbing into the speedboat, but she saw no reason to indulge Yu's questions. Instead, she turned back to the orcas, searching for any sign of M'cal. There was no trace of him. Perfectly logical, but it made her uneasy.

Kit closed her eyes, cradling her spirit around the quivering note resting in her heart—one shining shard of music not her own, but wholly M'cal. She pretended her grandmother was with her, hand to hand, voice in her ears. Whispering. Telling secrets.

A chill passed through Kit's shoulders. She opened her eyes. She half expected to see her grandmother, but no one was there. She was getting too used to miracles.

Kit raised her head to the wind, drinking in the salt, the cold. She looked again at the orcas, slicing the ocean some twenty feet behind the boat. One of them lifted itself just a little higher from the water—the pod leader, she thought—and inside Kit's heart, in that place where M'cal resided, she imagined something else taking root: connections and language, all bound up in a sense of protection, duty.

Images passed through her mind—herself jumping, orcas carrying her, biting the links binding her limbs. Taking her to freedom. To M'cal.

Come to us. We will carry you.

Kit stared. Felt like she was drowning above water, suffocating. Too much information, too much choice. But she grabbed the edge of the speedboat, hauling herself up on one foot. Looked out at the rushing ocean, the orcas. It would be a leap of faith. She would either live or die. But she was desperate enough. And she believed in magic now. Miracles. Kit set her jaw and tensed her legs.

A hand grabbed her hair and hauled back, slamming her into the deck. Kit lashed out, aiming her fingers at Yu's wild eyes. Poke and gouge—she remembered that much from her mother's lessons—but the cop batted her hand away, mouth contorted in a snarl that was part fury but mostly disbelief.

The woman dragged Kit to the front of the boat, cuffing her other hand to the railing behind the driver's seat. Several orcas bounded dangerously close. Yu took out her gun and fired at one of the creatures. Kit saw the impact; blood spurted. The orca dove. Yu whirled and slammed her hand on the accelerator, pushing it up to the maximum. The boat lurched, hurtling against the choppy waves. The orcas were left behind. And with them, Kit's chance of escape. Her disappointment tasted bitter.

After several minutes, Yu slowed the boat, driving close to a hulking precipice of rock jutting from the sea. What had seemed like a tiny island from far away felt, up close, like the opening strains of the Sacrificial Dance from the *Rite of Spring*. At the top of the sheer cliff, evergreens covered the island, tall and dark, holding shadows under the morning sun. The wind shrieked.

Yu steered them slowly around the rock face, following the broad curve of ragged rock. Ahead of them, Kit glimpsed a flat outcropping of stone. At first she thought it was a natural protrusion, but as they grew closer, she saw moorings, steps, a smooth, polished surface that was definitely man-made. A nice illusion, though.

Yu cut the engine, letting the boat drift up against the stone dock. Kit glimpsed movement at the end of it, along a path leading down from the tree line. There were four men in dark gear, guns strapped to their hips. They were short, with tough faces, carrying themselves with less ease than Yu but with more professionalism than Dutch and his cavemen friends.

As the men walked down the dock, Yu yanked up one of the seats, revealing a hidden compartment. She pulled out sweats and a T-shirt, tossed them to the deck beside Kit, and crouched to unlock her restraints. Kit did not ask, and Yu did not have to explain. Kit dressed fast, and was just tugging the sweats over her hips when the men arrived.

They looked at Kit with some interest, but nothing lascivious. *Professionals,* she thought again. Men used to this sort of thing, with a job to perform that had nothing to do with ogling.

Yu stripped off her earphones. An electric guitar

shrieked. The woman had orange molds in her ears, and she pulled those out, too, hitting a button at her waist. The music stopped.

"Put her with the others," Yu said. "Remember your instructions, Hartlett. All of you."

"Yes, ma'am," said one of the men. He was blond, with a thick neck and forearms roped by bulging veins. He looked Kit in the eye with absolutely no expression and hauled her out of the boat. Her hands got close to his gun—negligence, on his part—but she did not make a grab for it. Not yet. Too many people, all of them standing far too close. Any one of them could shoot her before she had a chance to pull the trigger. She was no Annie Oakley.

Hartlett took her arm and marched her up the stone dock. Kit glanced over her shoulder at the three men following them, and saw Yu watching them from the boat. Her hand was on her gun. She looked like she wanted to take a shot. Kit thought of Yu's partner, Dick, his brain bleeding out on the forest floor. She could not bring herself to feel remorse.

The dock bled into a set of rock stairs carved into the island. Kit kept pace with Hartlett, stealing glances at the sea. In the far distance she saw a ferry, some sailboats. No orcas. And, obviously, no M'cal. She tried to reach for him again and hit a wall. Stumbled.

Hartlett grunted, glancing sideways at her. Kit took the opening. "Why am I here? Who do you work for?"

Harlett did not answer, looked straight ahead and kept on walking. Kit thought again about his gun. She also thought about her own supposed power. Her . . . magic. M'cal said she could do extraordinary things. Her grandmother had told her the same, in more ways than one.

You can move the stars.

Move the stars with a song, so Old Jazz Marie had said. And while that was fine to hear, putting such a promise to practical use was another matter entirely. Could Kit free herself now? Make a run for it? Maybe steal that boat down below, or find another. Even jumping into the sea and risking hypothermia all over again would be better than whatever was waiting for her up ahead. She was certain of it.

The gris-gris bounced against her chest. The leather was soft, warm, like her grandmother's hands. Kit thought about the song Old Jazz Marie had made her listen to, the song of her soul, which had lurked in the background of her mind ever since that dream of the veranda and conch. Dawnlight and thunder, sleeping under the cover of her thoughts.

But when she tried to pull the music free, nothing happened. No surge of symphony, no melodic tumult. There was music in her head, but nothing with teeth. As though it were rote, mechanical, without inspiration. An odd sensation, totally unlike anything Kit had ever experienced. She was *always* on. Always inspired. And she could feel it still, waiting. Part of her, holding in that fire.

Not time, a small voice whispered. *Not time, yet.*

The climb was steep. Kit's legs burned, as did her lungs. The rock steps turned to hard-packed earth that was soft on her naked feet, except for the occasional stone and twig. The feeling of cold earth helped center and calm her; she focused on the sensation, pretending she was part of the soil, that her roots extended deep into the stone, winding with the trees and the sea. Breath to breeze, slow heartbeat to a slower tide.

The path curled into the forest, which was thick,

quiet. No birds. No breeze, though only moments before, the wind had swept off the ocean, somewhere between a fluttering wing and a cannon blast against her body. Here, everything was still. Hushed. Kit's gaze roamed, searching. She felt like someone was watching her. Not the men, either. They were not as dangerous as those eyes she imagined peeling back her skin.

Kit glimpsed structures—several of them—and moments later they entered a wide clearing. A log cabin squatted in the center. No windows. It was very large. Several outbuildings perched nearby, but they were nothing, barely noticeable. Kit's focus was only on the cabin. Looking at it felt like seeing a future victim of murder—as though a house could die—except all she saw was a shadow, an aura hovering over the entire structure like the hand of a giant ghost. Kit balked as Harlett tried to guide her close to it. He yanked on her upper arm, but she dug in her heels, fighting. Another man grabbed her shoulder and wrist, wrenching her arm behind her back. Kit bit back a cry of pain, took one stiff-legged step . . . and then dropped to her knees. The bastards were going to have to carry her in. She was not going to help them. Not into *that* place.

Harlett never said a word, and the men with him followed his example. He grabbed her shoulders, while two others each took an ankle in their hands. They picked her up. Hauled her in.

The interior of the log cabin was dark, with only a candle burning in a sconce nailed into the wall. The golden light flickered, casting eerie shadows in the air—dancing shapes that oozed with far too much life. Again Kit felt like she was entering Death; as though murder slept and she stood in its beating heart, waiting for it to wake. Or begin to dream.

There was no furniture. Hartlett and his men set her down. Her feet touched something soft, yielding. The sensation was a shock, and Kit looked down at the floor. It was covered in sand. White sand, finer than anything found on a beach—soft as silk, delicate as powdered sugar. For a moment, she considered the possibility of cocaine—a mountain of it—but that made even less sense, and she remembered with hard clarity her dream about M'cal and how he had lain in a circle of sand, restrained and tortured.

A deep chill struck Kit. She felt like she stood on a mass grave, except the people underneath were still not dead.

She had long stopped fighting the men. Three of them backed away, out of the log cabin. Hartlett gave Kit a hard look, but when she did not make any move to run, he pointed to her left, down a long corridor she had not noticed, and gestured for her to precede him. She did, fighting the beginning of a shudder. No use holding it in, though; her reaction to the cabin and the sand beneath her feet was too visceral.

The sand stopped at the edge of the room. They walked down a hall lined with closed doors; a horror movie mystery, Kit thought, with a monster hidden behind every door. And in front of her, looming like a shining tooth at the end of the corridor, was a metal door. Rubber seals lined its edges.

Hartlett had a set of keys in his pocket. He unlocked the door and yanked it open.

It was like unwrapping the interior of a blast furnace; hot air rolled out, searing Kit in the face. Worse was the smell—like being chin-deep in a hole full of rotting flesh and raw sewage, sun-baked and oozing.

Hartlett grabbed her around the waist and shoved.

Kit fought, tried grabbing his gun. He caught her wrist, twisting until her knees buckled and she staggered.

"In," he said, voice strained. He heaved her forward, and Kit fell hard on her knees, scrambling past the pain to stand and turn. Too late. The door had closed. It clicked, the seals making a sucking sound. Trapping her in darkness. She felt like Aida in the tomb, only there was no M'cal to be her Radames.

The air was suffocating, foul. Kit struggled not to gag—fought, too, the paralyzing terror that swept through her body like a wash of cold sea. Her throat locked up, as did her heart, stuttering itself into sickness. Kit grappled with herself, struggling for an anchor, control.

She found M'cal. Suddenly a flash—that sliver of his soul, a needle bright. Her mind latched tight to his presence, cradling in on itself to rock and rock, like a child lost in the dark. Feeling him with her, no matter how distant their separation, made the terror ease. Her breathing steadied. Her heartbeat slowed.

But Kit still shivered, despite the heat. Riding the edge of shock. Blind as a bat. She wondered if that was a good thing. As she calmed, she heard all around her the low rustle of bodies. Low rasps of breath.

Again, horror clawed up her throat. The bogeyman was rearing its ugly head, and she stepped backward until her shoulders pressed against the sweating metal of the door. She thought of M'cal. Wished for him. Heard nothing but silence inside her mind.

"Hello?" she called softly to those bodies shifting quietly unseen all around her. Like dying butterflies trapped in a cocoon.

No one answered. Kit stopped trying. She was afraid of the reply.

CHAPTER SIXTEEN

Down into places where the sun never reached, where cracks open in the earth—descending into oubliettes and graves for lost souls; another world, alien to the one above the sea, which took for granted the stationary and concrete, opposites of light and dark, whereas here there was only dark, the endless night, no sky or stars to set a dream upon—M'cal's captors took him into the abyss, more than twelve hundred feet down. His body adjusted to the pressure, as did his eyesight—a second lid fell over his pupils as the waters pushed and pushed. He began to grow physically uncomfortable, though; deeper waters meant less oxygen, and for the first time in a long while, he began to feel a hint of cold.

There were three Krackenis: two males, one female. All were fast, lean, hard; faces sharper than knives, more alien than even M'cal. His human blood had put curves into his bones, made his shoulders broader, larger. But he was not nearly as fast. A lifetime on shore, and he was weak in comparison. Soft, even. He had not realized—had been around so few of his kind, except his father.

Kitala, stay alive. Kitala, fight. Kitala, I will find you. He fought to reach her along the link between their souls, but it was difficult to focus; he was too enraged. Years of wishing for contact from his people—some acknowledgment that he was not alone—and now, this. Beaten and gagged, caught in a net, dragged away from the mate they must surely sense inside his heart—and there was no reason M'cal could think of why such a thing should happen. It made no sense.

At the ocean bottom, the Krackeni men tied strips of the net around craggy rocks, binding M'cal's arms above his head. Having secured him, they floated backward, staring. Their hair was long and pale, decorated with shells and precious stones. Black pearls the size of eyeballs looped around the waist of the woman, alongside a dagger cut from obsidian.

The men were pierced with bone. Long, curving shards laced through the skin of their forearms—horizontal spikes, an artful mutilation. Spears hung against their backs. All three of them shone with a faint pale glow: bioluminescence, good for the deep sea. Their eyes were large, too, and their nostrils small, their noses hardly visible. These weren't members of any colony that had ever mixed with humans; the evidence of their Krackeni blood was too alien. M'cal wondered if their bones were soft, too; if they were one of the deep-sea people. It was beginning to seem that way. It might not even be possible for them to ever mix with humans on land; their skeletons would be too soft, the cavities in their bodies not easy shifted.

The Krackenis hovered apart from him, whispering to each other with whistles and clicks—an intricate dance of sound. M'cal understood them, though the accent was peculiar. He also doubted his ability to speak fluently. It had been a long time.

Look at his hair, said one of the men, darting a glance at him. *Black as your knife.*

So human. His blood is thick with them. The woman bared her teeth with a sharp hiss and touched her dagger. *As is his heart. He has taken a human as his wife. Perhaps we should cut her out of him?*

The second male drifted close, peering at M'cal like he was some strange beast, hardly capable of emotion or intelligence. It was a disturbing sensation, far too familiar. Nor was the irony lost on M'cal. He was an object, even amongst his own kind. Always the outsider. And the sense of betrayal and loss associated with that was unexpected. He had not realized until this moment how strongly he had anticipated seeing other Krackenis again.

He tested his bonds, but the net was secure. The sponge was thick in his mouth. He thought of Kitala, tried singing inside his head, but whatever worked for her was clearly not the same for him, and all he did was become even more agitated. He stared at the Krackenis. Watched them stare back. Saw, with some uneasiness, how their eyes suddenly shifted to look at some spot over his shoulder.

He sensed movement behind him. A hand touched the net just above his face. On the hand was a ring. Golden. A wedding band.

M'cal closed his eyes.

A voice filled the water; music, a low, keening melody that sounded like the first edge of some endless sob, cutting ragged like teeth. It was a painful sound, stripped bare of any joy, rolling down into M'cal's heart and holding there, holding him just as surely as the witch. He felt that voice search his soul, held himself strong against that touch, and just when the music threatened to break him into something small and sad, the voice eased off, withdrew, and quieted into the silence of the sea.

He opened his eyes and through the net saw a face, pale and blond and strong; an older mirror of his own, though M'cal had gotten his coloring from his mother. No Krackeni of pure blood had dark hair.

The two men stared at each other. The others gathered close, also watching, no longer so distant or disdainful. M'cal did not care.

S'har Abreeni had aged since M'cal had last seen him. There were more lines in his face, sharp wrinkles that only served to accent his already angular features. He was built differently than the other Krackenis; his ancestors were from warmer seas, accustomed to living near the surface—a lifestyle his father still led, or had the last M'cal had heard. There was a world of uninhabited islands dotting the South Pacific, and those sandy shores were perfect for colonies who preferred mixing land with sea. Such Krackenis could also mingle more easily with humans if they wished. There, their features were not so alien.

His father gestured to the others. *Set him loose. He is safe.*

Not quite, M'cal thought. The Krackenis hesitated but did as they were told, loosening the knots of the net until he could move his arms. He tore the sponge from his mouth, fighting down a sudden burst of rage.

You did this, he said to his father, who watched him with shadowed eyes, his long, lean body holding off the currents with gentle movements of his hands and tail. His scales gleamed in the glow of the other Krackenis. They watched M'cal, too, but with a great deal more wariness.

He paid them no mind, staring only at his father—who remained impassive, as though it had not been ten years between them without a word.

I had to be sure, he said quietly. *I had to know it was not a trap.*

A trap? M'cal echoed, dazed, still unable to accept the presence of the man in front of him. His father's mouth settled into a hard line.

A trap. From the woman who put that *on you.* Fury danced through his face as he glanced at the bracelet—the rage was there and gone, swallowed up by a cool mask. He glanced at the other Krackenis and told them, *Leave us.*

No, replied the woman, fingering her dagger as the currents slid her pale hair in a tangle around her face. *There is a matter to be discussed, now that we have fulfilled our bargain.*

Bargain. An ominous word in M'cal's estimation. He had no time, though. No desire to be caught in yet more words. Not even for his father. He looked up and could not see the light of day, but he reached deep inside his heart and found Kitala. Good as sunlight, warm and sweet.

I must go, he said to his father. *Right now.*

You may not, said the woman, glancing at her fellow Krackenis. *Not until we have settled.*

M'cal briefly shut his eyes, the monster stirring inside his throat. *Settled what?*

Later, said his father, curtly.

No, said one of the men, glancing at M'cal. *He should be part of it, too.*

The female Krackeni gave him a disgusted look. *He is impure. To mix our blood—*

I said later, snarled M'cal's father. *Let my son go. Now.*

The outburst was shocking, raw, unlike anything M'cal remembered about his father, who had always been the cool one—unlike his wife, the firebrand; impulsive, ready for a fight.

The Krackenis stared at S'har, until only the woman made a sound, her mouth twisting into a sneer that was too much like the witch for M'cal's comfort. *You should never have taken a human as your mate, S'har. Bad, all around. And now he has done the same. A disgrace. Neither of you have fulfilled your duties as the others have.*

Duty? M'cal stared, clarity burning. *I have fulfilled my duty. Paid dearly for it. The things that have been done to me—*

Are your *fault.* The woman bared her teeth, which were almost as sharp as Ivan's. *You were weak. Your human blood, contaminating your abilities. If you had been strong enough, you would* never *have submitted—*

Enough! hissed S'har, his power striking through the water with such ferocity M'cal felt it vibrate in the marrow of his bones. The other Krackenis froze, paralyzed, their bodies instantly tilting and drifting in the current like stiff dolls.

You forget yourselves, M'cal's father continued, each word hard and dripping with power. *You forget who I am.* He released his hold. The Krackenis folded in on themselves, and he drifted backward, gesturing for M'cal to follow.

The woman said, with rather less ferocity, *You promised.*

And I will keep my promise. Later. He caught M'cal's eye, expression inscrutable, and the two of them began a swift ascent, leaving behind the other Krackenis.

The entire length of M'cal's body prickled; he felt like a moving target. But they did not follow.

Above, the world lightened. Fish darted past them; M'cal inhaled the taste of boat fuel and listened for the orcas. Listened for Kitala, too. He glanced sideways at his father, taking in the long, sharp face, those lines and the turn of his mouth. He was afraid of looking too long—afraid his father would look back—and all the pain and joy and fear he felt at being in S'har's presence again felt like an open wound rubbed with poison and salt.

What are you doing here? M'cal finally asked. *Why now?*

His father twisted, graceful as a dolphin. *You assume too much. I have been here for years. Ever since I learned of your misfortune.* As M'cal stopped swimming, his father slowed and gazed back at him with tired eyes. *There are no secrets in the sea. You should know that. And I had a friend nearby, watching you.*

The seal, M'cal replied, thinking of that constant gentle presence every time he entered the ocean.

Yes, said his father. *It was too dangerous to go near you. I tried once, and suffered for it.*

She wanted to isolate me.

You killed for her.

I did.

And now? S'har reached out and touched his son's chest. *Who is she?*

My life, M'cal told him. *She is my life.*

His father looked away. Somewhere distant, M'cal heard the orcas crying. Their voices were distressed.

One of the pod had been injured. A blast. M'cal reached out to their minds, pushing hard across the expanse between them, and caught an image of the black speedboat, Kitala ready to jump . . . and that woman, Yu, hauling her down. Firing a gun.

His father made a low clicking sound at the back of his throat. *You should go. Hurry.*

M'cal looked at him. *Will you come?*

His father said nothing, but M'cal held his gaze, heart screaming—for the both of them; for his mother, for Kitala.

Please forgive me, he whispered, holding out his hand. His father did not even look at it.

Go, S'har said, and without a backward glance descended into the darkness like a ghost. Gone, again. Almost as if he had never existed.

M'cal drifted in the water, staring. He did not try to follow. The orcas called to him. Kitala was out there, somewhere.

He began to swim away, felt a swirl behind him and turned just in time to catch a rush of scales and blond hair. He twisted, grabbing the slender wrist arching toward his shoulder, wrenched back and squeezed. Bone gave way—soft cartilage—and M'cal felt it tear like paper. A scream pounded the water. An obsidian dagger drifted down into the shadows.

M'cal did not let go. He swung the Krackeni female around and held her tight against his body. She did not struggle long—not when she looked into his eyes. He did not know what she saw, but he knew what he felt, and it was ugly, dangerous.

M'cal snarled, his voice whistling through the water with enough force to make her flinch. *I have done nothing to you. Nothing to deserve this.*

She threw back her chin. *It was not to be a killing blow. Merely a reminder. You are not of us, and never will be.*

And you care so much? Words would be enough.

No, she whispered, eyes narrowing. *I have been promised a child, a child of your father's blood. Your sibling. But when he is born, he will know nothing of you. You will not exist to him. I wanted you to know that. I wanted you to remember it, in your flesh.*

M'cal threw her away, disgusted. He caught movement from the corner of his eye, saw his father rising again from the shadows. For a moment M'cal wanted to use his voice, to hurt them both. To hurt them like he hurt. To make their hearts break. But he clamped his mouth shut, looked away from the growing triumph in the Krackeni female's eyes, and left. Swam fast. Did not look back to see if his father watched him go. He felt like a child again, and he could not afford that. Not now. Being here was poison.

He followed the song of the orcas, pushing through the sea as quickly as he could. He avoided sailboats, jet skis, felt the wake of their passage above his head as he raced out of sight beneath the waves. He threw aside his grief, focusing on Kitala, feeling her inside him, pulsing. His only home. The only one who mattered.

The orcas met him halfway, a tourist boat in hot pursuit. M'cal had to slow—they begged him—and he took a moment to check the wound of the female who had been shot, the orca sinking underwater out of view of the humans topside. The bullet had stopped within the top layer of fat. The wound continued to leak blood, but not enough to kill. M'cal was more concerned about removing the bullet. The risk of lead poisoning and infection was great, even to a creature so large.

His fingernails were hooked like claws. He asked for permission—received it—and placed a hand on the orca's side, humming a soothing melody. The pod leader led a small group away from them—a diversion, for the tourist boat—while the others gathered close, bracing the injured orca. M'cal steeled himself and dug his finger into the wound.

The orca whistled, jerking, but the others held her still and M'cal worked fast, grappling for the bullet. His fingernail hooked around it and he tugged, scraping out the flattened slug. More blood clouded the water, but again, nothing lethal. The wounded orca filled his mind with her thoughts and memories; images, fleeting: Kitala, dragged by her hair down the length of that boat; the wildness in her face as she watched the gun fired, every detail caught by sharp eyes.

M'cal pushed backward through the water. The orcas did not follow. He did not want them to. But they let him go with a song, and the warmth of their inclusion—as though he were one of them—was in such stark opposition to what he had just endured, he felt the warm sting of it in his throat.

He reached for Kitala again. The link was too new to him, and he was too inexperienced, to know exactly all that he could do with it, but he carried himself along the bond between them, letting it guide him in the same way he was guided by the witch—instinct, compulsion.

An island rose before him. Underwater, it was a rocky monolith riding down into the sea; above, more stone and trees, with smooth walls like a fortress. Too high to climb. Only one way in, and one way out—unless a person was prepared to jump.

There were no fish around the island. No life at all. The waters were empty. After a moment, M'cal understood why. He could feel, in the sea, a subtle push like shooing hands sinking deep into his mind, reinforcing the instinct to turn away. He recognized the feeling; the witch had used something similar to keep the curious from her yacht. It was a reverse compulsion, spread indiscriminately over a particular area, so subtle that most might never realize the manipulation. M'cal certainly would not have, not before the witch.

He could feel Kitala on the surface, though, pulsing like a second heartbeat in his chest. He circled the island and, halfway around, saw the hull of a boat above his head, moored to an outcropping of stone jutting up from the sea. M'cal surfaced carefully, his cheek pressed against the black hull. He listened for a moment, tasting the air for a soul. Diving again, he circled the speedboat and poked his head above the water beside the stone dock. From his vantage point, the boat appeared empty.

M'cal shifted his legs and climbed onto the dock. Nothing happened. No shots were fired, no cries of alarm. His skin prickled, though. He felt . . . watched.

A path led away from the dock. M'cal hesitated, still listening hard, but his options were limited and he started running up the rock steps, trying to be quiet, fast. The trees pressed around him. They made him feel vulnerable—he had always found forests unnerving. He appreciated the beauty, but their mystery was something foreign, indecipherable—unlike the sea, which could be counted on for its chaos, its simplicity of instinct, a lack of any barrier. There were no walls in the sea. Like soaring through the clouds above mountains, chasms, wrecks, and worries, the sea was utter, total freedom of body and in spirit.

Unless, of course, one incurred the loathing of fellow Krackenis. Which M'cal seemed to have done, just by breathing.

Sibling. A child promised. Bargain and settlement. Those words raced through his mind before he could set them aside. He did not want to think about his father right now. Or what his father had promised. The possibility was too disturbing—almost as disturbing as M'cal's memories of the witch's rape. It felt the same. He did not know why.

Music swelled in his head. He stopped on the path, testing the air, listening hard. He heard nothing, but instinct tugged him into the underbrush where he crouched behind thick ferns, his toes digging into soft black earth and moss.

Less than a minute later, two men walked past his hiding place. No warning; they made not a sound, moving easily, with dangerous grace. As they passed out of sight, M'cal opened his mouth, prepared to call them back. He could use some information.

A hand touched his shoulder. He flinched, spinning. Sucked in a deep breath, prepared to implode a brain. Prepared to do so regardless when he saw who it was.

"Hey," Koni whispered, glancing over M'cal's shoulder at the path. "About time you got here."

M'cal gritted his teeth. "Kitala?"

Koni slapped his shoulder. He was naked, too. "Come on. I'll show you."

The two men moved quickly through the underbrush; nettles slapped, thorns tore, rocks cut into feet. M'cal felt burdened by his body; it was clumsy, far too large for stealth. The forest was different from the sea, and worse, he'd been growing used to his old body after years of painful separation. Legs could not compare to the grace of cutting through water with fin and tail.

Koni did not seem so burdened. He moved silently, on light feet, like a ghost.

"Was she hurt?" M'cal asked him. "How many men?"

"Not hurt, but not happy," Koni replied curtly, "and I've counted only five individuals on this island. Might be more, but right now, that's the best I've got."

"How did you find her?"

"The guys and I made it back to the cove about an hour ago. Found out fast that something bad had happened. I asked around, and some seagulls pointed me in the right direction. I haven't been back to tell the others yet. Hari's probably shitting kittens."

"Two of our attackers were prepared for me," M'cal said. "Ear guards, to protect against my voice. I do not understand why the rest of the men with them were not similarly guarded."

"Pawns. Fodder." Koni glanced at him, golden eyes glittering. "A way of testing your strength, perhaps. Take your best guess."

M'cal did not want to. The implications were too disturbing. He pushed onward, struggling. Several minutes later, though, with their destination still not in sight, he said, "The island cannot be so big. Are you certain we are not lost?"

Koni hesitated, glancing back at him. "We should have been there by now. I'll check."

Golden light swarmed up through Koni's skin. M'cal reached out and touched him. "Wait."

M'cal felt odd. His skin tingled, as did the bracelet. Not with the old compulsion, but something different. He had the urge to sing—an overwhelming desire. He gave in only so far as to hum—faint, melodic, allow-ing the music to run its course through his voice as he released the notes softly into the air. He felt, for a moment, that his song had a life of its own—intelligence, purpose—and that it was searching for something.

The world around him wavered; the trees wiggled for one brief moment in an improbable zigzag motion that seemed less like dizziness or exhaustion and more like something from a B-movie adaptation of *Island of the Damned*. M'cal had seen enough television to know what *that* looked like.

Fake. Rough.

"An illusion," M'cal whispered with dreadful clarity. "This is not real."

"What?" Koni asked, but he stopped, staring at a tree. M'cal followed his gaze. The rough bark was glittering, leaking some black substance that looked like liquid hematite, or some thick oil filled with metal shards.

"Go," M'cal breathed, and then again: "*Go!*"

Golden light erupted from Koni's skin, black feathers sweeping across his exposed flesh, rippling and pushing like an earthquake. M'cal felt the physical heat of the shift as he turned to sweep his gaze through the forest—the now bleeding illusion. Koni threw back his head, face contorting, narrowing; his soul being reborn into another body.

The change done, Koni threw himself into the air . . . and hit the sky above their heads with a thud. It was a hard impact, totally unexpected. Koni almost fell to the ground, but he rallied himself and tried again. Several feet above M'cal's head, the shapeshifter ran into something hard enough to make him lose feathers. He plummeted, and M'cal caught him. Koni squawked. Blood seeped from the edge of his beak, and his eyes glowed with furious light.

The trees wavered. The sky flickered—then disappeared entirely.

A rush of cold air swept over M'cal's skin. He kept singing, reaching out with his voice, searching for some taste of souls. Anything, as the world was replaced with darkness, shadows cut with some distant flicker of natural light. He saw stone walls, rough-hewn. Dirt on the ground. A cave. A cave with a narrow iron grate barring the only way out. They had walked, blind and deceived, into a trap.

On the other side stood a woman. Headphones on. Gun out.

M'cal sang louder, pushing his voice, surrounding the woman like a cloud of mosquitoes buzzing, searching for a place to bite. He found nothing. She continued to stare, impassive, her mouth set in a hard, cold line. M'cal set Koni down in the shadows behind him—hoped he stayed a bird, a small, dark target—and walked up to the barrier.

Yu never blinked. M'cal stopped singing. He expected her to shoot him, but all she did was hold the gun, her finger loose and easy on the trigger. Behind her, movement. Four men. All of them were wearing protective gear over their ears.

M'cal turned back to Koni, who was still in his crow form. He did not worry about speaking softly when he said, "No matter what happens, stay small, quiet. Do nothing. Pretend you are dumb. Even if they know differently, it might save you. Please. Do not give them an excuse."

Someone has to survive this. Someone has to help Kitala.

Koni's eyes flashed, but he backed deeper into the

shadows, tucking his small body inside a shallow alcove. He blended perfectly.

The metal grate rasped. M'cal turned. Yu swung open the barrier. The four men preceded her, ranging out across the small space between them, weapons pointed at his head. M'cal did not sing. He watched their eyes. Wondered if he could move fast enough to rip off those earphones, from which trickled the low bass of some pounding music.

Yu gestured to the men. One of them—the only blond of the group—nodded curtly. He shot out M'cal's kneecap.

The roar of gunfire in such a small space rebounded like an explosion, drowning out his scream. M'cal managed to bite back his cries, but the pain dulled his brain to nothing but a thick slab of meat, his thoughts reduced entirely to instinct—and Kitala. She burned inside him. He clung to that fire, taking shelter.

Sanity returned in pieces; he thought of Koni, but heard nothing. No outburst. He did not dare look to see if the bird-man was still in the alcove, but focused on the feminine face swimming close to his own. Boots stood on his wrists. Hands held his ankles. His left leg felt loose, hardly connected to the rest of him.

Yu's face cleared in his vision. He watched her hand slide behind her back, under her shirt. M'cal heard a hissing sound, and her hand reappeared with an eight-inch curved blade. She looked M'cal in the eye, held his gaze . . . and jammed the knife into his chest, twisting hard. He fought so hard not to cry out that he felt like he broke something in his throat.

"I've never known a man who can't die," Yu finally

said, her voice thick, more raw than her eyes, which remained cold, hard. "But I guess I can learn to appreciate it."

And she twisted the knife again, aiming for his heart.

CHAPTER SEVENTEEN

Kit lost track of time, as well as her fear, though it lingered, pressing in upon her like the edge of a scream. After nothing stole in from the dark to hurt her, though, she began to feel slightly ridiculous about her initial terror. A calm head—that was what she needed.

Kit finally sat down. She did not want to, was afraid of how filthy the floor might be, but she was tired and her body ached. She gave in, and was relieved to find her section of the floor completely dry, free of whatever made the rest of the room reek. She could guess what that was—she needed to go to the bathroom so bad it hurt—but who else was in here with her, and why, was the big question.

She leaned against the door and closed her eyes. Passed the time. Thought of her parents, wishing very much she had called them. They might even be on a plane by now to Vancouver.

The darkness, too, was a reminder of her father. When she was twelve, he had temporarily given up his music to go back to Kentucky and work in the mines.

Too desperate for anything else. A bad year for Kit and her mother. Worrying about him, worrying about themselves. She remembered lying in bed at night with her eyes closed, pretending she was her father, deep underground. Suffering for money. Those long, elegant hands, those deft fingers, cutting rock instead of music.

But now it was Kit in the mine—a cave-in—fighting for her life instead of cold, hard cash. Not for the first time, she wished she could see her death, know for certain if murder was her fate. Not that it would help. She would still fight, even if it was. But she wanted to know.

She heard a cough. In front of her, to the left. Her first human sound since entering this place. It was low, feminine; almost a gasp for air.

"Hello?" Kit asked softly.

Silence. And then, barely a whisper: "Ms. Bell."

Kit closed her eyes, heart lurching. After everything she had gone through, it seemed impossible. "Alice. You're alive."

"Am I?" The woman sounded exhausted, ill. "That's too bad."

Kit stood, awkward. "Where are you?"

"Stay where you are. It's a . . . mess . . . over here."

She ignored her, edging into the darkness inch by inch; as if she were hanging in the abyss, surrounded by ghosts. Alice, nothing more than a spirit speaking from the void. Kit tried breathing through her mouth. Her feet touched something wet and she stopped, cringing.

Kit swallowed hard. "Talk to me. I need to know where you are."

"Please, don't."

"Are you restrained?"

"You're close enough."

"If you're tied, maybe there's something I can do."

Kit heard metal jingle. Alice said, "I doubt it. Please. Let me pretend to have some dignity."

Dignity. There was power in that word. Kit tightened her jaw and sidled back the way she had come, trying to dry her wet foot on the hard floor. When her back hit the door again, she asked, "What is this place and who is doing this?"

Alice said nothing. Kit closed her eyes again, shifting painfully. She was going to have an accident soon if she did not relieve herself.

Dignity, she thought. *More dignified not to wet your pants, right?*

Not when the only alternative was the floor. But Kit had a feeling there would be no potty breaks from this room, and she had no idea how long she would be here.

She walked to her right until she touched the wall. Moved forward until she had the sense that any farther would have her bumping into something. Swayed back a little, pulled down her sweats, and squatted. Her bladder would not work. Not right away. But she managed, and the sound seemed as loud as a gunshot. Pure fire crawled up her face; she felt dizzy with shame.

"I'm sorry," Kit said when she was finished. Her feet were wet.

"Don't be," Alice replied gently. "At least you can move away from it."

Kit did not reply. She could not. Her body felt misused, though she tried not to think of it that way. If this was the worst of the abuse she endured, it would be a blessing. Alice was certainly not doing as well. Kit had to assume the others locked in this room were suffering in a similar fashion, though their relative silence—and the smell of death—made her uneasy.

"You never answered my question," Kit said, voice quavering.

"I am afraid to," Alice replied, and then, softer: "I saw you. In my dreams. You came to me."

Kit hesitated. "You told me I was next. And then I was. Please, Alice, tell me what this is about. I deserve answers."

"You deserve not to be here. And that is my fault. I was stupid to involve you."

"No," Kit said, but Alice said nothing else, and Kit did not have the energy to push. Drained from the tips of her ears to her toes, and all the stress, all the struggle, slammed her so hard she wanted to cry. She held it in, though. Contemplated all the ways she might escape. Prayed a little. Wished for her grandmother and M'cal. Held the gris-gris tight in her hands and pretended it was her fiddle.

At some point, she fell asleep. A long time, a short time; there was no way to know. Only, she did not dream. And it was the sound of footsteps that woke her.

Alice whispered, "Careful. Be careful."

Kit stood, teetering. She listened to keys jangle, watched the door open slowly. She glimpsed a lithe figure, the outline of a bob. Officer Yu.

Two men stood behind her—not Hartlett, but some of his colleagues. Yu stood aside, wrinkling her nose, and gestured for Kit to precede her. The woman's hands were covered in blood. Blood was everywhere, Kit noticed—even on Yu's face. Specks of it darted across her cheek like large, sticky freckles.

Kit stared for a moment. Yu smiled. There was something feral and cold in her eyes, which were different than Kit remembered, even from the boat. As though part of the woman had gone so far down some dark, slippery road, something fundamental had changed in her heart, so much so that she could no longer hide it on her face. A physical transformation. Dark thoughts and actions, cutting new features. It was frightening to look upon.

The men still resembled soldiers: impassive, unblinking, though they grimaced at the stench and heat. They walked around Kit, entering the room. She watched. Flashlights blinked, and she caught glimpses of pale flesh, contorted and stiff and filthy. Corpses pressed against the living, who moved weakly without sound. Eyes flashed against the light, and then were lost in shadow.

The flashlight beams converged on one spot. Kit glimpsed blond hair before the men blocked her view. Chains rattled. Alice groaned softly.

And then the men were back, carrying Alice between them. She was still clothed in her white dress, but the lower half of it was stained and wet. Her fine hair was a rat's nest of tangles, and her face was so gaunt and red, she looked like a woman left in the desert to bake.

"You help her," Yu said to Kit, and gave the men a hard look. They let go of Alice immediately, and Kit had to rush to keep the woman from falling. Alice reeked, but Kit paid no mind. Just held her by the waist and tugged one skinny arm over her shoulders, holding her up on two feet.

Yu started walking. The men stood behind Kit and looked on, impassive. She wanted to scream at them and go for their guns, but she steeled herself and took a step. Alice walked with her, eyes heavy-lidded, mouth slack. A far cry from the woman in the room who had been far more talkative. Kit recalled her act in the police cruiser a lifetime past, and wondered if Alice was not playing another trick. Weak, helpless.

Kit peered up into her face. No one could see Alice's eyes but her. She squeezed the woman's waist, and Alice for one brief instant glanced sideways at her with sharp, piercing clarity.

Kit looked away before she could do anything stupid and stared resolutely at Yu's slender back and bloodstained hands. Felt the doors on either side of her looming, as though the wood carried faces watching her with hungry gazes. Kit imagined creatures breathing on the other side of those doors. Locked up. Waiting.

Ahead, sand. Kit's spirit balked at the sight, but her legs kept moving. There was a train wreck coming, with no brakes to pull. Full speed, collision course. She glanced at Alice again and saw that knife sticking out of her eye. Blood gushed from her face. Kit sucked in her breath and looked back at the men. One of them had a broken neck. The other was blue in the face, his hair drifting wildly. Drowned, sinking.

The vision passed. The two men gave her an odd look, and she tore her gaze away. Yu's back appeared no different at all. If she was going to be murdered, Kit still could not see it. She found it disturbing that she wanted to.

They entered the main room, every inch of the floor still covered in white sand. Alice balked, but the men shoved her, which carried her and Kit even deeper toward the center of the room. A large circle had been drawn there, the line made with something dark that glimmered wet beneath the flickering candlelight.

Blood. The word leapt into Kit's mind. Blood as ink. Blood as a line to be crossed, or not.

She thought of M'cal—her vision of him, trapped in such a circle—screaming. Nothing in this one—not yet—but Kit felt the promise. It was only a matter of time. She wished she had her fiddle.

Yu made Alice and Kit stop near the circle. At the far end of the room, in the shadows, someone moved. A hulking body. A round body. A body Kit knew well enough by heart, without needing to see the face.

Ivan moved into the light. Alice gasped. And then she made another sound—lower, harsher—as the witch appeared from behind her companion. She wore a pristine, silver robe—a kimono, flowing with silk ties. A gray silk veil was draped loosely around her face. Only her pale eyes showed, as well as her hair, which flowed long and shining to her waist.

Alice gave up all pretense of near-unconsciousness. She took a step forward, out of Kit's arms, her eyes wide, haunted. "No."

"Alice," said the witch, her voice muffled, silk veil puffing around her mouth. "Alice, how could you? Why?"

The young woman closed her eyes. "I had to. I was trying to prevent this."

The witch swayed forward, just one step, stopping so abruptly she looked caught by strings. Her eyes were raw, human. All the hate, all that cold charm Kit remembered—all was utterly wiped away when she looked at Alice. It was like seeing another woman. A normal woman. A woman without a mark upon her soul.

And it occurred to Kit, despite the witch's uncanny presence in this place, that she was innocent of this much: hurting Alice. Whatever else might be going on, that much Kit could be certain of. She hated the woman, but that hatred did not make her blind. Confused as hell, maybe, but that was another matter entirely.

"Only you," murmured the witch, gazing at Alice. "Only you would ever think I deserve mercy."

"Because she loves you," said a new voice, from behind Kit. "And it is amazing the foolhardiness done in the name of love."

Alice went very still. Kit turned. Behind Yu, on the other side of the room, was another corner full of shadows—and deep within those shadows, movement. Kit did not need to be told; she knew instantly what she was looking at.

Endgame. It. Someone bad.

Kit shivered. The voice was familiar; it had a rasping quality that ran right down her spine and reminded her of Ivan's teeth: sharp, hungry, and not just for show. She did not want to see—was afraid—but she forced herself to look hard into the darkness, squinting, and glimpsed a round body, a flash of long metal earrings, the fat edge of a headband jutting from a thick forehead.

And then her eyes adjusted a little more, and her mind caught up.

The old woman stepped into the candlelight with cats in cowboy hats still swinging from her ears. She looked the same—dressed the same—but as she took off her tinted glasses, Kit glimpsed a darkness so profound she wanted to scream.

"Edith," breathed Kit, sickness crawling up her throat. The old woman wore an aura like the heart of murder, pressed so thick over her shoulders it seemed part of her clothing. Her eyes were black, all the way through. Inhuman, alien. A sharp contrast to the pale gaze that had studied her only a day before. Youth counselor. Eccentric old woman. An illusion.

"What a sight this is," Edith murmured. "Women of power, gathered together. It has been a long time, Luanna. Too long."

"Long enough," said the witch, eyes glittering in that dangerous way Kit remembered; like her gaze was full of diamonds. "We all changed too much to ever be again as we were."

"We changed," agreed Edith, glancing at Ivan. "Some more than others. I suppose our father would be proud. All his scattered daughters, coming to fruition. Following his footsteps."

The witch narrowed her eyes. "I did not come here to talk. I want Alice. I want Kitala. I want what is mine."

Edith glanced at Yu, who nodded and walked to the front door. There was a black sack resting on the floor. She reached inside and pulled out a thick gob of bloody flesh. It looked like a heart. Yu carried it to Edith, who took it in her hand like a prize. She looked at Kit, and then the witch.

"This," said the old woman softly, "belongs to the both of you, I think."

It took Kit a moment to understand, and, like that, all the fear she felt washed away into a cold, hard spike of rage. She sank deep, searching for M'cal, whose presence rose like a star inside her heart; immediate, true. Still alive.

Edith tilted her head, studying Kit's face with unnerving intensity; unblinking, cold. "Or maybe just you. I think Luanna has lost her prize."

Kit shook her head. "What is this? What are *you?*"

"No," said the witch, moving forward, Ivan following close on her heels. She grabbed Alice's arm. "Enough, Edith."

"Enough?" Edith smiled, and it was ghastly, lips peeled back, teeth bared; like a mouth ready for a scream. "The circle is ready, Luanna. The time is right. All I have to do is open the door."

The witch took another step. "This is not you, Edith."

"Blood of my blood," whispered the old woman, and she held up her wrinkled hand to look at it, turning her palm against the candlelight. "Blood of power." She stopped, and looked at the witch. "I was going to spare you, Luanna."

"Not in place of Alice," said the witch. "Not her."

"She came to me so innocent. She had no idea who I was." Edith settled her gaze on Kit. "And you. You came as well. You and the merman."

"Me," Kit said in hard voice. "I don't know what the hell is going on here, but it is done. *You* are done."

Edith clicked her fingers. Kit felt heat spread across her throat, and then pressure. She tried to swallow and could not. Tried to breathe, and started choking. Panic swelled. She clawed at her throat, even as part of her spirit settled into a small, quiet ball, fiddle strings humming inside her mind. Kit clung to the music, feeling it swell inside her heart like thunder. The pressure on her throat eased; she took a shallow breath. Edith reared back, staring.

And then the witch was there, pushing Kit aside with a snarl. She raised her hands and light flashed, so bright it seared right down to Kit's brain. A rough hand grabbed her arm, pulling her away. It was Ivan. He yanked hard, reaching out for Alice. Sand kicked up beneath their feet, digging trenches. Kit looked down and saw a red stain in those fine grains. A stain that spread, welling up like an oil strike, a vein of water.

Blood. They were standing over blood.

Kit's vision flickered, strings snapping in her head. Ivan still pulled her. She did not resist. No strength was available, not when all her focus was on shadows and spirits and the wail of music screaming. There was a pattern there—she could feel it like the rhythm of a hard stroking jig, rising and falling on a pound and a beat; as though the spirit of this place was a taste and a heartbeat. Living, breathing, darkness. Something stirring. Growing. The belly of the beast.

And Kit felt herself answering back. She felt, on the tip of her tongue, a thrill of music so strong she wanted to cut herself with it. To spill her own blood, as if that would chase away the spirit she felt hovering over this place. All the murders she had ever seen—all the pain that fate could deliver—this, here, what she felt right now was the cause of it all. She could almost touch it.

Alice shouted. Kit's focus snapped back, tearing away from the spiritual to the physical—the sand and heat and blood and screams. The witch was on her knees in front of Edith, who had her hand pressed against the woman's shoulder. Smoke rose from the contact, the hint of sparks. The witch screamed and screamed—more defiance than pain—and Kit could see her dead, a vision, sprawled on the ground with her eyes open and staring—

Yu appeared in front of them with a gun in one hand and a knife in the other. The blade was sticky with blood. Kit knew who it belonged to. She lunged, but Ivan yanked her back, standing between them, blocking her view of the police officer. She could not see around him, but she glimpsed the two men flanking her, standing on either side of the door. Guns out. Eyes hard. Totally unnerved by the scene going on around them.

Alice screamed at Edith, still struggling to free herself, until suddenly, like a whip, she coiled around and fastened her teeth on Ivan's wrist, biting down hard. He must have been distracted, surprised; he let go, and Alice moved fast. Kit lunged after her, but Ivan still had hold of her wrist. She watched, helpless, as Alice threw herself at Edith.

Alice had guts, but she was about as good in a fight as Kit—and Edith, despite her apparent old age, moved like a viper. The young woman went down hard, and the witch cried out, reaching for her. Edith batted her away.

Ivan finally released Kit. She did not look back, only sprang across the sand and slammed into the old woman, who was just beginning to crouch over Alice's prone body. Edith snarled, mouth opening far too wide for anyone pretending to be human, and grabbed Kit around the throat.

Time stopped. Kit felt like she was floating. Edith's hand was around her neck, but it did not matter. She was back on the veranda with her grandmother, watching Old Jazz Marie's strong fingers sew the pouch of a gris-gris as her old dark eyes burned bright and hot.

Edith's hand exploded from Kit's throat. Literally.

It happened too fast to see, but Kit felt the heat, the blast, and suddenly her face was covered in hot blood and Edith was on the ground, cradling her arm, which stopped at the wrist. Blood spurted around a jagged lump of protruding bone. The old woman did not make a sound, but her eyes swallowed the candlelight when she looked at Kit.

Kit wasted no time being stunned. She yanked the witch to her feet, and they both grabbed Alice and began dragging her unconscious body to the door. Ivan joined them. He was bleeding, but one of the soldiers was sprawled on the ground with his head twisted all the way around. Fate. Yu and the other were gone.

Edith reached out with her remaining hand and hissed one long word. Alice stopped moving. Kit pulled with all her strength, crying out with the effort, but it was like hauling a two-ton slab of concrete. Dead weight. Kit had to drop her. The witch had her hands wrapped around Alice's wrist. She dug in her heels, the veins standing out in her neck. Edith bared her teeth and smiled.

The witch let go. She stared at Edith, and Kit could feel the power rolling off her in waves. It was not enough, though. Whatever—whoever—Edith was, she was too strong. The witch gazed down at Alice, snarled, and grabbed Kit's arm.

"Good," Edith said as the witch dragged Kit away. "Good, Luanna! She was already mine."

The witch did not say a word. Ivan opened the door, and within seconds they were stumbling out into a wash of cold air. It was night. Kit was surprised by the darkness, by the amount of time that had passed, but Ivan made a grunting sound and the witch tugged Kit into the forest. The ground hurt her feet, but it was better than walking in blood and shit and that terrible sand.

"Alice," Kit gasped, looking over her shoulder. She

saw nothing. Without any light escaping the structure, it was impossible to see in the darkness.

"We will save her," said the witch grimly, and Kit felt the woman's gaze track over her face. "All this time, you have been trying to help her. And you still do not know why."

"I had to," Kit said breathlessly, and then: "Who is she to you?"

Silence for one long moment. Kit stubbed her toes on a log and cursed, stumbling. The witch kept her from falling. "My granddaughter. Alice is my grand-daughter."

Too much had already happened for Kit to feel surprise; she was numb. "And Edith is your sister?"

"We had the same father," said the witch, her breathing ragged. "There are many of us who could claim that privilege. He was long-lived. Immortal."

"Was?"

"Dead now. Murdered. But he left his mark, in more ways than one. I doubt he ever knew the true extent of it. He was . . . focused on other things." The witch squeezed Kit's hand. "The world is bigger than you know. If you want to survive—"

"Cut the bullshit," Kit snapped. "You're the last person I want lecturing me about survival. You'd throw a baby in a volcano if it meant keeping your eyelids from falling."

"But not *my* baby. And not my granddaughter."

Ivan had disappeared, but the witch did not falter; she moved without hesitation through the night, and Kit kept getting hit in the face with branches, tearing her skin on thorns and rocks. Her feet felt like they were bleeding. The pain made her think of M'cal—his heart, the blood on Yu's hands. She gritted her teeth. "M'cal."

"We are going to him." The witch's eyes glowed for one brief instant. "He has what we need."

"You still want my soul," Kit said. "Jesus Christ. How could it possibly help you?"

The witch did not answer. Instead, she said, "Your grandmother loved you. She loved you enough to protect you tonight. Do you know the cost of that gift, Kitala? Do you understand the price of that love?"

Kit said nothing, touching the gris-gris where it bounced beneath her T-shirt. The witch looked at her again, and in a deathly quiet voice, said, "I am going to teach you, Kitala Bell. Tonight. You are going to learn the price of a grandmother's love."

CHAPTER EIGHTEEN

Returning to life was a slow process, depending on the wound, but when M'cal finally opened his eyes after losing his heart, the first face he saw was craggy and lean, with golden glowing eyes and hot breath that smelled like garlic. All things being equal, M'cal would have preferred something less . . . fetid.

"Koni," he rasped. "What happened?" He looked around. He was still in front of the grate, in front of the cave.

The shape-shifter blew out his breath. "Fuck. You're alive."

"What happened?" M'cal asked again, trying to sit up.

"Bitch carved you like a turkey. Never seen anything like it. Never seen anyone . . . enjoy it as much as she did. Like she was getting the taste in her mouth." Koni leaned back, sprawling on his side. He ran a hand through his hair and covered his eyes. "I listened to you, man. I stayed quiet. But it was fucking hard."

"Thank you," M'cal said. "Thank you for staying alive."

"Your love kept me going," he replied.

M'cal grunted at the sarcasm. "Enough people have died because of me, that is all."

Koni grunted and rolled to his feet. He tested the grate, shaking it. "You must be popular at parties."

M'cal sighed. "I do not suppose you have some lock pick hidden on you?"

The shape-shifter stared, then pointedly glanced down at his naked body. "I'm going to pretend I didn't hear that."

M'cal stood. His chest hurt. He touched his skin and found an indentation above his heart. He took a deep breath, clearing his head, and focused on Kitala. She was still nearby, and still alive. But he could feel, almost like a taste drifting on his tongue, the fine lines of some terrible stress. Something bad was happening.

He joined Koni, and the two pulled hard on the steel bars, the ends of which had been embedded in the rock face on either side. What light had been at the mouth of the cave was gone. Night had fallen.

"Some trap," Koni muttered. "I've never been tricked like that."

Neither had M'cal. He laced his fingers through the grate and pressed his forehead against the cold steel, breathing slow and deep. The gaps were too small for Koni to fit through in his other form. "Whoever captured us has considerable power, but not without limits."

"Hence the henchman?" Koni got down on his knees and poked at the ground. "This is just dirt. If we dig a hole, I could shift and crawl under."

M'cal did not say a word. He got down on his

knees, transformed his nails into long hooks, and started clawing at the hard-packed soil. Several minutes of hard work yielded a space big enough for a crow to squeeze through. Koni did just that, with M'cal pushing. A surreal moment, though brief.

Koni shook out his feathers, and with only a quick glance at M'cal, fluttered his wings and flew from the cave. No time to waste.

M'cal kept digging. His fingers began to bleed, but he did not slow. Simply clawed the earth, hard and fast, fighting to make room for his body beneath the grate. He did not pay attention to the passage of time, only to Kitala, pulsing in his heart.

Until, quite suddenly, he felt a change in their connection. Something made him stop and sit back, concentrating. Somewhere near, brush rattled. M'cal's breath caught, and he stood up so fast he made himself dizzy. He clutched at the bars, staring into the darkness, pushing his vision to adjust. His bracelet tingled.

A giant hulk appeared at the jagged, slanting mouth of the cave. Ivan was unmistakable. M'cal did not know how the man had reached the island—or escaped the sinking boat—but his presence was an unwelcome surprise. Ivan did not enter the cave, though. He stepped aside, and the witch pushed through, her face partially covered. A burn in the shape of a hand covered her right shoulder. Not that M'cal looked long—not when he saw who was following her.

Kitala. Alive. Covered in blood—but after a closer look, seemingly unharmed.

M'cal exhaled sharply, briefly closing his eyes. Warm hands grazed his fingers, and he made a sound. It was Kitala, blindly touching the grate. She came back to his hands and he latched on to her, tugging her tight through the bars. She stared past his face, her gaze stricken.

"You're alive," she whispered. "I knew you would be, but I saw your heart—"

"Shhh," he interrupted gently, glancing over her shoulder at the witch, who had no trouble seeing in the dark to look him in the eyes. "What happened?"

"I found Alice," Kitala said, and glanced over her shoulder at the witch. "*Her* granddaughter."

M'cal stared. The witch said, "No time. Edith will work fast."

"Edith," he echoed, not certain he was hearing correctly. Ivan pushed Kitala aside, and the witch stepped close to the lock and knelt.

She briefly glanced at M'cal. "For all I have done to you, right now let there be no grudges between us."

"No," M'cal said. "I will not promise that."

The witch tore away the veil covering her face. Her features had partially healed, but her nose was well and truly gone. He searched himself for regret and found none, though the lack of anger in her gaze made him feel odd. Her eyes were clear and steady.

"You will die beautiful," she said with such quiet thoughtfulness, it seemed to him that each word was a meditation, a promise. A reflection, too, on what she no longer could have. Her face was as ugly as her heart—which was a fine thing, as far as M'cal was concerned.

But the way she looked at him continued to be unnerving. Her hand touched the lock—he heard one word, whispered—and a loud click filled the cave. The grate swung open. M'cal reached immediately for Kitala, and pulled her gently to him, mindful of her blindness in darkness. Her body felt warm, good. His heart began to untwist.

The witch watched him, moving to Ivan's side. "You must do something for me, M'cal. One last thing, and you will be forever free."

"No," he said. "I will not give you Kitala."

"No," she replied softly. "But will you take me, M'cal? Will you kill me?"

M'cal stared. Kitala went very still. Even Ivan looked at the witch with something close to dismay. The woman gazed at them all, though her eyes lingered on Kitala the longest. She reached out and touched her face. Kitala flinched.

"I submit to you," said the witch, and held up her other hand. Took one step back and removed her rings. Held them in her palm. She turned to Ivan.

"I release you," she said, holding out one of the rings. Ivan shook his head. His mouth opened—air hissed, his throat gurgled—but there were no words he could say. None he was capable of uttering. The witch touched his chest and stood on her toes. She kissed his mouth. Pressed the ring into his hand. Ivan shut his eyes and the silver cuff around his wrist fell off.

The witch turned to M'cal and held out the second ring. He took it without hesitation and his own bracelet snapped, hitting the ground with a thud. He stared at it, unable to move or speak. He could not believe what was happening. Too much, too fast, and far too impossible. Not even in his wildest dreams had he imagined it would be like this.

"Why?" he breathed.

"Because I love my granddaughter," whispered the

witch. "And I cannot help her in this body. I realize that now. Kitala, however, is protected in ways I am not, and never will be. *She* is the proper vessel."

M'cal felt cold. "No."

"What?" Kitala asked.

"No," he said again, and then: "She wants me to take her soul and then give it you."

Kitala reared back as though struck. "What does that mean?"

"It means you will have my knowledge." The witch closed her eyes. "It means that before I dissipate, I will pass on to you all my secrets, my entire life."

"You will infect her," M'cal snapped. "You will try to control her."

Kitala touched his arm. "What will happen if Alice is killed? What is Edith planning?"

"I think you know," whispered the witch. "You felt the promise."

"Death and darkness." Kitala's eyes were haunted. Her fingers crept up M'cal's arm. "But why me? Why do you think I have a chance?"

"I think you know that, too." The witch's face hardened. "Do it, M'cal. Take my soul. Give it to Kitala."

He hesitated. Kitala squeezed his arm. "I'm willing."

"You do not understand what you are asking."

"I will still be me," she said to him, her voice dropping low and soft. "I will not be her, M'cal. I know that much. I know *me*. I know *us*."

He began to argue, and stopped. The witch was willing to die. Kitala was willing to fight. And there was nothing he could say to negate either of those two things. He could see it in their eyes.

He moved in quick, and the witch flinched. Ivan placed a hand on her shoulder. She clung to it, and the vulnerability in her face reminded M'cal of a time, long ago and far away, when he had believed in her. It had been a lie then. He did not think it was a lie now. But he hardened his heart and leaned close.

"Thank you for my freedom," he said at the last moment. He was compelled, though he did not know why. Perhaps it was the fear in her eyes. He searched his heart for pleasure and found none.

The witch held his gaze. "It was inevitable, M'cal. Fate takes its own, always."

He hesitated, but she was right. Fate was calling.

So he answered with a song.

Kit was blind, but her ears worked fine, and she listened to M'cal take the witch's soul. She could hear the difference in his voice—the curl and venom, the lure—and she remembered again what it was to be on the receiving end, to feel her soul peeled from its anchor. Only, there was no fear with the memory—it was like putting her ear to the soul of the world and hearing its lullaby; unearthly, intoxicating.

It ended fast. Kit heard the witch sigh, and Ivan made another choking sound. Then M'cal was there, his hands on her shoulders, and in a strained voice he said, "You can still change your mind."

But she could not, and she told him as much, feeling his unhappiness like a cut across her heart—inside the shard of his soul, still bright and warm. Her sense of him was growing stronger, as though their link was a muscle flexing.

M'cal did not ask again. He pressed his mouth over hers. Kit had no time to react. She felt the rush—like before, in the sea, receiving a piece of his soul—only this time on a much larger scale, pouring and pouring, like her body was a pitcher being filled to the top.

For a moment, Kit felt afraid. There was so much fear she shook with it, and finally she understood M'cal's concern. Her own soul felt crowded, pinched, but she fought back with vicious abandon, rearranging the witch, who tried to spread through Kit's body and exert control.

You must listen to me, said the witch. *This will be for nothing if you do not listen.*

Then learn your place, Kit replied. *This is my body. Not your second chance.*

But Kit felt the urgency all the same, and grabbed M'cal's hand, tugging. She could see him, as though there was an ambient light all around them, glowing. All because a switch had been turned on in her head; simple, something she hoped she would remember.

You will remember everything, the witch told her. *Now run.*

Kit did just that, dragging M'cal behind her. She did not look to see if Ivan followed, but focused on Edith and Alice, suffering a schizophrenic tumult of vying words, images, and personalities as she fought to keep herself whole inside the core of her heart. It was ugly, messy, but the music rose up like a thundercloud, and it was real this time, no holding back.

They raced through the forest. Kit's body felt light as air; no pain in her feet, no stumbling falls. She imagined that she was flying, and knew in her heart that she was so close to doing just that, there was hardly any difference.

She led them back to the clearing, guided by the witch, and found company waiting. Kit recognized Hartlett, and inside her head his death unfolded with such clarity she knew he was already standing with one foot in the grave. The three men at his side were little better. And far on their right was Officer Yu, who met Kit's gaze with a momentary expression of triumph—until she saw M'cal.

No headphones. None of them were protected.

Yu did not try to fight. She ran, and was gone into the forest even before M'cal had a chance to open his mouth. But he did, just as Hartlett and the others raised their guns, and his voice was sharp, biting. The men cried out, clutching their heads. M'cal twisted the melody, and all three of them collapsed. Dropped like puppets with their strings cut. Fast, clean, and easy. Breathing, but otherwise still.

The witch thought it was stupid to let them live. Kit ignored her. The dark aura that had covered the log cabin felt like a smear of hate—infectious, lethal—and as they approached, shadows peeled away from the night. Tall, slender, shaped like slips of paper dolls. They gathered like flimsy stems, some echo of creatures that could be human. And though it was dark, they stood out in stark relief as something deeper than night.

M'cal made Kit slow, his eyes hard, dangerous. He stared at the dark ghosts. Ivan, close behind, did the same. His pale gaze darted around the clearing, coming to rest briefly on Kit's face with an intensity that she thought had less to do with her than the woman currently inhabiting her body.

The shadow men moved closer. Kit could not imagine them causing real harm. An absence of light was not the same as flesh and blood.

You are wrong, said the witch, her voice so loud she could have been standing outside of Kit's body. *Edith has begun the ritual. Each moment she continues will strengthen these creatures. Even now they could kill you with a blow.*

How do we stop them?

Kill Edith. She had not finished the ritual. Until she does, her body is their only link to this world. Kill her, and you will send them back.

"Kitala," M'cal said, his voice full of warning.

"I have to kill Edith," she told him. "Otherwise, all you can do is slow these things down."

"We have to get you in there," he said, but before he could use his voice, Ivan picked Kit up his arms and barreled through the shadow men, tossing them aside in his wake. There were more of them than Kit had realized—and though Ivan moved fast, the sensation felt like a race on top of shallow quicksand, each step sucking, tugging. Shadows clung, arms shaped like swipes of ink—rained down, hard. She felt each blow like a slap of an open palm. Her face stung.

M'cal appeared, music pouring from his throat. The shadows fell aside. Not far—not like Hartlett and his men—but enough to clear a passage all the way to the door.

Ivan set her down, while M'cal kept singing. He tried to open the door but it was locked against them. Kit felt the barrier inside her mind—a projection from Edith—and cut it down like the first striking chorus of the Dies Irae from Verdi's *Requiem*, slicing through another stacked illusion that Edith threw upon them—images of even more shadow men, tall as the trees. The witch exercised her limited control, guiding Kit's use of her power with ruthless abandon, but Kit followed her own instincts, too, as the music became more frantic, rising higher and higher.

You dance that devil down, she remembered her grandmother saying. *You dance that bastard right back to Hell.*

Kit swung open the door. The earlier signs of fighting were still present, but the circle in the sand remained unbroken. At its center lay Alice. She was naked. Edith crouched over her body, a knife in her good hand. Her other was slung tight against her chest, wrapped in bloody bandages. The old woman did not appear at all slowed by the massive wound. One cut had already been made in Alice's arm. Her blood dripped into the sand.

A conduit, Kit heard, followed by a jumble of images that made no sense but were so disturbing she shut them away.

Edith glanced over her shoulder and snarled. Kit entered—took two steps across the sand—and the door slammed shut behind her. She started to go back, but stopped. No time. She had to do this on her own.

She turned to face Edith—and was overwhelmed with the sensation of terror and death, along with a feeling of awful hunger; a waiting hunger, like a starving man perched at the ready for a fat steak; to pounce and tear. Deeper, even; a soul hunger, starvation for life.

This life, the witch told her. *This entire world.*

Edith's face contorted against the candlelit shadows. She raised her dagger high above Alice's chest. The young woman's eyes opened.

Fight, said the witch. *Fight now.*

Power swelled inside Kit. Music roaring. She ran toward Edith and broke the circle.

When the door slammed shut behind Kitala, M'cal stopped singing. It was only for a moment—the time it took to ram his shoulder against the hard wood, shouting her name—but that was long enough. The shadows, these men made of night and darkness, swarmed upon him, and while a small part of his heart still wondered if this was yet another illusion, the blows felt real enough, as did the hands around his throat, cutting off his voice.

Demons, he thought, falling to his knees. *The shadows of them.*

M'cal was dimly aware of Ivan at his back, fighting his own losing battle with the vastly greater numbers. The only thing the big man had going for him was that he was still immortal—and M'cal most definitely was not.

Golden light streaked overhead—a crow bathed in fire—and suddenly there was another set of fists pummeling the shadows holding him down. M'cal broke free, and his voice rolled into the air like the scream of high winds on ocean waves. He shifted his tone just a note, and the shadows lurched backward even more. He kept singing, still trying to open the door behind him. Ivan waded deeper into the shadows, his giant fists sweeping left and right. Koni took a stand beside M'cal; farther away, at the edge of the forest, a cheetah burst from the trees and leapt into the fray, followed by two men. Both were familiar. One of them was shocking.

M'cal's father met his son's gaze across the roiling shadows, opening his mouth to sing. His voice wound through the air and power rumbled, their twin melodies braiding with no hint of discord; just low, smooth tones that laid the demons down, flat and hard. As M'cal sang with his father, he had a sense, for the first time in his life, of how it must have been in the old wars of magic, the ancient battles, when armies of his ancestors—voices linked—had cut through the ranks of gathered enemies. It was a heady power, intoxicating.

His father ran toward him through the shadow men, clicks and whistles entering his song; words and meanings winding through the melody.

Go to her. I will take care of this.

M'cal did not hesitate. He turned against the door, his voice rising to an ear-shattering shriek that sent Koni stumbling away, covering his ears. The wood vibrated. M'cal, desperate, latched on to his soul bond and clawed his way across it with both voice and will, struggling to reach Kitala.

She was still alive, fighting for her life. M'cal sensed the witch inside the echo of their connection, and he said, *Open the door. Hurry.*

A moment later he heard a click, and he tried the knob again. This time it worked, and he slammed through into a room of shadows and white sand, golden candlelight burning the air like some hazy fire. There was blood everywhere. Kitala stood in the center of a large circle with a naked woman at her feet and another across from her, one arm ending in nothing but ragged chunks, while her face—her *face*—

Edith. He finally understood who Kitala and the witch had been talking about. The name had meant nothing before, though he remembered the elderly counselor. His mind simply could not put the two together—not like this.

He ran forward, entering the circle, his voice twisting. Edith snarled at him, eyes black as pitch, and his power slid off her soul like water. Kitala stood beside him, the strain on her face enough to break, sweat rolling down her forehead; but both women stood unmoving, staring, a battle of wills roasting the air between them. Edith held a long knife. The woman below was blond, with a lovely face; she looked like the witch. The resemblance was uncanny. She caught M'cal's eyes, and hers were wild. Her body was paralyzed. He remembered the feeling. He had been in one of these circles before.

Instinct guided him, blood memory of older battles reawakening in his subconscious. He moved behind Kitala and placed his hands upon her shoulders, sinking deep into the bond, riding into her soul. She was screaming inside her mind—screaming with music—but there was a restraint there, doubt, and he saw in her mind a hunger for her fiddle, something to hold in her hands as she *danced that devil* and *cut the bastard down.*

Make your own fiddle, he told her, his palms sliding down her arms to her wrists. He picked up her hands and held them in front of her face. *Play, Kitala. Play your music.*

And she did. He felt her fingers move—slow, then fast—listened inside his head as power pulsed with every mental note. The witch had never been this strong—her power was great, but music was a conduit of greater complexity, added passion, and Kitala was a master of both.

Between Kit's hands light formed, pure and white: a fiddle made of sun and lightning. M'cal lent his voice, new insight guiding him as the monster reared inside his throat. It ripped deep into Edith's body, and the woman cried out, skin rippling across her face. She stared hard at him—he felt fingers against his throat, digging into his eyes—but the music in Kitala's head shrieked and cut, and the pressure eased. Edith snapped her teeth, black eyes rolling back in her skull. Her skin shriveled, splitting and cracking. Blood rolled down her cheeks, from her ears and nostrils.

It is not enough to kill her, whispered the witch. *You must trap the spirit holding her.*

Yes, M'cal heard Kitala say, and he felt the house shake around them as she played a solo symphony inside her head, power coursing through her music as she played for death, death down to an inferno. He felt her wrap a cocoon around Edith, binding it tighter and tighter—but even as she did, he sensed a change overcome the older woman, and he finally could see the heart of what they were fighting: a shadow that oozed up from her skin like oil from the pores of the earth, writhing against Kitala's bonds of light. A demon, M'cal realized. But nothing like the shadows that fought outside the cabin; this creature was something more, something beyond gender or description, a force of ancient desperate fury.

You cannot stop me, rasped the demon. *If not this gate, and this vessel, then another. We are strong again. We are coming. It is only a matter of time.*

Time, said M'cal to Kitala. *Are you ready?*

Yes, she said, and it was like feeling his soul melt inside its perfect opposite as his voice wrapped around her music. He tore the dark spirit loose from its bindings inside Edith—like stealing a soul—and threw it down into the ball of light arcing between Kitala's hands. Power roared through her, coursing along the music, and the demon, the ghost, the darkness, shrieked. As did Edith, reaching out to the dying creature that had consumed her body. Her hand touched the light; M'cal ripped into her with his voice—

Edith exploded. Her chest, her cheeks, her throat—the skin tore with such force, bits and pieces flew through the air. She screamed just once, then slumped, her heart jutting through a cracked well of bone. M'cal saw it beat one time, then go still.

Kitala collapsed to her knees. M'cal also went down hard. His legs were made of jellyfish, his throat raw. He tried to say something to her, but all he could do was rasp her name. So he crawled, wrapped his arm around her waist, and hauled her close.

Alice sat up, scooting away. Her eyes were haunted as she stared at Edith's mutilated body, and then her gaze fastened on Kitala. "Grandmother," she said, and the look in her eyes said she knew the truth, that she could see what had happened.

"Love has a price," Kitala whispered, hoarse. "And she loved you more than anything."

A disturbing revelation, M'cal thought. But he was free to live with it . . . and he thought he could.

CHAPTER NINETEEN

Ivan was gone. And there were survivors behind the metal door, though so near death it hardly counted.

"They were taken for blood and sacrifice," Alice told them bluntly, and that was all she would say. They were the only words she spoke for the rest of the night, even when M'cal and Kit led her to the cave where they had left her grandmother, and they discovered that her body—and Ivan—were missing.

"The witch is still alive," M'cal murmured to Kit when Alice was far out of hearing range. "Her body, that is. But that will not last long."

"And you can't put her back?"

"No," he replied. "It is a one-way trip."

I knew that, said the witch, a cool presence at the back of Kit's mind. *It was an acceptable sacrifice.*

Kit did not entirely believe her seemingly imperturbable serenity, but if the witch still wanted her secrets kept, that was fine. Truly, Kit did not want to know much about the woman anyway.

The survivors of Edith's torture were too weak to

be left alone. Hari made arrangements with his employer, announced that he and Amiri would stay behind, and sent the rest of them on their way. Kit had the very distinct feeling that the cops were not going to be involved in this matter. Or if they were, that Dirk & Steele had ways of keeping all the mysteries safe, without too many questions asked. As with the witch, Kit did not want to know too much.

Down at the dock, the speedboat was gone. Yu, still on the loose. Kit tried not to feel sick about that, focusing instead on the other boat docked in its place—a yacht. Standing on its deck, waiting for them, was Rik. His shirt was off, his ribs bandaged. Kit was very glad to see him. But there was another man at his side, and he was as tall as M'cal, with a face that was the same—if older, and more blond. His body was lean, strong; his narrow hips clad in tight swimming trunks. Kit hesitated, seeing him. So did M'cal.

Koni, who had somehow found a pair of sweatpants, led Alice below deck, presumably to clean up. Rik took the helm, accelerating the boat away from the dock. M'cal and Kit stayed topside, and after a few moments of silence, she was introduced to S'har Abreeni.

She noticed M'cal's father still wore his wedding ring—a human habit in honor of his late wife, Kit assumed. She said nothing, though. The tension between M'cal and his father was so thick she felt sick.

"Thank you," M'cal finally said. "I know it must have been difficult for you to set foot on land."

"I made a choice," said his father. "As did you."

Kit glanced at M'cal and found his expression strained. "And the other matter? Your promise?"

S'har's mask cracked. "All these years I would not

leave their waters. I had to stay close in my efforts to . . . watch over you. My promise was the only thing I could give them in return while I waited. Your mother, I think, would not hold it against me, given the goal and prize."

M'cal said nothing. Kit had no idea what they were talking about, but now was not the time to ask. She steeled herself as S'har turned his pale gaze on her face, examining her with an unblinking intensity that was difficult not to look away from. Kit remembered, with some embarrassment, that she was covered in blood, but she kept her gaze steady and after a time he nodded.

"She would like you," he said, and the honest simplicity of that statement, given what little M'cal had said of his father's love for his mother, made her eyes burn and her heart ache high in her throat.

S'har did not wait for a response. He walked to the edge of the yacht, wind blowing back his pale hair, and glanced over his shoulder at M'cal. "After I fulfill my duty here, I will return south. Perhaps . . . you and Kitala might visit one day."

"Yes," M'cal whispered. "Thank you."

S'har nodded curtly and gave Kit a long, steady look. "Take care of him."

"Yes," Kit breathed. "I will."

He hesitated, a silence that begged for more words. None came. M'cal's father leapt off the back of the yacht and disappeared beneath the waves. Kit stared at the choppy sea, lost in the darkness of night. Another world, down below. A whole civilization that was nothing but a fairy tale.

M'cal held Kit tight against him. They did not speak for quite some time.

* * *

Rik did not take the boat back to Vancouver. That night, they laid anchor beside another island, where Hari and Amiri found them late after supper. It was a cool night, but everyone sat topside with drinks in their hands, dessert plates scattered over the deck, talking quietly, enjoying the simple act of breathing, of being alive. No mention of violence or murder, just good things. Life.

Alice did not join them. She was below deck, resting. Kit went to find her.

She knocked softly on the cabin door, prepared to retreat, but Alice said, "Welcome," and Kit entered carefully.

Alice lay on the bed, one arm thrown against her forehead. She wore sweats and a T-shirt, and her hair was wet. Scrubbed clean of everything but her pain. Kit understood, though she felt nothing but weary when she looked at the young woman, who was still an enigma and more—the grandchild of a wicked woman, doubtless a person of no small power herself. Kit did not know whether to be wary, or to try—just this once—to be a friend.

She could use a friend, murmured the witch. *She has had so few.*

"I'm sorry," Alice said softly. "I want you to know that."

"It wasn't your fault." Kit peered down into Alice's eyes, searching for signs of death. She was not afraid of seeing the truth; facing down that demon had been worse than any murder, and she remembered—would always remember—the touch of the creature as it had tried, for one brief moment, to reach into her body in the instant before its death. Its touch had felt like a mouth swallowing the sun.

You were strong. Stronger then me, said the witch.

Perhaps Edith and her demon knew that. It was why she took M'cal's heart. She would have used it against you—exploited your bond to him—but she lost her chance.

"Edith tricked us all," Alice said, and for a moment Kit wondered if the young woman could read her mind and hear the witch. "So maybe you're right about fault. But I was still naïve, stupid. She lured me here on the pretense of saving my grandmother, telling me that she was in danger. I believed her. I would not have given you that card otherwise. It wasn't until later that I discovered the truth."

"You don't need to apologize," Kit said. "I understand."

"Do you?" Alice said. "I come from a long line of very bad people. My Uncle John was the kindest of them. The most . . . normal. I've tried to be the same. Ignored what I am, what I can do. Fought to be the opposite in every way from the people I was born to. But it seems as though every year I find out something more terrible, more heinous." She shut her eyes. "I did not like Edith, but I trusted her. I loved my grandmother, but I did *not* trust *her*."

Alice sat up, gazing at Kit. "Edith wanted you, in the end. The creature *possessing* her wanted you. You were going to replace Edith as its new vessel. She would have sacrificed me earlier, otherwise. But once she met you, her plans changed. She decided to wait until you were in her possession."

"Ah," Kit said, creeped out. "Well, it's already a bit crowded in here. I think that demon would have had a hard time fitting in."

A faint smile touched Alice's mouth. "Is she mad at me?"

No, whispered the witch.

"No," said Kit. "Not at all."

Alice nodded, taking a deep breath. "Good. That's . . . good."

Good that you want the love of a sadist and murderer? That you love a sadist and murderer without reservation? Or do you know? Do you know everything, Alice, that your grandmother did?

The witch settled heavy against Kit's heart. *She does not. I was careful to keep it that way.*

Liar.

Survivor, was the witch's reply.

Alice said, "So, you saw my death. And you believe we avoided it?"

"You were going to be stabbed through the eye. I think so."

Kit got ready to leave. As she touched the door, Alice said, "There's a problem, you know."

"Yes?"

"Edith wasn't aiming for my eye."

"Oh," Kit breathed. "Well, then."

"Yeah." Alice smiled, rueful. "Exactly."

Kit went to her room after that. Too much to think about. She was not alone for very long. M'cal joined her, and in his hands was her fiddle case. There was no sweeter sight she could imagine, though for the first time in her life, Kit was happier to see a man than her instrument.

The fiddle was still safe, without a scratch. Kit ran her fingernails down the strings and plucked a quick tune. It sounded like laughter, and felt as good.

"Courtesy of Rik. He forgot to give it to you earlier," M'cal said, but stopped and touched her face. "What is it?"

"Alice," Kit said, and told him. It did not take long, but by the time she was done they were both on the bed, curled tight around each other. They drifted inside each other's heads, following the bond between their souls, and Kit caught glimpses of the long night—Yu, cutting him open—Koni, wriggling under an iron grate—the sight of her bloodstained face as she entered the cave and his joy, his utter relief, that she was still alive.

"You love me," she said, with wonderment, with awe.

"And you love me," he replied.

Kit touched his face, pouring all her feelings for him into her fingers, into her eyes as she looked at him, into her lips as she kissed his mouth, into his soul and the bond connecting them. Her whole body was filled to burst, and the witch whispered, *You are both fools to pin so much of yourselves on one heart. It is impossible to find love without pain.*

I wouldn't want to, Kit replied, and M'cal said, *Anything, as long as it is with her.*

And it was with those sentiments that they closed their eyes—still rumbling inside each other's heads— and fell asleep.

Kit opened her eyes in Louisiana, on the edge of the swamp with frogs croaking and the air as warm as steam from a cup of tea. The veranda was full of evening sun, and her grandmother perched on her stool. The pouch she had been sewing was done, full and round, and only the very foolish would open it up to see what lay within.

Kit felt movement on her left: M'cal, opening his eyes. His black hair was tousled, the corner of his mouth curved, and he gazed around the veranda with curiosity and stark appreciation. When he saw Kit's grandmother, his smile widened, though with a surprising amount of ruefulness.

"Let me guess," Kit said. "She's visited you before."

The old woman chuckled. "Stop fussing with him and come here. Time's wasting."

Kit took M'cal's hand and pulled him off the wicker seat. Her grandmother watched, a smile playing on her mouth. "Lovely, so sweet and lovely. All a woman can ask for when thinking good thoughts for the ones who come after." She leaned close, her eyes as bright as stars. "Treasure it. Take nothing for granted."

She gestured for M'cal to step around the table, and slipped the newly made gris-gris over his head. She patted it against his chest. "To keep you safe."

"Like you kept me safe," Kit said, and then, softer: "The witch—Luanna—said you protected me with your love. But that there was a price you had to pay. What did she mean by that?"

The old woman shook her head, knocking her fist on the table. "She meant the truth, though it didn't need to be said. That I saw what you would face. I knew what was coming, glimpsed it in my waking hours and in my dreams—more details than I wanted to know. The darkness, the danger . . . I was already on my last ropes. Wouldn't have gone more than another year, and I figured one year was a good sacrifice for an entire life. Give some nine lives to a little cat. My Kitty Bella. So I put it all there in that gris-gris you wear. My protection, my last breath. Just like M'cal gave you his. All of us part of each other, in the ways that mean forever. Something *someone* could have used a lesson or two in." Old Jazz Marie glanced sideways. "You can come out now, Luanna."

A tall, silvered woman moved through the open French doors. She was not the witch Kit remembered. This woman was old, and though her spine was straight and strong, her face held a canyon of wrinkles traveling from her forehead down her neck. The only recognizable part was her eyes: pale, sharp, intelligent.

"Jazz Marie," said the witch.

"Luanna," said Kit's grandmother. "About time you croaked."

"My heart still beats. Somewhere."

"Don't mince words with me. You're good as dead, and it's time you started thinking that way."

"I could live on." She looked at Kit. "Your granddaughter and I are comfortable together."

"Not that comfortable," Kit replied dryly. "I would like it to remain that way."

The witch sighed, and settled her gaze on M'cal. "No final words?"

He shrugged. "Burn? Rot?"

"Good enough, I suppose." The witch glanced at Kit. "And you?"

"Thank you," Kit said grimly. "For wanting to kill me. I would never have met M'cal otherwise."

The witch shook her head. Kit's grandmother smiled and slid off her stool. "Well, come on, then. I'm here to take you where you're going."

"I don't suppose you'll give me a clue?"

"Oh," said Old Jazz Marie, "I think I'll let you be surprised."

She held open the veranda door and the witch walked down into the swamp. Kit's grandmother hesitated, looking back at Kit and M'cal. "Times won't be easy, you know. There will always be something."

"Ritual sacrifices?" Kit asked.

"Demonic armies?" M'cal added.

"Yet more sexual slavery?" She tapped him on the arm. "Oh, you are so totally mine."

Her grandmother shook her head. "Never mind. Both of you will be fine."

"Yes," M'cal said. "If I know anything, it is that."

Old Jazz Marie smiled and left the veranda. She did not look back at them, but raised her hand to wave as she swayed her hips into the swamp. Luanna was waiting for her. The two women disappeared behind a banyan tree.

Kit felt no sense of loss; her grandmother would be back. Death was not always the end. She realized that now.

She glanced at M'cal, and found him fingering the gris-gris pouch, his eyes thoughtful. She asked, "What are you thinking?"

A faint smile touched his mouth. "I was thinking . . . that life is strange and awful and lovely, and that to have one, you must have the others."

Kit leaned against him. "Regrets?"

"Some," he admitted. "None that have to do with you."

The sun was setting behind the swamp; clouds blushed rose and gold, like honey mixed with some warm dream. M'cal slowly exhaled, sliding his arm over her shoulders, and glanced down at the table beside them. Kit followed his gaze. Her fiddle lay on the hard battered surface, surrounded by dried chicken feet and bones and rocks.

He smiled. "Play me a song."

"Only if you'll sing."

"Magic, if we do it together."

Kit stood on her toes and brushed her lips against his cheek. "So, let's make magic."

M'cal laughed. "Only with you, Kitala. Only with each other."

She picked up her fiddle to hide the sudden burn of tears in her eyes. "Always, M'cal. You and I are so blessed."

We are indeed, he said, inside her mind, reaching down between their souls, holding her with a love that was wild as a thunderstorm and deeper than the sea. There was mystery between them; magic. Enough to move the stars.

Kit smiled and struck a note.

For those who love the
Carpathian novels of Christine Feehan,
here is a preview of a sweeping tale of
encroaching darkness and healing
light by an exciting new author.

C. L. WILSON

*Lord of the
Fading Lands*

AVAILABLE OCTOBER 2007

PROLOGUE

Loudly, proudly, tairen sing,
As they soar on mighty wings
Softly, sadly, mothers cry
To sing a tairen's lullabye.
—The Tairen's Lament, Fey Nursery Rhyme

The tairen were dying.

Rain Tairen Soul, king of the Fey, could no longer deny the truth. Nor, despite all his vast power and centuries of trying, could he figure a way to save either the creatures that were his soul-kin or the people who depended upon him to lead and defend them.

The tairen—those magnificent, magical, winged cats of the Fading Lands—had only one fertile female left in their pride, and she grew weaker by the day as she fed her strength to her six unhatched kitlings. With those tiny, unborn lives rested the last hope of a future for the tairen, and the last hope of a future for Rain's people, the Fey. But today, the painful truth had become clear. The mysterious, deadly wasting disease that had decimated the tairen over the last millennium had sunk its evil, invisible claws into yet another clutch of unhatched kits.

When the tairen died, so too would the Fey. The fates of the two species were forever intertwined, and had been since the misty time before memory.

Rain looked around the wide, empty expanse of the Hall of Tairen. Indeed, he thought grimly, the death of the immortal Fey had begun centuries ago.

Once, in a time he could still remember, the Hall had rung with the sound of hundreds of Fey Lords, warriors, *shei'dalins* and Tairen Souls arguing politics and debating treaties. Those days had long passed. The Hall was silent now, as silent as the long-abandoned cities of the Fey, as silent as Fey nurseries, as silent as the graves of all those Fey who had died in the Mage Wars a thousand years ago.

Now the last hope for both the tairen and the Fey was dying, and Rain sensed a growing darkness in the east, in the land of his ancient enemies, the Mages of Eld. He couldn't help believing the two events were somehow connected.

He turned to face the huge priceless globe of magical Tairen's Eye crystal called the Eye of Truth, which occupied the center of the room. Displayed on the wings of a man-high stand fashioned from three golden tairen, the Eye was an oracle in which a trained seer could search for answers in the past, the present, and the infinite possibilities of the future. The globe was ominously dark and murky now, the future a dim, forbidding shadow. If there was a way to halt the relentless extermination of his peoples, the answer lay there, within the Eye.

The Eye of Truth had been guarding its secrets, showing shadows but no clear visions. It had resisted the probes of even the most talented of the Fey's still living seers, played coy with even their most beguiling of magic weaves. The Eye was, after all, tairen-made. By its very nature, it combined pride with cunning, passion with often-wicked playfulness. Seers approached it with respect, humbly asked it for a viewing, courted its favor with their minds and their magic but never their touch.

The Eye of Truth was never to be touched.

It was a golden rule of childhood, drummed into the head of every Fey from infant to ancient.

The Eye held the concentrated magic of ages, power so pure and undiluted that laying hands upon the Eye would be like laying hands upon the Great Sun.

But the Eye was keeping secrets, and Rain Tairen Soul was a desperate king with no time to waste and no patience for protocol. The Eye of Truth *would* be touched. He was the king, and he would have his answers. He would wrest them from the oracle by force, if necessary.

His hands rose. He summoned power effortlessly and wove it with consummate skill. Silvery white Air formed magical webs that he laid upon the doors, walls, floor, and ceiling. A spidery network of lavender Spirit joined the Air, then Earth to seal all entrances to the Hall. None would enter to disturb him. No scream, no whisper, no mental cry could pass those shields. Come good or ill, he would wrest his answers from the Eye without interruption—and if it demanded a life for his impertinence, it would be unable to claim any but his.

He closed his eyes and cleared his mind of every thought not centered on his current purpose. His breathing became deep and even, going in and out of his lungs in a slow rhythm that kept time with the beat of his heart. His entire being contracted into a single shining blade of determination.

His eyes flashed open, and Rain Tairen Soul reached out both hands to grasp the Eye of Truth.

"Aaahh!" Power—immeasurable, immutable—arced through him. His head was flung back beneath its onslaught, his teeth bared, his throat straining with a scream of agony. Pain drilled his body like a thousand *sel'dor* blades, and despite twelve hundred years of learning to absorb pain, to embrace it and mute it, Rainier writhed in torment.

This pain was unlike any he had ever known.

This pain refused to be contained.

Fire seared his veins and scorched his skin. He felt his soul splinter and his bones melt. The Eye was angry at his daring affront. He had assaulted it with his bare hands and bare power, and such was not to be borne. Its fury screeched along his bones, vibrating down his spine, slashing at every nerve in his body until tears spilled from his eyes and blood dripped from his mouth where he bit his lip to keep from screaming.

"Nei," he gasped. "I am the Tairen Soul, and I will have my answer."

If the Eye wished to cement the extinction of both tairen and Fey, it would claim Rain's life. He was not afraid of death; rather he longed for it.

He surrendered himself to the Eye and forced his tortured body to relax. Power and pain flowed into him, through him, claiming him without resistance. And when the violent rush of power had invaded his every cell, when the pain filled his entire being, a strange calm settled over him. The agony was there, extreme and nearly overwhelming, but without resistance he was able to distance his mind from his body's torture, to disassociate the agony of the physical from the determination of the mental. He forced his lips to move, his voice a hoarse, cracked whisper of sound that spoke ancient words of power to capture the Eye's immense magic in flows of Air, Water, Fire, Earth, and Spirit.

His eyes opened, glowing bright as twin moons in the dark reflection of the Eye, burning like coals in a face bone white with pain.

With voice and mind combined, Rain Tairen Soul asked his question: "How can I save the tairen and the Fey?"

Relentlessly, absorbing the agony of direct contact with the Eye, he searched its raging depths for answers. Millions of possibilities flashed before his eyes, countless variations on possible futures, countless retellings of past events. Millennia passed in an instant, visions so rapid his physical sight could never have hoped to discern them, yet his mind, steadily commanding the threads of magic, absorbed the images and processed them with brutal clarity. He stood witness to the deaths of billions, the rise and fall of entire civilizations. Angry, unfettered magic grew wild in the world and Mages worked their evil deeds. Tairen shrieked in pain, immolating the world in their agony. Fey women wept oceans of tears, and Fey warriors fell helpless to their knees, as weak as infants. Rain's mind screamed to reject the visions, yet still his hands gripped the Eye of Truth, and still he voiced his question, demanding an answer.

"How can I save the tairen and the Fey?"

He saw himself in tairen form, raining death indiscriminately upon unarmed masses, his own tairen claws impaling Fey warriors.

"How can I save the tairen and the Fey?"

Sariel lay bloody and broken at his feet, pierced by hundreds of knives, half her face scorched black by Mage fire. She reached out to him, her burned and bloodied mouth forming his name. He watched in helpless paralysis as the flashing arc of an Elden Mage's black *sel'dor* blade sliced down across her neck. Bright red blood fountained. . . .

The unutterable pain of Sariel's death—tempered by centuries of life without her—surged back to life with soul-shredding rawness. Rage and bloodlust exploded within him, mindless, visceral, unstoppable. It was the Fey Wilding rage, fueled by a tairen's primal fury, unfettered emotions backed by lethal fangs, incinerating fire, and access to unimaginable power.

They would die! They had slain his mate, and they would all die for their crime! His shrieking soul grasped eagerly for the madness, the power to kill without remorse, to scorch the earth and leave nothing but smoldering ruins and death.

"Nei!" Rain yanked his hands from the Eye and flung up his arms to cover his face. His breath came in harsh pants as he battled to control his fury. Once before, in a moment

of madness and unendurable pain, he had unleashed the beast in his soul and rained death upon the world. He had slain thousands in mere moments, laid waste to half a continent within a few bells. It had taken the combined will of every still-living tairen and Fey to cage his madness.

"*Nei!* Please," he begged, clawing for self-possession. He released the weaves connecting him to the Eye in a frantic hope that shearing the tie would stop the rage fighting to claim him.

Instead, it was as if he had called Fire in an oil vault.

The world was suddenly bathed in blood as his vision turned red. The tairen in him shrieked for release. To his horror, he felt his body begin to dissolve, saw the black fur form, the lethal curve of tairen claws spear the air.

For the first time in twelve hundred years of life, Rainier vel'En Daris knew absolute terror.

The magic he'd woven throughout the Hall would never hold a Tairen Soul caught up in a Fey Wilding rage. All would die. The world would die.

The Tairen-Change moved over him in horrible slow motion, creeping up his limbs, taunting him with his inability to stop it. The small sane part of his mind watched like a stunned, helpless spectator, seeing his own death hurtling towards him and realizing with detached horror that he was going to die and there was nothing he could do to prevent it.

He had overestimated his own power and utterly underestimated that of the Eye of Truth.

"Stop," he shouted. "I beg you. Stop! Don't do this." Without pride or shame, he fell to his knees before the ancient oracle.

The rage left him as suddenly as it had come.

In a flash of light, his tairen-form disappeared. Flesh, sinew, and bone reformed into the lean, muscular lines of his Fey body. He collapsed face down on the floor, gasping for breath, the sweat of terror streaming from his pores, his muscles shaking uncontrollably.

Faint laughter whispered across the stone floor and danced on the intricately carved columns that lined either side of the Hall of Tairen.

The Eye mocked him for his arrogance.

"Aiyah," he whispered, his eyes closed. "I deserve it. But I am desperate. Our people—mine and yours both—face extinction. And now dark magic is rising again in Eld. Would you not also have dared any wrath to save our people?"

The laughter faded, and silence fell over the Hall, broken only by the wordless noises coming from Rain himself, the sobbing gasp of his breath, the quiet groans of pain he didn't have the strength to hold back. In the silence, power gathered. The fine hairs on his arms and the back of his neck stood on end. He became aware of light, a kaleidoscope of color bathing the Hall, flickering through the thin veil of his eyelids.

His eyes opened—then went wide with wonder.

There, from its perch atop the wings of three golden tairen, the Eye of Truth shone with resplendent clarity, a crystalline globe blazing with light. Prisms of radiant color beamed out in undulating waves.

Stunned, he struggled to his knees and reached out instinctively towards the Eye. It wasn't until his fingers were close enough to draw tiny stinging arcs of power from the stone that he came to his senses and snatched his hands back without touching the oracle's polished surface.

There had been something in the Eye's radiant depths— an image of what looked like a woman's face—but all he could make out were fading sparkles of lush green surrounded by orange flame. A fine mist formed in the center of the Eye, then slowly cleared as another vision formed. This image he saw clearly as it came into focus, and he recognized it instantly. It was a city he knew well, a city he despised. The second image faded and the Eye dimmed, but it was enough. Rain Tairen Soul had his answer. He knew his path.

With a groan, he rose slowly to his feet. His knees trembled, and he staggered back against the throne to collapse on the cushioned seat.

Rain gazed at the Eye of Truth with newfound respect. He was the Tairen Soul, the most powerful Fey alive, and yet the Eye had reduced him to a weeping infant in mere moments. If it had not decided to release him, it could have used him to destroy the world. Instead, once it had beaten the arrogance out of him, it had given up at least one of the secrets it was hiding.

He reached out to the Eye with a lightly woven stream of Air, Fire and Water and whisked away the faint smudges left behind by the fingers he had dared to place upon it.

«Sieks'ta. Thank you.» He filled his mental tone with genuine respect and was rewarded by the instant muting of his body's pain. With a bow to the Eye of Truth, he strode towards the massive carved wooden doors at the end of the Hall of Tairen and tore down his weaves.

«Marissya.» He sent the call to the Fey's strongest living *shei'dalin* even as he reached out with Air to swing open the Hall's heavy doors before him. The Fey warriors guarding the door to the Hall of Tairen nodded in response to the orders he issued with swift, flashing motions of his hands as he strode by, and the flurry of movement behind him assured him his orders were being carried out.

«Rain?» Marissya's mental voice was as soothing as her physical one, her curiosity mild and patient.

«A change of plans. I'm for Celieria in the morning and I'm doubling your guard. Let your kindred know the Feyreisen is coming with you.»

Even across the city, he could feel her shocked surprise, and it almost made him smile.

Half a continent away, in the mortal city of Celieria, Ellysetta Baristani huddled in the corner of her tiny bedroom room, tears running freely down her face, her body trembling uncontrollably.

The nightmare had been so real, the agony so intense.

Dozens of angry, stinging welts scored her skin ... self-inflicted claw marks that might have been worse had her fingernails been longer. But worse than the pain of the nightmare had been the helpless rage and the soul-shredding sense of loss, the raw animal fury of a mortally wounded heart. Her own soul had cried out in empathetic sorrow, feeling the tortured emotions as if they had been her own.

And then she'd sensed something else. Something dark and eager and evil. A crouching malevolent presence that had ripped her out of sleep, bringing her bolt upright in her bed, a smothered cry of familiar terror on her lips.

She covered her eyes with shaking hands. *Please, gods, not again.*